Praise for MICHAL'S WINDOW

"Ayala makes this Biblical tale come to life in a present-day, real life, oh-I-can-so-relate, way."
Holly Michael, *WritingStraight.com*

"Never has a story drew me in and took me to the past, but in a present kind of way, as this one has. We get to walk, run, fear, and most importantly, love as Michal does."
Melisa Hamling, Author

"A superb writing style, engaging characters and well worth reading!"
H. C. Elliston, Author

"It's easy to cheer for the tenacious Michal as she fights for the man she loves."
Chantel Rhondeau, Author

"The heroine of *Michal's Window* embodies the heated determination of *Outlander's* Claire. Coupled with the equally intense hero, David, the sparks fly."
Taylor West, Author

"RIVETING... a heartwrenching romance deftly evoking challenges between the sexes in Bible times."
Terry Long, Author

> > > < < <

>>><<<

"Ayala mixes sexuality, danger, and religious history to craft a unique, provocative romance novel."
Ivan Borodin, Actor and Author

"Excellent reading! Brought to life the Biblical characters for me. I could hardly put it down."
Flara Jean Rice Richards, Reader

"If you loved Claire in the *Outlander's* series, you'll find yourself drawn to Michal of *Michal's Window*. Both characters embody strong female characters willing to sacrifice for those they love."
Melisa Bailey, Author

"Ayala intertwines fact from the best selling book of time, the Bible, with a fast-paced, gripping story. Her portrayal of Princess Michal is one to remember."
Rebecca Berto, Writer and Editor

"Ayala's writing is crisp and fast-moving, drawing you in from the first line and tugging you along with wonderful rich characters and complications."
C.S. Lakin, Author

★★★★★ 5-Stars by Kristie I. for *Readers Favorite*
"In the past few years I have become a fan of Biblical fiction and Ayala's novel does not disappoint! This story is well-written as it is filled with vivid details, well-developed characters ... creating a complete picture of life as lived in Biblical times."

>>><<<

MICHAL'S WINDOW

Rachelle Ayala

ISBN-13: 978-1475081480

ISBN-10: 1475081480

Dedication

Melisa 'Michal' Hamling

CONTENTS

ACKNOWLEDGMENTS

Cover Art by Robin Ludwig of Robin Ludwig Designs Inc.

Edited by Cherie Reich of Surrounded by Books Editorial Services

Many thanks to my wonderful critique partners at CritiqueCircle.com who challenged my writing and pushed me to clarify and motivate my characters. Special praise to my first five readers, Melisa Hamling, Jennifer Comeaux, Aminah Grefer, Carla Barber, and Melissa Irwin, who stuck with me through multiple plot changes and drafts.

All errors and omissions are my sole responsibility.

PART I
Approximately 1000 B.C. in the land of Israel.

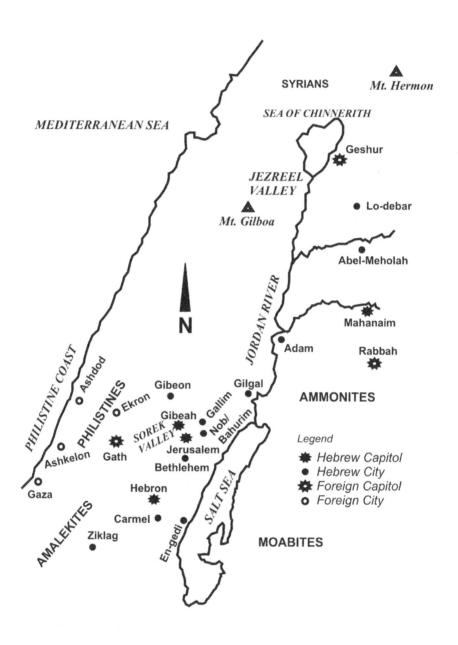

Map of Israel and surrounding nations around 1000 B.C.

CHAPTER 1

Psalm 78:70 He chose David also his servant, and took him from the sheepfolds

>>><<<

"Your music displeased King Saul. Useless cur!" Soldiers shoved a man to the ground in front of David.

The man writhed and begged, "Have mercy. I've a family to feed."

A soldier grabbed the man's arm and lashed it to a wooden block. David prayed silently on the man's behalf. The man shrieked as the soldier raised an axe and dropped it on the block, severing the hand. An old man dabbed hot pitch to the bloody stump while the man howled. Another soldier threw a reed flute in the dust. "That's mercy enough for begging."

The king's steward jerked his thumb at David. "You know what you're here for."

David's fingers turned cold and his breath hitched. He entered the courtyard and pulled out his harp. A band of sweat prickled his forehead as he tuned it. Rumor told of a king out of control, unable to lead battles to defend Israel. His physicians had searched the kingdom looking for musicians to calm him and soothe his spirit.

David finished adjusting the pegs. The departing screams of the flutist scratched a chill down his back. How many others had been maimed? He swallowed to wet his dry throat. His playing had better be perfect. *So help me, God.*

Brisk footsteps crunched on the path, and a servant announced, "Behold, Prince Jonathan."

A tall man with perceptive eyes greeted him. "So, you're the son of Jesse. How was your journey?"

"Fine, my lord." David bowed, wary of the prince's pleasant demeanor. Jonathan wore fine clothing: Egyptian linen, a prayer shawl with blue and silver tassels, and a leather sleeve slung across his chest. A golden crown highlighted his chestnut curls.

David tugged at his tattered shawl to hide the patches on his robe and followed the prince through the garden. Lilies danced in the breeze and the fragrance of jasmine poured over a whitewashed ledge.

Jonathan stopped in front of a wooden door and knocked. "Father, the harpist is here."

"Tell him to wait," a powerful voice called back. "My daughter is reading scripture to me."

Jonathan pushed open the door. "This man sings scripture and weaves the words with music. I promise you'll be delighted."

David gulped back fear. The young prince was so bold. But it wasn't his head on the line.

The king grunted for them to enter. David clutched his harp and stepped into the overheated chamber. The pungent odor of burnt hemp tightened his chest. King Saul, as large a man as rumored, slouched on a gilded couch.

A young woman placed a scroll on the table and stood to leave. David closed his mouth and dropped to the floor. Her stunning beauty drained any trace of composure from his heart.

"Michal, sit. You may stay," the king said.

Michal. David whispered her name. He closed his eyes and moistened his lips. "My king, I'm David, the son of Jesse, your servant."

Jonathan tapped David and pointed to a sheepskin-covered dais at the side of the couch. David took the seat and inhaled to quiet his speeding pulse. He forced his shoulders back and lifted his hands to strum, unable to keep from glancing at the princess. Her gaze drifted from his eyes, to his mouth, to his chest and hands. His throat tightened. How could he sing with her looking at him like that?

The king prodded his daughter, and she lowered her face. David willed his fingers to stretch and caress the taut strings. The harp responded with a sprinkling of chords, and he sang of God's glorious creation and marvelous works. Again, his eyes gravitated toward the princess. And he sang of beauty, grace, and God's loving-kindness.

The princess smiled, lifting an eyebrow. Her father looked at her and thumped his pipe on the table. David flinched, frozen in mid-strum. Panic speared his chest, and he pinpointed his gaze to the floor. The guards at the king's side did not move. Sweat trickled down the side of his face as he counted down the minutes of his life.

"Your music pleases me," the king said. "You're dismissed."

David bowed and backed out of the chamber. The princess stood, graceful and lithe. Her eyes were green and flecked with emotions he could not read. A cascade of rosewood-colored hair swept the challenging tilt of her face. She walked toward him. A thunderbolt slammed his heart, and he could barely breathe. *She belongs to me.*

She shut the door.

* * *

My elder sister, Merab, stepped into my room and poked me with her spindle. "Well, Michal, what do you think of Father's new servant?"

I tightened the threads on the loom and adjusted the weights. I had hoped Merab wouldn't notice David. But as usual, she made it her business to inquire about every young man who frequented the palace.

"He's a servant." I lifted my chin and swept a thread off my sleeve. "And besides, I'm not supposed to talk to him."

She twirled her spindle. "All the better. He can't refuse to talk to you. I've always found serving boys very accommodating."

"Well, if you're so interested, why don't you—" I didn't want Merab to toy with David. She had a way of stripping her suitors of their dignity before she refused bride prices rich enough to buy the daughter of Pharaoh.

She tapped my shoulder. "Way below my sights. A shabby servant. And you? Blushing and stammering already. I dare you to kiss him, baby sister. Don't forget to pay Mother's maid to look the other way."

She walked away with a dismissive laugh.

I set my weaving aside. Unlike my sister, I had never spoken to a man alone nor been kissed. But I had observed her tactics. And I was no longer a baby.

Perhaps I would approach David. He appeared humble and kind— and oh, so handsome. And when he sang, he showed a tenderness that made me tremble. And his fingers, solid yet fluid, caressed over chords as delicate as the morning dew.

David. His name meant 'beloved.' *Dah-veed.* I clicked my tongue and pinched my lower lip with a wet bite. David and Michal. I rolled the words and imagined long walks in the woods and lingering evenings in the moonlight.

I changed into a delicate, rose-colored dress and twisted my hair with a golden comb. A necklace of fiery rubies and matching earrings completed my outfit. Satisfied with my appearance, I opened my door and peered down the corridor.

It was the quiet time right before the evening meal when Mother napped and Father held court. Merab sang love songs in her room, mooning over Adriel, a married friend of our family. What my parents didn't know could fill a book.

I meandered through the garden and slipped past the kitchen to the servants' quarters. What luck! David sat alone on a bench, reading. I stepped to his side, cast my shadow over his scroll and startled him.

"Walk with me." I presented my hand, and he took it. But before he could press it to his lips, I withdrew. "You'll have to catch me first. There's an abandoned guard shack right above the granary on the old section of the palace wall."

Not waiting for a reply, I walked across the storage yard and skipped up the wooden steps. A new set of walls extended a hundred yards beyond, leaving this part of the battlements isolated. Here, I often spied on my brothers while they exercised in the training yard below. I also had a view of my parents' separate bedchambers.

A veiled woman entered my father's chamber. A few years older than I, she was given to my father to promote her father's position. I would have pitied her if she weren't so haughty, although being bed toy to the king was hardly a laudable accomplishment.

"I found you." David appeared at the top of the steps.

"I knew you'd come." I pursed my lips to hide a smile of delight. This was easier than I thought.

"Are you alone?"

"Why no. You're here, aren't you?" I held out my hand. "We haven't been properly introduced. Michal, daughter of Saul, of Gibeah."

He clasped my hand. "David, son of Jesse, of Bethlehem."

His voice as unyielding as his grasp, he swept my palm to his lips. Warm tingles radiated from his kiss. His honey-colored eyes brightened before lowering under gold-tipped lashes.

I leaned toward him. "Have you ever courted a maiden?"

He straightened to release my hand, but I squeezed his fingers and trapped him with my other hand. A fierce blush colored his face. "I've never courted a princess."

"You didn't answer my question."

"Would it matter?" He cocked his head and turned up a corner of his mouth.

"How dare you! Of course, it matters."

"Would it matter that I'm a poor man? A servant of your father?"

I dropped his hand and leaned over the windowsill. The scent of night jasmine wafted from the garden below. "It depends on what you wish for in your heart."

"My wishes or yours?"

"Yours first. Tell me."

He gazed at the horizon. He seemed an intelligent man with a masculine face. Not broad, but angular—strong brows over deep set eyes, a distinctive nose, and a crown of copper-brown hair unruly like my goat-hair pillow. When he settled his eyes on me, I hardly dared to breathe.

"Peace for Israel," he said.

"Is that possible?" I drew closer.

"Yes, if we have peace with God first."

His profound statement stirred my pulse and kindled a flame, an aching, twisting pang. Unable to sustain his probing gaze, I turned toward the setting sun. Its burnished rays bathed the jagged walls of our palace, dappling the rugged hills with shadows of gold, crimson, and brown.

"So you're a man of peace. Very good. What about love? Do you wish for love?"

He took my hand and traced my palm with his thumb.

Oh, my soul. A thrill shot straight to my heart. A lone hawk screeched, banked and crested toward the tip of the disappearing light.

"Princess, how old are you?" His voice deepened.

I hovered into the warmth of his chest. "Ancient. As old as these hills."

"Have you ever been courted?"

I shook my head.

"As old as you say you are and a princess too. Tell me, Michal, have you ever been in love?" He raised my hand to his lips but dropped it without kissing it.

Crickets serenaded the darkening sky with scratchy chirps, accompanied by the throaty croak of a persistent toad. I trembled, and David wrapped his arms around me. His scent pulsed hot with sandalwood, raking me with a newborn sense of longing. And his hands, oh, so firm, tightened around my waist, and his prayer shawl entangled my fingers, and his body, oh, the press of his body... made me want...

Voices sounded from the courtyard below, and I pulled back from the window ledge.

David turned me into the shadow of the wall. He brushed my lips so lightly I couldn't tell if he had touched me with his breath or his mouth. The wind gusted, and he was gone.

I clung to my shawl, holding in his warmth, the strength of his shoulders, the excitement of his chest. I had never allowed a man to hold me before. But David was different. He awoke strange and uncontrollable sensations. A tiny star shivered, wavered, and plummeted straight into my heart, mingling with my unspoken wish. And I knew at once why songs are sung and ballads told.

* * *

The sun broke through after a few days of rain. I donned a saffron gown trimmed with golden threads and pulled golden bracelets on my wrists. Mother braided my hair and insisted I wear a scarf. I pulled on a diaphanous one and headed for the wall to enjoy the sun. Unlike Merab, my olive complexioned skin did not burn easily. The small scroll of Ruth under my arm, I climbed the steps two at a time.

David looked up from the bench in the guard shack. His eyes widened, and a smile crept on his face. "Nice day, Princess."

I stopped at the top of the stairs. "I didn't expect to see you here."

"This is such a peaceful place. You don't mind sharing?" He moved his harp to make room.

"Not at all." I scooted next to him, slightly breathless, my body humming with an unsettling frisson. "What are you doing with your harp?"

"Changing strings. Wouldn't want them to break while I play for your father."

My father's temper had raged and thundered with the recent storm. I took David's hand and touched the blisters on the tips of his fingers. "Is my father feeling better?"

"Thankfully, he's settled down. I'm free for the rest of the day." His breath was a little too hot. I giggled and dropped his hand.

"What do you have there?" He pointed to my scroll.

"My favorite story. Ruth and Boaz."

He regarded me with a clandestine smile, shook his head, and pulled a new string onto his harp.

"What?" I shoved the scroll aside. "You know, David. You're on my bench." I removed my scarf and unbraided my hair. "I came here for some sun and quiet."

"Oh, excuse me for intruding." He gathered the loose strings and prepared to leave.

I pressed him down, one finger on his shoulder. "Since you're on my bench, you might as well show me a few things."

"Only a few?" He twirled a string between his thumb and forefinger.

I pointed to his harp, perched on his lap. "May I touch?"

"Um… sure, it's a shepherd's harp. My grandfather made it for me." He handed it to me.

I trailed my fingers over the smooth curves. The wood where his hands rested was well-worn and polished. "It's splendid. Lighter than I thought."

The scent was reminiscent of crushed bay leaves, clean and fresh. Swirls of tan, red, yellow and brown grain rippled along the contour of its body.

"It's made of myrtle wood," he said.

"And the strings?"

"Sheep gut." He laughed. "Go ahead, pluck them."

I picked the fibrous strings. The tones jarred. "Ooph. It sounds much better in your hands."

David took the harp back. "Forgive me, the strings are not tuned. I'll finish and show you how to play."

His nimble fingers made quick work of the restringing. With closed eyes, he plucked two strings at a time and adjusted the pegs until they rang true. His face took on an angelic aura, and his hair shimmered in the sunlight.

The harp tuned, he placed it on my lap, arranging my hands to hold it, and plucked a few strings to demonstrate. "The pitch of the longer string is deeper. Those from the shorter strings are higher. Some intervals sound nice when plucked together. If we skip a string or two… this string, this one, and this…"

My head swam with possibilities, and I could not catch his words. His hands touched my hands, his thigh pressed against mine, and his breath tickled my hair. My bracelets jangled as I strummed a cacophony of disharmony as wild and frothy as my feelings.

He was so close, I could barely breathe. My shoulders wobbled, and my fingers fluttered over the strings. Tempted to melt into his arms, I pushed the harp back and warned myself to behave as a princess should.

"Giving up already?" His lips curved with barely concealed amusement.

"No… I'm just hot. You know, the weather. Can you sing for me?"

I caught my breath as he sang and picked the strings to the cadence of a rippling brook. The earthy timbre of his voice wrapped around the clean tones of his instrument. Wooing, seducing, trapping—he held me with the promise of his song.

When he finished, he handed the harp to me, the frame still vibrating. His fingers toyed with my hair, and his warm breath caressed my face. His mouth drew near, eyes intent, seeking permission.

Hesitant, my lips parted. Curious, my eyes closed. And his lips brushed the corners of my mouth, an invitation to taste, to touch, to hold. I accepted and held my breath as his tongue slipped over mine. A flurry of tingles danced around my waist and trailed down to my toes.

I clutched the harp, unable to move. Everything was possible, and the world was mine, and life was glorious.

And at the center of it all was David.

CHAPTER 2

1 Samuel 14:49 Now the sons of Saul were Jonathan, and Ishui, and Melchishua: and the names of his two daughters were these; the name of the firstborn Merab, and the name of the younger Michal.

>>><<<

David followed Jonathan's servant to the stable. The sun brightened the morning haze. He breathed a prayer, half expecting to see Michal running through the yellow field of fennel, her laughter in flight, her cheeks rosy and fresh, her hair bouncing in the breeze.

He stroked the mane of a mare and fed her a cucumber. Jonathan had lent him clothes, asked him to ride with him. He was here to entertain the king, not fall in love with his daughter.

The memory of the kiss simmered, honey sweet, just beyond reach. He exhaled deeply. Michal. When would he chance upon her again?

Jonathan greeted him with a slap on the shoulder. "Ready to ride? My father is pleased with you and orders you to stay. You're going to train and become his armor bearer."

David's heartbeat jumped. Surely, God had opened this path for him. He could save the king's life, find favor with him, perhaps earn the hand of his daughter. He bowed. "My prince, I'm honored."

"Call me Jonathan and consider me a friend. Do you like it here in Gibeah?" Jonathan mounted his steed in a single leap.

"Oh, yes, I do," David said as he jumped onto the mare.

They trotted through a large grove of olive trees, ancient and full of dark purple fruit. The trees stood angular and bent like gnarly old soldiers. Their peppery scent saluted from mantles of grey-green leaves.

"Homesick?" Jonathan asked.

"A bit. But you've all been so kind to me."

David followed Jonathan across a stream and cantered up the meadow to the sheepfold. Had Michal ever ridden with Jonathan over these fields or hiked through the streambeds? Was she allowed to explore the village of Gibeah?

Two young women walked down the path with baskets full of grapes while others congregated at the well.

Jonathan grinned. "I know a few willing maidens in the village."

He cast a suggestive glance toward the women while David lowered his face.

"Your sister, Michal. How old is she?" His throat tightened the moment the words slipped out.

Jonathan's grin turned into a frown. "You're bold, aren't you? My father would run a spear through you rather than let you talk to her. She's his favorite child, only fourteen, and destined to wed a king."

David pressed his lips together, his heart dropping. She had flinched when he kissed her. Innocent. Lovely. Unattainable. *But mine!* His fists tightened.

Jonathan flicked the reins. "Besides, what bride price could you possibly offer a king? Stick to the village girls."

They jaunted through a small wooded area and emerged on a dry riverbed. Jonathan broke into a gallop. David kicked his horse sharply, buried his head down and charged ahead. By the time they arrived at the stables, both horses were lathered with sweat.

Jonathan handed him a circular comb and a stiff brush. "You're not a bad rider. Meet me at the exercise field after you've groomed the horses."

* * *

I wrapped a woolen cloak around my dress and climbed to the guard shack. The afternoon breeze buffeted my face. Below, David trained with my brothers. A peaceful man, he seemed out of place among my boisterous brothers.

Ever since becoming friends with Jonathan, David had avoided me. My mother's warnings echoed in my ears. I should have heeded them and not let him kiss me. But oh, how he kissed, so gentle and sweet that I wanted more. Lost in the moment, I tried to kiss him back, but he escaped so abruptly he left his harp in my lap.

Jonathan picked two wooden shafts and threw one to David. They squared off. In a single move, he slammed David across the chest and sent him to the ground. Melchishua and Ishui laughed and jumped into the fray.

I pulled my cloak tighter. They jabbed and punched David, jeering and calling him names. I cringed when he fell and cheered inwardly when he staggered back to the fight. They were stronger and more experienced, but David was more agile. His wiry body rolling with the punches, he ducked and feinted until my brothers tired.

When they finished, my brothers peeled off their armor and piled them on David, telling him to clean up. They jostled one another as they strode off, laughing and in good spirits.

I ran down the steps and found David dragging the weapons back to the armory. His hair matted with sweat, he mopped a hand across his forehead and flashed a disheveled grin.

"Were my brothers too tough on you?"

"They weren't too bad," he said. "It's nothing like being the youngest of eight brothers."

"Let me help." I reached for a shield.

"No, Princess. I'll get it." He took the shield and piled a breastplate and a pair of greaves on top of it.

I picked up a bow and a few arrows. "So, how's my father? Do you play for him every night?"

"Yes, he seems fine." He balanced the pile of armor and walked toward the armory.

"Does he treat you well?" I peeked sideways at him, wondering if he saw me unworthy of his attention now that he had Jonathan's friendship and my father's approval.

His lips thinned into an upturned line as his forehead wrinkled. "Well enough. He wants me to be his armor bearer."

"Indeed? Does that mean you're staying longer?" A flicker of hope stirred in my chest.

David looked at my feet. "As long as I please him."

We walked past the garden. He stumbled over a tree root and dropped one of the greaves.

I hurried to retrieve it and bumped my head on his. The rest of the armor tumbled as David caught my hand.

"Ow." I rubbed my head and giggled when he dropped my hand as if it were a hot firestone.

David set the shield down to reposition the armor. The tips of his ears reddened.

I tucked the greaves under my arm. "My father hasn't called me to read to him lately. I wonder if you've been reading scripture with him."

"No, he hasn't asked me to read."

"I have an idea. What if I read while you strum the harp?" I handed the greaves to the armor master and hung the bow and arrows on the rack. "I'll suggest it to him."

David didn't answer. I bent to pick up a short stick, and when I glanced back, he was staring at my hips.

My cheeks heated, unaccustomed to a man's intent stare. Yet I was pleased he had noticed me. I wagged the stick at him. "We'd make a fantastic team, wouldn't you say? Father always loved me over my brothers and sister, and he enjoys your music. All the servants are talking about you. I hear he calls you a son."

David blushed as he turned away from me to pick up the spears and sparring rods.

While he cleaned the weapons, I ran to the kitchen and returned with a water skin. He sat on a low wall with his elbows resting on his knees.

I handed him the water. "Will you be too tired to play for us tonight?"

David drank and wiped his mouth with the back of his hand. "No, I'll be fine. Will you—"

"David!" Jonathan crossed the courtyard. "What are you doing talking to my sister? My father expects you to play at dinner, and my manservant has set clothes out for you in my chamber."

Before Jonathan could say more, a servant scuttled to his side and handed him a message. He slid us a disapproving look and disappeared into the building.

David jumped to his feet. "I shouldn't be talking to you. Besides, you've put me in a difficult position."

"Why?"

"You won't tell anyone. Swear you'll say nothing."

"About what?" My heart chilled. He had to be referring to our kiss.

"Look, I must go." He handed me the skin. "Thank you for the water."

"David, wait. Did I do something wrong?"

"No, you haven't." He walked off.

My mouth hung open. I had been dismissed by a servant boy, and he wanted nothing to do with me.

* * *

Torches lined the hallway to the dining hall. David was already there, sitting next to Father. He did not appear to notice me as I made my way to Mother's side. She sat with her hands clasped, her knuckles bone-white. My father's concubine sipped wine at a side table.

David looked unbearably striking in my brother's princely robes. When Merab glided through the door, his mouth widened. Unbelievably, Father asked Merab to sit next to him. He stood to let her pass, his neck bobbing as he cleared his throat in obvious admiration.

Merab tapped David's arm and cupped her mouth to speak to him. They glanced at me briefly and laughed. My stomach grumbled and needle sharp pains stabbed my ribcage. I should never have been born. How could she flirt with him with no care for my feelings?

My brothers settled down as Father led the prayers. I peeked at David. His eyes were closed with a rosy blush on his freckled cheeks. He breathed evenly, and his mouth moved in obvious devotion to the LORD.

The prayer ended, and our eyes met. But he tightened his lips and turned away. The pit grew deeper in my stomach. I thought he liked me when he showed me his harp, but now he hated me.

The servants set platters of fish, parched corn, cucumbers, goat cheese, and bread on the table. My brothers dug into the food while my sister picked at her plate. David stared at his meal like a hungry wolf but did not start eating.

Mother elbowed me. "Eat, or the boy will starve."

I picked up a piece of flatbread and waited to catch his eye. Before he took notice, Merab offered him a piece of fish off her plate. Mother grimaced. "I don't know what's gotten into your father, letting a servant sit at our table."

Merab graced David with a phony smile. "Do we have the pleasure of your music tonight?"

David looked at my father, who nodded. A servant handed him his harp, and he settled on the bench between the tables. He smiled at Merab. She blushed and his eyes twinkled as he plucked a series of ascending chords. A dull ache spread from my heart to the tips of my fingers, but I couldn't pry my gaze from him.

His deep voice filled the room amidst rippling chords. My father's eyes were shut, his brows relaxed. Mother tapped her fingers and took a deep breath. Even Ishby, my youngest brother, had stopped fidgeting. A sigh slipped from my lips. I wanted David to be my friend, to walk with me through the meadows and hold my hand. We'd sit under a tree, and he'd play his harp and sing to me alone.

His voice lifted to praise the LORD for His goodness and wonderful works toward us. When he finished, Father tapped the table with his goblet and my brothers cheered. My heart jittery and pained, I jumped to my feet and clasped my hands. David cocked an eyebrow at me before Mother's censorious look pressed me down into my chair.

David took a bow and went back to his seat. Merab leaned over and said something that made him chuckle. Did he know she disdained him? Mocked his poverty and found him unsophisticated? Yet she batted her eyelashes and cooed as if she thought him attractive.

Servants refilled the goblets of wine and passed out honey cakes. My father ordered the pipers to play. My brothers sang a song of war, and Father dragged David around the room, high-stepping and kicking in a wild dance. Merab giggled and clapped, while I crumbled my honey cake into tiny pieces. Ishby flicked pieces of cake at Merab, landing a few in her hair. Mother would have stopped him, but her eyes were fixed on Father, and she wore a hopeful smile when he winked at her. David and my brothers refilled their wine goblets as Ishby threw a raisin into Merab's goblet. She jumped up and spilled her wine on David. Giggling, she dabbed a napkin on his robe.

Mother motioned to Ishby's nurse, and he ducked under the table to escape. During the commotion, I eased my chair next to Jonathan and wished David would take notice of me. But Father grabbed him. "Son of Jesse, you've been training with my sons, haven't you?"

David bowed. "Yes, my king."

Father held out his hand, and his armor bearer handed him a spear. He gestured to a wooden beam. "Can you hit the beam directly across the room? The one with the spear marks?" Handing the spear to David, he laughed. "Go ahead. Show me what my next armor bearer can do."

David took the spear and rubbed his hands. He looked at Merab for courage, and she graced him with a close-mouthed smile. Shifting from foot to foot, David set the spear back over his shoulder and threw it. Everyone gasped as it flew toward Mother's priceless Egyptian eggshell vase.

Mother shrieked. The spear thudded just a cubit short of the vase. My father's cousin Abner guffawed loudly. "Looks like the boy should stick to his harp."

Everyone laughed except for David and me. My father slapped his knees and stood. "Maybe he can sing the enemy to sleep."

David lowered his head and his face reddened. He yanked the spear from the wall and handed it to my father's armor bearer. Talk turned to the possibility of another war with the Philistines. I glanced at David while Father waved his hand and adjourned the dinner.

My father's concubine yawned loudly and headed out the door. I followed her and went around the side to wait on the path to the servants' quarters.

Merab's flirtatious laughter floated out the window. "Oh, David, you should have seen my mother's face."

They slid out the dining hall and walked around the fountain, arm in arm. She poked his side. "Do you know how much that vase is worth?"

David didn't reply. He seemed stiff and nervous. I followed them through the garden, staying well away so they couldn't see me in the light of the moon. Almost as tall as David, Merab wrapped her snake-like arms around his shoulders.

"Have you ever kissed a princess?" she said, her voice soft and seductive.

David shook his head. My heart crumbled, and I bit my lips, tasting blood.

"Would you like to?" She cupped his cheek and pulled him close. He didn't answer, so she leaned in and drew him to her lips. My frantic pulse hammered behind my ears. I gripped my fists to keep from crying. Merab had kissed many young men, driven them to obtain outrageous bride prices, only to cast them off as discarded rags.

No longer able to witness the destruction in front of me, I ran to my bedchamber. David wished to court my sister and was ashamed of having kissed me. A heavy stone crushed my chest, and I could not breathe. Blinking, dizzy, screaming inside, I stared out my window at the stars.

* * *

David stepped back from Merab. "I really shouldn't be here with you, Princess. Your father would object."

She tapped him with a pointed fingernail. "Stay away from my baby sister. I've seen you looking at her. You're a servant. Don't forget it."

Merab wrapped herself tightly in her shawl and walked away.

Shame burned his cheeks. He swallowed the growing lump in his throat and walked toward the servants' quarters. A fist clenched his heart, and he rubbed his temples. Who was he fooling? He had no right to court a king's daughter. A lowly servant dressed in borrowed clothing. Yet God had anointed him, chosen him to be the next king. Would God also grant him a wife?

He passed under an open window. A woman's breath hitched. Michal's face shone pale in the moonlight. David picked up a pebble and threw it at the corner of the window. She wiped her eyes and looked down, almost smiling before she furrowed her eyebrows and jutted out her lower lip.

His voice failed him while he stared at her. What could he say? Sorry I kissed your sister. Forget about me. I toyed with your affections. I wounded you.

She turned from the window and closed the shutters. David blinked. Their kiss vibrated in his memory. Her mouth, so sweet, had trembled, so enticingly. And her voice, the way she said his name, pure adoration. Such verve and persistence in a woman, a girl, was rare. Off-limits. No one but the Prophet Samuel knew of his destiny. She would not give him another chance.

David walked around the granary and up the wooden steps. He sat on the bench in the guard shack. Their bench. He smoothed his hand over the weathered wood. She had been kind and welcoming. She treated him as an equal. And he had been cruel, as if she had wronged him. Even worse, her father planned to marry her to a king, a foreign king. A daughter of the Law shouldn't be married to an idol worshipper. What could he do? The dragon of pain turned somersaults in his chest, and his breath steamed in his face. He looked to the heavens and pleaded with God.

CHAPTER 3

Psalm 9:14 That I may shew forth all thy praise in the gates of the daughter of Zion: I will rejoice in thy salvation.

>>><<<

Jonathan set me on his horse sideways and mounted behind me. "I've a few things to say to you, my sister."

I tugged my shawl against the biting wind. Merab had no doubt put him up to this. I hadn't spoken to her in days.

We rode at a walking pace out the gate of the palace. Despite my mood, I couldn't help but savor the scent of fresh cut grass and the damp earth, moist from the winter showers. Small white buds appeared on the grapevines, and tender green shoots sprang from grey branches.

I poked Jonathan. "Can we go a little faster? I want to fly across those fields and jump a creek."

"No, my sister. You are still a virgin."

I shifted on the swaying horse. "What does that have to do with anything?"

"It means I have to watch you and remind you that you're a princess. I've already told David to stay away from you." He tugged the reins. The horse waded across a small brook and headed up a rocky pathway lined with wildflowers.

"Then why does Merab get to talk to him?"

Jonathan snorted. "Merab's just playing. I'm not worried about her."

A cloud blocked the sun as we passed through a sheepfold. "David hates me anyway."

"It doesn't matter," Jonathan said. "Father wants to keep you for a major alliance to protect our borders."

I ground the inside of my cheeks. *So that's all they saw me as, a possession to be traded.* "Can we get off and walk? My legs are stiff."

Jonathan helped me dismount. I walked up the hillside with my arms crossed. He followed me. "You should stop acting like a baby."

I didn't want to hear him, so I ran. I tore across a ridge and scrambled around a stand of juniper trees. Did he care that my heart ached and that I thought only of David? My breathing grew ragged, my lungs struggled, and my legs burned. If only I could be free to fly away from the confines of the palace. I could be a warrior, or a poet. Not a pathetic girl destined to be bartered or sold.

Tears mixed with sweat trickled down my cheeks. I pumped my arms and ran faster, staring at my feet as I kicked clods of dirt. I rounded a stand of trees and stumbled, twisting my ankle. Three men on horseback blocked my path. The two in the front laughed and spoke in a foreign tongue. Philistines!

I turned and ran back the way I came. Hoof beats pounded behind me. My ankle throbbing, I veered off the path and tumbled down a steep slope. The horses stopped at the top, and a man dismounted. I screamed for Jonathan.

Footsteps chased me as I scrambled toward a brook. A sharp pain poked my sides, and my heart threatened to leap from my throat. Tripping and falling, I scraped my hands and landed in the water. I reached for a rock, but a hand grabbed my wrist.

I screamed and flailed to escape. My attacker held onto me, lifting me from the ground. He let go and stared at me. He was a boy—tall, but thin and gangly.

"Are you hurt?" he spoke in the trade language, his voice high pitched and reedy.

I coughed, trying to catch my breath. My dress was torn and my hands and knees bled. The boy sat on a rock and watched me. The banks were steep on both sides, and he was downstream from me. His companions could have surrounded me. I threw a rock at him but missed.

"Let me go," I said in Hebrew.

He lifted his palms and replied in Hebrew. "I'm not stopping you. You're bleeding."

"What are you doing in our land?"

The boy raised an eyebrow. "Your land?"

I walked past him. "If my brother catches you, he'll kill you."

He walked at my side and offered me his arm. "You're limping."

"You know, I don't need you to make stupid observations." I jutted my chin. "If you want to help me, show me how to get back to my palace."

His mouth broke into a lopsided grin. "Ah, so you're lost. And a princess too."

I glared at him and would have punched him had I not noticed the iron knife tucked in his belt. His long black hair fluttered in the wind, and

19

he wiped it from his beardless face. He pointed down the stream. "If you keep going, you'll come to the Sorek Valley. I live on the other side of the valley. You're welcome to my palace."

I turned around. "That means I go up the river. Goodbye."

"You're very pretty." His footfalls crunched behind me.

And you're very annoying. Well, maybe not, because he was friendly, and he hadn't hurt me. I wrapped my arms around my wet clothes. The sun was setting, and a chill traversed my spine.

My teeth had barely chattered when a warm cloak settled on my shoulders. "You're shivering," the boy said.

I cringed at accepting the cloak of a Philistine, but my body welcomed the warmth. "You're a Philistine. How is it you speak Hebrew?"

"I had a Hebrew nurse."

"Oh, I have a Philistine nurse." I hugged the cloak, smelling an outdoorsy scent mixed with oily food. "But the only words I know are milk, bread, and well… never mind. Was she a war captive?"

"Yes, but she loved me like a mother." He offered his hand again, and I took it, glad to take some weight off my sore ankle. We walked to where the bank was shallow and cut across a pasture, bypassing a grove of old olive trees.

"See the torchlight up on that mound?" He pointed. "That's your palace. Can you make it by yourself? If they capture me, they'll probably kill me."

"What are you, a spy?"

He smiled, his white teeth gleaming in contrast to his bronze skin. "I'm your friend."

I held his hand a bit longer. "I'm Michal, daughter of—"

The leaves rustled, and a man tackled the boy, knocking him to the ground.

"Run, Michal," David said. He drew a short sword and held it to the boy's neck. "Leave before I kill him."

I grabbed David's shoulders. "No, he's only a boy."

"Boys grow to become men. Please turn around unless you want blood on you."

"No, David. Let him go. He helped me."

"His companions hurt your brother, sliced his arm."

I gasped and covered my mouth. "Jonathan's hurt?"

David nodded. "Not badly. He was still able to kill them. Move aside and let me finish the job."

The boy choked, and his lips shuddered. "My brothers are dead?"

"They attacked first." David sheathed his sword and pulled the crying boy up. "Now, go. Remember, I had mercy on you."

The boy ran, his long legs flying and his hair bouncing in the wind.

David pulled me into his warm chest and hugged me. "What happened to you? They came back to the palace yelling about you being kidnapped by Philistines. Your father's guards headed west on horseback."

The events of the day tumbled over me. My knees weakened, and my head swirled. David tucked the boy's cloak over my shoulders and picked me up. "You shouldn't scare me like this."

"You mean you care? You're not angry with me?" I pulled one arm around his neck and the other over his shoulder. His eyes were dark with concern.

"Not at you," he said. "I was wrong to kiss you. You're the daughter of the king."

"Doesn't mean I can't have friends." I rested my head against his neck. He smelled like leather, my father's smoke, and excitement.

His whiskers brushed across my temple. "You're hurt and cold. I have to take you back to the palace."

"Can you take me away to your palace? Somewhere far away across the sea. Maybe a land of green hills or black forests. I heard my nurse tell a story." I lifted my face to his chin, and my pulse churned with affection.

"Oh, I'd take you anywhere, if I could." His voice gravelly, he lowered his lips to mine, whispered my name, and kissed me, soft, safe, mouth relaxed, but closed, as if I were beyond reach. I waited, my breath barely held, aware of the hiss of his breath growing more agitated.

He murmured my name again, and his mouth grazed against mine, simply touching, not taking. I pressed up to him and slipped a taste when his lips parted on the second syllable. He shivered, tightening his embrace and stopped walking.

I climbed higher in his arms as he placed me on a slope so I could be level with him.

"What can I do to earn your hand?" His eyes glistened in the moonlight.

It is enough if you love me. But I knew my place as a princess was difficult. I caressed the soft spot beneath his jaw and said, "Bring peace to Israel."

His fingers tangled in my hair. "You are truly the most expensive girl in all God's creation. And the most precious. I don't know what I would have done had you been taken captive."

Our faces drew closer, nose to nose. I wrapped my arms around his neck and teased his hair. His breath fanned my face, sweet, a hint of spice, and full of heat. "I want you, David, beloved."

A groan rumbled in his chest, and he was over the edge, bending my head back, his mouth encompassing mine, inhaling my breath, my spirit, capturing my heart.

21

* * *

David almost lost consciousness the moment Michal confessed her desire. Forget the rules, the laws, the kingdom, and the price. He needed her in a way that felt elemental, as if she had always been a part of him, that missing rib. His feelings too intense, he pulled his body back, but she followed and clung to him, her wet clothes dampening his skin.

The tangy, salty scent of blood and mud, and the sunshiny sweat of the Philistine boy underneath her jasmine flavor stirred his emotions into a rushing torrent. He ripped off the cloak and threw it on the ground, then wrapped her with his tattered prayer shawl. She shuddered, her flesh raised with goose bumps.

Angry voices and hoof beats punctured the rhythm of the chirping insects. David jumped and pushed Michal back so abruptly that she stumbled. The metallic swish of drawn swords cut through the air. Men holding torches shouted. "Who's there?"

David raised his hands as he knelt to the ground.

Michal stepped forward, picking up the cloak. "Princess Michal. This man found me."

* * *

I woke the next morning with a cough and sore throat. Mother was displeased with me and suspected David of tearing my dress and causing the scrapes on my hands and arms. Around the palace, men sharpened their bronze weapons and patched their shields. Father prowled the corridors like an injured lion. The killing of two Philistines so close to the palace had everyone on edge, prepared for war.

The evening approached. My nerves jolted with every footfall, and my heart pounded inside my throbbing head. I hadn't seen David all day. Would he go to war? I rushed to the servants' quarters, but his room was bare, emptied out. He wouldn't have left without saying goodbye. I waited until the changing of the guards and ran up the stairs to the abandoned guard shack, hoping to see David or receive a note.

Tinkling notes of the harp lifted my heart. I skipped up the last few steps. David set his harp on the bench and hugged me, his eyes solemn. "I have something for you."

"Don't tell me you're leaving." I twisted the edge of my robe.

He licked his lips and swallowed, placing a smooth stone in my hand.

"What's this for?"

"I picked it out of the brook. See the pretty patterns? It's green, flecked with brown, like your eyes. It's not valuable."

I put the cool stone to my cheek. "Oh, David, I'll treasure it, but does it mean you're going to war?"

He kissed my forehead. "Not to war. Your father dismissed me."

Panic spurred through my chest. "But he loves your songs. He can't send you away."

"Songs are only a dream, but pain lingers."

"What pain?"

He pulled me into his arms. "Of never seeing you again."

"No, it can't be." I clutched him tightly. "Take me with you."

"I can't. Your father will hunt us down like animals."

"Da-vid." My breath hitched and tears followed. "I don't care. I just want to be with you."

He stroked my hair softly. "I'll come back for you. I don't know how, but I will."

I clutched his robe. "Promise?"

"Yes." He touched my cheek. "Don't cry, Princess."

He held me for a long moment and kissed me until my lips were swollen and my eyes ran dry of tears. When the guards departed from the gate and marched toward the back, David swung his leg over the side of the wall and was gone.

He left his harp.

CHAPTER 4

1st Samuel 18:14 And David behaved himself wisely in all his ways; and the LORD was with him.

>>><<<

I waited on top of the wall and watched for David. He'd been gone more than a month and Father's army had been stalled in a valley, a standoff against the Philistines.

Merab tapped my shoulder. "Sister, I know how you feel."

I blew out a breath. Every day, she tried to make up to me. But I couldn't erase the image of her kissing David. I gritted my teeth and wished she'd leave.

She took a seat on my bench, put her arm around me and kissed my temple. "You're in love with David."

"Then why did you kiss him?" I wiped my eyes quickly.

"To test him." She swung her face in front of mine. "You don't understand, do you?"

Tears trickled through my fingers. What was there to understand? David had been banished, never to see me again.

Merab rocked my shoulders. "Don't let him hurt you. He was only looking to advance himself. He won't be the last man who'll make eyes at you to gain a position."

"David's not like that." I almost moaned, but caught my breath.

"If he truly cared about you, he wouldn't have kissed me. He's just a man like all the others." She took my hand, spread out my fingers and dried them with her scarf. "This was your first experience. Be glad he was only a servant. Next time, do not let him know how you feel. Men never want what they can easily get."

I bent my head to my lap, my face burning with shame. "I shouldn't have let him kiss me?"

"Exactly. I've never let Adriel kiss me." She heaved her shoulders. "He couldn't meet the bride price anyways. Well, cheer up. There's always another prince. Father is saving us for worthwhile alliances."

"Like who?"

Merab sighed. "Don't know. Jonathan mentioned the Ammonites or Syrians. He just killed the two possible Philistine princes."

A hot flush spilled up my throat. "Foreigners? Father would marry us to idolators?"

She patted my back. "Don't worry. Father's demands are too many. No one can meet his price."

I pulled at the roots of my hair. "I wish I weren't a princess."

"Wishing never helped anyone. Don't think about David. He's not worth it." She turned with a jangling of bracelets and floated down the stairs.

* * *

Mother met me in the hallway in front of Merab's bedchamber. Her brows were crinkled with a sharp line between them. "Where's your sister?"

"Maybe in the garden? Why?"

She ground her lips and sighed. "Your father wants Merab brought to the frontline. He has promised her hand to whichever brute will bring him the head of the giant, Goliath. Your father is about to—"

"Giant? I heard stories from Ishby. I thought he was fibbing."

"Unfortunately not. There's a Philistine who challenged your father to find a man to fight him. So far, no one dares and he's been taunting us close to forty days."

"Isn't Jonathan well enough to fight?" My brother had single-handedly killed twenty Philistines.

Mother pinched my arm. "Don't be silly. Jonathan's the heir to the throne."

"But what happens if no one fights him or the Philistines win?"

Mother's eyes hardened like flint. "We'll be made slaves. It's worse for women. I might be killed immediately, but the virgins will be taken as war captives or sold to men to do as they please."

"No!" The sensation of icy spiders crawled over my shoulders, and I fell into her arms. She rubbed my back. "Child, it hasn't happened yet. Pray God gives us a champion."

Merab entered her room and stopped when she saw us. "What's going on?"

Mother let me go and put a hand on my sister's shoulder. "Put on your best gown, the one you got for your eighteenth birthday, while Michal packs your personal items."

My lips trembled, and I drew in a shuddering breath, blinking back tears.

Merab's eyes widened. "Why my best gown?"

"Be brave, daughter. You have to go to the frontline and rally the men of war."

"Why me?" Merab stepped back, her eyes darted from me to Mother and back.

"Your father is offering your hand to the man who slays Goliath."

Merab's excruciating wail stung me clear to the bone. She threw herself against the wall. I ran and grabbed her from the back, my head on her shoulder and held her as she crumpled to her knees.

"Stop crying and get dressed." Mother pinched Merab's cheek and dragged her to the dressing area. "The bearers are waiting at the gate."

She snapped her skirts and swept from the room.

Merab slumped on her bed. "I have cramps, and I'll never be able to sit in that hot, dusty litter. Why don't you go? It might be fun."

"Fun? But I don't want to marry a soldier."

"Neither do I. But maybe David will be there." Her eyebrows perked. "What if he fights the giant?"

"David?" My heart bounded up three steps. "But he hardly knows how to fight."

"Even if he doesn't fight, maybe you'll see him." She handed me her finest gown, a jade green silk with golden vines embroidered around the edges.

"But, I don't look like you. Wouldn't Father notice?"

"Pshaw." She waved her hands. "You're close enough. Besides, the veil will cover your face. No one will get too close if you stay in the covered litter."

I worried her gown would be too long for me, but I donned it anyways. It dragged on the floor a few inches.

Merab wrapped me with her forest green cloak. Placing a golden shawl over my head and shoulders, she handed me a thick veil.

After I dressed, she opened the door. "Quickly, go to the front gate and jump in the litter. You're the best sister ever."

I lingered. "Merab?"

She waved her hand. "Hurry, before Mother comes back."

I hugged her. "I'm so scared. What if David gets hurt or killed?"

She pushed me into the hall. "Don't worry. Likely Father will end up killing the giant himself, and you certainly can't marry him. It'll just turn out to be an adventure for you. Hurry before Mother returns. I'll sleep in your room tonight." She lifted the veil and kissed my cheek. "I'll make it up to you. I promise."

* * *

"Behold, the daughter of Saul." The herald announced my arrival. Hot and sweating inside the stifling litter, I fanned my face and coughed to clear my dry throat.

Uncle Abner, my father's general, approached the litter. "Merab, I'm glad you're here. The men need courage."

I didn't reply, afraid my voice would give me away. He noticed my fanning and asked a servant to give me water. Father headed my direction. A pesky fly buzzed around me. I swatted at it, almost upsetting the bearers.

"Uncover the litter and take my daughter around the camps," Father said. "I want every man to see the prize I'm willing to sacrifice to vanquish this heathen Philistine."

Thankfully, a servant brought a water skin as the bearers knelt to remove the cover. I gulped the water, unmindful of how unladylike I appeared. Besides, they all thought I was Merab.

The bearers jostled me amongst the troops. Uncle Abner walked before me. "Behold, the daughter of King Saul. Whosoever brings the giant's head shall have her hand."

Dirty, stinking men leered at my form. "Unveil her. How do we know she's the daughter of Saul?"

Some followed the litter, reaching up to touch me. One insolent fellow prodded me with the end of his spear shaft. The guards pushed the throng back.

"Men of Benjamin," Abner shouted. "Who will kill Goliath and win the king's daughter?"

"Off with the veil. Off with the veil." The men chanted.

Abner looked toward Father's direction, and he shook his head.

"You cowards," Abner said. "Step forward before I offer her to another tribe."

The men threw up their shields and thumped their spears as my litter wove through the camp, but no one volunteered.

My face grew hotter underneath the sweltering veil. Did I look like a ridiculous lump of clothes? I could be a maid servant for all they knew. I pulled the veil open a sliver and scanned the hordes of men.

Abner led the way. "Men of Judah, the king demands your attention. Kill the dirty Philistine and receive the king's daughter."

As the men milled, gawking and pointing, one set of eyes stared at me. My heart leapt, and I sat straighter. David. Without thinking, I flipped the veil off my face and gazed at him.

His eyes widened, and his mouth popped open. The men around him whistled and hooted, but when Abner glared their direction, they turned their faces. Again, no man raised his hand. I looked back at Father. He stood with his arms crossed, his face red with fury.

My cheeks heated. I had ruined Father's venture. Without the dazzling beauty of Merab, no one would step forth to fight the giant, and we'd all be slaves of the Philistines. I placed the veil on my face to hide my shame. Uncle Abner grunted and ordered the bearers to keep walking. "Perhaps the tribe of Gad has a valiant man."

My veil securely fastened, I looked after David. He argued with several young men. They pushed and shoved him. One shook a finger at him and poked his chest. He hadn't wanted me enough, but I couldn't blame him. He was no warrior. The bearers brought me away from the camp of Judah toward the camp of Gad.

A hush fell across the men, and all eyes turned toward the ridge. A Philistine warrior swaggered on a rock pile high above a dry riverbed. Muscular and over nine feet tall, he was clad with a bronze breastplate and leather greaves. Brandishing a stout spear, he shouted, "Where's your champion? If he kills me, we will be your slaves. If I kill him, you become our slaves."

After waiting a few moments, he looked over the crowd and bellowed with laughter. "What? Is there no valiant man in all of Israel? Where's your god? You don't even have enough gold to make him an image!" The entire Philistine army guffawed and jeered.

Angry murmurs smoldered through our ranks, but no man stepped up. The bearers waded through a sea of cowards, taking me to the center of the formation.

The Philistine pounded his breastplate. "I am Goliath of Gath, and I challenge the God of Israel to find me a worthy opponent."

The Philistine host howled and banged their shields with a deafening clamor.

A sudden commotion stopped the heckling. David stretched his palms to the sky and yelled, "Dare this man reproach our God and live? Who is this uncircumcised Philistine to defy the armies of the living God?"

Soldiers on both sides stared at him. He lifted his hands again and yelled. "Is. There. Not. A. Cause?"

Not a man answered.

He wound his way to the base of my litter, between the two front bearers. I leaned forward and lifted my veil.

"Michal, is there not a cause?" His voice lowered intimately.

"There is, David. God's cause." I touched his hand. "God be with you."

He held my fingers and my gaze. "And you. Pray for me."

Abner pulled him back. "Do not touch the princess."

David brushed off his robe and spread his hands toward my father. "Let no man's heart fail because of him. Today, your servant will slay this Philistine, for the LORD, our God, will surely grant us victory."

I craned my neck, thrilled with David's boldness, but my heartbeat spiked, and my fingertips grew numb. David was so small compared to the giant. What if he were injured or worse?

He stepped into my father's tent. Moments later, he emerged without armor or weapon. Dressed in a shepherd's robe and carrying a staff, David washed his hands in a brook at the base of the camp.

My scalp ringed with cold sweat, I closed my eyes and prayed. *Dear LORD God, bring us the victory through Your servant, David. Place Your hand on him and deliver him from the hand of the Philistine. Be with David, always. In Your name, LORD.*

Across the ridge, the Philistine clambered down with his armor bearer, a muscular man who carried a huge shield before him. He shouted, "Am I a dog? That you come to me with staves? My gods curse you, boy. Come now. And I will give your flesh to the birds of prey and to the beasts of the field."

My heart pounding to escape my chest, I twisted the skin on my arms, gasping for air. How would David go against him with a thin shepherd's staff? I couldn't look. My David. So foolhardy. The giant's spear was thicker than his leg and the tip as large as his head.

Goliath advanced with the Philistine troops behind him. "This is the best of Israel? In Dagon's name, you shall perish."

David stood alone. "I come to you in the name of the Living God, the LORD of Israel. Today, He will deliver you into my hand, and the entire world shall know there is a God in Israel."

Goliath raised his spear and charged. My pulse knocked furiously in my ears, and I felt as if I were jumping out of my skin. I peeked under flickering eyelids, my hands clasped to my face.

David ran toward the giant, his flaming hair a beacon amongst the shrubs and bushes. The giant raised his spear and aimed the tip at him. A silent scream crawled to my throat. What was David doing? He took out a leather tie and swung it over his head.

Oh, God! A whip could do nothing against an iron spear. Goliath braced his leg and hoisted his heavy spear to his powerful shoulders. I squeezed my eyelids and choked to catch my breath.

David flicked his wrist. The giant's neck jerked backward, and the spear flew toward David. It fell short. A collective gasp swept the crowd. Goliath's knees buckled, and he crumpled forward. David jumped and shook his fist in the air.

He charged the remaining distance, drew Goliath's sword, hacked off his head and raised it up for all to see. The Philistines dropped their weapons and fled.

David knelt and lifted his eyes toward heaven. "The battle is the LORD's."

An ear-splitting cheer rose from our side, and the men of Israel rushed to pursue the panicked Philistines. Only David hiked to me, holding the head of Goliath by his hair. Blood covered his forearms and chest. When he reached the front of the litter, he smiled sideways at me. "Think your father will invite me back now?"

* * *

I returned to the palace, sweaty and dust-streaked, ready for a long, hot bath. I could hardly wait to tell Merab. David was the hero, and I would be his bride. I kissed my own hand and bounced down the hall to her chamber.

Merab met me at the door. "You won't believe how angry Mother was. She was fit to tear out my hair. So, tell me, what happened?"

I skipped up and down, kissing her. "David killed the giant, and I'm going to marry him."

She squealed and hugged me. "Oh, this is what you wanted. Will he be good to you?"

While the maids drew water, I told her everything. She tapped me with her fingernail. "And I endured three days of Mother pinching my arms. How are you going to repay me?"

"Repay you?" I slapped her with the tie of my robe. "You told me you'd make it up to me for taking your place."

Mother's maid bustled toward us, clapping. "Your mother said to wear your finest gowns for the victory banquet. Hurry, into your baths."

When Merab did not move, the maid said, "You too, elder princess."

Bubbling over and hardly able to stay still, I squirmed into a transparent turquoise gown layered over a white linen dress. The maids pinned my hair in loose coils and adorned me with pearls and moonstones. Wrapped in a silken shawl with silver threads, I followed a maid into the hallway.

Merab appeared in a pale-green gown decorated with golden figs. She twisted her lips wryly. "I don't understand why I have to dress up for your betrothal."

"Payback for going on the adventure." I pushed her playfully, and she giggled.

My father's guards escorted us to the banquet hall. I walked as if on golden clouds. By the end of the evening, I would be David's, and we'd have the rest of our long lives together.

Merab sat next to me and adjusted her shawl. Neither of us talked. Mother had warned us to keep our eyes down, but I peeked at David as he entered the hall.

My breath caught deep in my ribcage. He was dressed in princely attire and sat next to my father. Dancers, accompanied by flutes, viols, and drums, entertained the assembly. A minstrel pantomimed David's heroics: swung a leather sling and sliced off an imaginary head. While they paraded Goliath's severed head around the hall, I caught David staring at me.

His brows furrowed, and his eyes smoldered for a heartbeat before he deliberately averted his face, his jaw set for a fight. A gust of fear raised tingles through my scalp. What happened? What had I done? Why did he look at me like he hated me?

Tears threatened. I gripped the edge of my shawl. Merab's eyes widened with confusion and concern, and she rubbed my shaking hand.

I yanked away from her. Had David changed his mind and asked Father to give him my sister? I turned my face to the wall. Blinking, I recalled his grin of victory and the touch of his hand. How could I have been so wrong? Obviously the elder princess bestowed more prestige than the younger.

"Behold, my servant David," Father said. "You have vanquished our mortal enemy, the Philistine, Goliath, and brought victory to Israel."

The crowd cheered. They pounded the tables and stomped their feet. My heart skipped beats, and my stomach clenched. Hope fought with despair, and I dreaded the next minute. Merab fiddled with her shawl and bit her lips. Her expression was both sympathetic and worried.

Father clapped a hand on David. "Tonight, I give you my daughter for wife. Only be valiant for me and fight the LORD's battles."

All eyes turned toward us. Father approached our table and took Merab's arm. My heart tore into shreds, and I chewed the sides of my tongue raw. Murmurs of approval shuddered through the assembly as my father and Merab walked to David's side.

I held my breath, wanting to look away, but like the rest of the crowd, I stared at David. He bowed to the ground. "Who am I, and who is my father's family in Israel, that I should be son-in-law to the king?"

"My son, David, you have found favor with me." Father lifted him to stand. "Let it be known, that I, King Saul, am a man who keeps his vow. My daughter for the head of Goliath, and my daughter you shall have."

He joined my sister's hand with David's to signify their betrothal and handed him a light veil for her to wear during the year before the wedding.

My stomach twisted into a Minoan knot, and my heart tolled like a mourning bell. A soundless wail strangled my throat. How could David be so cruel?

He placed the betrothal veil on Merab and led her around the hall to be congratulated. Anguish crawled from my reeling head to my cringing toes. I pulled my face into a mask of indifference and stared at the giant tapestry framed on the wall. It bore a tree of life, florid and fruitful, quite the opposite of my bleak and barren future. David would never be more than a brother.

* * *

David slipped away from Merab as soon as the celebration finished. Merab walked to her mother's side while Michal hurried from the room. She had stared at the wall as if the entire evening bored her.

How could he have misread her? The king had laughed when he asked for her hand, told him Michal had refused. Had she meant it when she told him she wanted him? Or did she play with him and mock him with that ridiculous bride price, throwing the peace of Israel in his face?

He pounded a fist into the stone wall. He should leave well alone. After all, she had rejected him. But he had to know why.

He found Michal sitting on the bench in the guard shack, wrapped in the black Philistine cloak. Her shoulders shook with suppressed sobs as she prayed. He waited for her to finish. Her sweet jasmine fragrance awakened a longing to pull her into his arms.

"Michal." His voice was pinched.

She jumped and clutched her necklace. He swallowed the lump, but it grew and filled his throat. She was so beautiful, dressed for the special occasion of her sister's betrothal. He held his hand out, but she shrank from him.

"What happened?" he asked.

She turned to the wall and ignored him. He resolved to save face. She'd deny it anyway, as if he had any right to question her.

He crossed into the guard shack. "I wish you happiness. I'm sorry if I behaved inappropriately with you. If I'm going to marry your sister, we cannot have misunderstandings."

She brushed by him toward the stairs. "I'll give my sister your harp."

"Keep it. I want you to have it." He tugged her elbow.

"Why?" Her lower lip quivered. "I already threw away your stupid stone."

Her words cut his heart. She had said she would treasure it. Obviously she had used him, found him amusing and tossed him like a piece of dirt.

"It wasn't stupid," he replied lamely.

She jerked her arm from his grasp. "Leave me alone. You're marrying my sister, and she's not happy either. Why did you have to come to our palace? To ruin our lives?"

David clenched his fists and straightened his shoulders. "Your father invited me, and I earned my reward."

She narrowed her eyes. "I hope you're happy. Too bad she doesn't love you."

David's jaw tightened. "Love has nothing to do with this. I earned the privilege of being son-in-law to the king."

Her face twisted as if she were in pain. "I hate you. You're so stupid. You should have a wife who loves you."

"And what did you want? A husband who would be king? Even an idol worshipper?" He tore the Philistine cloak from her shoulders. "Why are you wearing this?"

"I'll scream, David. Give it back."

He waved it over her head and threw it over the wall. Tears overflowed his eyelids, and his heart slammed into his stomach with a hollow well of agony. Michal had rejected him for the young Philistine prince. It all made sense now.

She lifted her chin and looked at the moon, her jaw jutting defiantly, her hair fluttering in the breeze. The transparent turquoise gown outlined a figure he yearned to hold, the woman he thought God had given to him.

He rushed down the stairs and looked up for the last time. She only wept because her sister was forced to marry him, a commoner. He'd show them. Wasn't he God's chosen king?

The next morning he departed to fight the LORD's battles.

CHAPTER 5

1st Samuel 18:20 And Michal Saul's daughter loved David: and they told Saul, and the thing pleased him.

>>><<<

I stepped into Father's bedchamber and hesitated, struck by his appearance. Greasy hair hung over sweating jowls under red-rimmed eyes. The room reeked of wine and burnt hemp.

"Come in, daughter." He gripped my shoulders. "David sent a message asking for his bride. It's a pity your mother talked me into marrying Merab to Adriel."

"What will you tell him?" I rubbed my fingers over tingling palms.

"Why does he think he deserves a king's daughter, unless it's to make himself king? If the people didn't love him so much, I'd have him killed already. What do you think about that, my sweet?"

His words brought a chill to my spine. I lowered my face and waited. Despite Father's jealous anger, my heartbeat quickened. David had been gone over a year. No one told him Merab had married Adriel after his wife died in childbirth. Would David settle for me?

"I'm a man of my word. I promised him a daughter." He touched my cheek. "I should offer him another chance. Would you like to be the bait?"

I blinked at the floor and twisted the side of my robe. My father could be laying a trap. Although David had wounded me, I wanted no part in harming him.

Father traced my cheekbone with his rough finger. "Let me look at you." His breath hot against my face, he asked, "How old are you?"

"Sixteen."

He cradled my face with both hands. "She was sixteen. A goddess in a pool of water. Blue-green eyes." His gaze blurred into a faraway look. "She was lively, impertinent, and never one to stop teasing. I can see her in you."

"Who was she?"

"She left her heart in that river, the brook where…" His voice trailed, a solitary leaf fluttering into the past. He shut his eyes and furrowed his fingers down my face. "If I could see her again… Like a dream, so fleeting. Let me look in your eyes."

Sweat popped over my forehead. Who was father seeing in his vision? He had been tormented by spirits, and without David's music, he could not sleep.

I stepped back. "I'll get Mother."

"No, not your mother." He swallowed a draught of wine. "So, you think you're ready for marriage? I had plans for you, my darling, to make peace with the Philistines. Their prince is two years younger than you. I had wanted to wait."

I had no wish to marry for peace, especially to a foreign idol worshipper. Merab had held out. No matter how many times she had been promised, at the end, Father allowed her to decide.

He thumbed my cheek. "But alas, this David has to be dealt with. Perhaps there's still a chance."

My heart jumped at the opportunity. I clutched my father's sleeve. "I should like to marry David, if you'd permit."

He pushed me aside and pounded a fist on the oaken table. "If he thinks he'll usurp my crown with my daughter's body, he shall pay dearly."

My heartbeat jittered. "Didn't he already pay with the head of Goliath?"

"That was for Merab. And she cheated him. That girl always got her way." He tapped his chin. "Yes, I will extract a heavy bride-price from him. One hundred freshly slaughtered Philistine foreskins."

Disgusting. I clapped my hand on my mouth. Why would he want such a price?

My father chuckled through a slurred grin. "He has to do the task alone, and he has one year. But don't worry, my doll, he won't succeed."

I stared at him, unbelieving. I wanted David, but I wanted more for him to live.

* * *

One spring morning, about nine months later, my youngest brother, Ishbaal, shuffled to my side. "David is back with the bride price in a bloody bag."

My heart jumped like a playful kitten. "You've seen him? Where?"

"He's going to see Father." He waved his hands and dragged his club foot. "Do you want to watch him count it?"

I made a face and rushed to my dressing room. Thank God! David had survived, and he wanted me. But what would Father do? He had sent David into danger by asking for the bride price. Would he allow me to marry him? Or would he find some reason to thwart him?

Trailing my hand through my gowns, I chose a shimmery silver-colored dress. A maid tucked my hair under a sequined headband. For jewelry, I donned a simple strand of pearls and shell earrings. After a dusting of jasmine powder, I wrapped myself in a jade-green shawl with a fluttery fringe and headed for Father's audience chamber to hear the news.

"Burn it," my father ordered as he exited the chamber. He came toward me, followed by my mother. I froze. Father's brows furrowed, and he shoved me against a wall. "Explain why he brought two hundred foreskins. Have you been playing the harlot?"

"What do you mean?"

"A double bride price is given for a defiled daughter."

I clenched my fists in front of my chest. "But I never saw him. How could he defile me?"

Father glared at me, his dark hair pummeled in his eyes. "By bringing double, he's telling the world he's taken your virginity. Sly fox. He's outmaneuvered me."

My knees shook, and I would have dropped to the ground if he hadn't held me up. Mother placed a hand on his arm. "There's nothing we can do about it now. Saul, let it go."

She pried Father's fingers off me and led him away.

I rubbed my shoulder and ran to the garden. Father resented the people when they cheered for David. And David behaved wisely and charmed all Father's servants. Was I just a bartering chip in this dangerous rivalry? I slowed my pace and let the sweet, spicy scent of cut fennel calm my mind.

David stood under the shade of an ancient olive tree. He looked different, stronger and sturdier. His hand poised over the large sword at his waist, he surveyed the courtyard like a lion regarding his pride.

His wave was commanding and deliberate. I refused to run to him, to act like a lovesick girl. My heart knotted in remembrance of his last words, his only concern that he was properly rewarded by the king. I turned and glided toward the lily pond. A light breeze ruffled the leaves of the bay laurels, and the piquant fragrance of crushed leaves stiffened the hairs on the back of my head.

Footsteps crunched on the gravel behind me.

"Princess." And there he was, the man who had hunted two hundred men to win the remaining daughter of Saul. My heart fluttered, contrary to my resolve, and when he offered his arm, I took it and walked with him around the pond. The warmth of his touch wet my lips, and I fought the urge to lean on him, to conform to his strength.

"Are you happy to see me?" A smile lit his face, and his eyes seemed to dance.

I picked a lily and twirled it in his face. "Shouldn't you be disappointed?"

His brows crinkled briefly, and he let go of my hand. "About what?"

"I suppose you were disappointed to find my sister married." I hid the lily behind my back.

"No, I was worried you'd be married before I could earn the bride price."

The golden-brown eyes seemed sincere, but I couldn't succumb so easily. I pouted and looked at him sideways. "I didn't care whether you got it or not."

"You didn't care if I was hurt or killed?"

My lips trembled. I stared at the veins bulging between the knuckles of his strong, square hand. The thought of David injured had kept me up many nights. "I only prayed for you and wished you well."

His smile broadened, and he grabbed my hand. "So, you *are* happy to see me."

I flung the lily at him. "You assume too much."

The sides of his mouth dropped, and his shoulders slumped while he ran a hand through his ruddy locks. I turned toward the stand of myrtle trees near the back gate.

A few footfalls later, he caught my shawl and swung me around. "Michal, I don't understand. Am I not good enough for you?"

I gasped and coughed to cover my surprise. He acted as if I had hurt him. I pushed him aside and hugged myself, fighting for composure.

"Talk to me." He touched my chin with the tip of his finger.

"You didn't want me." My voice came out too small—girl-like. "You wanted my sister."

His mouth opened, and he shook his head. "No, your father said you refused."

A swell of pressure washed over my shoulders. "He never asked me."

David's face hardened. "But why would your father lie about something like this?"

I couldn't tell him of my father's hatred, or his suspicions that David would usurp his crown. I dared not believe he wanted me, or did he?

David took my hand. "I doubled your bride price. It shows how much I value you."

"Oh, I bet." I bit back a smile. "I don't suppose it to be a fair trade. You're going to have to offer something more than a putrid sack."

His eyes twinkled. "Come, let's take a walk. I can see you're still hesitant."

He offered me his arm, and I reluctantly took it. Was it me he valued? Or did he only wish to be son-in-law to the king?

We walked out the back gate, circled a hillock and stepped over a meadow. Sheep grazed in peaceful clumps. The twitters of sparrows trilled through tangled leaves, and dragonflies flitted between the reeds that swayed alongside a glistening brook.

He led me down the bank and turned me to face him. "Remember that night I found you? And you told me your price?"

My cheeks heated, and I could not meet his eye. I wanted him so much, but the pain of rejection stung my heart.

He twirled the ends of my hair. "I mean to deliver peace to Israel, not a bloody sack. But before I can do that, would my heart be enough?"

"What are you saying?" My fingers tingled with feathery pulses.

He kissed my forehead. "Michal, my heart for yours, is that a fair trade?"

I raised my eyes. He stared at me so intently that my throat went dry. His honey-brown eyes beckoned an invitation to his soul.

"But what if I do not please you?" I said.

"I'll always be pleased with you, no matter what happens. Do you believe me?"

I yearned to believe, to trust, and to cast my fate to his. His embrace soothed me, and I needed his acceptance. Warmth crept over my shoulders where he held me, and my breathing steadied as I leaned against him.

He caressed my face and kissed my cheek, his beard calming and reassuring. "You don't have to answer me today. I'll wait and stay as long as your father tolerates me."

He led me through the meadows and back to the palace. We climbed the steps to our spot on the wall behind the abandoned guard shack.

Warblers flitted among the treetops, and clouds swirled in soft trailing wisps. High above, a pair of hawks glided in circles, their paths crossing, intersecting oh, so close, and then parting and coming around to almost touch again. David embraced me, his chest to my back, and pulled his cloak around my shoulders to shield me from the evening breeze.

His arms felt safe and his heartbeat promised security. And even though I had cried many tears while he was gone, he now offered me his heart. I tilted my face. "I'll answer you now."

He dropped slowly to one knee. "Michal, you're everything I want in a wife. Will you marry me?"

"Yes. Yes, David, I'll marry you." A smile sprang from my heart, and I bounced on my heels.

"You will?" he asked, his voice excited like a young boy's.

I nodded again, and he bowed his head. "LORD God, I thank You this day for granting my heart's desire to marry Michal. May we both abide in Your Laws and cleave to each other, by faith, as husband and wife. In Your name, LORD."

He swung me around, and we stared at each other, giggling.

"I can't wait another day," he said. "Let's skip the betrothal and go straight to the wedding before your father changes his mind."

"I'd love nothing better."

The troth promised and sealed, we kissed.

* * *

Decked in multiple layers of cloth, beads, and jewelry, I took my father's arm and walked with him to the wedding pavilion. My heart leapt at my first glimpse of David through the threads of my bridal veil. He stood, erect as a prince, a bridegroom's crown glinting over his thick red-brown hair. A blue and white prayer shawl wrapped his broad shoulders, and his luminous eyes tracked my path.

At the canopy, he walked around me three times and lifted my veil, as was custom, to assure my identity. I licked my dry lips and stared at the fringes of his shawl, but couldn't restrain the corners of my mouth from twitching. The sun beamed brighter, and the colors of his robe jumped sharply. His shallow breathing fanned my face, and I could almost hear his heart thump, or was it my own pulse? His hand trembled slightly as he clasped mine.

Elihu, the priest, read the seven blessings describing God's creation of the universe, of mankind, of Israel, and of husband and wife. He finished with the final blessing. "Blessed are You, LORD, who grants joy to David by giving him Michal as wife, a help meet for him."

David looked at the sky and said, "Blessed are You, LORD, our God, sovereign of the universe, who gave me life and blessed my path."

He dropped his gaze to mine. "Michal, I take you as my wife of the covenant; I take you uprightly according to the Law of Moses. You are forevermore consecrated unto me. Blessed are You, LORD, who mercifully grants that we may grow old together."

Warmth encircled my heart at his declaration. I belonged to him forever, my David.

Elihu produced a scroll, the book of our marriage covenant. He offered the reed to David, who signed his name and passed it to me. Our marriage was officially sealed before God and witnesses. David and I faced the assembly to receive the blessings.

Father spoke first, "Blessed are you, my children. May peace and harmony always be between you. Blessed be the LORD God, for His mercy endures forever."

David's father, Jesse, approached us with his arms open. "Blessed are you, my son and my daughter, when you fear the LORD God. May you be content with the fruit of your labor, and may you be fruitful as a well-tended vine. Blessed be the LORD God, who shall preserve your steps from this time forth and forevermore."

Jonathan held our hands. "Blessed are you, my brother, David, and my sister, Michal. Today, may your heart and soul be knit as one. May you be joined on this day and forevermore. Blessed be the LORD God, may nothing pull you asunder."

As tears wet my eyes, musicians sang a hymn of praise and thanksgiving. Jonathan handed David a vase, and he smashed it on the ground to signal the end of the ceremony. The guests paraded to the banquet tables, and Mother let down the covers of the wedding canopy to leave us alone for the customary quarter of an hour.

The fragrance of jasmine mixed with the heady scent of sandalwood emboldened me. I clasped my arms around David and squeezed him tightly, breathing my vows in his ears. "David, Ishi, I bestow myself to you today and always, to love only you, to pray for you, and to be a help meet for you."

"And likewise, I to you," he said. "Isha, only you, my wife…"

Our lips joined as husband and wife, and I kissed him, inhaling the joy of belonging and the security of desire. So enveloped was I in his presence, that it took me a few moments to feel my mother's jabs in my back. I smoothed my dress and followed her to the wedding feast.

We sat at a table laden with platters of fish in lemon sauce, herbed roast pheasants with garlic and leeks, lamb shanks cooked in cumin and cilantro, and an assortment of honey and date cakes. David enjoyed the food and insisted on feeding me each bite from his hand. How blessed to belong to a man, one so loving and solicitous, who cared for me and pledged his protection.

My sister walked by, kissed me and whispered, "The man has quite an appetite—and large hands. Enjoy."

CHAPTER 6

Isaiah 62:5 For as a young man marrieth a virgin, so shall thy sons marry thee: and as the bridegroom rejoiceth over the bride, so shall thy God rejoice over thee.

>>><<<

Late in the evening, my parents led us to the wedding tent for the consummation. Father lifted the flap, and David pulled me in with his fringed prayer shawl over my head. A stark white cloth spread over a bed covered with pillows and skins.

"What happens now?" My voice trembled, and a sudden chill washed over me. Mother had warned me that the marriage night would be unpleasant, something to be endured through closed eyes, especially the staining of the virginity cloth.

"Sit with me a bit." He touched my elbow and gestured to the bed. After he uncrossed my arms, he removed my beaded headdress and bridal shawl. "With that out of the way, I can properly kiss you."

Tiny kisses encircled my lips, and he bathed me with his warm breath. His lips trailed over my mouth and down my neck to caress my breasts through the silk of my dress. Firm hands slipped the tinkling bracelets off my wrists and slowly untangled the layers of fabrics and beads adorning my wedding gown. Heat spread across my belly, and I pressed against his solid body. He lifted my dress and wedged one knee between my legs while touching me in places no one had ever handled. I held my breath. The sensations were too concentrated, too intense.

He shifted his weight and gently unclasped my fists. "Did you think we would fight?"

"Of course not." I threaded my fingers between his.

"There's no rush." He pulled me to a sitting position. His quickened breathing belied his calm words.

My tongue stuck to the roof of my mouth. He held my hand and smiled, his honey-colored eyes twinkling. The hand he held became moist, and I swallowed several times to calm my fluttering heart. I had dreamed of this moment, waited in anticipation. But I wanted it to be perfect for him. And I was ruining it. I reached for a cloth to dab my face, afraid the kohl and rouge would smear.

"It's warm in here, isn't it? Would you like to take a walk to cool off? Or shall we play a game?"

"Game?" A giggle bubbled in my throat. He looked so eager, like a young boy out to play ball.

"First to undress the other wins. I'm ahead because I've taken off your headdress and your shawl. Watch my quick hands." He unhinged a heavy gold and carnelian collar and dropped it to the table.

"Wait, wait." I lifted the bridegroom's crown off his head.

"You catch on fast. Now, untie my sash."

I unknotted his sash with some difficulty and looped it around his neck, boldly reeling him in for a kiss.

He lingered on the kiss before moving my hands to his shoulders. "Take my robe off. With your mouth."

I clutched at the silken groom's robe between my teeth. It was a bit more difficult than I thought. I nibbled at the edges near his neck, and he squirmed to help me. But each time I tugged one side, the other side tightened.

"It might help if you started lower," he suggested with a sly smile.

I moved my face to his chest. The robe already hung partially open, exposing the linen tunic he wore as an inner garment. His torrid male scent stirred my insides like drunken butterflies, and I lingered before pulling one side of the robe back. David slid his arm out and dropped the other side.

I couldn't help noticing the bulging tent underneath his tunic. My pulse quickened, and I wondered about the things Merab told me the night before.

David placed my hands on his chest. "Now, strip me."

Tempted, I trickled my fingers under his shirt, surprised at the smoothness of his skin with its sprinkling of soft, springy hair. He raised his arms for me to remove the garment. Goosebumps popped over his flesh, and I tickled him until he could barely breathe.

"Enough, enough." He flipped me on my back. "My turn."

He grasped my waist and removed a beaded apron. I squirmed, but he propped on his elbows and plucked the combs from my hair, one by one. Laughing, he rumpled my wavy locks. "Did I ruin your hair? I bet it took hours to fix."

I leaned forward to untangle my hair from a beaded fringe. When I looked back, he had kicked off his breeches. I averted my eyes but couldn't help what I'd seen. A tangle of nerves fluttered deep in my belly.

"You win." He pulled me to his muscular chest. I twisted out of his grasp and stumbled behind the table.

"Come back here." He laughed. "Do you want a closer look?"

Curious, yet shy, I turned away, resisting the surprising urge to touch. As he caught the hem of my gown, I grabbed a jar of water and poured it over his head. His eyes popped and he wiped his face, sputtering. Still clothed in my wedding dress, I ran to the tent flap.

"You're afraid, aren't you?" he called from the wet rug.

"Not at all." I threw a bracelet at him. "Bet you can't catch me." I stepped out of the tent.

A crowd of guests gawked, their mouths open, as if I were a creature from a Sumerian legend.

Father grabbed my arm. "Michal, what's going on? Have you disgraced us?"

Behind him, Mother fanned her face, her eyes wide.

"No, Father, we were playing a game. I—"

A sharp slap spun my head and threw me to the ground.

"Is he putting you away, found you unsuitable?" Father's voice rumbled.

Pain and shame welled in my face, and I backed away from his towering rage.

David rushed out of the tent in a hastily tied robe. His cheeks burnished with anger, he shoved my father into my mother. My brothers grabbed David and held him while my father drew his sword.

I flung myself at his feet. "Father!"

He pointed his sword at David. My brothers released him, and David fell on his face. "My king, have mercy."

"Father," I cried, "please, forgive me. It's my fault."

He brandished the sword. "Son of Jesse, I could have your head as a wedding present for your bride."

The onlookers gasped.

"No!" I covered David. "Please don't hurt him."

Mother pulled Father's arm and murmured, "Saul. It's their wedding. The boy is young."

Father glared at the crowd of relatives and dignitaries who looked aside and pretended nothing had happened. I wheezed and trembled with David beneath me.

"Get up, Michal." Father pulled me, but I wouldn't let go of David.

"Listen to your father," David said softly. "He told you to get up."

Mother grabbed me, and I clutched her shoulders, hiding my face in her robe.

"This is my wedding present to you," Father said.

"No, Father, don't hurt him," I cried as Mother tugged me away from him.

The crowd groaned. I couldn't look, but I did.

Blood dripped down David's left cheek. Father shoved him toward me. "Now, take my daughter and give her mother the cloth."

David nodded. "Yes, my lord, king."

Father had cut David's cheek with the tip of his sword. Head down, I followed David into the tent. An uneasy silence descended on the wedding party.

"I'm so sorry," I whispered. "My father has lost his mind."

"Don't say that. He's the LORD's anointed king."

"He's not the same man he used to be." I dipped a napkin in a bowl of water and dabbed his face while he gingerly touched my throbbing cheek. Tender, loving feelings flowed from my heart through my hands as I ministered to him. The cut began to clot, but he would bear a scar, forever wounded for me.

"Why did Father hurt us, and on our wedding day?"

"I don't pretend to understand him. Maybe he's upset we're finally married. He didn't think I would obtain the bride price."

Tears rimmed my eyes. "He said you'd put me away, divorce me."

David put his arms around me and shushed me. "I'll never do that. Your parents think it's a disgrace for you to marry me, a poor man. But when I doubled the bride price, it guaranteed that you'd be mine forever. The Law says a man who pays the double bride price may never put his wife away."

"Never?"

"Never. Looks like you're stuck with me. Are you happy?"

"Yes, David." I yawned and rubbed my eyes, drained by the excitement. The party had terminated with the fight, and it was deathly quiet outside. "Do we still have to give my mother the virginity cloth?"

David grinned. "We have seven nights, but if you're ready…"

"I… ahh… sure." I chirped, a little too brightly.

He thumbed my chin and kissed me. "I want it to be special for you. It's late. Do you want to sleep in the tent with me or back in your bedchamber?"

I hugged him, my face in his neck. "With you."

David stepped out of the tent and asked for Naomi, my maid. After she tended to me, I climbed into the bed, dressed in my sleeping gown. He put out the oil lamps and cradled me to his chest. The thump of his heartbeat calmed me.

"I love you, David."

He whispered my name, and I wasn't sure whether he said he loved me or not. Perhaps I only dreamt it.

* * *

The morning light peeked through the seams of the tent.

"My bride is awake," David said. "Ah… your eyes. Did you know they change with your mood?"

I yawned and covered myself with the sheets, but David yanked them off me.

"Open up." He teased. "You're relaxed and happy. They're clear pools of dark jade. When you were frightened, the brown flecks expanded."

I blinked, uneasy to be so transparent.

"Now you're worried," he said. "The brown specks are dancing. And last night they were muddy with anger. You know, you fascinate me?"

I touched the edge of his cheek. The mark was swollen with a dark red crust. "Does your face still hurt?"

"Yes, especially when I smile. But you've made me smile a lot, and I don't mind. Are you ready to have breakfast with my parents?"

"As long as I don't look like a creature from a nightmare."

"Hardly. You are beauty personified." He kissed me, opened the tent flap and led me out.

I went with Naomi to take care of my grooming. After a warm bath and cold compresses on my swollen eye, I sat at the table with his family.

They graciously pretended not to notice anything amiss. His mother comforted me with her warm presence, and his father recited the entire love story of his grandparents Boaz and Ruth to my great delight. David's brothers dragged him to the side with wide grins, punctuated gestures and loud chuckles. Every so often, they looked over, laughed, shook their heads, and cupped their hands to whisper.

David's mother took my hand and rubbed it. "You have nothing to worry about. My son cares deeply about you. I know."

"He wouldn't have married you if he didn't," his father said. "He never looked at any maidens. We thought he'd never marry."

His mother smiled. "He's a good boy, always mindful of what's right. He never gave us any trouble, such a sweet disposition."

"And he loves God. We're so proud of him."

"Oh, look how we go on." His mother patted my hand.

His father stood and grabbed his cane. "We should let you two get back to your business in the wedding tent. You have six more nights to determine if you'd like to keep him." He winked as he hobbled away.

David put his hands on my shoulders. "While they rest, let's sneak out and go for a walk."

He took my hand, and we scampered to the back gate. I lifted my skirts to hike through the grassy meadow. David wove strands of honeysuckle in my hair, and we lay under an acacia tree to nap. I snuggled in the crook of his arm and stroked his chest and shoulders, admiring his muscular build.

He twirled my hair, an impish smile on his face. "Lower, I've something harder." He took my hand and guided me toward his loins. "I know you wanted to touch."

I held back. "I didn't, I mean, I just wondered…"

A fluttering, coiled skein dropped on my face. I shrieked and swatted at the giant insect. It cheeped shrilly.

David laughed and thumped his head on the tree trunk. "Ow!"

The mass of blue and grey squawked. A baby bird with a collar of white pins around his neck and sticks for wings opened his mouth and cried plaintively. Above us, the parents screeched while they zipped from branch to branch. One dived toward us and swooped up when David raised his arm.

I pointed to a nest high in the feathery leaves. "Oh, he must have fallen."

David picked up the baby bird. Thorns and dry branches surrounded the lower canopy. The bird cheeped in his palm. He swung a leg up to climb the tree using only one hand. His clothes tore, and he made exclamations of pain all the way up. I waited with my hand over my mouth. The parent birds buzzed his head to drive him away.

After he put the bird back in the nest, he scuffled down the tree and dropped at my knees.

"My hero." I rewarded him with a hug and helped him flick ants off his robe. I couldn't keep the smile off my face as I kissed every scratch while the birds shrilled and squawked. Such a kind, caring man, he'd make a wonderful father.

* * *

After dinner, my parents stationed themselves at the tent flap. David's parents shook their heads and retired to more comfortable accommodations in the palace. My brothers laughed and sang bawdy love songs. David's brothers took bets. Guests, filled with mirth, sloshed wine on one another. Drums, flutes and viols plied sweet melodies in the air, and perfumed incense rivaled the fragrance of the flowery garlands. Professional chanters keened, clapped their hands and swayed to the beat of the drums.

When David and I reentered the tent, my stomach fluttered. "What did your father mean by six more nights to figure out if I'd like to keep you?"

He pinched my cheek lightly. "I don't know what he meant, but I aim to capture your whole heart and never let you go."

I hugged him and laid my head on his shoulder. My gaze shifted to the tent flap. "They're still waiting."

"Let them wait. I'll take my time so my touch will be as natural to you as your own." He lit the oil lamps and smoothed the cloth over the bed before pulling me into his lap.

His kisses probed deeper, desiring, wanting, and his tongue rolled with mine in a rhythm that hypnotized me. Leaning forward, he lowered his mouth to my neck and pressed me to the bed with his hard body. When he caressed my breasts, I tensed and waited.

"Don't be frightened, my love. It's me, your David."

I took deep breaths and willed myself to relax. "I want you to be pleased with me."

"I already am, more than you know. I know you're pure. You have nothing to worry about." He placed his hands in mine. "Move my hands, wherever you want. Think of them as yours."

A deep breath eased my jitters, and I held his large, strong hands and placed them over my shoulders. Tentatively, I dragged them to the opening of my robe. And when he did not grab, I became bolder. I knew where he wanted to go, but his hands remained relaxed. I picked them up and placed them under my robe.

His gaze intently on me, I loosened the sash to my robe and moved his hands to the side of my hips. I trembled with a strange, soft feeling. My expression must have changed because his eyes grew hazy, half-closed, and his breath quickened.

He flexed his fingers so gently that I could barely feel them move. Needing more, I grasped his hands and caressed them into the silks covering my flesh, awakening my desire. *I can do this.*

He drew over me, his face etched with care and complete concentration. I relaxed and allowed him to complete our union, the flash of pain replaced immediately with a sense of fulfillment. A cloud of peace descended; a warm glow of well-being anointed me, washing me with a swelling of affection. I held him with a fierce tenderness, my face plastered to his chest, our bodies entwined, husband and wife.

CHAPTER 7

1ˢᵗ Samuel 18:28-29 And Saul saw and knew that the LORD was with David, and that Michal Saul's daughter loved him. And Saul was yet the more afraid of David; and Saul became David's enemy continually.

>>><<<

David ran up the stairs and stepped through the door of the apartment he shared with his new wife. Little more than an expanded guard station, it perched high on a section of the palace wall away from the courtyard and toward the back gate. The privacy of the location suited him. He could almost believe he and Michal had their own home. He caught his breath as she stepped toward him with a rustle of gowns.

She kissed him. "How's my father?"

"He fell asleep after I played love songs."

She laughed and slid a finger up his arm. "Do you have a love song for me?"

"I might, if you promise you won't fall asleep on me." He rubbed her nose with his.

"You might have to do a bit more than just sing if you want my complete attention." She tugged his robe open. "I'm glad he let you leave early."

"Yes, better than scowling and thumping his spear at me."

"Your playing can't be that bad." She lifted the harp off his back and placed it in the corner near the door. "Or does he suspect?"

"Suspect what? I'm merely his son-in-law." He handed her his robe, and she hung it at the side of the bed.

"You can tell me. I'm your wife."

He studied her eyes, the brown flecks retreated and pools of green jade shimmered, enticing. "There's nothing to tell."

She caressed his shoulders, smoothing out the tension knots. "What about the time the Prophet Samuel visited you? Was it to anoint you king?"

48

"Who told you?" His blood slithered like ice water. "It's treason to speak of such things. Your father is the king."

"You talk in your sleep." She drew soft hands around his waist. "I won't betray you."

He was sure she wouldn't deliberately betray him. But she was a young lady, prone to excitement. He stared at her, trying to discern her motivation. "What's this all about?"

"Trust. Love. You know I love you, don't you?" She blinked, her eyes expectant.

David jerked his face the direction of her father's bedchamber. "Would you side with me against your father? If it came to it?"

She cupped his chin and stroked the soft, vulnerable spot under his jaw. "Why would you doubt me?"

The tender look on her face reassured him. He sank onto the couch and pulled her into his lap. "Your father can't know about this. He hates me enough already."

"He seems to be calmer now that we're married." Her soft breath fanned his beard, and her fingers danced light circles on his chest. "I want to know everything, how it happened, and how you felt."

David closed his eyes and breathed steadily through his nose. He wanted to trust her and know she'd be on his side. He took her hand and placed it over his heart. "I'll never forget that moment as long as I live. I stood in the meadow and watched the sheep. The sun went down and the sky glowed red, the last rays slipping over the horizon like golden swords. I marveled at God's glory and prayed for peace in Israel. A chorus of a thousand voices in pure harmony rang over the sound of the bleating sheep."

He peeked at her. She seemed awestruck, her eyes dreamy. A lock of hair strayed across her brow. David smoothed it back and continued. "An old man with a white beard and a staff asked me for a drink of water. I held the water skin for him, and he refreshed himself. He asked my name, and I told him. He put his arm around me and said, 'The LORD looks not on the outward appearance but in the heart. Tell me, David, what is in your heart?'"

"What did you tell him?"

"That I love the LORD God with all my heart, all my soul, and all my mind."

"That's lovely." Michal pressed her ear on his chest.

"The Prophet brought me in front of my father and all my brothers. And he said, 'Behold, the LORD has provided Himself a king, a man after His own heart. My son, David, this is he whom the LORD has anointed.' And taking a horn of oil, he poured it on my head. The cold oil heated as it ran down my hair and my face, until it burned in my chest like a mighty flame, filling me with a tremendous sense of exhilaration and tranquility."

She squeezed him tighter. "So beautiful. I wonder if I'll ever feel that burning for the LORD."

"You can, if you trust and believe Him. Do you?"

"Yes, I've always believed in God, but I don't know Him. He's behind a cloud. I wish to feel as you do." Michal rubbed her face on his chest as if she could borrow some of the fire. "Why has the LORD regarded me, to let me be your wife? To love a man after His own heart?"

The longing look on her face told him more than he could bear. What expectations would she have of him? He swallowed hard and leaned over to kiss her before she could say more.

* * *

Alone, I wandered the expansive corridors of my father's palace. I pressed my flat belly. Merab was expecting a second child. She claimed he was conceived the night of my wedding. They had appeared with their firstborn son, Joel, and Mother had kept him all night. I barely had time with David before Father ordered him to war with the Philistines. He had been gone six long months, but with winter upon us, I hoped we could spend it together at his home in Bethlehem.

Shouts resounded down the hallway.

"What kind of a son are you? Everything I do is to preserve your kingdom." Father's heavy steps pounded toward me.

"God anoints the next king. And I shall gladly serve him." Jonathan's angry retort shattered my calm, and a sudden chill blanketed my face. What if Father guessed David was the anointed? Would David be in danger?

They barreled around the alcove and stopped when they spied me. Father clapped an arm around Jonathan. "Perhaps we better get to the frontline so we can return victorious."

Jonathan grunted and flashed me a smile. "No worries, my sister. We'll make sure David comes back safely."

A few days later, the village women's repeated chants heralded their return. "Saul has killed a thousand. David has slain ten thousands!"

I cringed, fearing my father's response. He would no doubt fly into a rage and accuse David of stealing the people's hearts. I ran down the steps and toward the gate, but Jonathan caught David's arm and led him toward the audience chamber. David scanned the crowd, and even though I jumped and waved my scarf, he didn't see me through the throngs of men and dust.

Disappointed, I climbed to the top of the wall near our apartment. The afternoon sun gleamed over the village. Hawks coasted lazily in the wind currents. I laughed at a young boy who yanked a red-brown calf that reared and resisted his tugs with loud grunts.

A man's strong hand covered my eyes, and his bearded lips kissed me deeply.

"Michal, do you go around letting strange men kiss you sight unseen?"

I poked his ribs. "Are you telling me you're a stranger?"

"You're supposed to say, 'I'd know you anywhere.'" David bent my head back for another kiss while carrying me to the bedchamber.

My lips still locked on his, I untied his sash and thrust my hands under his tunic.

"Wait, wait." He squirmed from my grasp and fumbled in his pocket. "Close your eyes."

I shut them and bounced on my heels. The weight of a light chain dangled around my neck.

"Now, open them."

A single round emerald, the size of a partridge's egg, lay on my chest. "Oh, David!"

"Do you like it? I mean, you probably have lots of jewels and everything."

"Oh, it is lovely. I shall never take it off." I knew how hard he had worked for this. The gold and silver he obtained for Goliath's head had paid off his family's debts. My father did not pay him to serve as his captain; soldiers lived off loot taken from the enemy.

"I hope it's the only thing you won't take off." He fingered my dress and swept me onto the soft, downy bed.

* * *

David stood with King Saul at the victory celebration. The king placed his hand on his shoulder. "The LORD has wrought a great victory for all of Israel. Today, the Philistines were pushed further toward the sea. One day, David will rid our land of these beasts. David has been a godsend to us all."

He raised his tankard. "Behold, my son, David!"

The cheers rang long and loud as the people stood to applaud. David shifted in his seat. The king had pointedly exaggerated every pronouncement, eyeing him to watch his reaction. A drop of sweat wormed down the side of David's temple. Michal had told him about her father's envy, how he felt God had abandoned him for David.

David's gaze drifted to his wife. No matter what happened with the kingdom, God had gifted him this wonderful creature. After the celebration was adjourned, he grasped her hand and led her quickly to their bedchamber. The tightness in his abdomen hummed in tune with the tingling in his hands as he undressed her.

Insistent raps on the door interrupted them. David groaned and pulled a sheet over her body.

A sharp voice shouted through the closed door. "The king summons you to his bedchamber. He cannot sleep. Bring your harp."

David pulled on his clothes. "I'll be back as soon as I can. Hold that warm spot for me?"

She blushed and squeezed his hand before settling down on the pillow.

He grabbed his harp and followed the manservant to the king's quarters, tamping down the edge of resentment in his chest. Perhaps Michal was right. He could serve the king from the battlefield and move her to Bethlehem to stay with his parents.

The king sat in a gilded chair, a spear in his right hand. He thumped the floor with the shaft. "Son of Jesse, you think you're some kind of hero, boy?"

He tilted his face, and David kissed his beard. "Show me you're still my servant by playing for me. All. Night." The pitch of his voice sank low and menacing.

David strummed the harp strings and sang. Hours passed, but the king stayed alert, keeping beat with the tapping of his spear. David's face sweltered with sweat. His voice grew hoarse and then raw. His throat tightened, and he sought a place to escape. Escape the stifling odors, the rank, sweet smell of the water-pipe. Escape the scent of terror and jealousy swirling in the room. Escape the pounding in his head, the beat of death.

A gentle breeze stirred the moisture on his shoulders, his neck, his arms. His wife waited in her bed. Her breath, panting, warm, hot. Her hands tracing the ridges on his stomach, following the line of hair pointing to pleasures below. *I love you, David. I love you. Do you love me?*

David's breath hitched, and he missed a chord. He caught the king's piercing look and dodged. Something whooshed past his ear. A spear thudded into the wall where his head had been. David dropped his harp and plunged out the door.

"Return to me, my son," King Saul bellowed. "I meant you no harm."

David stumbled past the servants and into the garden. He put his hands around his head and took deep breaths. Saul had once loved him, called him a son. He had once leaned on the king's chest and strummed his harp, and Saul had found peace. But there was no peace tonight, no calm, no comfort. Tonight was a night ripe for murder.

* * *

Hurried knocking roused me.

My maid, Naomi, stood at the door, her cheeks flushed. "My lady, the king seeks to slay your husband. He told his guards to set a watch on your house and kill him in the morning."

A fierce jolt in my chest almost knocked me over. "Where is he? Is he all right?"

"I don't know, my lady. Please, don't let anyone know I told you." She ran from the room.

I pulled on my outer robe and cloak and peeked out the door. David walked toward me followed by guards. They stationed themselves at our door as David entered.

I shut the door. "Naomi just told me. What happened?"

He moved away from the door. "Your father threw a spear at me."

"He told his guards to kill you in the morning. You must leave now."

David clutched my arms. "How will we get out of here? They're standing at the door."

"The window. It drops outside the wall. It's the only way." I looked at the bed sheets. "I'll hold the sheet and let you down."

"But what about you? I can't leave you here."

"Don't worry. He won't kill me. I'm his daughter." I helped David knot the sheets together.

"Oh, Michal, I'm not such a coward to run. What will become of us?" He secured the tied sheets to the foot of the bed.

"Come back for me when his anger has cooled."

"Haven't I served him well? Could I have done better?"

"You've been good to us all. He's afraid of you because the LORD is with you." I rubbed his beard with both hands, grasping for the fuzzy reassurance that it represented.

"I'll be back as soon as I can. If you need anything, let Jonathan know." He kissed me, his eyes moist.

Cold sweat broke on my forehead, as a hollow feeling sunk into my heart. "You must go now, while there's time."

"Not yet." Breathing unevenly, he planted his mouth on mine. The kiss was full of questions, stumbling, tripping, and gasping without answers. My nose bumped his, and he fumbled with my robe. Sobs hitching my chest, I pawed and clutched at him, begging, shaking, out of my mind.

He bent me back to the bed, his mouth swallowing my sobs. Shuddering, trembling, wheezing, my chest tightened under his weight. I clamped my legs around him, his solid flesh consoling, as he comforted me, urgent in anguish, but tender in leave-taking. Our hearts and pulses joined, we stroked each other, imprinting, and memorizing every contour, every loving detail.

Marching footfalls alerted us—the changing of the guard. David jumped from the bed and tied his robe. I pulled my clothes together and crept to the window to time the path of the guards. When they had strolled under our window and headed toward the main gate, I motioned to him.

It was time. We clasped hands, fingers intertwined, and stared at each other through the stream of moonlight. A tear slid down his cheek, followed by another and another.

"David, you must leave now," I said, "before the dawn, or my father will be upon you."

I let the sheets down.

He looked at the jagged rocks below. "Come with me. Can you make the jump?"

"They'll be back in a few minutes. Go now, before anyone sees you. I have to pull the sheets back up." *This can't be happening. My father will cool off. Everything will be fine. It's just a bad dream.*

He swung a leg out. "Wait. Give me a blessing, as my wife, my beloved."

I stared deep into his eyes. "The LORD bless thee and keep thee."

"The LORD make His face shine upon thee and be gracious unto thee," he replied.

"The LORD lift up His countenance upon thee and give thee peace."

He brushed my cheek and tried to smile. "Don't cry, or I won't leave."

Tears dripped to my lips. "David, you'll come for me, won't you?"

"Yes, yes. I promise." His throat rippled, and he kissed me on the temple.

"I love you, David."

"I… do, too." His gaze held mine, unblinking, and he lowered himself slowly.

Tears streamed down my face as I held onto the taut rope of sheets. He dropped onto the rock pile with a slap of his sandals and waved. I yanked the sheets up as he ran toward the hills. My last glimpse was a flash of copper swallowed by the murky tree line.

Footsteps outside the door roused me to action. I rolled an Asherah pole carved from cedar, a wedding present, onto the bed. After I untied the bed sheets, I arranged the idol of the goddess with a pillow of goat's hair, ruffling it to resemble David's. I covered everything with a blanket and sat down in the corner of my room. *David, David, my love. Where are you now? I should have gone with you. When will I see you again?*

A few minutes later, a voice shouted through the door. "David, son of Jesse, the king summons you!"

I opened the door a crack, putting on a stiff and imperious expression. "What is the meaning of this? He's ill and should not be disturbed."

The two guards in the front craned a look over my shoulder. They backed away. "Sorry, Princess."

I shut the door and bent on my knees. *O LORD God, be with David, don't let Father's men find him. How fast can he run? Please, dear God, let David get away safely.*

Unable to sleep, I watched the morning star fade into the horizon and the rosy cone of dawn glow in the east. I prayed David had found shelter. Rough footsteps approached the door.

"Why has he not responded to my summons?" Father's voice boomed down the hallway.

"He's ill, my king," one of the guards said.

"I don't care. He won't be ill when he's dead."

Father ordered his servants to break the door down. I cowered in the corner while he rushed in, raised his javelin and plunged it into the figure.

The shock of cracking wood jolted his wrist, and he roared with anger. He grabbed me and shook me. "Why have you deceived me and helped my enemy to escape?"

In one motion, he held me over the window. "You daughter of a perverse woman, how dare you turn against me? Answer me or I'll throw you to the wolves."

I latched onto his shoulders and cried, "He… he… said to let him go, or he'd kill me. Father, I'm sorry. I was scared."

"Ungrateful daughter." He pulled me from the window and slammed me against the wooden figure.

My head buzzed with dizziness, and my ribcage radiated sharp pain. I hugged the wooden goddess and cried into the goat-hair pillow. *Oh, why did I lie about David? He would never have hurt me. Oh, God, forgive me.*

PART II

CHAPTER 8

Lamentations 3:49 Mine eye trickleth down, and ceaseth not, without any intermission.

>>><<<

David's sandals squelched on the muddy path. Everything had happened too fast. Michal's sad farewell echoed in his ear. She had clutched the window frame, her face contorted, her knuckles white. A single teardrop had fallen on his nose. He ran until his sides ached and his legs burned. Would he ever see her again? Could he steal her away someday?

The day dawned, drizzly and grey. A shepherd boy pointed him to Samuel the Prophet's house, a small mud-brick structure surrounded by old-growth oaks. Plastered with rain and sweat, David knocked on the door.

A servant opened it. "Who disturbs the prophet at this hour? Know you not how late he stayed at the sacrifice?"

David lowered his head. "Pray tell him his servant David is in need of him. But do not wake him on my account. I can wait."

A shuffle and a grunt greeted him. "Oh, my bones. David, son of Jesse."

David bowed to the dirt floor. "Great Prophet, I am running for my life."

"Stand, my boy. So, marriage to a princess does not suit you?" He chuckled and called his servant, "Bring some towels, a change of clothing and some food."

After David changed out of his wet clothes, he sat at a table piled with scrolls.

"My son," Samuel said. "What troubles you?"

"King Saul wants my life, but I have not done anything to warrant it."

Samuel huffed and shifted his weight. "I'm not surprised. He must know God has chosen you to be the next king."

"But how? My wife did not tell him. She said she'd keep my secret. And the only other person who knows is Jonathan, my best friend."

"Well, it's the only explanation. Otherwise, why kill you? You've led his troops to victory, served him loyally, even married his daughter, although regrettably, it seems."

David squeezed his eyes shut and rolled his head in his hands. "Why would you say that?"

The prophet wagged his staff. "Let this be a lesson to you. Do not let women enwrap you with their charms. Remember Samson."

"Michal would never betray me."

Samuel's eyes narrowed. "Think Delilah told Samson the truth?"

A cloud of doubt dampened David's face. He gripped the side of the table. *It's impossible. She loves me, she's mine. I'm sure of it.*

Samuel leaned on his staff and clunked to the shelf. He picked up a scroll and opened it. "My son, read from the Word of the LORD daily. Meditate on it and pray. The LORD will lead you. The road to your kingdom does not go through Saul. God has rejected Saul and his entire house. He has chosen you."

A sharp pain stabbed David's heart. *Michal? Rejected by God? No! But God spoke through prophets. If Samuel was right…*

He kneaded the bridge of his nose. "The LORD has not told me exactly what to do."

"You must trust Him and wait on His timing. Do not trust in man. Forget about them. They've shown you how wicked they are."

"Not Michal. She saved my life."

"She is his seed. The seed of the serpent should not mix with the sons of God." Samuel patted his shoulder. "The LORD will lead you one step at a time. Do not keep company with the evil and wicked. Be not overcome with evil, but overcome evil with good. Keep your heart pure and love God above all else."

The door shook with heavy pounding. "Open up. The king demands the return of his servant."

David glanced around, but there was no place to hide in the sparse one-room house.

Samuel answered the door, gazed at the sky, and raised his staff. An unseen power knocked the ten men to the ground. They rolled in the wet earth and chanted, "Praise the LORD, give praise to His glory, and to His mercy and loving-kindness."

David's eyes widened, awed at the display of God's power. After the men departed, Samuel's servant gave him a pack of food and a bundle with his wet clothes.

"You must go now, my son," Samuel said. "And may the LORD bless you and keep you. May He make his face shine upon you and grant you peace."

* * *

I paced my room, stopping at the window at the end of each circuit. Had David eluded my father's guards? They had taken off on horseback in all four directions. David had no weapon, nothing but the clothes he wore. Had he found shelter? It had rained all night.

The throbbing in my head clamored louder and louder. What could I have done? Why didn't I pack him a bag of food? If I had distracted the guard, he might have gotten to the stables and grabbed a horse, maybe even found a weapon. I raked my hair and pinched my cheeks. The weight on my chest constricted my ribs, my breath squeezed in shallow puffs.

Alone, the hours passed. Naomi brought a platter of food. I picked at it and could not bring a morsel to my mouth. David. Alone in the wilderness, hungry and cold. I pushed the tray and leaned against the window. What did I expect to see? David on a white horse? Or my father's men with David trussed like a spring lamb. Sapped and sleepless, I crumbled to the floor, my heart a hollow husk. Alone, without David.

His harp sat in the corner. While he was here, we had shared everything. He would place the harp on my thighs, encircle me with his arms. Our voices would blend, flirt around the melody and dance in harmony. His warm breath would caress my neck and he'd gaze in my eyes. Plucking a few strings, I picked a chord. It sounded listless, dull, dead.

I drew a breath to sing. David loved my voice. With him, I was uninhibited and alive. He taught me songs, and we'd sing until kissing consumed our tune. I choked back a sob and pressed my lips together. I would sing no more.

When the weather cleared, I climbed to the old guard shack and sat on our bench. I tapped the wood and stared at the foothills. Jonathan had to help. He loved David as I did. He could come and go freely, and he knew his way around Israel. I shaded my eyes against the sun's glare. Watchmen guarded every approach. I was foolish and silly to expect David to come back. The palace was a trap, and I was the bait.

* * *

The day Jonathan returned with his spies, I ran to the garden to meet him.

He held out his arms. "My sister, how good to see you."

I kissed his jaw. "Have you news? How's David?"

"I've spoken to him. He's well. But he cannot come back."

"Did he ask after me?"

Jonathan put an arm around my shoulder. "He wants me to watch over you."

"Can I go to him? Will you bring me?"

"No, it's too dangerous. Our father hunts him from one side of Israel to the other. He is ever in danger. He cannot rest."

"Why is this happening? Why?"

Lowering his voice to a rasp, he said, "We're under the curse of the LORD. Father failed to wipe out the Amalekites when God ordered him to. Samuel rebuked Father, and God tore the kingdom away from him. After that, Father started to hear voices and suffer headaches."

A grinding pit tightened my stomach. "What shall we do?"

"You'll need to be strong. Wait until David becomes the king."

"How long will that be?" How could I possibly wait, lonely and childless?

"I don't know. David has promised me he'll do only good to me and my children. I'm sure he will come for you as soon as he can. But our father is a tough and determined adversary. He will stop at nothing until David's head is on a stake."

"He can't!" I shuddered and covered my face. "I shall die."

Jonathan hugged me. "Have faith. David will prevail. I'm sure of that. And when he does, we can all be happy again."

I tried to focus on a sliver of hope. Father loved me. Did he not see how unhappy I was? I tapped Jonathan. "But will Father not relent? Didn't he once love David as his own son?"

"Father cannot help himself," he said. "He's tormented by an evil spirit. But I will try again for your sake. Perhaps he will give David another chance."

"Oh, thank you." I squeezed his arm and hugged him.

He walked off, and I lowered my head to pray.

A footstep crunched on the gravel. I lifted my head with a start.

A powerfully built man stepped into the courtyard. He pierced me with a predatory stare and caught my arm. "I shall hunt him down, and after I'm through with you, I'll kill him."

I tried to shake him off. "Unhand me. Who are you?"

"I'm your next husband." He tightened his grip and dug into my flesh. "You want to know a secret? I saw David with the priests of Nob, and we're on our way to kill him."

His rough laughter grated my ears and sent an icy spear through my heart. He shoved me aside and swaggered out the gate.

Fear knotted my stomach, and I tore into the palace. Father wished to make me a widow. I'd rather die than remarry. I bumped into Merab, who was visiting for the New Moon Feast.

"What's wrong?" she said.

"I have to get away from here." My hands fluttered in small circles. "Can you help me?"

She pushed a finger on my lip. "Calm down. Mother needs you."

Taking my hand, she dragged me to Mother's bedchamber. I stopped short and gasped. Broken plates and vase shards littered the floor. "What happened?"

"Your father tried to kill Jonathan," Mother cried. "He blames me for everything."

I gaped at Mother, then Merab, and back. "How can he do that? Jonathan is his heir."

Mother grabbed my shoulders. Her face contorted as if in pain. "Your father is throwing me out."

Heavy sobs choked her, and she couldn't continue.

Merab patted her back and said to me, "Jonathan and Father had a fight about David, and he's putting our mother away to marry Rizpah."

"But doesn't Father love you?" I clung to my mother. "He can't do this."

"He's the king. He can do whatever he wants." Her shoulders heaved. "After all these years and all the children I bare him."

"But where will you go?" I asked.

"She's coming to live with me," Merab said.

I hugged Mother. "May I go with you to Merab's?"

"No, daughter," she said. "Your father does not want to let you out of his control. As long as you are at the palace, David might try to come for you, and then he'll be trapped."

I stepped back. "Why do you all hate David so much? What has he done to you?"

Mother pinched my arm. "He wants your father's throne. And he's ruined your life. I cannot believe you still care for him. He threatened to kill you. He's nothing but a criminal."

"No, I lied. David loves me."

Merab patted my shoulder. "After Father catches David, we'll get you a real husband, someone who loves you."

I threw myself against the wall. "You don't understand. I love David."

"Oh, dear sister. It doesn't work that way. A woman is to reverence and serve a husband who loves her, not the other way around." She patted me as if I were a spitting kitten.

I stomped away. I would rather have lived a single day with the man I loved than to be adored by dozens of men I cared nothing for. *Oh, God. When will I see David again? How long will I have to wait?*

A few days later, Adriel came with his wagon. I waved a tearful farewell to Mother and Merab. I spied Rizpah, my father's main concubine, eyeing Mother's bedchamber. She was the real reason for Mother's banishment. No doubt she had bewitched Father. Milky white with long black hair, lustrous and smooth, she looked down her nose at me with a she-devil's unearthly blue eyes while rubbing her pregnant belly.

I rued my flat stomach, empty inside, with nothing to tie my destiny to David's except his promise. My bleak future washed over me like tears over a trail of snails.

* * *

David's body was sticky with blood. Angry men lunged with spears. He sliced one, and another attacked him. Wild men, Amalekites intent on plunder, swooped in from the desert. David saw no soldiers, no one to defend the village.

The last attacker dispatched, David gazed in the sky at the cawing of the birds of prey. The dead lay strewn around him. Boys descended from the hills to collect the spoil. All the villagers were dead, and so were the Amalekites. It made no difference whose bodies they robbed. Beyond the scavengers, feral dogs loitered in packs, their tongues lolling.

He stepped over a trail of bodies to examine a farmhouse. A solitary cat darted out of the barn and leapt to the rafter above.

An iron mattock lay in a manger. His ears pricked. A sob rattled, followed by a snuffle. He unsheathed his sword.

Two quick steps brought him to the nearest haystack. He swept the top with the side of his sword and uncovered a young woman, eyes wide with fear. She cowered and balled her fists in front of her face. David brushed the hay from her hair. Her eyes moistened and full lips trembled.

He reached for her hand. "Come, I won't hurt you."

"Stay away from me," she cried.

"I'm an Israelite. You're safe with me." He carried her in his arms, his armor and tunic caked with dried blood. The mattock lay forgotten.

"What is your name?" he asked, observing her graceful curves, her long, straight hair, black as the night.

"Ahinoam."

* * *

The commotion of a returning war party startled me. The men's wild whoops and cheers vibrated the palace walls. Even as I feared the news, I needed to know. I pulled on a cloak and went toward Father's audience chamber and hid among the juniper bushes near the window.

"Doeg, you have proven yourself loyal by executing the men who disobeyed my orders concerning David." My father's voice sounded through the open window.

"Yes, my king. I, and only I, will return with the head of the son of Jesse."

"You shall have your reward," my father said. "Go, while we have him trapped."

The man slapped his shoulder in salute and swiveled out the doorway. I stepped back, but not in time. Doeg caught my arm and leered with a bone-grinding smile. "Daughter of Saul, my prize."

I jerked my arm, but he twisted it behind my back.

"We know where that dog is," he said. "And it's only a matter of time before we catch him."

"Let me go. You're my father's servant. Keep your hands off me."

He grabbed both my wrists and pushed me against the wall. "The king has promised you as wife to the man who brings him David's head. And I, Doeg the Edomite, will be your next husband, and you shall bend in front of me like the bitch you are."

His breath reeked of stale meat. My stomach turned, and my pulse clawed in my ears. Doeg had singlehandedly killed the priests of the LORD and slaughtered the entire city of Nob because they had aided David's escape.

He forced his cruel mouth over mine, and I struggled and spit to elude him. When Father stepped out of his audience chamber, Doeg released me and bowed to him.

Father ignored me and puffed on his pipe. "My enemy is trapped at Maon, harassing a nobleman's house. Catch him tomorrow."

My knees wobbled. The chill of defeat sank through me. I stumbled back to my room, my nerves shrieking at a high pitch. Father would not protect me. I'd throw myself off the palace wall than let Doeg take me as his wife.

* * *

"My lord." The young woman bowed her head and crouched. David squinted toward the entrance as her shadow closed in.

"Call me David."

"Yes, my lord." She handed him a platter with a few pieces of flatbread, a cluster of grapes and a water skin.

David leaned against the cool, damp wall inside the cavern and enjoyed a few moments of respite. Yesterday, they had been trapped, boxed in, surrounded by the king's men. But before Saul's men could launch the attack, a messenger had arrived with news of a Philistine invasion. The king's troops retreated, leaving a few spies. David would have to move further into the wilderness toward the Salt Sea. It would be a grueling journey through burning desert.

"Ahinoam, do you have family? Anywhere you can go?"

"No, my lord. Everyone is dead. Why do you ask?"

"Today we leave for the Salt Sea, a harsh and dry land. You sure you have nowhere to go?"

She shuddered. "I have no one. My betrothed is dead."

"Are you a virgin?"

"Why would I not be? You haven't touched me."

David shifted his weight, his left leg numb on the cold cave floor. "I can find you a husband. My way is treacherous, and my life is forfeit. Hunted to be killed. It's not safe to stay in my cave. Not after last night."

She crept to his side. "Don't make me leave."

Her hands smoothed his tunic and raised the hair on the back of his neck. She kissed his beard, her lips soft and dewy. "I've not known a man, and I want it to be you."

"There is nothing but suffering with me. Hunger, want, cold, fear. Let me take you to a village and find you a home. The king knows where we're camping. He'll be back as soon as he finishes with the Philistines."

"I will suffer with you, my lord. Every step of the way."

She wrapped her arms around him and kissed his lips. Her scent, like sweet oranges, stirred his loins with longing and despair. Jonathan said Michal was remarrying—no doubt waiting for the highest bidder. Their love, but a vapor, vanished in the wind.

"My lord, I'm yours, if you'll have me," the woman murmured. "I'll never leave you."

He fingered the back of her neck. He'd never give his heart to another woman. Pretty faces and beautiful words were but the gall of asps, the dust of death.

* * *

My prayers were answered. Father returned without David's head. After a subdued banquet, Father called me to his bedchamber. Rizpah lounged, half-dressed on the bed, popping grapes into her mouth.

Father pulled me into his arms and patted my back. "Michal, you are getting on in years. Why pine away for a dog that has deserted you?"

I pulled away. "He hasn't deserted me. You're the one who's keeping him from me."

A smile congealed on his face. "You're too naïve. Did you think he would come for you? I hate to tell you, but I spoke to him in the wilderness across a divide. He looked well, rugged, and hearty. He had women and children with him. Bunch of filthy vagabonds. I found the caves where they camped."

Cold sweat dampened my face as he continued. "David has remarried, not once, but twice. One of them is a widow of a man of wealth, a Nabal of Carmel, a loyal subject of mine. With his grave still warm, David made off with his wife."

I shook my head so hard my teeth chattered. "No. No. David wouldn't do this. He promised he would come back for me."

"Oh, Michal," Father drawled. "He's been gone two years already."

"But... he asked me to wait. I don't believe it. You hate him."

Rizpah snickered loudly. "It's not like some big secret. Jonathan knew, but your father did not want to tell you until he had confirmed it. Besides, men get as many wives as they can afford, and I suppose your David has become quite a warlord."

I crumpled to the floor. This couldn't be true. David had promised me so earnestly. Oh, David! I pounded my head against the tiles and wailed. Father placed me on his lap like he used to when I woke from a nightmare. "I should not have let that dog hurt you. I'll find you another husband. Do not despair."

My heart burst like an old wineskin and bled into my gut. I wept, giant gulps, choking, screaming, dying on his shoulders. How could David forsake me? Didn't he love me?

God, kill me now. Let me melt away like an untimely birth, never to feel the sun on my face, never to taste a drop of sweet milk, never to rock in my mother's arms. Let my mouth be filled with thorns and break my teeth, O LORD, for You have hated me and ripped me like filthy rags and cracked my heart, a broken leaf blown into a firepot.

Rizpah scraped her fingers across my back. "Michal, daughter, we're here for you." Her voice slurred like syrup in the frost. "Let your father find you a worthy husband—someone loyal to him."

I wrung my fingers over my swollen eyes. "I still want David, even if he doesn't want me."

They both clucked and shushed as if I were a stubborn child.

"David has forsaken you," Rizpah crooned. "You'll need to remarry."

"I have a man for you," Father said. "Doeg."

I panicked. "No! Please, not a bloody man. Somebody peaceful and nice. Not a warrior."

Father kissed my forehead. "Not a warrior, not someone like David."

CHAPTER 9

Song of Solomon 5:6 I opened to my beloved; but my beloved had withdrawn himself, and was gone: my soul failed when he spake: I sought him, but I could not find him; I called him, but he gave me no answer

>>><<<

"Your father asked Jonathan to find you a husband." Rizpah ran a comb through my hair.

My father could be lying. Hadn't he lied to David and told him I refused to marry him? How could David take other wives when he still loved me? There had to be a misunderstanding.

"I'm not remarrying." I crossed my arms. "Did my father actually see David's wives? Or were they maid servants?"

Rizpah clicked her tongue. "If he cared about you, wouldn't he have sent a message?"

I lowered my head and allowed Rizpah to rub lotus oil into my hair. Jonathan had met David several times without Father's knowledge. Never once did he bring a message. And the replies he gave to my questions were vague.

"I still don't want to remarry." I jutted out my lower lip and clenched my teeth. "I'll wait for David to look in my face and explain."

Rizpah eyed me in the bronze mirror. "Better to marry than to remain vulnerable. Doeg has asked for your hand. Let's hope Jonathan finds you a peaceful man, one who won't hurt you."

I shuddered as a cold spear pierced my insides. I'd fall off the wall before I let Doeg touch me.

A few weeks later, Jonathan returned to the palace with a young man. Square-shouldered and tall, he stood level with my father and brother. His large, soulful eyes lighted on me, and my heart tugged, despite my reluctance.

Rizpah fanned herself and pinched me. "I wish your brother was my matchmaker."

I shuffled and looked down, feeling guilty. Why couldn't David be with me? Why had Father driven him away? I coughed as if a piece of dry bread had lodged in my throat.

Jonathan brought the man over. "Rizpah, Michal. This is Phalti, son of Laish, a scribe."

Rizpah blushed and simpered. "How nice to meet you. My daughter, step-daughter, for I'm not old enough to... well, Michal..." She nudged me.

Large dark-brown eyes regarded me under a cascade of wavy brown hair. An aquiline nose sloped straight down his smooth forehead. He smiled and took my hand and brought it to his lips. "Princess, I'm honored to meet you."

A rush of warmth ambushed me. Phalti held my hand gently, and perversely, I did not want him to let go. He wore a tender expression, humble and kind. I tightened my lips in a polite smile and jerked my hand away, wiping it on my skirt.

"Princess, I understand your predicament." He lowered his voice and guided me away from Rizpah's side.

"I am a married woman, yes."

"Jonathan and Elihu have told me your situation, and I agreed to respect your wishes." He locked my gaze, eyes deep and warm.

"Will you help me find my husband?"

"If it's what you want," he said. "I'm your friend. Besides, I'd hate for Doeg to harm you."

I dragged a smile across my face. "Then I will pretend to marry you. And I thank you."

The wedding was a hastily done affair, no party, tent, guests, or feast. Elihu, my father's priest, presided, while Father and Rizpah were witnesses. Elihu agreed to escort me to Phalti's house the same afternoon. While Naomi packed our things, I took leave of my father, Rizpah and their two young sons. They walked with me to the gate.

"Goodbye, Michal." My father's voice choked. "I wish you happiness with your new husband. He'll be good to you."

His eyes were clear and at that moment, he was once again the father I had before the demons hounded him. A tear crept down his rugged face. He took my hand. "Forgive me," he whispered.

My fingers slipped slowly to my side. "Goodbye, Father."

* * *

David's lungs burned and his sides ached. Footsteps pounded through the forest. He stumbled down a creek bed.

A shout. They had spotted him. He headed for the rocks. *Oh God, let there be a crack, a hiding place.* He scrambled over a boulder. An arrow whizzed by. He dove behind a rock wall. They had boxed him in.

He struggled for breath, his arms and legs twitching. He wanted to lie down, let fate take him, but the warrior in him urged him to keep moving, to fight, to live. He surged out of the crack, leapt to another boulder, scrambled up the face. An arrow struck above. Too close.

He pivoted, found a foothold and pulled himself into a crevice, climbed it like a chimney, his back against the wall, his feet pushing off the opposite wall. Above him, sunlight. He stretched. *Preserve me, O God, for in thee do I put my trust.*

Angry shouts popped in the air. *Push, David, push.* He reached for the ledge, but a large rock struck him. He fell and knocked the air out of his lungs. *Michal!* His last conscious thought spiraled to the sand below.

* * *

Phalti lived in Gallim, a tiny village, more remote and rustic than Gibeah. A few clusters of mud-brick houses spread between patches of farmland and rolling meadows. His house sat near the village well. Its small shuttered windows and peeling walls had a pastoral charm reminiscent of warm earth and fresh grass.

He helped me off the mule and gave me his arm. "Welcome to my home, wife. I know this isn't what you're used to, but please consider me your servant."

He brought a basin, and Naomi bent to wash my feet.

While Phalti went to the pantry, I asked Elihu, "I'm not really married to Phalti, right?"

"Yes and no." He rolled his lips and fingered his white beard. "If David had not abandoned you, then you are still his wife. You still have the scroll of your covenant?"

"Oh yes, I do." I patted my satchel. "But what do you mean abandoned?"

"A man who deserts his wife, puts her away, or removes himself from the covenant of God by joining and serving another god has no right to a daughter of the Law."

David had not really abandoned me. He was banished by my father. But I did not argue the point with Elihu. I needed his help.

"We should give him another chance," I said. "Can you send a message?"

Elihu pulled his robe as he eased his way into a chair for Naomi to wash his feet. "Sure, don't see any harm. I'm hungry."

Phalti came back from the pantry with bread, butter, honey and wine. He set the food on the table and straddled a chair backward. "My wife, please accept my hospitality."

I smiled to keep from gritting my teeth too hard. "Do you know where David is? Can you take me to him?"

Elihu and Phalti glanced at each other. Elihu coughed and buttered a piece of bread. "If we knew and took you, your father would be sure to find him. He could have Doeg follow us."

Elihu's explanation sent a sobering chill down my back. Doeg had lurked in the shadow of the wall, sharpening his knife and watching me out of the side of his eye.

"We'll send a message to David and ask him to come for you," Phalti said.

"But how? If you don't know where he is."

"We go through the prophets," Elihu said. "My servant will deliver your message inside a scroll to a young prophet from Ramah, Samuel's hometown. He'll then pass it to Abiathar, who escaped to serve David after the slaughter of priests at Nob."

"And then? What then?"

"We wait." Elihu looked at Phalti again.

"Yes, we wait," Phalti said. "We're not warriors, and we can do no more."

I slammed my hands on the table. "Wait, wait, wait. Why can't Jonathan show us where David is? I know he's met him in the wilderness."

Again, Phalti and Elihu stared at each other.

I crossed my arms and tapped my foot. "What are you two up to? Answer me."

"Jonathan refuses." Elihu spread his palms up. "He doesn't want to endanger David."

"So why did he find you, Phalti?" I glared at him.

Phalti rubbed the back of his neck. "To help you. To keep you safe. Do you wish to endanger David?"

I steadied myself at the side of the table. Whose side was Phalti on? And Elihu? I should not have trusted them so easily. No matter, I'd get that note to David and be done with them.

"David promised he'd come for me," I said. "Hand me the reed."

Phalti's eyebrows shot up. "You know how to write?"

Elihu winked. "Ah yes, she does. I taught her. Tell David you're staying in Gallim with Phalti, son of Laish. He knows the area." He turned to his meal.

As they ate, I penned these words:

Dearest Love, my husband David, I am freed from the palace and my father. I am in Gallim, eagerly awaiting you. Look for the house of Phalti, son of Laish. Come quickly, for I miss you and love you more than ever. Your wife, Michal.

I handed the parchment to Elihu, who glanced at it briefly before he tucked it in his pocket. Naomi and I retreated to our room to sleep. Whatever misgivings I had about David's two wives, I ignored them. As soon as he received my message, he would lose no time and come to me.

I savored the night air and looked to God, calling on His glory. *LORD, You've kept David safe and out of harm's reach; please let me be with him. You answered my prayer to be his wife. I want to be by his side, to love him and to help him as a wife should.*

* * *

Elihu and his servant left the next day for Ramah with my message. I waited a week, and then another week. Surely, now that I was away from the palace, David could chance to come for me. The women at the well said he had attended Samuel's funeral. Even though Father's men had guarded Samuel's house, the townsfolk swore David had come and gone.

Phalti spread his hands across my doorframe.

"My dear wife, do you find the accommodations unsuitable for you?"

Dear wife, indeed.

"Phalti, you've been more than kind," I said, "lodging us while we wait for David. Don't worry about us."

"I'd like to see you settle in, make a home here, maybe make a few friends."

"That is kind of you, but I don't see the point. David will be coming for me soon."

Naomi excused herself to go to the well, and Phalti stepped into the room. Even though he was nonthreatening, my heartbeat unraveled. I stepped aside to let him pass.

"Let me help you unpack." He opened the wardrobe and drawers in the corner of the room.

"It's unnecessary. I need to be gone at a moment's notice."

"Do you always sleep with the windows open?" He latched it and opened his arms. "Come, let's go for a walk. I'd like to be your friend."

I clutched my shawl and brushed by him. "Actually, I need to help Naomi with the water. Thank you."

Why was I rude to him? He only tried to be friendly. But oh, he was so handsome, and he made my insides quiver. And he seemed to look through me, or at least through my clothes.

I caught up with Naomi who gossiped with a handful of village women. They stared at me as if I were a walking apparition.

"Ladies, this is my mistress. Please, do not gawk at her." Naomi spoke in a firm but friendly voice.

"A princess…"

"Is it really she?"

I tilted my head and stared each one in the eyes. They turned away—a harmless and foolish bunch. One set of determined eyes remained steady. I held her gaze and waited for her to blink.

She was an older woman, perhaps in her mid to late-thirties. Her eyes were blue-green like the pool at my father's palace. She had light complexion, and her hair was a mixture of brown and red highlights. She floated toward me.

I crossed my arms. "Do I know you?"

Undeterred, the woman held out her hand. "Come, come, my dear." Her voice held a melodious quality, the sing-song lilting of a Philistine accent.

"Who are you?" My throat tightened.

The woman bowed her head. "I apologize for intruding. My name is Jada, the healer. If you ever need my services, you can find me in a valley tucked behind a grove of oaks, near a brook, a small brook."

"What makes you think I would countenance your services?"

"You are Princess Michal, aren't you?" Her voice warbled like a songbird.

"No, I'm the new wife of Phalti of Gallim." I spat the words out. As hard as it was for me to admit it, I couldn't jeopardize David by mentioning his name, especially to a Philistine.

The woman lifted an eyebrow and smiled. "I'm also a midwife. Should the happy occasion arise, I would be glad to assist."

"I don't know you, and you don't know me." I turned my back.

"It is true that you do not know me, but I know you. You're hoping to meet someone in secret." Her musical voice trailed into laughter, like silvery tinkling bells.

My eardrums pulsed. With a chilling sensation prickling my back, I marched back to Phalti's house. The woman had to be a sorceress.

* * *

David squinted toward the cave entrance. Uriah, a recruit from the Hittites, dropped to his knee. "My lord, we've captured the king's son. Shall we execute him?"

David jerked upright. "Where is he?"

He bounded to the entrance.

Two guards kicked at a disheveled man lying face down in the dirt.

"Prince Jonathan." David raised his friend and slapped an arm around his shoulder.

Jonathan brushed his robe. "I expected a heartier welcome from these ruffians. At least they didn't take my head."

"It's good to see you." David motioned to his men to return Jonathan's weapons. "Come into my throne room."

Jonathan bent his lanky frame and crouched into the cave.

"Abigail," David said to his third wife. "Bring my guest some wine and food."

She pulled her shawl and scuttled to the back. Jonathan stared after her.

"It's not what you think," David hastened to explain. "She helped me at her own jeopardy."

"You don't know what I think, do you?" Jonathan grinned. "She's beautiful."

David's face heated. "I had to take her in. Your father put a price on her head. She was the wife of Nabal, the Carmelite, remember him?"

"Ah yes, my father's loyal informer. He gave away your position, but I misled my father and gave him the wrong directions."

"What can I do to thank you?" David handed him a wine cup while Abigail poured.

"Give me your solemn oath before the LORD," Jonathan said, "that when you become the king, you shall preserve my descendants."

David clasped his hand. "I make a vow before the LORD not to harm a hair of your seed."

They kissed each other, once on each cheek.

After Abigail retired to the back of the cave, David leaned forward. "How's Michal? Did she get my last message?"

Jonathan's eyes shifted. "She can't travel like you do. Besides, she's married now."

David dropped his cup. It shattered on the stone floor. "Married? Already? Who?"

A sinking feeling wrung his stomach and ground it in the dust. He clenched his knees to steady his erratic heartbeat.

"It's for the better," Jonathan said. "My sister needs a stable life. I found her a scribe. It was either that or Doeg the Edomite."

David shook Jonathan's shoulder. "Did she want to marry or did you force her?"

"Listen to me. My father wished to marry her to the man who brings him your head. It took some doing to convince my father to marry her to a scribe. But it's the best way to keep her safe and away from the dangerous men who loiter around the palace."

David closed his eyes and pinched the bridge of his nose. By not answering his question, Jonathan had indicated Michal was willing. "She has no message for me? No explanation?"

"David, my friend. What's done is done. Leave her be and let her find a life with her new husband. Besides, you remarried twice."

"It's not the same. I rescued Ahinoam from the Amalekites. She had nowhere to go. And Abigail was a widow who helped me."

Jonathan's eyes twinkled. "Look, my friend. I'm not judging you. A man can have many wives."

"Who is this man and does he treat her well?" David tried to hide the waver in his throat.

Jonathan ran his fingers through his hair. "I shall not tell you his name. You'd only endanger yourself. But I've paid him well to take good care of her. She will not be mistreated."

"Thanks for informing me." David stiffened his jaw and clapped a casual hand on Jonathan's shoulder. "Now, what are your plans? Why not join me? We can be brothers again."

Jonathan drew his brows and shook his head. "I must honor my father. It is a commandment of the LORD. When you are king, I shall be your loyal subject. But until then, my loyalty is to my father, and I will not betray him."

* * *

I placed the reed pen down on the writing table and rubbed my cramped wrist. Six months had passed, and I had settled into village life. Naomi and I tended a small garden of vegetables and herbs. Other than the occasional traveler, no news reached Gallim and certainly no message from David.

A flock of sheep grazed in the meadow, and the silvery green leaves of the olive trees swayed in the breeze. Phalti walked up the path with a satchel of scrolls and a serene smile on his face. I had become friends with him. In the evenings, we enjoyed long walks where we'd talk and share our thoughts and feelings without reserve. I even allowed him to hold my hand.

He dropped the packet on the table and bent to kiss my cheek. "Your script is beautiful—graceful, full of life. Like you, my wife."

I held my tongue. My covenant with David still stood, whether he came back or not. In silence, I brought a basin of water and peeled off Phalti's dusty sandals. As I smoothed water on his sturdy feet, I wondered if I'd ever get a chance to serve David in this manner.

Phalti pulled me close. He held my wrist and stroked it. "You work too hard." His firm fingers soothed the tightness. Warmth replaced the cramp as he worked his way up my arm. My body hummed in response. I squirmed under his gaze, his dark lashes and serious eyebrows probed my inner thoughts.

"Michal, why do you still wait?" His already deep voice lowered.

Why indeed? The man staring at me was attractive and kind-hearted. It would be so easy to retreat into his arms—arms that tempted me and could comfort me—so easy, except my heart gnawed continually for David.

I pulled away and stood. "He promised he would come for me. I believe he meant it."

"He might have meant it then. I don't doubt it. However, would he not want you to be happy?"

I closed my eyes. How long without a message, a word? Happiness, fulfillment, how is it measured?

"I don't know if I can be happy," I said.

"You can try. You can count your blessings. Go ahead, name a blessing."

I swallowed the lump forming in the back of my throat. "I don't know."

He drew closer. "I'll start. God has blessed me by making me an Israelite, a partaker of His Covenant. Your turn."

"God has blessed me by making me a daughter of the Law."

"That's a good one," he said. "And God has blessed me by teaching me how to read His Law."

"And God has blessed me by having Elihu teach me how to write." I grasped his hand, wondering how such delicate and flourishing script could come from hands so large. Safe, that's what Phalti was. Not a man of war, not given to violence. Not my true husband. I dropped his hand.

"God has blessed me," he said, his voice deepening, "in having you stay with me, help me, and be my companion."

His brown eyes beckoned and he moved, almost imperceptibly, toward my lips. Pressing a finger to his upper lip, I traced the line below his mustache, keeping him at bay. "God has blessed me with your friendship and a safe place away from my father."

His generous mouth curved as he wet his lips. With one hand around my neck and the other at my hip, he drew me to his face until our noses touched. My legs wobbling with uncertainty, I held his arms to steady myself.

He lowered his eyelids. "God has blessed me and made me love you with all my heart."

My heart skipped and fluttered like an injured bird. A tiny gasp escaped as I opened my mouth. I clutched his shoulders, needing to recoil, yet drawn at the same time.

"I can make you happy." Phalti's voice tapered, waiting for my response.

"I'm still married to David."

"I'll never hurt you. In my heart, you're married to me, and only me."

He loved me. This beautiful man, dark hair swept at an angle over his eyes, gave me an open invitation straight to his heart.

He caressed my hair and massaged the back of my neck. A deep and comforting murmur rose in his throat, and he kissed my temple, my jaw, my cheek—winding kisses to my lips. A shower of shooting stars skittered across my neck, and I pressed my parted lips over his.

Phalti carried me to my bed. His sensual lips begged to taste, to consume, to possess. Devoured by his kisses, I drank in sweet and powerful sensations, dark and velvety. And the scent of a man, animalistic, intoxicated me. My body ached with yearning. *David, let me feel your touch, taste your heat, savor your scent. Oh, David, hold me and don't let me go.*

Like a cloud of incense, he descended over me, his breath on my face, his lips on my neck, and his solid length against my belly, pressed over the folds of my dress. My fingers crawled through his hair and down his chest and under his tunic. He kicked off his breeches and moved my hand to touch him. Shocked at my brazenness, I recoiled to my elbows and opened my eyes.

Phalti's face fell with my reaction. He rolled to the side and covered his face with his arm, his breathing uneven. "I'm sorry."

Shuddering with frustration and unspent need, I leaned out the window. The night air blew away the embers of guilt. I collapsed on the windowsill and cried under my breath, "David, David, David…"

CHAPTER 10

Lamentations 3:25 The LORD is good unto them that wait for him, to the soul that seeketh him.

>>><<<

David squinted in the fading sunlight and scanned the western horizon. Grim-faced men stood next to him, hiding disapproval behind stoic expressions. He lifted his sword, Goliath's sword. "We have no choice but to escape to the land of the Philistines. Saul cannot catch us there."

No one replied.

He turned to his nephews. "Joab, lead a scouting party to search the land while I meet the Philistine king directly. Abishai, stay with the people and set up defensive positions."

Joab brushed rust-colored hair out of his eyes. "Alone? Last time they threw you out as a lunatic. I say we all go with you."

David glared at him. "If six hundred armed men go, would the Philistines not fear an invasion? Believe us part of Saul's army?"

He untied the sheath and handed Goliath's sword to Joab. "Take this. I will go unarmed."

"With all respect, Uncle, they will kill you. Why Gath?"

David grinned. A sense of perverseness flooded his chest. "It's Goliath's hometown. Saul would never expect us to move there. Enough talking, let's go."

The rains had failed again, and the underbrush crackled dry under his feet. Remembrance of naked hunger gnawed his ribs. Ahead, around a hillock, the city of Gath loomed above the countryside. Perched on a natural fortress of rock, it appeared as fierce and impregnable as the legendary giant had once been.

David forced his feet forward. He'd become a Philistine ally. The dream had been a mirage. He was never meant to be king. He'd throw his lot with the enemies of Saul. Leave Israel behind. Leave Michal behind. Leave God behind?

Crazy, stupid crazy. That's what she did to him. The image of a man between her thighs pierced his heart with pain and sorrow and loss. *You should have a wife who loves you, who loves you, who loves you.* David tried to stomp the mocking voice from his head.

Back upright and shoulders squared, he strode to the gate and stood in front of the barrel-chested guards.

"Who goes there?" a guard called.

"David, son of Jesse, requests an audience with King Achish."

Beady eyes scanned his body. Another pair of hands checked for weapons. "Did you say, David? As in the Hebrew David?"

"Take me to your king." He stared at the first guard and did not flinch at the sound of drawn swords.

A blade poked his back. "Shall we slay this madman and leave his blood for the dogs?"

"Perhaps the king may have objections," David said in a flat, monotone voice.

"Why would that be, Slayer of Goliath? Know you not that he was kin to the king?"

"I dare suggest you let the king decide," David replied.

Feet shuffled behind him, and weapons dropped to the ground. The first blow landed between his shoulder blades, the second in his kidneys. His head lolled, his face marred and swollen, they plucked his beard. Two hundred bruises for two hundred men. He deserved every blow—killed them for a worthless prize, a woman who no longer loved him. Blood seeped from his broken nose and cracked lips.

"Ho, what goes there?" A sharp voice split the air.

The men dropped David to the ground. "Prince Ittai, we've captured the man who killed Goliath and murdered two hundred stout men."

The Philistine prince lifted David's head and stared in his eyes. "So, you're the man. What do you want?"

"To seek asylum, my lord." Words gurgled through bloody lips.

The crowd of gawkers jeered, "String him up. Execute him. His blood be on his own hands. Avenge our kin." They surged with axes and sticks.

"Step back," Prince Ittai ordered. "The king will decide his fate."

Ittai dragged him to his feet, led him bound into the palace, and cast him into a prison cell. At midnight, he set meat before him and washed his wounds. Then he kissed him on both cheeks and said, "I remember your mercy."

* * *

I walked to the well, alone.

Jada grasped my hand. Her face shone with a calming smile. "I knew you would come."

"I am not in need of healing, but of wisdom," I said. "I've prayed incessantly to my God, but my heart is troubled, and I cannot see a way."

"Come, child. Let's walk to my house. You are under a great weight, and a burden clouds your face. Come and pour it out on me."

We walked arm in arm.

"Are you a Philistine?" I asked.

"My father might have been an Israelite, but then again, maybe it was a legend. This much I know. My mother and I lived in a house in the Valley of Sorek. She was a healer and an enchantress. She taught me the arts of medicine, magic, and love."

"Love? Is there an art for love?"

"Oh, yes," she replied. "There are techniques and spells. Would you like to know?"

"Yes, definitely. Have you a man who loves you? Are you happy?"

Jada's laughter trickled like a peal of bells. "Oh, Michal, I may know the art of love, but love and happiness are two completely different creatures."

"My mother always said, 'To be loved is to be happy, and to be happy is to be loved.'"

Jada stopped and faced me. "Let me ask you. Was your mother both loved and happy?"

"Neither. But her parents arranged her marriage. As for me, I married for love."

"Are you happy?" Blue-green eyes searched my face.

My chest tightened, and I shifted my face to the side. "No, I was happy while my husband and I were together—every moment, until my father drove him away. Now I have to find him."

We walked along a small footpath through a grove of oaks, alive with the breath of honeysuckle and the song of a lark. Jada gave me a sidelong smile. "So, the handsome scribe's a ruse?"

"He's insufferable. He won't take me to David, and he won't allow me to leave and find him myself."

"Never count on men." She picked bay leaves off a tree. "No matter how well intentioned, they want to imprison you in one form or another."

"Is that why you have no man? You wish to be free?"

Her eyes grew as big as pools. "No, child, the man I love let me go, even as I wished he would bind me with chains. Perhaps it is the same with you."

"I don't wish to be free of David, ever."

Her eyebrows bunched together, almost tenting in the center of her forehead as she placed a consoling hand on my arm. "Tell me what's in your heart. You'll find I'm a good listener."

We entered her house, a cozy one with walls of mortared river stone topped with thatch. She plied me with sweet wine and tea. I lay on a couch and told her my life story, starting in my mother's lap and ending at David's escape from my window.

Her fragrance, like warm honey in jasmine tea, pulled me into her arms. My heart ached for my mother's touch, and a pang of loneliness clung to my breast. She stroked my head and muttered soothing sounds. "I'll help you in any way I can."

"Can you see for me?" I took off a bracelet, gold set with carnelian, which had belonged to my mother. "Take this."

"No, no, dear Michal. Let's not discuss payment. Let me hear you first."

I placed it on the table and stared at the bottom of the wine goblet. "I have prayed night and day to my God, and He has chosen not to answer me. Perhaps He does not regard love as a proper motivation for prayer. To hear Elihu and Phalti talk, the desires of a mere woman do not move our God, not when He has kings to raise and princes to punish."

Jada poured more wine. "Asherah is the goddess of love. Nothing is more in her heart than the plight of lovers. You want to know about your husband, where he is, whether he loves you, and when he'll come for you. Stay here while I consult her."

She headed for the beaded curtain that led to another room.

"May I come with you?"

"You are a daughter of the Law, no? You must not appear in her presence. Is there anything else you want?"

"Yes, ask her to send a message in his dreams."

"What would you like to tell him?"

"That I, his wife, love him. Not to despair. I will seek him and find him and come to him." I closed my eyes and pressed my fingers to my breast. "I love him so much it hurts."

Jada hugged me. "I once loved a man as much as you love your David. But as much as we loved each other, we could not be together."

"Why is that?"

"Your Law forbids it. I'm a strange woman, and your God hates us. It has been this way since your people entered our land."

"But many men violate this law. I see it all the time. As much as Samuel detested it, they still marry those of the land."

Jada sniffed. "Not the man I love. He feared the curses. I would give anything to see him before I die. But he's forgotten me. May the goddess grant all your desires and return you to the man you love."

She stepped behind the beaded curtain. Incense bloomed spicy and gentle green. She sang a lilting melody that lifted the skin on the back of my neck. Tears wet my eyes. The rope of regret wound around my heart and pulled me to my knees. *Dear God, help me.*

Jada returned from her incantations and fingered my hair. "Give me a lock of your hair."

Running her fingers through my hair, she unlocked the thick braids and snipped off a long wavy lock. "Now I'll add a little henna to give you some copper highlights."

Deftly, she worked the powder into my hair and finished with a dusting of jasmine. She handed me a mirror. My hair undulated like a waterfall of tortoiseshell colored snakes, dark brown, streaked with amber.

I pressed her hand to my lips. "I must go. Phalti might be worried."

"You're a good girl. Come back after the next full moon. I shall have an answer for you."

* * *

The moon waxed fuller night after night. David, are you looking at the moon? Do you know how I long for you? Have you dreamed about me yet?

I approached Phalti's house and quieted my steps. The rooms were darkened. Not bothering to light a lamp, I gathered a few crusts of bread and cold meat. Lately Phalti and I had been avoiding each other.

"Michal?" His voice startled me. "Where did you go? You've been gone all day."

I stared at the table and fingered the whorls and knots in the wood. "I went to the forest to collect plants. I'm sorry I didn't prepare your dinner."

He pulled his chair closer. "I've been busy, too."

The damp silence hung awkwardly. I glanced at his chest. His body warmed the space between us, but his eyes closed warily, and he gripped his hands so tightly his knuckles whitened.

"Has something happened?" My voice stalked out of my constricted throat. "You look frightened, why's that?"

He stared at the table. "The king's men came today while you were out."

I drew my breath sharply. "What did they want?"

"There's no good way to say this." He avoided my gaze.

I grabbed his hands. Panic shot through my heart. "Have they caught David?"

"No, they haven't."

I exhaled in relief. "Then what?"

He palmed my hands and rubbed them. "David has forsaken the covenant, and you've been granted a divorce."

"What?" A gaping emptiness hollowed my stomach, and I pushed from the table. "I don't believe you."

Phalti pulled a scroll from his robe. "Read it."

Michal, David has deserted the covenant of God and left the land of Israel to serve the Philistine king. I hereby grant you a divorce. Elihu, priest of the LORD.

A cold shiver grabbed my shoulders and throttled my neck. I threw the scroll on the floor. "No, this cannot be. He loves God more than himself. He would never serve the enemy. He killed Goliath and hundreds of Philistines. His greatest desire is peace in Israel, a land freed from our enemies and the people worshipping God as he does."

Phalti gaped. "I don't know what to say. Your father is furious, but since he can't catch David, he's put a price on his head."

I glared at him. "How do I know this note's not a forgery? You're a scribe. Easy for you to imitate an old man's writing."

"Michal! How can you accuse me? I'm your friend." He tried to grab me, but I jerked away from him.

"No, you promised to help me. I bet none of my notes were delivered."

"I gave them to Jonathan. I swear. Michal, don't look at me like that." He fell to his knees and hugged my legs. "I'll send another one begging David to come back for your sake. I know how much you love him."

He looked so distraught I hated myself. Of course he had not lied. Why did I mistreat him? I patted him. "I'm sorry. You tried."

I didn't believe he could get a message to David, but I allowed him to think he could help. "I'll leave a note on the table. Don't stay up on my account."

His mouth turned down. "I'll be gone before dawn. I won't disturb you."

He lumbered from the room.

I bit my lip as my heart ached for him. I'd been too hurtful to him. It would be better if I left.

* * *

I woke early the next morning and waited for Phalti to leave. As soon as the hoof beats faded down the lane, I hastened to the stable and fastened my bags to the back of a mule.

"Where are you going?" Naomi's voice was quiet and tremulous.

"You can't come with me."

"You're going after David, aren't you?"

"Yes, and you can help me by not raising an alarm. When Phalti returns, tell him I went to visit Jada for a few days. That should give me plenty of time to get away."

"But how will you know where to go?"

I pulled out my emerald pendant. "My heart will lead me to David, do not worry."

Two fat tears rolled down her cheeks. "I shall miss you. Please send for me when you can."

"Of course I will. You're more a sister to me than a servant." I kissed her on both cheeks and hugged her. Naomi had been gifted to me on my wedding day. No one knew who her parents were or how old she was, but I imagined her to be the younger sister I never had.

I mounted the mule and headed up the river toward the valley behind the grove of oaks. Jada sat on her haunches, washing pans at the brook under a terebinth tree.

She clasped her chest and stood. "I'm so glad you came."

"What's the matter?" I dismounted and rushed into her arms. "Did you have a vision?"

"Help me pack my things. I have to leave right away. King Saul has given orders to slaughter all who deal with familiar spirits. Last night, after you left, a friend from the village told me about a man with a map. He marked my house. In a few short days, it will be burned to the ground, and I with it, should I remain."

"But you're a healer, a seer. Do you also channel spirits and talk to the dead?"

"My dear, there are many things you do not know about me. Come, let's go. I need to be gone before the king's men return."

I hitched Phalti's mule to the tree and followed her into the house. "I'm coming with you."

She kissed my cheek. "I knew you would. There's a trapdoor behind the storeroom. Take as much of the gold, silver, and jewelry you can carry and bury the rest for me—these urns, packets of herbs, and medicines."

We spent the next few hours rearranging everything in her house, burying most of her medicines and tools. I piled rocks over the trapdoor.

Jada packed a bag, a few clothes, some sandals, herbs, and salves. She showed me a purse made of silver tapestry with scarlet threads. "My mother's treasures are in here. A few locks of hair, hers, and my father's. I've woven them together. If anything happens to me, take it from my body and keep it in remembrance of me."

She took out the weaving. It was finely done. The sun's pale rays pushed against the black mat of the night.

"Nothing will happen to you," I said.

"Just promise me."

"I will. Do you have kin, anyone I should deliver it to?"

She fixed me with a pointed stare. "I trust you'll know who should keep this. Now, we must go."

I had no idea what she hinted at, but I let it go. We mounted the mule and rode down the trail away from the village.

"Did your goddess tell you where David is?" I asked.

"No, she didn't. But the ladies in the village said he has joined the Philistines and pledged his loyalty to King Achish."

A sharp chill prickled my scalp, and I berated myself for blaming Phalti. "But why? David is an enemy of the Philistines."

"Common enemies make strange bedfellows. Your father is a more deadly threat to David than King Achish. We'll inquire of the Philistines and find him easily."

"Why would it be easy when we couldn't find him in Israel?"

"Silly child, everything is easy in Philistia. We are a joyous people, unburdened by sin and scruples. With my gold and silver and my divination bowl, I can buy and sell information. And my goddess Asherah shines her face on lovers, true lovers."

"Oh, Jada. You're wonderful. Did she place my message into David's dreams?"

"She will, in the right time." Soft laughter cascaded from her lips. "So, are we going or not?"

"Oh yes." I puffed my chest and kicked the mule. "David, your wife is coming."

CHAPTER 11

Job 6:20 They were confounded because they had hoped; they came thither, and were ashamed.

>>><<<

I dragged the mule and followed Jada through tall grass. We passed a row of towering trees and stopped in front of a broken wall. A tumble-down house appeared, covered with green vines and grey thorns. The roofless courtyard was overgrown with weeds and brambles, and birds perched in the rafters.

I stepped over the threshold, or what was left of it. Part of the roof overhung a set of pillars, the door long gone. Blackened walls stood as sentinels toward the back.

I tied the mule to a tree. "This place has been burnt."

"Yes, but it'll do. We have at least a part of a roof over our heads." Jada took snares and nets from her bags and placed them in the corner near the doorframe. "There's a stream nearby where we can draw water and catch fish."

Shards of pottery lay embedded in the hard packed soil. The stone floor smelled sour and dusty. I picked my way to the blackened wall. "Oh look, the fire-pits and fire stones are still here, and there's a brick oven."

"Then we have all we need," she said. "Let's gather thatch to repair the roof."

I stepped over the rubble and wiped aside cobwebs. A cold breeze blew the pungent odor of rotten figs through the window opening. I jumped at a skittering sound in a pile of dried leaves.

"How do we find David?" I asked.

Jada squeezed my shoulders reassuringly. "Tomorrow I will go to the village of Sorek and put out my bowls near the well. News will come, sooner or later."

We walked to the river bank and gathered thatch and reeds. Wordlessly, we tidied up the house, ate some of our provisions, and settled for the night. Jada spread a few blankets on a mat of rushes and beckoned me to lie at her side.

I expelled a deep breath, exhausted. "Do you think David dreams about me?"

"I'm sure he does. Do you dream about him?"

"Yes, although lately, it has begun to fade. He's been gone three years. I wonder what he looks like and whether he still remembers me."

Jada raised her hands, fingers intertwined, and stretched. "You have to work on keeping his face in your mind. Pick a particular event and think of it over and over again. His touch, do you remember? How about his scent? And his kisses, the tang of his breath, the prickle of his beard."

"We used to play the harp and sing together," I said. "He stood like a prince at our wedding. Then there was his anguished face at window, just before he dropped to the ground."

"Not to worry," she said. "When you're in his arms, it'll come back as if you had always been together."

"But what about his other two wives? Wouldn't he think of them more?"

Jada turned to her side and stared at me, her blue-green eyes flared larger. "Each woman is different, like a carved musical instrument. No two are alike, in tone color, response, voice or timbre. Isn't that the same for you? You'd never confuse Phalti and David, would you?"

My face burned and I coughed. "Ah. No, but I never. I mean. No."

She tickled my cheek. "Why all the sputtering? Phalti is as much your husband as David. And I've seen you taking long walks with him in the evening and sitting with your heads together at the well in the moonlight."

"I, ah, wasn't kissing him. We only... talked." A bead of sweat trickled down my face despite the cool night.

"Darling, you needn't be ashamed. Phalti is Asherah's gift. The young man adores you."

"But it would be wrong. I took a vow with David. What if he thinks I've been unfaithful?"

Jada flicked a twig out of my hair. "Pshaw, you Hebrews, so uptight. Let him think. It'll make him even hotter."

"I just want David to love me." My voice sounded pitiful even to myself.

"Are you saying he doesn't? Let me ask you, what do you love about him?"

I squirmed and turned my back to her, closing my eyes. "I'm nothing without him. God anointed him, a man after His own heart, and I'm fortunate to be his wife."

She smoothed my hair. "One thing I've learned. Never spurn Asherah's gift when it's right in front of you."

* * *

Jada used a blade to cut through the tangled brush. I slapped at the flying insects darting in front of my face. Plant life grew abundantly, and small animals rustled in the bushes. Warblers and thrushes flitted and chirped in the trees above.

We reached the village around mid-morning. I wandered around the vendor stalls while Jada headed to the well. She approached a woman and asked for a drink of water. The woman lowered her pitcher to pour. Jada took out her bowl. "Sister, pour the water here and let me divine your future."

Soon, a crowd of women gathered. She told their fortunes and collected many silver pieces, chickens, eggs, wine, and bread.

We went back many more days as winter approached. Every woman had heard a rumor, knew someone who'd seen him, told a story about a chance encounter, and whispered dread about imagined curses, but we were no closer to finding him than when we left Gallim.

I had no heart to berate Jada. She taught me her lore of medicine, herbs, and basic skills, how to cook, snare, skin, fish, and plant. And she took me to villages where she went to heal and occasionally deliver a baby. She dressed me as a Philistine, bright reds, woven with gold and blue in spiral and circular patterns.

At night, she taught me Philistine words, told stories, and sang songs. An island amongst a sea of dolphins, priestesses with snakes on long boats, a mountain of fire, the wrath of the gods, and the sojourn awaiting the bull king's return. She talked of love, of men, and the many ways to snare, to entrap, and to haunt. And she braided and unbraided my hair, and curled it and straightened it, and washed it, and oiled it. And she showed me a mother's love, and she called me the daughter of her heart.

* * *

"Michal, don't look back. Someone's following us." Jada pushed aside a fig branch.

My palms tingling with sweat, I quickened my pace. Instead of approaching our house, we turned abruptly at the creek, crossed it, and trekked up the hill.

"Hide over there." She pointed to a rock.

I crouched obediently and clenched my fist in my shawl. "What are you going to do?"

"Find out who the man is and what he wants. I don't want him to find you. Hurry."

Jada walked along the creek, skipped up the bank, and stepped into a clearing.

A man stopped at the edge of the forest, hidden in the shadows.

"Stand back, for I am a priestess." Jada waved her arms like snakes in front of his face.

The man bowed. "I am Ittai, son of King Achish. I mean no harm."

"What is your business, Prince Ittai?"

"I wish you to see for me, Priestess. I'm looking for a woman."

Jada laughed, a high-pitched shriek designed to unsettle the man. "You've taken a wrong turn. The Sorek Grove is down the river. You can worship fiery redheads from the northlands or sultry nymphs of the Nile, as well as the more affordable local variety."

"I'm not looking for a grove. I'm looking for a princess, an Israelite." His smooth voice sent a rush of blood to my ears.

"I know not about whom you speak. Show yourself." Jada waved sharply.

I held my breath. A young man stepped into the clearing. Tall, muscular, and tanned, his bronze skin shone. Straight, glossy hair, so black it held shades of blue, flowed over his broad shoulders. A Philistine, he wore no beard on his strong, angular jaw. Butterflies took wings in my stomach. What reason could he have for seeking me? Did he know where David lived?

"Madame Priestess." He bowed. "I seek a princess. Her hair flowing streams of curly mahogany, her eyes green like a wooded vale, her skin golden like a lioness."

"There are many young women who fit your description," Jada said. "What makes you think I've seen her?"

"Honored Priestess, there is a young woman who follows you. She's the one I'm looking for."

"And who sent you?"

"Her husband." He waved a parchment and handed it to her. "You may examine this note. It is written by the hand of the princess."

My heartbeat accelerated, and I flapped my hands, almost jumping up. David had sent him! He hadn't forgotten me. A warm swoon like fresh wine bathed my chest. He still loved me.

Jada examined it with a swift turn of her wrist. "I do not read Hebrew."

"She does, ask her," the man said.

"I did not tell you I know of her. I will meet you here tomorrow."

"Madame Priestess." He handed her a sack of coins. "Bring her to me, and you shall have another one heavier."

I tipped at the edge of my toes, straining from behind the bushes to see his evidence. Could he be trusted? He spoke well, and I desperately hoped he'd be the one to take me to David.

After Ittai disappeared into the woods, I hurried to Jada, brushing burrs from my robe. She handed the note to me.

"Yes, it is my writing." I thanked Phalti in my heart while cheerful tingles engulfed my head and shoulders. "I'll be seeing David soon."

I hugged Jada and swung her around, dancing. "My husband wants me."

Laughter bubbled over my throat, and I skipped and hollered down the path. Everything looked brighter and prettier. The house was adorable, the trees were majestic, and the river sparkled. I yelled to the sky, "David, oh, David. Let me ride up on that cloud with you."

Jada placed a motherly hand around my shoulder. "Let me do your hair and pretty you up for tomorrow."

That night she sang a familiar song my nurse had used to lull me to sleep. She cradled my head to her breast and sobbed, kissing my forehead and cheeks. I wanted to ask her why she cried, if her heart had been broken, or if she had lost a child. But my eyelids danced with images of David, and when I drifted off, she blessed me by her goddess.

* * *

We woke early the next morning. After I said my prayers, I dressed in my own clothes and returned Jada's to her bag. She eyed me quizzically. "Are you sure you should dress as a Hebrew? Will you be safe?"

I tightened my sash and pinned my robe tightly over my breast. "David would not approve of immodest clothing. Do you think he'll come for me himself?"

Jada touched my cheekbone, grazing it with her fingertips. "A few days ago, I had a vision and saw a man with long black hair. The spirit of peace and friendship enveloped the two of you. When I saw Prince Ittai, I knew he was the one. He'll be good to you."

Her cheeks dimpled, and she kissed me. "I must go. The prince's father and I are not exactly friends."

The thundering of hoof beats alerted me. Ittai jumped off his horse, and his wide mouth broke into a smooth grin. "You are more beautiful than he described."

He kissed my hand with a flourish. "Let me help with your things."

Jada motioned Ittai toward the house. "There are still a few bags back there."

Ittai handed Jada a large bag of coins before following her to the house.

I pulled the note out of my pocket and perused it. David had not written anything on the back of it. But he must have remembered me and sent Ittai to fetch me. A smile tickled my cheeks as I stuffed the note into my bag.

Jada took my hand. Her eyes pooled. "Dear Michal, may your way be blessed."

I latched onto her, unable to swallow the lump in my throat and bear the sudden ache in my chest. "Will I see you again?"

A tear trickled down her face, and she made no effort to wipe it. She twisted a strand of my hair behind my ear. "I'll find you when you least expect. My destiny lies in Israel, in the valley of Jezreel. Look for me if you travel there."

Ittai helped her on the mule, and she rode away, the glint of her coppery-brown hair vanished into the greenery.

Ittai pointed to the bags he'd tied to his horse. "Princess, you're carrying a king's ransom."

"What do you mean?"

He opened the bag.

My head spun, dazzled by the glitter of gold and jewelry. "This belongs to Jada. We must catch her."

"She told me it belonged to you. I wouldn't argue if I were you. Come, let's get on the horse." He clasped my hand.

I hesitated, taken back by his deep midnight eyes, the rakish curve of his upper lip, and the heat seeping into my hand from his strong, hard grasp. He lifted me to sit sideways on the horse while he straddled it in one fluid motion and arranged my legs over one of his muscular thighs. Uneasy being nestled so close to a stranger, I leaned as far as I could toward the horse's neck.

Ittai grabbed the reins and spurred his horse. "Hold on, Princess."

"I can't." I bounced so high, I almost fell. Because I sat sideways, I could not grip the horse with my thighs. It was either this, or hike my skirts to straddle the horse.

"Then let me hold you." He clasped a strong arm around my waist and slowed to a trot.

I squirmed breathlessly. "Take your hands off me."

"But you might fall. I'm sorry. He's a bit hard to control. He's not used to having a princess ride him." He laughed and tightened his grip.

I elbowed him. "This is highly improper. I should not even be alone with you."

"Ah, but your mother seemed quite eager to leave you. She has a price on her head."

"She's not my mother, she's my friend. And what do you mean by a price on her head?"

His eyes bounced like a skittish colt. "It means I get a reward if I capture her."

He paused and licked his lips. "But I prefer a pretty, young princess to an old sorceress any day. Less trouble."

"How do you know I'm less trouble?"

"I don't, but I'd like to find out."

"Well, my husband isn't going to be happy if you don't take me to him safely and in one piece." I twisted and threw his arms from my waist for breathing room.

He responded by grappling me closer. "Which is exactly what I propose to do."

He rubbed his face in my hair and inhaled.

I threw my elbow into him harder. "Get your face out of my hair, you naughty boy."

"You're calling me a boy?"

"Yes, look at you," I said. "You don't even have a beard."

"Ah, but if you look closely, you'll see."

"I don't want to. Now, unhand me, you ruffian."

"You mean it?"

"Yes, take your grubby hands off me right now."

He raised his hands into the air. "Fine by me. But don't blame me if you fall." He kicked his horse.

The horse leapt forward. By reflex, I grabbed Ittai's arms and held on.

"See, Princess? You need me to hold you." He slowed the horse to a walk and flashed a triumphant grin.

I shot him a you-can't-be-serious scowl. "You shouldn't have kicked your horse. Do you know how rude it is? I'll have you know that I'm a princess."

He winked and raised a single eyebrow. "And, I'm a prince. So we're well-matched. Now…" He fingered the chain around my neck. "Let me see that gem, and we'll be on our way."

I slapped his hand. "Don't touch my gem. Don't even think of taking it, or… or, I'll curse you."

He gaped and made a circle with his mouth. "No, no, dear witch, don't curse me. Anything but a curse." He fluttered his thick, curly eyelashes and flapped his hands rapidly.

"You. Are. Not. Funny." I poked each word onto his chest.

Instead of faltering, the shameless boy moved his gaze to the line between my breasts. "David told me to look for a green emerald—one with brownish flecks that matches your eyes."

My heart jolted at his mention of David. But Ittai's greedy eyes angered me. I clapped my hand over my robe and tugged it tighter. "I'm not letting you look at anything."

He turned his head toward the sky and whistled. "How do I know you're David's wife? What if I go to all this trouble to bring you to his tent and it turns out I've caught the wrong wildcat?"

"Of course I'm David's wife." I wanted to claw his eyes out. "What would I be doing in this god-forsaken forest if I weren't?"

A gale of laughter blew from his mouth, and he doubled over. "You're exactly like he said." His shoulders jiggled so hard I thought they'd fly off.

"And what exactly does he say about me?"

"Oh, that you're headstrong, impetuous, irresistible, and maybe a little irascible."

"Did he say that? It doesn't seem like a particularly flattering thing to say."

"No, but you're not nice, so it doesn't matter." He winked and blew me a kiss.

I couldn't let that one pass. I jutted my chin and glared at his impertinent face. "And what else do you know about me?"

Amusement danced in his eyes. "I know what he tells me." He mocked in a sing-song voice.

"Oh, really. Did he tell you how he feels about me?"

Ittai frowned and rubbed his chin. "That depends."

"On what?"

"On my interpretation." He grabbed the back of my neck and kissed me, his lips massaging mine for several heartbeats, pooling guilt between my legs.

Breathless, I pushed back and slapped his face. "What did you do that for?"

He grabbed my hand and rubbed it across his lips. "Honing my interpretation." He rolled his thumb in my palm. "Yes, he loves you. He definitely loves you."

I twisted my hand out of his grasp and elbowed him again. "Why should I believe you?"

"Um… because you have no choice?"

I poked his belly. "Fine, just keep your hands from wandering."

He spurred his horse to a trot. I couldn't help but notice his short kilt and how much skin he exposed. I clamped my hands firmly under my elbows and fretted at his proximity, wiggling to relieve the tension.

He gripped me tighter. "Don't move, or you'll fall."

"Then I shouldn't be riding sideways."

"Hike up your skirts and straddle." Ittai wiggled his brazen eyebrows. I glared at him until he looked away, chuckling under his breath. "Relax, and I'll tell you what David says about you."

"What does he say?" I sounded like a flustered ninny.

"He said there's not a woman in the world like you. You're brave, courageous, and you love so hot. He misses you all the time. There's not a night that goes by when he doesn't look at the moon and the stars and think about you. He wants you so badly he'd go to the ends of the earth to find you. He delights in your smile, revels in your laughter. You thrill him so much."

I peeked at him. His eyes were closed, and a dreamy smile caressed his face. I tapped him with my elbow. "This doesn't sound like David."

His large eyes blinked markedly. "What? You mean you don't believe me?"

"I know him better than you. He'd never tell another man how he feels. He doesn't even tell me."

"Everything I said is true. You are brave, courageous, and thrilling."

"And you're a silver-tongued flatterer." I laughed.

"See, it is true, your smile delights, your laughter thrills." His gaze rested on me, and he flicked his tongue over his lips before swallowing, his neck rippling noticeably.

"I'm not sure David would be pleased with you flirting with his wife."

"Ah, but I'd rather please his wife." He crooned in my ear.

"And I'd rather flirt with my husband." I crooned right back.

He averted his gaze and settled for whistling a tune that made me want to crack the gleaming white teeth out of his jaw, one by one.

I stared at the surrounding countryside as we meandered out of the forest, past fields and meadows dotted with tiny villages, to the flat plain. The Philistines held well-watered land, rich and abundant with crops and game, quite unlike the rocky, hard-scrabble terrain of my homeland.

Around midday, we stopped at a small village. Ittai rummaged in his bags and pulled out a veil. "Sorry, Princess, you're going to have to put this on."

I yanked it from him. "Maybe you should have given it to me before you kissed me so impudently."

"Keep your voice down. There are bad men here."

"And how do I know you're not a bad man?" I adjusted the veil over my face.

"You have to trust me." He dismounted and led the horse to a well. "Now, you're my bride. Do not speak to anyone. Stay with the horse while I get something for us to eat."

I nodded sullenly, not daring to glance about. Philistine warriors, with their brass helmets decorated with red feathered plumes, hovered around the marketplace. Their stony eyes shifted and scanned over me. I lowered my head and ran my hands over the horse's mane as they approached me.

"Hebrew woman," the lead man said in the trade language.

I stared at the bronze plates on his chest. Cold sweat ringed my scalp.

"Eh, are you mute?" The man waved a hand in front of my face.

I pulled my veil tighter and pointed to my mouth while shaking my head, wondering where my dark-haired savior had gone.

"She's not from these parts." Ittai's voice rang behind them.

"Prince Ittai." The men scooted back in deference. "Your father sent us to bring his treaty bride. Might this be King Saul's daughter?"

Ittai threw his head back and roared in laughter. "Her? Does she look like a princess to you? She can't even speak, mute and deaf. Well, maybe not quite deaf, she reads lips. But only my lips. And she's mine."

An elderly gentleman hobbled over from the side of the well. "Do you always dress your women like Hebrews?" He chuckled, his jowls jiggling. "I've watched you two. She seems a little too feisty to be a maid." He rubbed his hands as if palming coins.

"Hebrew clothing keeps leering eyes off my property, especially useful for transporting my bride." Ittai slapped the side of his saddlebag.

"Ah, 'tis a bride you have?" the old man said. "Taking after your father already, aren't you? How many brides do you have, eh?"

Ittai grinned broadly, pulled his shoulders back and trained his gaze over the soldiers. "Being prince has benefits. Now be gone and make haste to find that missing princess. You know my father's temper."

As soon as the soldiers tramped into the woods, Ittai pulled a coin out of his pocket and palmed the old man's hand. "You keep dreaming. She's a wildcat, that one." He pushed the old man toward the poppy vendor.

How dare he claim me as his? This Philistine had no manners, no finesse, no… He licked a smooth tongue over his lips, plopped me on his horse and the basket of food on my lap. Without acknowledging me, he led us off the trail to a riverbed in the scrubland. He hitched the horse to a tree behind a thicket of bushes and reached to help me.

I slid from the horse, tore off my veil, and punched him. "Mute? Deaf? Reads your lips only? You despicable boy."

He mouthed 'wildcat' and wrestled me to the ground. Gripping both my wrists over my head, he grinned. "What are you going to do now?"

I struggled under his weight. "You better let me go. What were those men talking about?"

"Nothing you should worry about."

"I happen to understand your language," I said. "Mute, deaf, my sandals!"

"Oh, Princess, you are definitely… not mute." He muttered a few choice phrases under his breath and smacked his lips a mere inch from mine.

"You are a bad man. You've humiliated me, satisfied?" I choked back tears, not wishing to give him anything to gloat over.

His face hardened. "Apologize for your nasty temper. Go ahead."

"I don't apologize, especially to the likes of you. You insulted me. I'm not your property, and I'm definitely not your bride."

His eyes softened, and for a moment, I thought he would kiss me again.

"That's a pity," he said and helped me up. "Here, have something to eat."

He handed me meat, olives, and bread and sat on a log next to me.

I tapped him. "Sorry. And thanks."

He grunted and spit out an olive pit, his shoulders slumped over his knees. We sat side-by-side in silence and finished our meal.

He took his horse to the river, and I followed to wash my hands and face. The horse snorted and stomped his hooves. Ittai waved me to his side.

"We should be going." His eyebrows darkened over his high-bridged nose. "A few soldiers have backtracked. Hurry."

He helped me mount, and I glanced back at him. "And what's this about me being a treaty bride for your father?"

"My father will marry you in exchange for a deal with your father," he said.

"Deal? What kind of deal?"

"They didn't tell me. But it must be important because you have a huge price on your head."

Alarmed, I shook his arm. "Is that the reward you're claiming?"

He looked at me for a long moment. A stream of emotions played over his face: pride, fear, anger, and sadness, and then finally, nothing.

"My reward will be altogether different," he said.

"That doesn't answer my question," I said. "What exactly are you going to do with me?"

He avoided my gaze and sucked in his cheeks.

I prodded him. "What aren't you telling me? Are you trying to irritate me?"

"I've told you too much already." His mood darkened, completely opposite to his playful behavior earlier.

A chill traveled down my back. "Ittai, you're not turning me over to your father, are you?"

"Trust me," he said.

"How can I? I don't even know you."

He hastened his horse into a gallop. "There's not much you can do about it now."

I gripped the horse's mane and wished I didn't need to lean on him while I fought the nausea in my stomach.

We wound our way down the valley and met a contingent of warriors.

"Ho, Prince Ittai." The lead man pulled his horse. "Did you find her? The Hebrew princess?"

Ittai kept his horse moving. I hid my face in the crook of his neck.

The other man said, "Who's the girl?"

"Mine," Ittai said. "You want the princess, you better move to the east. Rumor has it she's crossed the border back to Israel already."

"Oh, I see." The man broke away from us.

I closed my eyes and clung to his warmth. Would he really take me to David, or did he want me for himself? What if Jada had set me up? Oh, God. What have I gotten myself into?

CHAPTER 12

Isaiah 1:8 And the daughter of Zion is left as a cottage in a vineyard, as a lodge in a garden of cucumbers, as a besieged city.

>>><<<

The city of Gath stood starkly on a lofty cliff, approachable only from the north. Massive walls encircled it with no spaces or gaps. Everything about the city appeared rock hard, a military fortress. As we drew near the gate, Ittai asked me to close my eyes.

"Why?" I strained my neck. Gruesome figures were impaled on poles driven into the ground. My stomach lurched, and I pressed my face to his chest.

He cradled my head and whispered, "I warned you."

The guards hailed him at the gate. "Ho, Prince Ittai."

"Peace," Ittai said in a firm voice.

They bowed low. "The king will be pleased. Enter."

As soon as we cleared the gate, I asked, "Are you taking me to David?"

"Not yet. We have to find you a place to hide. Tomorrow morning, I'll take you, promise." His demeanor changed, and he seemed to relax. He kissed my cheek. "I know what I'm doing. Don't worry."

Too tired to fret, I slumped against him. His warmth comforted me, even if it was temporary.

We arrived at a tiny stone house behind a walled courtyard. Ittai hitched his horse and helped me dismount.

"Ho, Auntie Kyra," he said.

A middle-aged woman set her fan on the bench she was sitting on. "Another one of your lady friends?"

Ittai flushed. "She'll need a room for the night and a bath." He handed her a silver coin. "Promise me you won't say anything about her."

She cackled. "Seeing as you haven't told me her name, no, I have nothing to say."

She looked me over with a somewhat disapproving eye. "Come in, young one. When are you to be presented to the king?"

I halted at the threshold. "Wait, I need a word with Ittai."

I grabbed his arm and hustled him around the corner of the house. "What are you doing?"

"Getting someone to clean you up. Would you like to meet David smelling like horse sweat and dust?" He bent over my neck and took a sniff before I palmed his face and gave it a firm shove.

"Who is she? Why did she ask if I were going to the king?"

"I'm not taking you to the king," he said.

"How can I know that?"

"If I wanted to betray you, I would have marched you to the palace already and collected my reward." He lifted one roguish eyebrow for emphasis. "You're fortunate I found you, because I'm the only one in the entire world who'd take you where you want to go."

"How can I believe you?"

"My reward is neither silver nor gold, but a hope and a song."

"Stop talking in riddles and tell me."

He didn't reply. His eyes intently on me, he looped a strand of my hair around his finger. I stood paralyzed when his lips touched mine. Deceptively gentle, definitely not tentative, the kiss tasted like a challenge, a deliberate provocation. A pulse beat of affection swirled and tangled my breath with his tongue. Moments later, consciousness caught up, and I inhaled sharply. "I can't."

He rubbed my chin with his thumb and whispered, "Trust me," before stepping out of the courtyard.

What had come over me? My face heated and a sigh escaped my lips before I took several deep breaths to compose myself. I walked to Kyra's door.

"Young one, do you have a name?" she asked.

"For now, no."

"I shall call you Princess, because Prince Ittai brought you." She called for a maid to fetch water and led me to a room lit with oil lamps. It was small, but well-appointed: a mahogany chest, a leather couch, and an oak table. A platter of fruit and a bowl of water sat on top of the table. A bronze mirror lay on the chest, and the couch sported a woolen throw and several pillows.

The maids returned with hot water and filled the tub while Kyra peeled off my clothes. She palmed the emerald and hefted its weight. "This is an exquisite stone."

"Yes, it is." I kept my tone casual as prickles crawled down my spine.

She eyed me. "Where did Ittai find you?"

I sunk into the tub, keeping one hand over the emerald. "I wonder. Does Ittai have a lot of lady friends?"

She leaned over, and her big teeth gleamed. "Now, why would a waif like you be interested in a prince?"

I jerked my face away from her, grabbed a sponge, and scrubbed my arms.

She twirled her finger in the water. "You're more high-minded than I thought. Very well, in case you're interested, he's not betrothed."

"He's the king's son," I said, wondering if he were the prince my father had wanted me to marry. "Wouldn't his father plan a political marriage for him?"

"He's headstrong, that one. He wants to choose his own bride. That's why every princess ends up in his father's harem. Besides, he doesn't want someone to marry him because he's the king's son."

"Oh, I understand—" I bit my tongue and splashed water on my hair. Would David have married me if I weren't the king's daughter?

While I toweled my hair, Kyra toyed with her bracelet and glanced at my pendant again. She handed me a robe. "Tora will bring your meal."

After I dressed, a maid wrapped in a veiled shawl set a platter of food on the table.

"Shalom," she said in Hebrew and headed quickly out the door. I stared after her. An Israelite, here?

* * *

I awoke sore and aching. The horseback ride had been uncomfortable, especially one with a half-naked man who threatened to kiss me at every turn. Sunlight streamed through a tiny window high above me. Within moments, Kyra peeked in and told me Ittai was waiting in the courtyard. I sorted through the garments in my bag. Sometimes when a woman could not pay for Jada's reading, she slipped us an article of clothing.

I pulled on a plain dress and a Philistine skirt over my underclothes, and completed my outfit with a roughly spun cloak, tying everything together with a leather sash. It would be better to go through the city in disguise and not advertise my Hebrew origin. Donning my veil, I glanced at myself in the bronze mirror. Looking more like a vagabond than a princess, I looped my heavy bag over my shoulder and went out the door.

Ittai greeted me, his bronze skin in contrast with the crisp white linen stretched over his broad shoulders. His sparse kilt flapped, and I wondered whether he wore anything underneath. My gaze lingered a little too long on his sculpted thighs before traveling to his face.

White teeth gleamed from his wolfish smile, and I couldn't help but return it. He took the bag from me and held out his arm. "Ready to meet your lord?"

With a leisurely swagger, Ittai guided me through the streets. Foreign sights and sounds surrounded me: a cacophony of sing-song voices, young women in tight, revealing clothes, street merchants hawking their wares, mothers walking their children, older men in long skirts discoursing loudly over drinks, and leather-kilted soldiers patrolling the streets.

He stopped near a fountain in the marketplace and took a sip of water. Several lanes converged there, and he turned and scanned as if trying to decide the direction to take.

"Do you know the way?" I asked.

His wide mouth stretched into a grin. "Offer me a reward."

"Why should I?"

"I might conveniently get lost. Gath is a big city." He bowed low. "I'm at your service."

"Fine, what would you wish me to confer upon you, humble servant?"

"A kiss."

"Despite what you seem to believe, I do not simply bestow kisses on every Ittai, Joash, or Kenan."

He leaned closer to my veiled face and peeked in. "You liked it so much before."

I snapped the veil tightly and huffed. "You impudent boy. You... you... forced..."

"I forced you? Does David know what a sharp tongue you have?"

I marched away from him, and he muttered, "Sharp and yummy."

I shook my fist. "I heard that, you imp."

"So long, Princess," he yelled. "See you in Gaza. The beaches are nice this time of year."

Several soldiers leered at me and stepped over to take a closer look.

"Having trouble with your bride?" one said to Ittai.

"Where did you get her? Does your father know?" said another.

The first soldier clapped Ittai's back. "Cousin, I didn't know you were betrothed. I thought you weren't the marrying kind. That's what you told the king last spring when he brought you the Princess Raya."

"Ha, the old king ended up marrying her himself. So who's your bride?" the second soldier said. "Or, is she your father's treaty bride? She looks Hebrew."

Ittai shook his head. "Does she look Hebrew to you? Too pretty and dainty to be Hebrew. Frankly, I don't understand why Father would want the daughter of Saul. From what I heard, she's a real bear. Hairy, too, with feet as big as Goliath's."

They guffawed and slapped their thighs.

"So, who is this young lady? Can I look?" Ittai's cousin grabbed my arm.

"She's mine. A vagabond and no one important. I found her on one of my expeditions." Ittai jerked me to his side and peeled his cousin's paws off me.

"You're supposed to be looking for the bear woman, not gallivanting around with pretty gazelles." The cousin huffed. "All the better, I'll get the reward. What did you say she looked like, this daughter of Saul?"

Ittai choked back laughter. "Her husband, who's very happy he escaped, says she's got a huge bump on her nose, her teeth are yellow and jagged, and she's cross-eyed. Oh, there's also a mole at the base of her jaw and hair grows out of it. Thick, black hair."

"Ugh…" The men laughed raucously and walked off making gagging motions.

"Don't forget the mole," Ittai yelled after them. "It's important. Make sure to check under the veil."

As soon as the men turned the corner, I punched Ittai, who leaned against a low wall, doubled up with laughter. I stomped my foot and waited for him to catch his breath. "I'll draw a mole on your insolent face, you."

"Did I upset you?" He chuckled and took my hand, swinging it in a wide arc. "Come, my bride, I'll take you to David now. But beware. His two wives may not look kindly on your intrusion."

I shook my fist. "I don't take kindly to their existence."

* * *

My heart raced and plummeted as we descended the higher parts of the city and made our way through the poorer section of town. Miserable, wretched beggars, eyes devoid of hope, sprawled in the doorways. Harlots, painted and jangling, beckoned at their windows. The street clamored with the barking of dogs and the cries of hungry children.

We left the town and crossed a meadow to a field of ruins. Broken houses, foundations, and piles of rubble obscured our path. Clusters of bedraggled people squatted around tattered tents.

"Hebrews," Ittai said. "Do you recognize anyone?"

"Who goes there?" A menacing-looking man with dirty red hair and an unkempt beard blocked our path.

"Tell your leader, David, that Ittai, son of Achish, has someone for him."

"He is out inspecting the flock." The man gestured toward a cloud of dust. "And who is this young lady?"

"She's my sister."

"You would bring your sister? You Philistines are unbelievable." The man leered at me. "I'll show you to his tent. You may wait outside."

After winding through ruins, rubble and flapping tents, we came to a large one that stood toward the periphery, backed up against a ruined wall under a large palm tree. I took a swig of water to clear my dusty throat.

The man departed, and Ittai opened the flap. "Why don't you sit in the tent, and I'll wait here."

"Wouldn't David be angry?" I hesitated. My nerves jumped, and my heart skipped. The big moment was finally here. "What if someone's in there?"

Ittai took a peek. "No one's here. Now's your chance. He'll be overjoyed to see you. Trust me."

I almost hugged the dear boy, but I clamped my hands under my arms and stepped through the opening. The dusty, acrid smell of unwashed clothing greeted me. Two sleeping areas lay on the packed floor. The area in the back had two pillows and two cloaks on top of goatskins. Unfinished needlework lay on one of the cloaks, and a small brass mirror was propped on the other pillow. I stepped back quickly, wishing I could light a fire to their things.

He'd get rid of them. I had only to ask. I crawled to the front area consisting of a leather pad topped with sheepskins and a goat-hair pillow. A harp lay near the pillow. I plucked the strings. They were out of tune.

I crawled into his bed and held his blankets to my face, inhaling the warm, male scent of his musky sweat. Minutes crept by. Two large flies buzzed while my pulse thumped in my ears.

The chattering of female voices knocked me out of my trance.

"Ho there, wives of David." Ittai's shadow blocked the entrance.

The women fell silent, and heavy footsteps approached.

"Wives, why aren't you getting my dinner ready?" David's voice grated. My heartbeat sped, and I wiped my moist palms on my robe. "And what are you doing here?"

"David, my brother," Ittai said. "Please tell your wives to fetch water or wash pots at the stream. Send them away until sundown."

David grunted. "I don't have time for jokes. My wives are tired. My feet ache, and I'm starving."

"Tell them to go away for a bit. It's important. Please."

"Ahi, Abi, go to Rebekah and borrow some lentils." David's voice held displeasure.

They scuttled away without protest.

Sounds of shuffling and pushing came through the tent flap. "I'm not in a good mood," David said. "What's going on?"

"Do you ever think about your real wife?" Ittai said.

"Of course I do. I told you all about her."

"Yes, and you told me that if I found her, you'd give me a reward."

"I was humoring you," David said. "Seems like you never tired of hearing about her. If I didn't know how young you were, I'd think you were in love with her yourself."

"I'm eighteen, and I was dead serious about finding her."

"What are you saying?" David's voice took on a guarded tone.

"You owe me a reward, that's all."

"Don't play with me," David said. "Don't even try. Son of Achish or not, don't you toy with me." An ache vibrated deep in the core of his voice, and I held his pillow tightly.

"I dare you to step into your tent," Ittai said.

David flew through the tent flap and stumbled. "Michal, what are you doing here?"

"David." I jumped into his arms.

"Let me look at you." He pulled off my veil. "Oh, my Michal."

I faltered under his concerned gaze. All the sweet words I had rehearsed were forgotten. I tasted his lips, honey pouring into mine, so heavenly, so divine. His kisses dissolved all my fears and misgivings.

He held me to his possessive chest and rubbed my shoulders and back. "I've missed you so much. I thought you forgot about me, that you no longer cared."

His words and anguished tone roused me from my cloud of serenity. "Didn't you get my notes? You were supposed to come for me, remember?"

"You sent me notes? Didn't Jonathan give you my messages?" His voice sharpened.

"No, he didn't. But why?"

"He always says you were doing well, so I thought you stopped caring. I didn't dream you'd find me." He brushed his hand across my forehead. "How did you know I was here?"

"You mean you didn't send Ittai?"

He gaped. "No, what are you talking about?"

Jealousy twisted itself like a snake through my heart. "Of course, you married again, twice."

"You also remarried."

"A ploy, to get away from my father so you could come for me."

"Look, I didn't marry. I just took them in." His voice hardened.

"Well, I never slept with him."

David stiffened, and I pushed away.

"David? Did you?"

His lips pursed in a firm line. He glowered and turned his face. "I'm a man."

I punched him in the gut. "Did you forget me so easily? You told me you were mine."

"I still am."

"Then send them away."

"Hold your voice down." His gaze shifted to the tent entrance.

"You liar. Liar."

"Where are you staying?" He grabbed my shoulders.

"Nowhere. I came to stay with you."

"You can't stay here. Look around. Is there room for you?"

"If they left, there would be."

"Look carefully," he said. "Is this how you'd live? You're a princess. You're used to better things. Listen to me. You can't stay here."

"I'm your rightful wife, not them."

"You can't stay. It's too dangerous."

"Then why is it safe for those two?" Large teardrops burned a trail down my face.

"They're not princesses. They're unknown women. Do you know what you are? A political pawn, a possible hostage. Jonathan arranged a hiding place for you. Why won't you wait there until I come to fetch you?"

"I'm tired of waiting." I tugged at his sleeve. "I love you so much it hurts. Why can't we run away together?"

He exhaled harshly. "I'm tired of running. Ahi and Abi are tired. They haven't had a day's rest for years. They've suffered too much already."

I pushed him and almost slapped him, except he caught my wrist. "So, that's it? You care more about them than about me. Maybe I shouldn't have come. Maybe I should have remembered how little you love me."

"They obey me without a word," he said. "Maybe it's time you obey me as your husband and lord. Go with Ittai."

"But where?" I reached for him desperately. "You need to help me."

He loosened my hold, none too gently, and walked out of the tent.

Ittai beckoned from the entrance. "Come on. David wants you out of here."

The curtain came down on my courage. "David!" I tried to run after him, but Ittai stopped me. "Oh, David." Pain shot through my stomach, and I doubled over. "Don't leave me."

"He cares about you," Ittai said. "He's embarrassed. He wants you as a queen, not here in the dust."

"But I love him so much," I wailed as tears streamed down my face. The ache in my gut spread to my chest and throbbed in my head. I couldn't have felt worse if a mule trod on my skull.

Ittai hugged me tenderly, my face in his chest. "He loves you, Michal. But he can't bear to see you suffer. He wants you safe in Israel, even if it means being away from you. It's because he cares too much for you."

"Then why didn't he tell me himself?"

"He has too much pride. Put on your veil, and come with me."

I donned the veil and crawled out of the tent. David turned his back, intent on consoling his wives, no doubt assuring them that I would be gone. Why didn't he care? The man who used to look at me with tender love had turned into a cold, hard monster.

Ittai grabbed my bag, put his arm around me, and led me back the way we came. The sun dipped low on the horizon. Purple clouds streaked with crimson heralded the end of the day—the day that had dawned with much hope ended in the dusk of confusion and despair.

CHAPTER 13

Malachi 3:3 And he shall sit as a refiner and purifier of silver: and he shall purify the sons of Levi, and purge them as gold and silver, that they may offer unto the LORD an offering in righteousness.

>>><<<

Waking late the next morning, I pulled my clothing together and walked to the back courtyard to breathe some fresh air and think about my predicament. I should have told David about my father's deal with Achish. He would have helped me. He always wanted to do good, and he had a kind heart. I shouldn't have bothered him about the two wives. That had set him off. Mother had said never to show jealousy, that it was a weakness and drove men away. I wiped my hands on my robe and sighed.

Maybe, if I charmed Ittai, he'd take me back to David instead of turning me over to his father. I needed another chance to make David care, a more opportune moment. *David, you haven't seen the last of me.*

I stepped through the courtyard and found Ittai at the forge near the end of the yard. The sound of blowing air drew me to investigate. Ittai stood shirtless in front of the oven. The muscles on his glistening back rippled as he pumped air into the fire. I inhaled sharply and clutched the opening of my robe.

He picked up a pair of tongs, drew a red hot piece of metal and laid it on a shiny block. Taking a hammer, he pounded on the metal, his muscles tight and corded. Trickles of sweat dribbled between his shoulder blades, and moved, oh, so slowly down the hollow of his back to the line behind his low hanging kilt.

I eased as close as I dared. The heat of the oven repelled me, yet the alluring vision drew me. So, this was what my father's kingdom lacked, the secret of forging iron weapons. Weapons so superior to our bronze, that the Philistines were, in truth, our overlords, and controlled all production and sharpening of iron farm tools in our land.

His face in total concentration, Ittai dropped the worked blade into a tub of water, enveloping the shack with a hissing mist. He raised the blade and studied it, turning it in the sunlight. My gaze swept his smooth chest, crawled down the ridges of his abdomen before dragging back to his face.

"Michal." He came toward me, the gleaming blade in front of him. Cool, dark, unsmiling eyes pinned me to the stone wall. "Touch it."

My breath latched in the back of my throat.

He took my hand and stroked it over the blunt side of the blade, smooth, hard, threatening. Cold tingles lifted the hair on my scalp and prickled my skin. He moved my hand to his bare chest, wet, hot, and alive, the pounding sensation of his heartbeat weakening my legs.

"So, you've discovered our secret. With iron, we forge swords and spearheads, construct chariots with spiked wheels and shoes for our horses. With iron, we dominate you Hebrews and control our destiny. So, Princess, what would you give for iron?"

I staggered against the wall. He ran the flat side of the blade from my neck down between my breasts and over my abdomen, leaving a trail of tremors. My breath in shallow shudders, I raised my eyes, drawn to the simmering heat of his masculinity as a moth to a lamp. He cupped my face, stroking underneath my chin, the invigorating scent of fresh bay leaves and mint enticed me, seductive. Our noses touched. I inhaled the masculine aura and licked a bead of sweat from his upper lip. He turned his head and kissed my lips, passing his tongue to the corners of my mouth.

I twined my fingers into his hair and lost my breath. He probed deeper and drew my body hard against his. My hands traveled down the glistening shoulders, following the trails of sweat down the small of his back. Losing all conscious thought, I arched against his hardness, encouraging, entreating, emboldening.

With a lingering nip, he lifted his head. "You do love so hot. I've a tent, too…"

Guilt flushed my face, and I pushed away. "I'm a married woman."

"Your husband didn't seem to think so." He licked his lips as they curved into a satisfied smirk. "Tell me, what happens now? Where will you go?"

I clutched my shawl and glanced across the yard in time to see his aunt regard us with her hands on her hips. "How long will she let me stay?"

He moved into my line of sight. "As long as you want, although most young women stay thirty days."

"Why thirty days?"

"You mean you don't know? The rule of war captives. Thirty days to ensure you're free of a child, are properly purified, and then you go to the king."

"The king? You told me you weren't taking me to him."

"And I didn't, did I? I took you to your husband, but he has repudiated you." He rubbed my hand in his warm calloused palm. "Does this mean you're free?"

I pinched his knuckles and peeled my hand from his grip. "He'll come around. I'll try again."

"You don't give up, do you?"

"I'll never give up on David." I stared at his darkened eyes.

He exhaled with a hiss. Releasing me, he pulled on a tunic. "Perhaps you're right. Let me wash the soot off, and I'll take you back to him."

He squeezed my hand before walking off.

Kyra called to me. "Tora will bring your meal. Are you hungry?"

A few minutes later, a maid entered and set a tray on the table. She clutched the shawl around her face.

"Shalom," she said, before turning to the door.

"Wait." I called to her in Hebrew. "Come and sit with me."

She crept to the edge of the couch.

"Please, eat with me." I gestured to the table. "I need some company."

She hesitated before dropping her shawl. Ugly welts and scars traversed her face. Her nose, or what was left of it, gaped grotesquely, and her lip had been cut in half. One of her eyes stared unseeing, clouded over and blank. I blinked and tried hard to keep my face still. She looked to be in her late thirties.

"Have I made you lose your appetite?" Her mouth stretched over the scars in a crooked tilt.

"No, no... What happened to you? Are you a daughter of the Law?"

"Yes, with a name like Tora, what else would I be? I grew up in Gibeah."

"Well, so did... I also grew up in Israel. Whose daughter are you?"

"Ribai, of the children of Benjamin," she said.

I handed her a cluster of grapes. "Please, eat. How did you come to work for the purification inn?"

"The Philistines captured me on a raid while I visited my sister near Elon," she said. "They killed everyone and saved the virgins for war captives."

A chill clawed my back as I thought of how close to Gibeah they had come.

"They brought us to inns like this to be cleansed and purified," she said. "King Achish chose first and distributed the rest of the captives among his men."

"How did you end up here?"

She grimaced and popped a grape into her mouth. "King Achish favored me at first, especially when I bore him a son. But one day when my son was four years old, he told his father he was Moses, and he would free the slaves."

She gulped and reached for a cup of water. Taking a deep breath, she looked down at her hands.

I put my hand on hers. "It's okay. You don't have to tell me."

"I want to tell you so you'll escape my fate. Do you want to know who did this to me? Who cut my face?"

"King Achish?"

"Yes," she said. "He cut me in front of my son and told him I was a disobedient slave, not his mother."

She lowered her head to the table and let out a sob that tore my heart. "I can still hear his cries, begging his father to stop."

I averted my gaze and blinked back tears.

Struggling for breath, she wiped her face with her shawl. "He took my son and gave him to his eldest wife, a Philistine, to raise as her own—as a Philistine prince."

"Does your son know you?"

Ittai stood at the door, his face contorted with a strange expression.

She shook her head, not seeing him. "The king said he would kill my son should he ever find out his mother was a Hebrew slave."

When I next looked, Ittai had left.

* * *

David grabbed Ittai's tunic and pushed him against the trunk of the palm tree. "Why did you bring her yesterday?"

Ittai's jaw clenched. "Why did you send her away?"

Anger boiled in David's chest. "She's my wife and none of your concern."

"Look, Jonathan sent me. He wants you to come back to Israel with Michal. He'll hide you." Ittai waved the note in his face.

David yanked it and read. *My dearest David. Every day we're apart, I love you more. Please come back to me. I'm in Gallim with my friend, Phalti, son of Laish. Yours always, Michal.*

Guilt and regret coiled in David's heart. She had always loved him, and he'd turned into a rogue and betrayed her. No matter, he was destined to wander the wilderness. A princess should not be consigned to a vagabond, forever exiled.

"Jonathan has no business meddling." David glared at Ittai. "I've pledged to serve your father. I don't need this trouble."

Ittai's eyes narrowed. "So, you've forsaken her?"

David pushed past Ittai. This wasn't how he envisioned it. He would have bestowed his riches and kingdom to her. Her beauty unsurpassed, she would be his queen. And Israel would be at peace under the feet of Almighty God.

He kicked the pebbles and bloodied his fist into the tree trunk. She wasn't supposed to see the squalor, smell the stench, taste his weakness. The dream was gone, finished.

David stepped into his tent. His two wives stared at him. Dusty faces, worn expressions, cracked lips. "Why did you come with me? I'm not the future king no matter what rumors you've heard."

He kicked dirt into their bedding and overturned their pillows. "I'm the enemy. Leave!"

Michal was Israel, the land of God's blessing. Her father had driven him away like a dog. David crushed her note and threw it in the ash heap.

* * *

A week passed, and Ittai did not return. I asked Kyra where he had gone. She said, "He told me to ask you to wait. He is arranging something for you. Once you're purified from your monthly uncleanness, you'll be ready to meet the king."

"Why do you say that?"

"Of course you will be brought to him. But you'll have to wait, as you have not bled. I was once his wife, but as I was barren, he has set me to run this inn. You're not barren, are you?"

I sputtered and shook my head. "I mean, I don't know. But what does it matter? I'm already a man's wife."

She stared at me. "I know who you are, the daughter of Saul. I am to complete your days of purification and keep you safe."

"Is that why your nephew brought me here?" My words spat through gritted teeth.

"He's a smart boy, isn't he? He has gone, no doubt to collect his reward, and you, my dear, are my responsibility. Come, relax your face and smile. This is no way to please the mighty king of our land."

Even as I smiled, I planned my escape. How could I have been so stupid? So naïve? Ittai had betrayed me with his smooth tongue and easy grin. If I ever lay hands on him, I'd squeeze… I shook my head. He was of no consequence. David would help me. He was my last hope.

I sidled up to Kyra. "Since I'm going to meet the king, what can I do to thank you for your kindness?" I lathered my words like honey on warm bread.

"There's no need. The king pays me for purification of war captives."

"But, I would like to do something for you and those of your household, the maidens, and the young men who stand guard. You have all been most kind to me, even though I'm not from your land."

"We're kind to any young woman who comes through here. Who knows if you will become the next queen? We want you to be happy here."

"Very well," I said. "I'd be happy if I could prepare a feast for your household. I will cook a meal and serve you, all your maidens and your young men. Wouldn't that be a story to tell your relatives, the night the future queen served you?"

She laughed and patted herself on the chest. "Oh, Princess, you must not think so highly of us. We are merely the king's servants."

"But, Kyra, you'll insult me if you don't allow me to make you a feast. If I'm to be queen, I must show gratitude for the care you've given me."

"Oh, you are too kind. Can Ittai attend? After all, if it weren't for him, you wouldn't have the chance to be the king's wife."

"Most certainly. I wouldn't want him to miss his reward." I laughed gaily, and she trilled like a meadowlark.

He'll get his reward all right when I throttle his handsome neck with my bare hands.

How could Kyra withstand my entreaties? Fluttering happily, she ordered her servants to take me to the market. In addition to the food, I bought a costly ball of cooked opium with my own gold.

I spent the entire day with the serving maids, preparing the feast, plucking the chickens, dressing the lamb, peeling the vegetables, chopping and steaming. The young guards found their way into the kitchen more often than not.

"Out, out." I shooed them. "If any of you play music, go get your instrument. We'll have singing and dancing tonight."

The feasting extended deep into the night. The young men played flutes, whistles, and drums. The young maidens danced with tabrets and rattles. I served everyone spiced wine laced with honey and powdered opium.

Kyra cried over my shoulder. "No one has ever done this for me. What an honor you've brought to my purification inn. From now on, the king's men will send every maiden my way."

"Have some more wine. I'll never forget you, dear Kyra, or your wonderful nephew." I almost bit my tongue with that last phrase. Oh, how I wanted to scratch that insolent grin off his face. Unfortunately, he had decided not to show.

"Oh, Princess, it is a shame Ittai is too young for you. Perhaps the king will relent and give you to him." She let out a maudlin moan. "Poor Ittai, if only you weren't the daughter of Saul, it might have been." She slumped over the table with a sob.

The young men and maidens disappeared, two by two, with wobbling gaits to dark hidden corners or behind low hanging trees.

I slipped a golden bracelet on Kyra's limp arm and walked casually to my room. With my bag over my shoulder, I sneaked to the courtyard. A hand touched me. Tora.

"Let me go," I whispered. "For the love of the God of Israel, don't give me away."

She grasped my hands. "Let my father know. Ribai of Gibeah."

"Ribai of Gibeah. I won't forget. Do you want him to rescue you?"

She shook her head, waving her hand like a wounded bird. "No, as long as my son lives, I will stay here, even as a slave."

I hugged her, feeling her pain and sadness.

"Shalom. Go in peace, daughter of the Law." She pushed me toward the gate. I fumbled in my bag and placed gold into her hands.

"No, no. I need no gold, no silver," she said. "Remember me and my fate. May yours never be as mine. Will you pray for me?"

I placed a golden chain dripping with garnets around her neck. "Remember me, David's wife."

She disappeared into the shadows. I glanced around, saw no one, and stepped out of the courtyard.

CHAPTER 14

Jeremiah 33:14 Behold, the days come, saith the LORD, that I will perform that good thing which I have promised unto the house of Israel and to the house of Judah.

>>><<<

I walked through the dark streets, chilled by the damp fog. A few drunks loitered, but they were too inebriated to pay attention to me. Once or twice, a harlot darted between doorways. Fortunately, the moon provided enough light for me to find my way to the edge of the town. I dimly recalled my bearings and picked my path through the rubble, avoiding the broken bricks, piles of refuse and burnt fire pits.

"Who goes there?" A rough voice shouted in Hebrew.

"David's wife."

Two filthy men with untrimmed beards and greasy hair stepped toward me from the shadow. "David's wives are with him. Who are you? A harlot?"

I propped my hands on my hips and raised my chin. "I'll have you know that I'm his true wife, King Saul's daughter. Take me to him."

They turned to each other. "Is she a crazy woman?"

"Maybe we'd better take her to the chief."

"This late at night?"

One shoved the other. "You go."

I stomped my foot. "Never mind. I remember the way."

Surprisingly, they stepped aside. I made my way through the camp to the tent under the palm tree. It fluttered in the breeze.

I stilled my breathing. Was David asleep or entangled with one or both of his wives? All seemed quiet enough, so I crept into the tent.

As my eyes adjusted to the dimness, I spied David asleep with a woman in his arms, her long black hair spread like a net across his naked chest.

MICHAL'S WINDOW

Twin shafts of anger and jealousy drilled through my temples. I staggered and dropped my bag, knocking over a cooking pot.

David sat up. "Ahi, go to the back."

She pulled on a robe and crawled to the side where his other wife slept.

David unsheathed a knife. I froze. I could feel him scan the dim interior lit by a shaft of moonlight. My anxious wheeze betrayed my location. He leapt and grabbed me.

"David, don't hurt me," I exhaled.

The knife fell to the floor. "What are you doing here?"

"I want to be with you." I threw my arms around him.

"Oh, Michal, I want you so much." He grabbed both sides of my head and pressed his lips over mine. A rush of warmth flooded me. My heart responded to his caresses, and I melted into his embrace.

Before I lost all conscious thought, I pushed myself upright. "You have to help me. The innkeeper is turning me over to the Philistine king to join his harem. I've just escaped."

"Were you seen coming here?" He pulled on a robe and motioned me out of the tent.

"Yes, two of your guards accosted me. They wouldn't let me pass until I told them my name. But they're Hebrews, so we needn't worry."

David groaned. "Hebrew or not, they can get the reward, and you're still in danger. Ittai has gone to seek help from your brother."

"What? Why?" My mouth dried, and I couldn't clear my tightened throat.

"To rescue you. He didn't think he could get you back to Israel by himself."

A tight shiver passed through my shoulders. Ittai had not betrayed me. But why would he involve himself against his own father?

"My place is with you," I said. "Let's run away together."

"We have to say goodbye, for now." His words twisted and wrenched my heart.

"But why?"

"Because I can't protect you." His voice broke. "I can't keep you out of Achish's hands. And I can't take you back to Israel because your father will hunt me down."

"But I love you. Don't let me go." My voice ripped as the fraying of a garment.

He put his finger over my lips and took my arm. We walked around the wall, following a small brook past the sheepfold.

He spread his cloak on the ground behind a hillock and pulled me into his lap. "If I were a king, I would never have to say goodbye. I could keep you in a palace, deck you in finery, and roll you in rivers of jewels."

113

I grabbed his cheeks with both hands. "I don't want that. I only want you, David. Do you love me?"

"I can't bear it if something were to happen to you," he said. "Do you think it's easy for me to be away from you?"

"Then I'd rather die. I'll—"

David covered my mouth. "Don't ever say that. I was never worthy of your love. You should have forgotten me, put me out of your mind."

"What are you saying?" My voice betrayed my dying heart.

"I wish I could take you, but I'm not a brave enough man. I can't see you suffering. Do you know what it's like to be hungry, or to be sick and miscarry in a cave?"

He bent over me, his honey-brown eyes soft and pained in the moonlight. "Please believe me. Will you trust me, Michal? Trust that I know what's best for you?"

"Do you still trust God?"

"Sometimes I do, and sometimes I doubt," he said.

"He will make you king over all of Israel. Do you believe that?"

He lowered his gaze. "I don't know. I'm not sure if Samuel even knew. Perhaps he anointed me in error. Maybe he was angry at your father."

"David, you will be the king." I stroked his beard and noticed an indentation over the bridge of his nose. At some point, it had been broken.

"More like a hunted partridge, a step from death." He shook his head slowly. "Your brother Jonathan deserves to be the next king. He's a military strategist, a valiant man, a diplomat and a commander. He is more capable than I. In this, I agree with your father."

I tapped his chest. "Don't say that. God does not make mistakes. What He says He will do, He will."

"I'd like to believe that," he said, "just as I'd like to believe we'd live together happily, forever. I'm so tired of fighting, tired of running. I wish I could be a child again and find comfort in stories and dreams."

"No pain, right? Just dreams and stories with happy endings." I stroked his beard.

He snorted and smiled. "Yes, sometimes when I sleep, I could almost believe it."

I traced the line of his strong jaw. "When your kingdom comes, will you think of me?"

He bent forward to kiss me, but stopped short, his eyes suddenly strong. "Yes, the first thing I will do is fetch you. And I will never let you go. I promise you."

"No matter what happens?"

"No matter what. I promise." He spoke each word heavily and firmly to impress his intentions in my mind.

"I'll wait for you then." I touched two fingers to his lips, and he kissed them.

"Put your mind to rest." He held me closely. "You are the only woman I married in front of God, and the only one I made a covenant with. And your title, David's wife, will I allow no one else to use."

The tattered edges of my heart knitted with his loving words, and my body swooned into his caring arms. His lips found mine, warm and compliant. He caressed me as he would a lamb and laid me down on soft pasture. With tender hands, he removed my clothes and loved me as calm as still water. And like a long, slow burning log, he anointed me with his love, and my cup overflowed with sweet and long lasting billows of delight, permeating every pore of my body and capturing the depths of my heart. Oh, if I could follow him all the days of my life, I would surely dwell in his arms forever.

* * *

We slept like two mated doves, nestled under a cold, misty blanket. When I woke, David brushed dewdrops off my hair. "Michal, don't forget me. Don't forget this moment, this night. Whatever happens."

"I won't. I promise." I rubbed my eyes as the image of David with a slender, long-haired woman sleeping in his arms jumped unbidden into my mind.

David put his hand on my shoulder and led me back to the entrance of his tent. His two wives whispered to themselves in the back. Little more than skin and bones, their faces were weathered, and their clothes ragged. They both appeared older than me, although it could be due to the hardship they endured. I pitied them, but I could never share a bed with them or be two cubits away while he gratified himself with one or the other.

I opened my bag and set aside silver, medicine, herbs, and salves. I then took the bulk of Jada's jewelry and gold and the finest gowns I had and pushed them under David's bedding. With winter approaching, his wives could use some warmer clothes, and the gold would buy a better tent.

David stared at me from the tent flap. He asked one of his wives to serve breakfast. She kept her gaze averted from me and bowed as she set the plate in front of me. After we had eaten, he led me by the hand. "Let's hope Ittai's back. I sent a messenger to him to meet us at the edge of the camp. I'll walk you there."

"Why is Ittai helping me? Are you sure he's not taking me to King Achish?"

"He's my friend. I trust him."

"Can you come part way with me to Israel? I'd like it if you would."

He lowered his eyelids and sighed. "I wish I could, but I am here as a liege to King Achish. Ittai is liable to get punished severely for helping you. I cannot take this risk because I'm responsible for six hundred men and their families. We need Achish to grant us land in Ziklag, a place to live where I'm safe from your father."

I traced the ugly scar on his cheek. "Always my father, isn't it?"

"It doesn't change how I feel about you." He kissed the side of my temple and caressed my hair. I wished he'd say more, but he cleared his throat and led me around the rubble and dust.

Ittai stood under a craggy olive tree, his long hair flowing in the breeze, his short kilt flapping dangerously. He unhitched his horse and came toward us.

David stopped and turned his back on Ittai. "Isha, don't get hurt or killed."

"Ishi, you'll be king some day and come for me."

He lingered, holding my face. "Thank you for your faith in me and in God." He kissed me slowly and tenderly. "Remember my promise."

"I will, David. I will."

Ittai helped me sit sideways on his horse. I looked at David, still hoping he'd call me back or grab a horse to accompany me. But he stood under the olive tree and waved. The lump hardened in my throat. Through blurry eyes I stared at him until he was just a dot among the ruins.

* * *

Ittai covered my face with a heavy veil. We cantered through the town and exited the city without incident. Once outside the gate, he set me down and pulled me up to ride behind him so we could gallop if needed. I hiked my gown and straddled the horse. The saddle blanket itched beneath my bare legs.

Ahead lay rolling hills and meadows with scattered rock outcroppings—exposed, without tree cover. We meandered along a creek and headed for a small hill. Only then did I dare to look back, too far to see the gruesome figures hanging on the wooden poles at the gate.

A plume of dust and wild cries followed us. Two men rode hard.

"Not good." Ittai warned me.

"I know. Let's fly." I gripped the horse tightly between my thighs and wrapped my arms around his waist.

Ittai kicked his horse into a gallop.

I looked back. "They're gaining on us."

"Then we're going to have to jump."

We leapt over a cleft, but the men also jumped. Our horse slowed, tiring under the weight of two people.

"This might get bloody." He unsheathed his sword. "I'm going to drop you near those rocks. Climb up and stay away from where the horses can get to you."

He pulled his horse to a halt. I slid to the ground and scrambled up the rock pile.

Ittai wheeled around and waved his sword. The men drew their swords. They were the two ruffians who guarded David's camp.

Ittai charged and knocked the closest man off his horse with a slice that cut his arm. The other man bumped Ittai's horse, causing it to rear. Ittai rolled off. The man on the ground attacked with his sword. Ittai ducked and knocked the man's sword away.

The man on the horse charged Ittai who dodged out of his way. The other man climbed after me. I lunged and jumped, barely hanging on a ledge. Kicking off the wall, I hoisted myself up and over. The man glared at me from below. I heaved stones at him. A rock the size of a man's head knocked him back. He fell and lay writhing on the ground. I cringed with cold sweat at what I had done.

Meanwhile, the horseman charged Ittai. Instead of backing away, Ittai barreled toward him on foot, his sword in the air. He slashed and cut the horse's throat. The horse collapsed with an unearthly, almost human scream. The man jumped off his dying mount. Ittai opened the man's belly, and the man's sword cut Ittai across the chest.

Ittai clutched his chest and walked toward me. "Strip their weapons and clothes."

I scrambled down and touched the man at the foot of the rockpile. Still alive, he twitched and foamed from the mouth. I removed his weapons, the leather sheathes, belts and water skins, then turned him over and yanked off his pants, tunic, robe, and sandals. I wrapped everything in the dead horse's saddle blanket.

Ittai grabbed the reins of the uninjured horse and handed it to me. "Do you know how to ride?"

"Yes, I can ride a mule. A horse shouldn't be different."

A stain of crimson red spread across the front of Ittai's torn tunic.

"You're hurt." I touched his chest.

"No time to worry. Get on the horse. There may be others." He strapped the extra weapons and clothes on my horse and went in search of his.

CHAPTER 15

Psalm 56:8 Thou tellest my wanderings: put thou my tears into thy bottle: are they not in thy book?

>>><<<

Ittai and I rode alongside a creek and turned up a dense forest trail. The trees shaded us, but brambles cut our legs and tore our clothing. Ittai swayed from side to side on his horse, his shoulders slumped as if he could tumble off at any moment. A dark splotch of blood spread over his tunic.

Toward evening, I recognized the clearing and the brook. I picked up the familiar trail and forged ahead, ignoring fallen logs, thick vines and the thickets of thorny bushes that sprang every which way. "I know of a house nearby, or at least what's left of the house."

"But I'm supposed to find Jonathan." His voice slurred.

"You're injured. Let's rest here."

We rode up the trail to the broken walls. The old fruit trees welcomed us with bent boughs. I dismounted and ducked into the weed-infested courtyard. Everything was exactly as Jada and I had left it.

The evening breeze sent a sudden gust that threw dirt in my face. I hitched the horses and helped Ittai dismount. He slid into my arms, his body smeared with blood, warm and sticky with a tangy, salty scent. I helped him over the threshold and laid him on the bedding Jada left behind.

After fetching water from the brook, I peeled off his stiff, blood encrusted garments, taking care to separate it gently from his wounds. A gash stretched from the top of his left shoulder to the line of his right hip. The wound was surface, but deep enough that the skin had separated. I ripped a linen tunic into strips to clean his wound and returned to the brook several times for fresh water. Sweat popped over his face, and he hissed through his clenched teeth in pain. I held his head in my lap and wiped his hair with a wet cloth until his breathing quieted.

The weather turned drizzly. Jada and I had repaired the roof, so we had shelter from above, but drafts blew through the holes in the wall. I wrapped my arms around Ittai and waited for his warmth to stop my chattering teeth. A wolf howled, sending chills down my spine. I drew the blanket over my face and held him, afraid to rouse him, despite my hammering heart. A tear slid down my cheek. He had been wounded to protect me.

Ittai groaned throughout the night and woke feverish. His wounds screamed raw and angry. Within days, his fever worsened, and he turned delirious. I had used up Jada's herbs and salves and had no choice but to heat a knife and burn the pus out of his wounds. The smell of searing flesh sickened me, and I cried and prayed as I drew the flat side of the blade over his skin. He screamed and howled freely, unable to hide his pain.

Every night I held him, fearing it would be his last. I sang to him, sponged him with water and rubbed my face against his soft, downy beard. I talked to him, told him my heart, my love for David, and his promises to me. And because I couldn't control myself, I kissed him in his helplessness. Desirous, delectable, delirious, he would not remember.

At night I sang. Songs my mother taught me, songs my Philistine nurse crooned—words of comfort danced and blended with an imaginary voice in the wind.

One night, when his beard grew full, he returned my kiss. His fevered hand snaked around my neck, and his gaze bore into mine. "Kiss me again."

"No. It's not right." I ran my hand on the side of his face, noting his strong square jaw, his chiseled cheeks, his sharp nose, a sculpture in flesh.

"Then sing to me, the song of our people in the old language. My mother sang it to me, to help me sleep. It's a love song."

"Mine also, only not my mother." I hummed the familiar tune Jada had sung to me. Blue-green eyes, fragrant skin, comforting hands. Could she be the woman in my father's visions?

"Now, sing me a Hebrew song," he said.

A song welled in my throat.

Float, O son of Israel
Your Father's hand shall guide.
Deliver, O son of Israel
Your Father's chosen people.
Write, O son of Israel
Your Father's Holy Law.
Sleep, O son of Israel
Your Father's glory wake.

"Eemah…" Ittai cried and raised his hands to the stars. "Mother!"

His eyes fluttered back in his head. His fever boiled. I went to the water pitcher, wet a cloth and bathed his face. He lapsed back into delirium.

"No, Father, no, no, no." He pounded the air with his fists.

I poured water on his head and lay on top of him, pressing him down and holding his hands. The cool water mingled with his sweat and tears, heating it up. He relaxed under my weight. I lowered my lips to his, soft and lazy. His tongue burned with licks of fire. Too hot.

Reluctantly I tore myself away and went to the water pitcher.

"I hate him." His voice floated like a sultry breeze. "I know who she is."

"Tora's your mother?"

His tears were answer enough.

* * *

I walked to the Philistine village of Sorek to buy milk and cheese. Our horses had wandered away shortly after we arrived. When I returned, Ittai sat against the wall, his long hair wet. I dropped my basket and hurried to his side, pleased he had recovered.

He stretched out his arms. "I've just been to the river and washed. Where are the horses?"

"Gone. I'm sorry. I was tending to you. I must not have tied them."

"We'll have to walk then." He hugged me. "How are we doing on food?"

I laughed and pinched his bearded cheek. "I have been keeping us supplied with meat and fish, vegetables, nuts and berries. There were few things I needed to buy at the village. This forest is so rich. I wonder why no one has claimed this house."

The tangled vines, the cracked walls, and the moss that grew on the floor stones all pointed to a once beautiful home, maybe filled with a happy family. In my mind's eye, children tumbled around the porch and danced around the fig trees. A dog scratched itself near the hearth, and cats chased mice around the low wall of the courtyard.

Ittai took my hand. "Sit with me, and I'll tell you."

I slid down the wall beside him.

"It belonged to a sorceress." He waved his hands. "And she haunts these hills, especially this house. That is why no one has bothered us."

"You're amusing. I lived here with Jada and never heard a thing."

He pulled me into his lap. "Do you feel chills at night? Do you hear her cry?"

I leaned against him. "Not over the sound of your moaning and mumbling. It's a wonder I get any sleep."

120

"I promise to be quiet tonight. We can listen for the ghost together."

"You talk nonsense. Are you sure the fever has left?" I wiped my hand across his forehead.

He put his hand on my lips and whispered, "Be careful how you speak about her—she was an ensnarer, a destroyer."

"My people don't believe in spirits. We have a God who is invisible and all powerful."

He tickled my ear with his beard. "This woman brought down a man of your people, a champion, one whom your God endowed with superhuman strength."

"Are you talking about Samson?"

He paused for effect. "Yes, and the ghost who haunts this place is none other than his lover, Delilah."

"Wait, if she brought him down, why would she cry? From what I heard, she received eleven hundred pieces of silver. Why would she hang out in this dump?"

"Shh, Michal. You insult her without knowing. Look around, this house was built with love. A beautiful home lies hidden beneath the weeds and cracks. Birds chirped in the courtyard, with a vineyard in back, and fig trees. Samson hewed the stones himself. Every detail, every corner, for the woman he loved."

"A woman who betrayed him, it seems. So tell me why does she cry?"

"Because she loved him."

"Delilah loved Samson? This I find hard to believe."

Ittai tipped my chin to face him. "Delilah was a slave, brought from the north, as white as the snow. Her price, eleven hundred pieces of silver, the price of the sun. He built this house to live with her. Once he paid off her master, he planned to marry her."

"But he was caught, blinded, and killed."

"He didn't believe his god would leave him. Yet his god betrayed him when he needed him most. So Delilah cries. She walks these parts draped in a veil, made with the seven locks of his hair, woven with her own. Sea grass and straw, night and day."

He drew me down to the bedding. "Now lay still and listen."

The closeness of his warmth mesmerized me with smoky tendrils of desire. He cradled me to his recently healed chest. The breeze rustled through the treetops. His breathing and steady heartbeat lulled me.

A faint sob, a catching of the breath tickled my ear. Ittai hadn't moved, but a sudden intake of air told me he had heard. The sobbing came closer. *David. What if God let him down? What if his kingdom would never come? What if he were to wander the wilderness forever with his twin wives?*

The sob was so sad, profoundly sad. I clutched Ittai's chest, oblivious of his healing wounds. Another sob broke from my own throat, my heart broken as Delilah's. A solitary form floated above, wearing a veil of human hair, woven, dark and light. Her hands reached for the moon. She yearned for her love and sang—separated from him for all eternity.

Ittai shook me. "Michal, wake up."

I blinked. *Gone. She is forever separated from him. He has gone with God to Heaven, and she walks below, lost.*

He touched my face. "You look so sad. I'm sorry I told you the story."

"I know what it's like to be separated, torn away, and banished."

"You'll see him again. You will. He promised."

"He's only a man, like Samson, only a man."

"Will you be able to sleep tonight, to get some rest?" He shifted his weight and cupped my face, looking like he wanted to kiss me.

I stood. "First, let's take a walk in the moonlight."

We walked around the courtyard and to the orchard, my sandals squishing over fallen fruit. Ittai peeled a ripe fig and squeezed it between my lips. A lover's fruit, subtle, somewhat musky. He moved the plump pulp over my tongue and traced the leathery skin over my upper lip. I licked its sweet succulence and kissed the fleshy pad of his thumb.

He backed me to a wall, my fingers clutching the mortar plastered with love. An uncontrollable pang, a mixture of longing and grief washed over me. I crunched the flesh of the fig and swallowed, and my knees crumbled along with my resolve. My back to the cold wall, my breasts to his heated chest, I wrapped my arms around him, my breath entangling with his hot puffs.

"You have me, Michal. You will always have me." His eyes shone in the moonlight, starry glints in the night sky. "I owe my life to you. According to the law of the ancients, I'm your slave."

He drew me inexorably to his lips, as firm and fleshy as the fig. His kisses trailed from my lips to my neck.

I broke away. "No, I can't. David."

His grin turned into a long smirk. "Am I so bad a kisser? After all the practice you gave me?"

My face burned. "I thought you were delirious. I thought you wouldn't remember."

"Goddess, you made me delirious. Every night I'd wait for you to bathe me, to dress my wounds and feed me. And I'd lay very still, waiting for you, listening to you talk." He nuzzled me with his beard, close to my ear. "And when you finished talking, you would rub your face on mine and ravish me with your lips."

He tilted my chin with his thumb. "It was all I could do to lay still. You made me so hot, so very hot for you."

He gasped and moaned loudly, too loud to be genuine.

I pushed him. "You... you tricked me. You impertinent trickster."

"Me? I tricked you into kissing me while I lay at death's door?" He caught my arm. "Admit you like me. Admit you need me. Admit you want my loving."

"Never. You're a bad boy." I sputtered, even as my traitorous thighs shook in assent.

Ittai grabbed me from the back and blew into my ear. "Goddess, I will serve you and worship you forever."

My body wanted to melt against him, but I tore out of his arms, ran into the woods and jumped into the river. David made a promise to me, and I would wait for him, no matter what.

* * *

David settled his family in Ziklag, recently emptied of all its inhabitants by an Amalekite raid. He smiled at his two wives. They would finally have a place to stay, separate beds and separate rooms. Abigail's feet bled, and she leaned on Ahinoam the entire way. *Hear my voice, O God, in my prayer; preserve my life from fear of the enemy.*

He picked up Abigail and kissed Ahinoam. "Come, let's get settled."

Michal's gold bought all the supplies for six hundred men and their families. And her gowns were precious to his wives. He would honor her and keep his promise, as soon as God willed.

That night, he slept alone on the roof, the night air wafting over him. He stared at the moon. Michal. Was she looking at the moon, thinking of him? He cupped his hands around his mouth.

"Hello, Michal!" He yelled and waited for her voice to echo. It did not return.

* * *

Ittai covered my eyes and hugged me from behind. "Quiet, we don't want to disturb the spirits."

He had everything packed. In the morning, we'd hike to Jerusalem. The Jebusites lived there, and we would be safe from my father. But he wanted to show me something, so I humored him. The evening breeze cooled the sheen of sweat from my forehead, and I shook off a sense of foreboding. "Where are we going?"

He hummed and did not answer. Instead, he nuzzled his nose into my hair and inhaled.

Tempting heat flushed my skin. Ittai turned my head and kissed me, his tongue darting a question that begged for an answer. I allowed my lips to linger a little longer than I should have. Reluctantly, I twisted away and covered my mouth; his spicy, piquant taste tingling my tongue.

"Why did you stop?" He rubbed my shoulder.

I closed my eyes and sighed. "I'm still David's wife."

We walked hand in hand and stopped under a large terebinth tree. The lemony-balsamic fragrance of its leaves, reminiscent of fennel, heightened my affection.

He squeezed my hand. "I want you as more than a friend. You must know by now."

My treacherous pulse pounded in my ears, but I cooled my head with a silent prayer. "I'm tempted, too. But I won't sin. David trusted you to take me back to Israel."

Ittai drew in a sharp breath and pouted exaggeratedly. "Your poor Ittai. See how sad he is?" He sniffed and rubbed his eyes, but couldn't hide the smile.

I slapped his arm. "Now, stop trying to guilt me."

"Ah, so you are guilty. I knew it." He jabbed his fingers into my waist and tickled me.

I pushed away from him. "You can't touch me there."

"Just watch me. Before the night is out, I'll be touching a lot more of you." He picked up a handful of twigs and seeds and threw it at me.

"You!" I brushed my robe. "What do you think you're doing?" I threw pebbles back at him.

He scrambled up the giant tree and squawked. "Bet you can't catch me."

Long arms and legs alternated on a network of branches. Soon he was a mere shadow hidden amongst the leaves.

I punched my hands to my hips and stomped my foot.

"You're scared, aren't you?" He hooted from the treetop. "Have you never climbed a tree?"

Truthfully, yes. Admit it to him? Never.

I loosened my robe and tightened my sandals. "You better beware. When I catch you, I'm going to tickle you until you fall off your perch. You arrogant little, little…" I caught myself. There was nothing little about Ittai, nothing.

My knees and elbows scraping on the rough trunk, I placed hand over hand and foot over foot. Somewhat breathless, I pulled myself to his branch. It creaked and swayed under our combined weight.

"Not bad for a princess," he said.

I raised my fist to wipe the smirk off his face when he caught my wrist and pulled me into a tight embrace.

"You are an annoying boy. That's what you are. You're so annoying you drive me crazy. I'll have your—"

His mouth covered mine with a deep, hot kiss. I staggered at the pounding of my heart and the crushing wave of heat and desire that pooled between my legs.

Hardly able to think, I disengaged from him. The heady, resinous scent dizzied my senses. "Why did you bring me here?"

His eyes grew serious in the dusk of the setting sun. "This is the wishing tree."

He pointed to the west as a reddish glow tinted the clouds, sable and lavender. "We make a wish as the sun sets, and kiss a leaf, then tear the leaf in half. I keep one half, and you keep the other half here, in your robe, next to your heart. And someday our wishes will come true."

"Do we have to wish the same thing?"

He shook his head. "That's the beauty of this tree. We can wish our own desires, and it'll still fulfill both of our wishes."

"That doesn't make sense," I said. "What if I wished to never see you again and you wished to always be by my side?"

He chuckled. "Then I'd say you'd better be careful because you'll be struck blind, and I'll be your guide."

"Then I'd better think of every loophole, shouldn't I?"

He gestured at the sun, whose last rays shafted from the ridge and kindled the leaves and branches afire. "You'd better think fast."

"Ready?" He plucked a leaf.

"Yes."

He put his arm around me, and we looked at the sun as it dipped below the horizon. Then he pressed the leaf to my mouth, and we kissed it at the same time. Slowly and deliberately, he tore the leaf down the vein and handed me my half, while tucking his into his inner robe.

"Do we tell our wishes?" I plucked a seedpod out of his glossy, black hair.

"Either way. Do you want to tell me?" His voice mesmerized me with a deep rumble.

I shook my head. "I wouldn't want you to know because you might avoid making it come true."

"Then I won't tell you either." He stuck his tongue out and blew a disgusting sound.

We sat in silence as the night air rose. Crickets chirped, and fireflies flitted below us. The diffuse, sweetish-citrony fragrance of the flowers cleared my irritations and soothed me with a sense of peace and contentment. Undisturbed by worries, Ittai and I clung to each other, breathing deeply of the dreams tucked away in the comforting branches of the wishing tree.

CHAPTER 16

Psalm 40:17 But I am poor and needy; yet the Lord thinketh upon me: thou art my help and my deliverer; make no tarrying, O my God.

>>><<<

A twig cracked and the sound of a drawn sword awakened me. I pushed Ittai, and he felt for his weapons. A low breeze howled through the trees, but the rhythmic rustle of dried leaves made my hair stand on end.

"They must be here somewhere." A voice grumbled from the woods.

"Quick, hide in the vineyard," Ittai whispered. "I'll jump up and surprise them."

I scuttled to the back of the house and crept behind a pillar. Shadowy figures circled at the fringes of the orchard. A man cleared his throat and spat.

"Aye, the fire pit's still warm." Another voice said.

The shadows of several men advanced toward the broken wall where Ittai hid. I edged through the weeds and crouched under a fig tree. A horse's nicker surprised me. I called to it with smooching noises.

The men stepped into the courtyard. Ittai's sword flashed. A man screamed. The air weighed heavily with huffs and groans and the clang of clashing metal.

Footsteps thudded behind me. I gulped and crawled on my hands and knees toward a juniper bush. Someone lifted me by the waist and swung me over his shoulder.

"Where are you taking me? Let me go." I pounded on his back and kicked at his stomach.

He slammed me against a tree trunk. The air in my lungs gushed from the impact. I bore my weight to the ground and pushed against his chest, but he clamped my head under his armpit and dragged me over the dry leaves.

Another man led a horse toward us. "Get her on the horse."

My captor unclamped my mouth to grab the horse. I let out a long scream.

"Look, they're taking her away." One of the men fighting Ittai yelled.

Several pairs of feet pounded toward us. My captors forced me to the ground and turned to fight the incoming men. Grunts and curses exploded from the mass of fists and swords.

I ran for the horse and grabbed its reins, halfway looping my legs over his back before the man who captured me yanked me off. He tied my hands, gagged me, and threw me face down across the horse.

Without waiting for his partner, he kicked the horse and tore off in a gallop into the dark woods. Pain pounded through my belly and chest as I flopped on the horse's back, pinned by his hand. The screams of the men left fighting faded into the distance, along with any hope of knowing Ittai's fate.

A few miles later, my captor slowed the horse, sat me upright and held me with a strong grip. I swallowed bile and dropped my head. Had Ittai been hurt, or God forbid, killed? My breathing convulsed into rapid sobs that choked against my throat. *Oh, merciful God, don't let Ittai be injured or killed. My friend, Ittai. My dear friend.*

We weaved through the shadowy forest threaded by streaks of moonlight. My captor rode with one hand around my waist, but did not harass me. I slumped against the horse, unable to speak because of the gag. Who was he and where would he take me?

* * *

I woke cramped and sore, my wrists still bound, but the gag removed. A man wearing a blue and white fringed shawl sat in front of a fire a few feet from me. His angular features flickered, and he appeared to be praying.

"You're an Israelite?" My voice croaked in Hebrew.

Before he could answer, a familiar voice cut in. "Michal, you look horrible."

My brother Jonathan sauntered over and lifted me from the ground.

I jerked my head. "What's going on here? Why am I tied up? And why did you attack Ittai?"

"We didn't attack anyone," my captor said. "They attacked us. When we approached the house, we saw a group of men trying to capture your sister."

Jonathan slashed my bonds and waved his hand. "One of us has to go back for Reuben."

"What about Ittai? Let me go back," I said. "He might have been hurt." I snatched Jonathan's sleeve, but he pulled away from me.

"He's not our concern," Jonathan said. "Go to the river and wash."

I knelt at his feet. "I plead with you, dear brother."

"You go first," Jonathan said to the man who captured me. "I'll take care of my sister."

"I shouldn't have left him," the man said and cast a disdainful look at me. "But you said to fetch your sister, no matter what."

"You did the right thing," Jonathan said.

"Don't kill Ittai, whatever you do." I yelled after him. "He helped me. He was injured because of me. Please."

My captor glared at me, straightened his sword in his sheath, and strode to his horse.

I ran after Jonathan's long strides. "Let me go and help Ittai. He said he's your friend. He saved my life and…"

Jonathan turned on his heels. "And what, my sister? What trouble have you gotten into now?"

"I care a great deal about him. I can't bear to think of him lying face down in a pool of blood. Please, dear brother, if you love me, even a little." I clasped my hands in front of his face. "He's David's friend too."

Jonathan frowned and clamped his hands on my shoulders. "Go to the river and wash. I'll find you some clean clothes."

I trudged to the riverbank and sat on a smooth slab of slate. Splashing cool water over my face and head, I berated my brother. Why did he send his men? Why hadn't he come himself and found us? And what had happened to Ittai?

Jonathan handed me clean clothes and a veil. He pushed me behind a screen of bushes. "Put on the veil and do not say anything to anyone."

I emerged from the screen, and he lifted me on his horse and mounted behind me. "Don't do anything to attract attention. You're in a lot of danger, for I have to hide you from both the Philistines and Father's men."

"Why are you so angry? Ittai and I didn't do anything. He tried to find you, but he was injured."

"I'm not angry at Ittai. It's you. Your little jaunt to Philistia was reckless. You're a disobedient wife, and you put both David and Phalti in great danger." He paused and said, "And Ittai too. If he's injured or killed, it's because of you."

His words burned a hole in my heart. The three men I cared for most had been harmed because of me.

"What happened to Phalti?" I said. "I saw the note he delivered."

"Whipped thirty-nine times and left to die."

A whirlwind of pain bowled me over. "Phalti? Is he?"

"He's alive. I stopped the beating and talked Father out of executing him. We both knew how difficult you could be. He's recovered, although he lost all his fields and livestock because he didn't keep his part of the bargain."

"What bargain?"

Jonathan kicked his horse. "To keep you safe."

"It wasn't his fault. He's the most kind and gentle man I know. He didn't deserve this."

Jonathan made no sound, nor did he try to comfort me.

"Jonathan?" I drew my veil aside and peeked at him. "I'm sorry."

He made one of those indeterminate grunts between assent and forgiveness, then steered the horse down a narrow trail overgrown with bushes. Leaving the sandy soil near the river, we climbed the stark ridges toward Israel, the horse's hooves stirring dust as they clopped over the rock-strewn path.

The valley of Sorek spread below, a lush grove with a meandering stream trickling in a crooked line toward the Great Sea. Behind me, the gaiety of balmy bazaars with their sing-song voices and dreamy songs faded. Ahead of me lay the stern hand of the Law, dry prophets, and retribution for my sins. I swallowed a dusty lump and asked God to forgive me and watch over Ittai and Tora. When I could no longer see the enchanted valley, I leaned against Jonathan's chest and sobbed.

* * *

Once we crossed a series of ridges, we followed a road patrolled by Father's men. Jonathan adjusted my veil and placed me sideways. "Dry your tears and don't say a word, for you are to act as my bride."

We passed other travelers, several contingents of Philistines marching in broad daylight on our road, as well as soldiers from our side. Our appearance as an Israelite warrior and his bride brought no inquiries, and we encountered no mishaps.

Around noontime, we stopped at the side of a large cistern to refill our water skins. A few women sat under a tree, and a knot of children played nearby. After watering the horse, we rested under the shade of a large oak tree where we ate our midday meal.

Jonathan pulled off my veil and shook out the dust. He rubbed my head and kissed my cheek. "No matter what, you're still my baby sister. You may talk now. There are only a few old women and shepherds hanging over near the cistern."

He handed me food from his satchel and a wineskin.

"Why didn't you give David my message?" I asked.

He chewed on a piece of bread and did not answer. I tugged his sleeve. "Jonathan, why would you not help? David said he sent messages through you, and you never told me."

RACHELLE AYALA

"That hothead wanted to raid the palace and get himself killed. I lied to him so he'd stay away. I'm sorry, but I told him you were happily married to Phalti to make him give up on you."

His words slammed my heart like a thunderclap, and I doubled over as if punched in the stomach. "But, Jonathan, he took two more wives."

His lips turned down in a thin line. "There's nothing we can do about that now. The important thing is to keep you safe, and that means far away from David."

"Why?"

He heaved a deep sigh. "Anyone who captures you captures David. And anyone who has David's head has you for a bride. Therefore the two of you cannot be together. Why do you think Achish refused to turn David over to Father?"

"Because he didn't have the bride?"

"Exactly. And if he had you, who do you think would try to rescue you?"

"David?"

"Yes. Now you see why David wanted Ittai to take you back to Israel and hide you."

The realization left me with a warm feeling. So David did care about me. And Ittai? Oh, Ittai. I tugged his robe. "Will you help Ittai?"

"Yes, I will go back for him as soon as I see you safely to Merab's house. Father will not look for you there because he thinks you're still in Philistia. And Merab lives too far inland for the Philistines to travel there."

"And why do the Philistines march into our territory without opposition?"

Jonathan's lip curled into a grimace. "Iron. Iron cuts through bronze like a hot knife through fat. When we fight them, we are truly like a few bees harassing a bear. We get in a few stings, maybe drive them out of a village or two, but they come back. The other people in the land, the Gibeonites, the Hivites, and the Canaanites have peace with the Philistines, allowing them garrisons, strongholds and forges."

"Ittai works with iron," I said. "I saw him hammer a blade. It was cold and sharp. He's my friend."

Jonathan eyed me a bit, adjusted the bags on the horse and handed me the veil. "You're a married woman."

* * *

In the evening, we stopped at an inn. Groggy from my nap, I stretched and stepped into the room and flung off the heavy veil.

Jonathan unpacked a basket of lamb, lentils, and bread he had bought from the innkeeper. I studied his profile while he ate. The small lines etching the corners of his eyes gave him a harried look. He was my eldest brother, and the years had not been kind to him.

I broke a crust off the bread. "Why is Father so mad he'd exchange me for David's head?"

He stopped chewing and tapped the table. "You shouldn't say such things. No matter how you feel, Father is the king and you must reverence him."

"But, Jonathan, kings do not always do what's right, unless they follow God's will."

"Yes, I suppose that's the problem with kings. The LORD God warned us about kings when the tribes demanded one. Kings have incredible pressure to protect their people and fight their wars, and yet at the same time, boundless power. Such power can blind a man to what is decent and good. Power that can snuff out a life, wed a maid against her desire, crush a son or daughter, and destroy a family and a nation."

"David would not do this if he were king," I said, somewhat smugly.

He smashed a fist to the table. "David will never become king. He is a traitor and pledged to serve the Philistines."

"No, you can't say that about him. He's only hiding from Father."

"I sent your note to him to try to get him to return to Israel. Instead, he sends you back with a Philistine spy."

I rubbed my eyes. "Ittai never gave him the note. He used the note to find me, so it was not David's fault."

Jonathan grabbed his head with both hands. "You don't know how it hurts me. I loved him as a brother. We were the best of friends. And now he is my enemy."

I patted his shoulder. "David still loves you. I'm sure he would never betray you."

"I wish that were true. Fear and doubt can change men's hearts. Since he serves Achish, he was obligated to hand you over to him."

My breath caught. "He wouldn't do that."

"And he didn't. I assured him Phalti took a vow to never touch you, and he consented to your return. But he wouldn't return himself."

"Of course not! Father would kill him. Besides, David doesn't serve the enemy. He's a refugee, biding his time."

He pushed the table. "You are blissfully unaware of David's double-dealing. Perhaps I should tell you why it took so long for me to find you. We had to fend off David's men in the south of Judah to protect the Kenites and the Jerahmeelites."

"You mean he attacked our own people?"

"Not exactly. He's been raiding foreign villages in the south, killing all inhabitants, robbing them, and buying off the elders of Judah. At the same time, he told King Achish that he leveled Israelite villages, leading the Philistine king to believe David would go to war on his behalf."

"Then David's only tricking Achish." I lifted my chin and sniffed. "I believe in David."

"I don't know what to believe. It would have been better for David to die in honor as God's anointed than to be a dog lapping at the feet of the Philistine king." A tear slipped down the corner of his eye, and he swiped it away with the back of his fist.

I waited for him to regain composure. "David still loves you. I know it."

After a few moments, he raised his eyes. "My sister, the best thing for you is to stay with Merab and Adriel. Promise me you'll stay out of trouble?"

I rubbed his slumped shoulders. "Yes, for you, dear brother, I promise, as long as trouble doesn't find me."

"My little sister, ever since you were a tiny tot, trouble has always found you. Let's get some sleep. We have a long journey tomorrow. You sleep on the bed. I'll lie down on my cloak."

I washed my face and cleaned my teeth at the basin and remembered Tora. "Jonathan, there's one more thing. Ribai of Gibeah, tell him his daughter Tora lives. She lives in Gath but does not want to be rescued. She wants him to know she is well."

He yawned and rubbed his eyes. "I will make inquiry."

"And tell him that he has a grandson. Ittai."

"Ittai? Isn't he King Achish's son? His mother is the queen?"

"No, his mother is a slave. Like Moses, he was raised in the king's palace. You have to find him and bring him to his grandfather." Weariness crept over my bones, and I slumped on the bed. "He's one of us."

Jonathan winked. "I couldn't let you carry on in front of my men. Ittai is my friend also."

He pulled a scroll from the leather tube he wore at his chest and read to me from the Book of the Law until I fell asleep.

CHAPTER 17

Ruth 2:10 Then she fell on her face, and bowed herself to the ground, and said unto him, Why have I found grace in thine eyes, that thou shouldest take knowledge of me, seeing I am a stranger?

>>><<<

Jonathan and I crossed the Jordan River and followed a smaller river due east. The full moon cast moving shadows through windblown trees. I drew my cloak over my face as we arrived at Abel-Meholah and stood in front of Adriel's house.

An elderly servant blocked the gate. "Who goes there?"

"Prince Jonathan with his sister Michal. We've come to call on our brother Adriel."

He opened the gate and called to a boy. "Go to the main house and tell the master his brother and sister are here."

The door flung open, and Adriel's tall, lanky form flew down the path. "Jonathan! What a surprise! What are you doing in these parts?"

He turned to me. "Michal?"

I extended my hand. "Adriel, it's been so long."

He kissed my hand and shocked me with a warm embrace. Leading us into the parlor, he called, "Merab, your sister is here."

I shook out my wet cloak and rubbed my hands in front of a crackling fire.

Merab came out of her room with a baby in her arms. I hugged her tightly and kissed her. "You look wonderful. Who's the little one?"

"This is Eliah, number three. You look remarkably well. We thought you were getting married again."

"No, not this time."

"Mother will be so happy." She handed the baby to a maid and knocked on a closed door.

Servants set food and drink in front of us, and soon Mother bustled into the kitchen and tried to hug both Jonathan and me at the same time.

"Jonathan, you were so brave to rescue her. Michal, my darling daughter. My prayers are answered. I couldn't bear to think of you bearing the child of a Philistine while your father glories in the peace treaty he signed over your body." She smothered me with kisses and stepped back to study me.

Slightly nervous under her scrutiny, I waved my hand. "Mother, don't be so dramatic. I'm fine, and Father received nothing because I escaped from Gath."

"You must tell me everything," Mother said. "How did Jonathan rescue you? I was sure they'd have you guarded well."

I glanced at Jonathan, hoping he wouldn't mention Ittai.

He coughed. "Actually, Michal had already gotten away when I met her on the road."

All eyes turned to me.

"Escaped? You don't say."

"How? Michal, how did do it?"

"Did you see David? Did he help you?"

I raised my hand to silence them. "Please, one question at a time. Yes, I did see David. But he would not help me."

Merab narrowed her eyes. "Why not? I told you he wasn't good for you."

"He sought asylum with the Philistine king," I said. "So obviously he couldn't help me."

Merab tapped Jonathan. "But I thought you kept track of David. How is it he's gone to the Philistines?"

Jonathan's eyebrows lowered. "Apparently he's given up. Father's forces hunted him all over Israel. I thought to use Michal to lure him back. But he'd already remarried, twice."

Mother pressed her lips. "Bad move. Michal also remarried. And you sent your sister into danger for David?"

"No, it's not like that. I sent a spy to take a note to him asking him to return. But before he got the message, Michal turned up."

Mother grasped my arm. "How did you get there? Why didn't you stay with Phalti?"

I made patterns on the floor with the tip of my sandal. Before I could answer, Jonathan said, "No doubt, our Michal took it upon herself to find David."

"Michal!" Merab's eyes widened.

"So how did you get away?" Mother grabbed my sleeve.

I looked sideways and twisted my robe from her. "There's always bribery. I met a woman in Gallim, and she gave me her gold and jewels. She was the village healer, and she took a liking to me."

Mother frowned. "A woman? What was she like?"

"A friend. She helped me escape, that's all, by bribing the guards. Anyway, I'm just glad to be back."

Merab laid her hand on my shoulder. "We're glad you're here, too. Are you going back to Gallim?"

Jonathan cut in. "It's too dangerous. The Philistines will surely look for her there. I'm going back to warn Phalti."

Adriel opened his arms. "Michal, you must stay. We're tucked many miles away from the border. They'll never think to look for you here."

Merab and Mother joined in. "Yes, stay."

Adriel clapped a hand on Jonathan's shoulder. "And when you see Phalti, tell him he's welcome to join his wife. I'm sure we can find work for him." His friendly voice rang with finality.

Mention of Phalti wrenched my heart. I had been so cruel to him. How could I face him when he'd been punished so severely? A choking sensation flooded my chest and tears threatened. I grumbled about being tired, and Merab asked a servant to prepare a room.

* * *

One morning, after the new moon, I woke sick and dizzy. As I sat in bed, a wave of nausea rippled through me. I stumbled to the chamber pot, trying to remember what I had for dinner.

A note from Phalti lay on the table. *My dearest Michal, I thank God you are well. As soon as I settle my business, I will hasten to your side. With warmest affection and lots of kisses, your Phalti.*

Regret and guilt coursed through my veins. Phalti had looked so despondent the last time I spoke to him. I had disbelieved him, accused him of lying and forging the note of divorcement. And he'd been hurt on my behalf. What could I possibly say to him?

A few minutes later, the queasiness was gone. I dressed and went to the kitchen and found Merab tending her children. I took the baby from her arms while she gathered the two toddlers and fed them breakfast.

After they were settled, I lifted a jar and followed her to the stable to help her milk the goats. My sister, a former princess, worked harder than a maid. As wealthy as Adriel was, times were hard, and crops had not been abundant because of the dry weather. The presence of bandits made trade difficult, and sometimes Adriel's grapes and olives rotted before making it to market.

"Merab, you're looking weary today, is everything all right?"

"I've been more tired than usual," she said. "My back aches from carrying the babe around. I sure could use a good night's rest."

"I can care for the baby at night. Show me what to do."

"You would? Oh, Michal, you've grown to be a gracious and thoughtful woman. I don't know why I didn't appreciate you earlier." She squeezed and pulled at the goat's udder while I rubbed its head, thinking of David's goat hair pillow.

"Ha, I was a spoiled and willful child, and I followed you around. But no matter, I'm glad we're together again."

I helped her carry the milk jug, and she showed me how to funnel the milk into the skins from which the baby would suckle on during the day.

"He's ready to wean," she said. "His nurse had to leave early, but this milk will keep him happy. He also eats little pieces of raisin cakes, chopped vegetables and meat."

Merab set Eliah on my lap. He wiggled and squirmed, the milk dribbled and spilled, and more food fell on the floor than in his mouth. He bit me with his two front teeth, laughing and squealing. A surge of affection warmed me. I blew and tickled his fat belly and kissed his chubby cheeks. A tear formed in my eye when I thought about all the nights I had prayed for a baby with David. Could it be? I shook the thought away, fearing another disappointment.

I handed Eliah back to Merab, and another wave of nausea overtook me. Cold sweat dampened my nose. The mess of curdled milk, squashed fruit, vegetables, and spit up meat took my appetite away. I swallowed hard, not wanting to be sick in front of everyone. Mother raised an eyebrow and asked if I were ill. Assuring her I was fine, I raced toward my room.

She followed and asked if I'd like to do some weaving with her. Wrinkling her nose at the sour odor, she yelled for a servant to change the chamber pot. I rummaged through the piles of thread, my fingers shaking.

Mother stepped in and shut the door. Her stare drilled through me. "We're alone. You can tell me what happened."

I tied threads to the top of the loom and attached stone weights to the ends. "I'm happy to be back. Do you have to lecture me?"

She swiped the thread from my hand. "What did you think you were doing running off from Phalti?"

"Mother, I'm sorry..."

She shook a finger at me. "Have you any idea what he suffered because he lost you? They whipped him and burned his fields, drove his livestock away. Your father almost executed him had Jonathan not intervened."

Flexing hammers pounded my head and rushed blood to my ears. Nausea swept over me, and I bent my head between my knees and swallowed until it subsided. My forehead broke in sweat. I stumbled to the bed.

"Your brother found you a dependable husband, and you endanger him for a traitor?"

I slapped the bed. "David is not a traitor. He's my husband."

"No, he has forfeited you. Abandoned you. Thank God, Merab did not marry him. All he wanted was your father's crown. We should never have allowed him into the palace."

I put a hand over my mouth. "Mother, I'm not feeling well. Can you let me rest? You never understood David."

I beat back a queasy rumbling from my stomach and hunched over the clean pot.

"Are you ill?" Her voice softened.

"No, just tired." I vomited and heaved until nothing remained but bile.

Mother wiped my mouth and swept errant strands of hair from my sweaty face. "Could you be pregnant?"

A flash of pride curled my lip. "I don't know."

"How do your breasts feel? Are they heavier, tender at the tip?"

"Maybe."

Mother rubbed my head. "How about your monthly blood? When was the last time?"

"I don't remember. I never kept track."

She sighed. "You've always been irregular, and I worried if you'd be barren. Did you last have it at Phalti's house or on the road?"

"Phalti's house. But what happens now?" I sank into the bed. "What will Phalti think?"

She clasped my hands. "If you are pregnant, he'd be overjoyed. Jonathan says Phalti practically worships you. He was worried sick when you went missing."

She rubbed my back. "Feeling better?"

"Yes, thanks, Mother." I closed my eyes while my stomach settled. "Now, about the weaving, I've learned some new patterns."

I dared not hope. But if I were pregnant, I would have David's son. My heart bubbled, and I wanted to jump and scream. David would certainly want me now. I had his heir tucked inside of me. A secret smile lit my heart. We would be so happy, the three of us.

* * *

Around noontime, Adriel returned from the fields with a broad smile. "Your husband approaches. He's crossed the ridge and should be nearing our gate soon."

I stood, a swarm of dots danced around my eyes like buzzing bees. Voices hovered above me.

137

"She's so excited she fainted," a female voice said.

"Michal, can you hear me?" A man's deep voice sounded near my ear.

Cold water splashed my face, and I swatted at the hands that swabbed my forehead. A set of bearded lips kissed me on the cheek. "Wake up. I'm here."

Phalti's face loomed above me. Naomi looked over his shoulders.

"She's been ill all morning," Merab said. "Looking forward to your arrival, no doubt."

"You're not well?" Phalti held me in his lap, fussed over my hair, and wiped the water off my face.

"I'm fine. Don't worry," I mumbled, embarrassed by his mushy display in front of my family.

Mother smiled and crinkled her forehead, as Merab placed a tray of food in front of us. Everyone sat around and asked Phalti for the news. He fed me small pieces of cheese that sent my stomach spinning. Discreetly, I pressed his hands away from my mouth. While they talked, I leaned my head on his chest, feeling miserable.

"The Philistines are more aggressive," Phalti said. "I'm afraid there's going to be war soon."

"How is the king reacting?" Adriel questioned him, his gaze darting back and forth.

"The king? He is scouring high and wide for Michal to deliver her to the Philistine king and secure David's head. Apparently they want to make some sort of alliance for peace." He draped a protective arm over my shoulder and rubbed my back.

"But that is ridiculous. Why is Father so stubborn?" Merab exclaimed.

"The Philistine king is furious," Phalti said. "He accused your father of stealing his bride."

I lifted my head. "Is that what he thinks?"

"Maybe, and maybe not," Phalti said. "But it's the official story. I hear at the well his own son betrayed him. Michal, is that so?"

Everyone turned astonished faces at me. My stomach fluttered and heat rushed through my chest. I could not betray Ittai. He had sacrificed so much for me.

"How did you get away?" Phalti demanded.

I pushed out of his embrace. "I bribed my way out. It doesn't take a genius to figure out guards blind themselves for gold."

Phalti gripped my arm. "You don't have to snap at me. I think you're tired."

Everyone assented, and I went back to my room and flounced on the bed, queasy and upset, but determined to hide it.

I didn't nap long. Phalti bustled around the room arranging the furniture. He stood David's harp in the corner and piled our scrolls next to it. When he saw me looking at him, he handed me a small scroll. It was the covenant of my marriage to David.

"This is temporary. I'm going to find a small house to rent for the two of us. I can help the villagers with their scribal needs. I'll get one with two bedchambers. You needn't worry about me bothering you." He unrolled a blanket and placed it on the floor near the door.

"Let's not worry about all that right now," I said. "Tell me about your journey."

He sat on my bed. "I'm so glad you're here. I had a dream. It was so vivid and unbelievable. The sun glinted behind you, all golden and red. You opened your arms and ran toward me. You said... you..." He rubbed the back of his neck and blushed. "It seemed real at the time."

"Why are you so kind to me?" I said. "Aren't you mad at me for leaving and stealing your mule?"

He held my elbow. "I was so worried. Why didn't you tell me where you were going?"

"You wouldn't have let me go."

"And I would have been right."

"Phalti?" I touched his beard. "Thank you, and I'm sorry about the mule."

A shock of hair fell over his eyes. Making no attempt to brush it back, he smiled. "Don't worry about the mule." His voice hoarse, he paused and cleared his throat. "Michal, can you at least like me a little?"

Warmth spread in my cheeks, and my heart fluttered. I squeezed his knuckles and tickled the hair on the back of his hand. "I like you more than a little." I leaned over and kissed his beard. "Did they hurt you badly?"

He lowered his eyelids, and his cheeks turned pink. "You care?"

I poked his chest. "You big oaf, of course I care. I'm sorry for everything that happened to you."

"How sorry?"

"Um... well, how sorry do you want me to be?"

A daft grin draped his lips. "Sorry enough for a kiss?"

I fingered his robe, picturing the matted hair on his chest. Glad that I'd cleaned my mouth with mint, I wrapped my fingers around the nape of his neck and kissed him lightly. Drawing back, I inhaled his scent, like warm leather and baked bread, and a tingling shiver caressed my spine. His lips dropped to mine, gently sucking my lower lip and then my upper lip. I tilted my head, and he nuzzled my neck, his hands seeking my breasts.

Tenderness and pain greeted me. I cringed and brushed his probing thumb away. Mother was right. I broke from his embrace when nausea roiled my belly.

"What's wrong?" Phalti bent over me. I clutched my middle, swallowing and rocking myself to calm my stomach.

Anxiety mixed with elation. How would Phalti react to David's baby?

"Are you sick?" Phalti rubbed my back.

"Get me a bowl, please." He had barely time to bring it to me when I threw up, splattering his feet.

"I'm so sorry." I cried.

His hands trembled. "No, don't be. I'll clean it for you."

I flopped on the bed, drained and sweaty.

Phalti returned with the clean bowl and wiped the floor. "What's wrong? You look so pale."

I probed his gaze. Could I tell him? I closed my eyes. David would come for me if he knew. He would take me back. Perhaps Phalti could send a message. "You're my friend?"

"You know I am," he replied evenly.

"Do you think you can get a message to David for me?"

"What kind of message?" His tightened voice scratched like dry pebbles.

"A delicate message. I need him to—"

"I'm your friend, but I'm no traitor," he said. "Jonathan told me all about David, how he received an entire city from King Achish in exchange for his loyalty. And frankly, I would not be welcome there, nor do I wish to cross enemy lines. Not even for you."

My head swirled with dizziness, and I grasped my impossible situation. David would not believe me. He'd think the baby was Phalti's. I choked back tears as my stomach clenched and tumbled.

"Phalti, the bowl."

He brought it and held me while I retched. With nothing in my stomach, the pain tore through my sides, and I moaned miserably. *David, when will I see you again? When will you meet your son?*

Phalti set the bowl down and clasped my shoulder. "You were with David?"

I nodded, holding my stomach with misery.

"And you're pregnant?"

"I don't know. But what if he thinks the baby is yours, and he divorces me?"

Phalti's lips thinned. "Is that all you're thinking about right now? What about me? Or how I feel? My wife runs off to a foreign country and gets pregnant."

"No one has to know. My mother thinks the baby is yours."

"What? You told her already?"

"You know how mothers are. Nothing gets past them. I'm sorry."

He grimaced, pulled his beard, and tugged at his robe.

"What are you going to do?" I pinned my hands under my armpits.

With downturned lips, he wiped his brow and opened the door. "I'm going to take a walk, alone."

He shut the door firmly.

* * *

After he left, I buried my head in the blankets. I needed to let David know, but who could help me? Could I bother Adriel?

Merab stuck her head in the room. "How are you feeling? Mother says you're ill, and your husband looks like a mule kicked him."

"Where did he go?" I pulled on a cloak and jumped to the door.

"Did you two have a fight? He headed for the river that separates Adriel's property from Auntie's."

I remembered the brook well. Merab and I had practiced jumping the stones while she snuck over to Adriel's orchards to spy on him. I ran out the door, more anxious to escape Merab's questioning than to find Phalti. Fresh air would clear my mind and help me conceive a plan.

Phalti sat on a rock overlooking the brook. He whittled a branch with a carving knife, and threw pieces of wood into water swollen with winter rains. My steps rustled the carpet of leaves. He did not look up, but his shoulders stiffened.

I gathered my skirts, climbed onto the rock, and knelt by his side. "I'm sorry. I understand if you never want to see me again."

He grunted and splintered a chunk off the stick.

"Look, it's not your problem," I said. "You did all you could for me, and I appreciate it. Do you wish to go back to Gallim?"

"I have nothing to go back to. I have no parents, no siblings. My only uncle died, and your father's men burned my fields and stole my livestock." His lower lip trembled, and he turned his head away from me. "All I ever wanted was a family of my own. But I was too poor. My uncle taught me to write and earn money, and when Jonathan found me to be your husband, I thought God had smiled on my face. I agreed to all his terms. I wanted a wife, someone to love."

He threw the branch into the water. We watched it float, tossing and bobbing over the rocks until it disappeared amongst the tangled vines.

I rubbed his shoulders and the back of his neck. "I'm sorry I disappointed you. Maybe Adriel will lend you some money. I don't have any gold on me, but when I do, I'll send it to you."

My fingers slipped to the emerald around my neck. It was the only item of value I possessed. I pulled it over my head and dropped it in his hand.

He stared at it and pressed it back to my palm. "I don't want anything from you."

"What will you do?"

He sheathed his knife and pulled me between his legs, my back to his chest. "Stay here and take care of you. I've already found the woman I love."

How could he love me when I'd played him for a fool? Phalti, you lovable man, I could lean in your arms forever, if only... My empty stomach complained loudly.

"You've been starving the baby." He kissed the back of my neck. "Michal, as long as you'll have me, I'll be yours and never leave you."

Taking the emerald from my palm, he looped it over my head and placed it back under my robe. "Let's go back to the house and find some food. I'm starving, too."

When we appeared at the kitchen, everyone turned toward us. Mother beamed with a sly smile, and Merab opened her arms to kiss me.

"I've wonderful news," she said. Adriel placed a hand on her shoulder and kissed her cheek. Mother stopped feeding Eliah, and Naomi quieted the other two boys.

"Mother, Michal," she said. "I'm expecting another baby. I think he'll arrive near the olive harvest."

The room erupted in laughter and cheers. Little Joel, Merab's eldest, danced up and down, singing, "I want a sister."

Adriel grinned and kissed her again, this time on the lips.

Mother hugged Merab. "You are so fruitful, my dear. Did I tell you how much I love you?"

Phalti and I took turns hugging her. Naomi gave my arm a squeeze and said, "My, this is one big, happy family."

Merab collared us. "Don't you two have something to say?"

Phalti sputtered and looked like a fish gasping for a breath. "Oh, you're... I'm... we're so happy for you."

Merab tilted her head. "And? Is there more?"

Phalti blushed, the tips of his ears reddening. His mouth opened and closed, and he gaped at me for help.

I shook my head to deflect Merab and spare Phalti embarrassment. "I'm with Joel. I hope it's a girl."

Mother grabbed Phalti's big hands and shook them. "But I'm sure you'd want a boy."

He sputtered, "I'm sure she'd be happy either way."

Merab wagged her index finger. "I saw you two lovebirds sitting on a rock. Come on, spill it. Mother's been exasperating with her hinting and blinking."

Adriel clapped Phalti's back. "So, big man, don't keep us in suspense. Are you two also expecting a baby?"

Phalti's jaw dropped, but he recovered quickly. He swept me into his arms and hugged me tightly. "It was unexpected, but I'm happy about it, if she's happy."

Merab clapped her hands and bounced on her heels. "When is he due? We'll have such fun making baby clothes together. Oh, I have the best midwife."

A deluge of nausea overtook me. I signaled to Phalti and rushed back to my room. *Now I'd done it, passing off the baby as Phalti's. Oh God, please forgive me.*

CHAPTER 18

Job 14:9 Yet through the scent of water it will bud, and bring forth boughs like a plant.

>>><<<

Merab and I budded in the spring, bloomed through the summer, and ripened in autumn. We did everything together, sewing baby clothes, and caring for her three older sons. We spent many enjoyable afternoons weaving fringes for circumcision gowns. In the evenings, Adriel serenaded us with the smooth, sultry notes of his viol. Merab and I hung on each other, dreamy eyed and content, lulled by the earthy timbre of the instrument, resembling the crooning of a woman in love.

One stormy night, Merab came to the kitchen, clutching her swollen belly. "I think it's starting."

I crouched over the stone tiles, wiping the water that spilled from me. "My water broke. What happens now?"

"Call the midwife." She bent on her hands and knees and moaned.

I wiped my sweaty palms on my robe. I recalled the pain I'd witnessed and shuddered at the thought of death. *Oh, God. Please be with me and my baby. Oh, David…*

While Phalti fetched the midwife, Adriel sent the older children to their bedchamber. Thunder roared and lightning cracked. Huge gales of rain pelted the house and rattled the trees. By the time the midwife arrived, my pain had pierced through my screams. They set my feet on a pair of long bricks and rested me on the edge of a wooden plank. Naomi crouched in back of me, her arms around me, propping me up. Mother wet a piece of wool and held it to my lips.

Large billows of red clouded my vision. Sharp claws clamped my body, squeezing, tossing, and casting me about. I blew ragged puffs, dreading the next advance. It came, rolling and rolling until it had completely wrung my insides like a wet dishcloth.

Mother wiped my head with cold water. "Hold on, Michal, hold on…"

The ravening motion came more furious than before. I clung to Mother and trembled until it mercifully ebbed, only to surge again. A giant hand pressed and wrestled and pummeled my womb. The burning between my legs radiated outward, and my screams contracted over and over and over against the wet fleece in my mouth.

"Push, Michal, push it out. Push." Firm hands grasped my shoulders and supported me on the birthing plank.

I arched my back, panting and gasping, and bore down. A spire of pain pushed through me, and a warm gush propelled David's baby out.

Silence. A few cubits away, Merab moaned. I pushed up to catch my breath. "Mother, the baby."

A smaller contraction cast the afterbirth. "My baby," I shouted. "Why isn't he crying?"

Naomi held me down, her arms tightening around me. She made snuffling sounds. The midwife pressed on my baby's chest, a boy, bluish. She slapped him and poked his feet.

My heart tightened, and my fingernails dug into Naomi's arms. *No. No. Dear God, he can't be dead. David's son can't die. I prayed for him daily, asked God for him. Samuel. I'll name him Samuel, and God will spare him. Dear LORD, let Samuel live before you. LORD God, please.*

I rocked in Naomi's arms while the midwife bent over and sucked Samuel's mouth and nose. Several panicked heartbeats of blowing and sucking and still no sound. She put her ear to his chest, and her gaze speared my heart to the wall. "There is no life in him. I'm sorry."

The world slowed to a halt as a shroud floated over my leaden chest. The midwife wrapped Samuel in a blanket and handed him to me. My son Samuel: a perfectly formed boy, translucent skin, reddish wisps of hair, a face as sweet as an angel.

David would never know. Oh, dear David. I've failed you so, so miserably.

Mother hugged me, her face mirrored my distress. "I better tell Phalti."

I held Samuel to my face, unable to respond, my heart as sodden as the bloody mess around my legs. My breasts tingled hot, yet my blood ran cold.

My sister, still battling her labor pains, slumped against her maid. Her pale, frightened face crumpled as our eyes met.

Phalti crept silently to my side. "Come, let me help you to bed."

"No." I held Samuel tightly against my chest. "I can't leave my sister."

Phalti's ashen face quivered, and he bent to kiss me. "May I see him?"

I squeezed Samuel tighter, my breath stuttering between my sobs.

He held me, with Samuel between us, and rubbed circles on my back. "It's not your fault. These things happen. I'll take care of you."

I leaned on him and wept.

Merab's screams grew louder and more insistent, laced with panic. She rocked back and forth, her sweating face contorted. Sound slowed into a hollow cave, my sister screaming, my mother comforting, my maid crying. Merab stared at me, pleading, her hand in a claw of pain.

"Phalti, I have to help her. Hold my baby."

Phalti cradled my son in the crock of his elbow and placed his large hand over him protectively. "He's precious. Our son. What did you name him?"

"Samuel."

"Samuel." Phalti stared at the baby's still face. "We've asked of God for you, and now we must give you back to Him." He bowed his head, a large tear trailed down his face.

Sounds of alarm emitted from Merab's side. I scrambled over and crowded around the other women. Merab's skin turned clammy and grey. I held her hand. It was cool, too cool. "Merab, you can do it." I joined the chorus. "Stay with me, stay with me."

Even as the contractions wracked her body, the baby would not move. "He's still too high up and turned the wrong way," the midwife yelled. She pressed her hands on Merab's abdomen to turn the baby.

My sister whimpered, barely able to breathe. Her eyes constricted with dread. "Michal, take my baby. Raise my sons as your own."

"No, no." I shook my head. "You're going to come through this. I'll help you raise your sons, but you must stay." I pleaded even as her head lolled and coldness crept up her face.

Her eyes clouded. "Take my boys."

She turned to Mother. "Ee...mah..."

Mother wailed and clasped Merab to her chest. The midwife held a long knife. Each cruel contraction lodged the baby more firmly behind Merab's hips and squeezed more of her life away.

"Adriel, Adriel," we yelled when the tip of Merab's nose turned blue and her breathing rattled.

My chest tightened. My throat squeezed into itself. *Oh, God, this can't be happening. Oh, God, save her!* "Merab, my sister, my sister."

Adriel rushed in. "Wife, my love, don't leave me, don't leave. Oh, Merab, let me die for you. No!!!"

He covered her with kisses, frantically trying to love her back from the brink, his tears mingling with her blood.

Merab's eyes fluttered into her head. The midwife cut her open as her last breath departed and her spirit went to God. She pulled out a baby boy who screamed lustily. She cleaned him, cut the cord and handed him to Adriel.

I bent over Merab and kissed her, holding onto her from the back like I used to when I tagged along after her. My sister, my big sister. How could you leave us? A rolling movement startled me. Merab's open eyes stared blankly at the ceiling. The movement came from her abdomen.

I slid my hands into the gash and snatched a blood-covered baby from her womb. He was blue. I pressed his chest and slapped him, while the midwife cut the cord. Without letting her take him, I sucked the mucus and blood out of his mouth and nose and blew air into his lungs. He coughed and made a small mewing sound.

Everyone crowded around me. I put the babe to my chest. His hair ruffled in every direction, tufts of red and gold. His little hands clawed at me, and his lips latched on my breast. He blinked. Golden eyes poured honey into my soul.

* * *

The day dawned warm and sunny. Golden, red and brown leaves flurried from the stately trees. The bright sky and chirping birds were an incongruous setting for Merab and Samuel's burial. I dressed Samuel in his circumcision outfit decorated with a fringe of red and gold, the colors of the tribe of Judah. I clung to him, not wanting to let him go, but when the time came, I let Phalti take him.

They walked down the path lined with olive trees toward the burial cave tucked in the golden-brown foothills. The pungent, oily scent of the olive harvest smeared the air with an overbearing heaviness. I stumbled back to my bedchamber and hugged the two babies. Their suckling brought small twinges of comfort. The little black-haired one nursed more aggressively than his brother, so I switched sides every feeding. They stared with contentment, and their sweet, puffy scent soothed the deep ache in my heart.

The gatekeeper shuffled up the path around mid-morning. I had just finished changing the babies and tucked them into their cradles. He rapped on my window. "There's a messenger from Prince Jonathan. Should I let him in?"

I wiped my hands on my dress, tied my robe, and followed him to the courtyard. A warrior bounded through the gate and was upon me before I could catch my breath.

"Michal."

"Ittai." My heart squeezed, and I stood still. "You're alive."

The gatekeeper shuffled off, muttering under his breath.

I ushered Ittai into the house. He seemed so silent and stiff.

He wrung his hands. "I don't know how to tell you."

"What has happened? Where is my brother?" Panic spurted into my chest. Ittai's eyes brimmed with tears.

"Sit down. Sit down." He motioned me to the couch and grabbed my hands. "There was a battle…"

A knife sunk into my bowels. "A battle? Jonathan? My father?"

He cleared his throat. "They died fighting for Israel on the top of Mt. Gilboa. Your father and all your brothers except Ishbaal are gone."

The drumbeat of blood in my ears tore the screams from my throat.

Ittai held me tightly. "They fought valiantly. Your brothers were so valiant, but the storm hampered us, and we ran out of arrows. I tried to drag Jonathan away when they injured him, but he would not run. Like the hero he was, he took down more than twenty men, before he lost his sword, his arm cleaved off."

He rocked me and cried in my hair. "Jonathan died in my arms. He was such a good man. He died in my arms. I should have died with him, I should not have left him, but my uncles drove me away."

Died, died, died, all around me was death. I looked down on myself from the ceiling. What sins I must have committed to deserve so much death and brokenness—Father, Jonathan, Merab, Melchishua, Ishui, Samuel—more members of my family dead than living.

Ittai rubbed my back and held me. When my breathing steadied, he pulled a packet from his robe and handed me a ring and a blood-stained tube.

"Jonathan wanted you to have it. He said that you alone of all Saul's children would see David again. Give the ring to David and keep the leather tube and wear it on your side. The ring is to remind David of his promises, and the scripture in the tube is to remind you to read God's Word daily."

The babies wailed in unison.

Ittai drew a sharp breath. "Babies?"

I set Jonathan's treasures on the table and stumbled to their cradles. My knees wobbled, and I shook so violently I could not manage them. They screamed and kicked, their faces red and their mouths rooting for the breasts.

Ittai picked up the red-haired one. "Is this David's son? Lie down, and I'll arrange him. Don't be shy." The babe resembled my sister, whose coloring matched David's.

I tucked the baby underneath my robe. He nursed greedily as I cupped his little head and stroked his cheek. Ittai held the black-haired one. The babe stopped crying and gurgled. His tiny hand grasped Ittai's little finger.

Ittai tilted his head back. A deep laugh rumbled and broke the remnant of his sobs. "David will be so pleased. Look how strong he is." He tickled the babe who kicked and swung his hands in the air. "Twin sons, what a lucky man."

I said nothing. The explanation would be too painful.

Ittai's smile widened. "This is a wonderful surprise, coming from such sad news." He cuddled the babe. "Do you have a name for him?"

I wiped my eyes. "They'll be circumcised soon. I suppose I should name them." Adriel had granted both his sons to me as Merab's last wish. "But I haven't given much thought. My family just left for the funeral."

"What happened?"

"My sister died last night." My voice trailed off. *God, how many have died, and how many more will die?* I prayed for peace in Israel, and I prayed for David, and I grieved for the son he'd never know and the life I'd never have with him.

Naomi handed us plates of food. Ittai and I sat on the couch, a baby on each lap, and ate.

"I worried about you so much, not knowing," I said.

"I'm not as good with the sword as I thought. Thankfully, Jonathan came back and told me you were safe."

"Jonathan. I miss him."

"He was a really good man." Ittai's voice choked. "Why did he have to die?"

"There's been too much death. I feel like I'm floating on a cloud, and it isn't me here. That I'm the one who's dead."

"No, don't say that." He leaned over me, a baby asleep at his chest, and his lips touched mine, kissing me softly, almost reverently. The babes squirmed but did not wake. "I've always loved you," he said.

"But..."

He put a finger to my lip. "Don't say 'but.' Just for this moment—"

I pulled away. "I'm a married woman."

The baby in his arms let out a yelp. "It doesn't make a difference to how I feel about you," he said.

I pulled the baby from him and tucked them in their cradles. Ittai followed me and put his hand on my shoulder. "Someday, you'll see. I'll get my reward."

I stiffened and hugged my chest. "I don't know why you keep talking about rewards. I'm tired, and I need to rest before my mother returns from the burial."

Ittai turned me to face him. His brows drawn down, he said, "I shouldn't have made you uncomfortable. Do you want any other news before I leave?"

"Yes." We walked back to the couch and sat side by side. "Have you seen David?"

Ittai's lips twitched, and he tugged on his beard. "I last saw him lined up with King Achish against your father."

"Against my father?"

"The lords of the Philistines confronted him and forced him to leave," he said. "They were afraid David would turn on the Philistines in the middle of the battle."

"So David did not fight for the Philistines?"

"No, he didn't lift a sword."

A wave of relief spread over me. "Thank God. Where is he now?"

"I suppose he's gone home. One of his wives had an estate outside of Hebron."

"Which one? Ahi or Abi?"

"Abigail, wife of Nabal the Carmelite," he said. "He was a wealthy man, but loyal to your father. Fortunately for David, he died."

Unfortunately for me, since David had married her.

"And where will you go?" I said. "Certainly you can't go back to the Philistines."

"No, I can't. My father seeks my life. I've dishonored him by helping you escape." He took my hand.

I squeezed his hand and rubbed the hard calluses in his palm. "So where will you go?"

He implored me with his deep, black eyes. "I will go to David and serve him as my king."

My breath snagged. "But, I'm still in confinement. The babies are too young."

He cradled my face between two large hands. "When you're able to travel, I'll ask David to let me come back for you. Right now, it's too unsettled. I still have to move my mother to Hebron. I left her in Gibeah where it isn't safe."

"Your mother. I prayed for her. She's well? I like her."

"She likes you too. Told me to always watch for you and take care of you. She also prays for you." He twirled a strand of my hair. "You are a remarkably kind-hearted woman."

Before his demeanor got too mushy, I tapped his shoulder. "My mother told me I should have names for the babies before she returns. Want to help?"

I led him back to the cradles. The babies made soft, high-pitched snoring noises in tandem, so incredibly darling. I blinked back tears. Samuel had never taken a single breath.

"What about Jonathan?" Ittai said.

I sniffled. "It would be a fitting tribute, but I'd grieve every time I think of him."

"Yes, it is too soon. Maybe Joshua? Or Moses?"

I twirled it in my mind. "I like Joshua. The LORD God saves."

At that moment, the little black-haired babe yawned and shook his fist. Ittai rocked the cradle. "He's going to be a mighty fine warrior. Was he born first or second?"

I rubbed his downy black hair, and he opened his eyes. "First. Go back to sleep, Joshua."

I tickled his stomach. He made a squeaking noise. His brother startled, clasped both hands, clutched the air, and woke crying. I put him over my shoulder to rub his back. "And what shall I name you?"

"He looks like how I'd picture David as a baby." Ittai tickled the baby's face. "Look at those darling red curls."

I swallowed a surge of acid. Could I pull this off? No. Adriel would speak up. So would Phalti and Mother. The babe burped and calmed as I cradled him. His golden-brown eyes focused on mine, and he reached for my breast. "Out of many calamities you came and gave me joy."

I tucked him in my bosom and kissed the top of his head. "Beraiah. My special little boy. You almost died, didn't you?" I wiped my tears on his forehead. Samuel and Merab lay cold and stiff inside a sepulcher. *Oh, God, will this day never end?*

A loud bang from the gate announced my returning family. I hustled Ittai toward the door, but he rushed to my bedroom. He looked out the window and said, "Abner's messenger is with them. Let me grab my horse and be on my way to David."

"Are you sure David will receive you?"

He smiled, and his white teeth gleamed. "He trusted me with you, and now I trust him as God's anointed king. And besides, there's iron. He needs me to bring iron working to Israel."

"Don't tell him about the babies yet." It was one thing for Ittai to believe they were David's, but should David try to claim them, Adriel would tell him the truth.

Ittai raised an eyebrow. "But wouldn't David want to know?"

I held his hand. "Not now. I want to tell him myself. Promise me?"

He put one leg over the ledge and held my face. "Don't worry, I will come again and take you to David when the time is right."

He mouthed 'I love you' before drawing his face to mine. His eyelashes fluttered on my cheek, and he trailed kisses up my neck, to my ear, persuading my lips to open. The salt of my tears mixed with his warm, spicy taste, and I kissed him deeply. And for a moment, my heart opened and grief fell away.

The front door bumped, and footsteps shuffled into the front room. Abner's messenger announced himself. Mother's piercing shrieks vibrated through the house. I broke from Ittai's embrace. "I need to comfort my mother."

He flipped his other leg over the windowsill and saluted me, his grin as wide as his face. Phalti stepped into the room, and when I looked again, Ittai had disappeared. The taste of sweet bay leaves lingered on my tongue. Phalti wrapped me in his arms. "Have you heard?"

Overcome with a deluge of grief, I rested my face in his chest and sobbed. The mournful dirge of Adriel's viol permeated the walls. The day had finally tolled to an end.

CHAPTER 19

2nd Samuel 3:1 Now there was long war between the house of Saul and the house of David: but David waxed stronger and stronger, and the house of Saul waxed weaker and weaker.

>>><<<

On the morning of the eighth day, I rose after a sleepless night to prepare for the trip to Mahanaim where my babies would be circumcised. Joshua and Beraiah waved their tiny hands and squirmed while I dressed them in the circumcision gowns Merab had made. She had woven several borders to try the patterns Jada had taught me, spirals and mazes and checkered crosses.

Naomi helped me finish the partially completed gowns, and I selected two of the fringed wraps. I shut my eyes briefly, recalling Samuel the day Phalti took him to the burial cave. The golden-red hair darkened with oil, his face had shone like alabaster, his tiny mouth puckered in a frozen kiss. And Merab, my beautiful sister had lain shrouded in her wedding gown, radiant even in death.

Joshua yelped as I attached the bold black and white crossed collar. "Hold still, little one."

I couldn't help but smile and tickle him. His beady, black eyes sparkled in the slant of the morning sun. I blew a kiss on his belly. "Eemah's happy and sad." I smoothed his hair with olive oil and rubbed his bronze face. His feet kicked nonstop, a ball of energy.

Beside him, Beraiah slept. His tiny eyes fluttered under his pink, almost transparent eyelids. "What are you dreaming about? Are you seeing your mother?" His mouth made tiny sucking motions that caused my breasts to tighten and drip.

Phalti slipped quietly to my side and took Joshua, leaving me to nurse Beraiah. The cherubic face pinked, and his honey-brown eyes poured sweetness into my heart. I loved him to the point of aching, as if he were Samuel and not my sister's baby. I imagined David as a tiny infant, nursing at his mother's breast. I kissed the soft spot on his head and rubbed my nose in the wispy, downy hair, inhaling his fluffy, powdery scent.

Our entire family set out toward Mahanaim where my brother Ishbaal reigned as king in place of my father. Adriel hired litters for Mother, the babies and me. I held onto little Joshua, his eyes laughing in the warm sunshine. Mother held Beraiah, her face relaxed, although tears rimmed her reddened eyes.

She kissed Beraiah's forehead. "I see Merab in this little one. Eyes like honey, milky skin. Merab was such a pretty baby. And she slipped out so easily. I barely felt any pain. And Joshua is so much like both his grandfathers. Dark and strong."

She squeezed my hand. "Joshua is a good name for your son."

"Yes, my son." I mouthed the words and hugged Joshua closer. My son. The thorn of pain pricked my heart. This would have been Samuel's day, too. He would have been in my arms. And Merab should have been here with lilies twirled in her chestnut hair and her face pink with joy. She would have made fun of my fumbling with the babies and more likely than not, taken advantage of my breast. She hated nursing and had joked more than once to make me her wet nurse.

"My sons." I untied my robe and tucked Joshua to my breast. His suckling would ease the raw, ripping ache in my empty womb.

Mother's eyes watered. "I remember the day we circumcised Jonathan. It was the happiest day in my life. He kept me so busy. I reused his gown for all the rest of my boys." Her voice broke. "And now, they're gone, their bones scattered without a resting place."

"We'll bring them back someday." I didn't know what I promised. The men of Jabesh-Gilead had taken their headless bodies off the wall of the Philistine temple and buried their bones under an oak tree. At least that was what Adriel told us.

"They should be in their grandfather Kish's burial chamber. Does Phalti's family have a cave? I wondered why he allowed Samuel to rest with Merab."

"Mother, do we have to speak on these things? Gibeah and Gallim are overrun with Philistines." Samuel should be with David's people. But there was no point correcting her now. I wiped the milk off Joshua's face and burped him. Beraiah squirmed and fussed in Mother's arms, and she exchanged him for Joshua.

"Well, it's all David's fault." Mother's voice hardened. "He went with the Philistines. I wouldn't be surprised if he cut down your father himself. To think we nursed a viper in our midst."

"Mother." I twisted the fringe on Beraiah's gown and rearranged him under my robe to nurse. "David didn't do anything."

Her breath hissed. "Your father's dead, and you dare defend David? Oh, I should have remembered what kind of daughter you are." She pulled her sleeve up and hugged Joshua so tightly he shrieked.

Beraiah popped from my breast and cried in sympathy with his brother. I cuddled him over my shoulder. Joshua's cries turned into rage.

"Give him back." I reached for him, but she swerved so suddenly the litter almost tilted.

"No, stay away from me. You're not my daughter. I supposed you're glad. Now David can become king."

"Mother, don't say that." I held Beraiah and cried into his gown, my heart lacerated with pain.

The bearers lowered the litter, and Phalti helped me out while Adriel retrieved Mother and Joshua. Phalti led me to the shade of an oak, a few paces away.

"She didn't mean it," Phalti said, hugging me along with Beraiah.

I stared at my shaking hands. "I wish I were dead like Samuel and lying at his side. Why did I live and Merab die?"

Phalti handed me a water skin and took Beraiah from me. "Rest on that rock for a bit."

I lowered my head to my lap. My fingernails dug into my knees as I tried to block out the pain whose tentacles spread to my fingertips and toes. Phalti rubbed my back and rocked me until I calmed.

They put me back in the litter with Joshua and Beraiah. Adriel hired another one to take Mother home. She no longer wished to attend the circumcision and share a litter with me. I swallowed a hard, rising lump. Maybe she wished I had died instead of my sister.

We resumed our journey toward Mahanaim, a walled city about fifteen miles south of Abel-Meholah, where the rest of my remaining family had been evacuated. My father's cousin Abner and my brother, Ishbaal, met us at the altar. After I made a sacrifice for my days of uncleanness, we took the babies to the priests for their circumcision.

Uncle Abner sat for my father and held Joshua and then Beraiah in his lap as the priest performed the circumcision. Adriel and Phalti made sacrifices and signed a pact. They joined arms as brothers and made a vow to protect and provide for our family in exile. I adopted Merab's sons. The priests wrote their names in Adriel's family scroll along with my name next to Merab's name. The boys were now mine.

* * *

Naomi burped Beraiah while I nursed Joshua. "Have you heard?" she said. "David has been proclaimed king of Judah and reigns in Hebron."

I tucked Joshua inside my robe and went to the kitchen. A group of loud men sat around the table with Adriel and Phalti.

"Ishbaal is the rightful king. We won't support that upstart."

"He's an ally of the Philistines and the Ammonites."

"There'll be a civil war, mark my words. We'll not have a king who treats foreigners better than his own people."

"But what can we do? David's allies surround us and have taken all the land west of the Jordan. We are wedged in by the Ammonites."

"We need to make an alliance with the king to the north, the Geshurites."

"But Ishbaal is too weak. He just plays at being king. It's Abner who's in charge."

My head swung back and forth between the men's angry faces.

Naomi tugged me. "Come, let's go back to your room. There's nothing you can do."

Joshua belched and clenched his face to cry. I hurried back and shut the door, refusing to believe the words I had heard. David would never turn against us. Didn't David once love my father? And would he remember me now that he was king?

* * *

Weeks went by. I jumped at every noise at my window and looked at each traveler who came through town, expecting to hear Ittai's chuckle or spy his smirk. My fingers tingled with needle pricks. How could I escape when Phalti hovered near me constantly? And my mother hated me. She acted as if I were dead.

When more time passed with no news, I despaired. I lay in bed and did not move other than to nurse my babies. I lived for their smiles, their kicks, and their tiny squeals. Everything they did reminded me of what Samuel would be doing.

Samuel. My perfect baby. He'd never know the warmth of the sun on his face nor the sweet contentment of a belly full of milk. He'd never feel the touch of my kiss nor the caress of my hand. He'd never enjoy the pleasures of being a child: the first taste of honey-cake, grubby hands and face smeared with dirt, laughing and toddling in the tall grass, splashing and squealing in a warm bath. And he'd never feel his father's hug nor doze to the melodies of his harp.

Someone else would have David's firstborn. Someone else would bask in his love and adoration. Someone else would be his queen. He had been made king, but he had forgotten me.

* * *

That winter, Mother fell sick and died. She never forgave me for defending David and refused to speak to me, even from her deathbed. A few weeks later, Adriel was killed by bandits not more than two miles from our gate.

We returned from Adriel's burial. The boys clung to me, Phalti, and Naomi, their faces like stone, their cries muffled and weak.

After we put them down to nap, I sat with Phalti at the kitchen table. I rubbed my face with heavy hands. "What are we going to do? We have five boys under the age of five, two of them babies. Robbers and bandits rule the roads. I'm afraid."

He poured me a cup of wine. "We'll need to buy protection. There is no other choice. Or we move to Mahanaim under Abner's protection."

"Abner is fighting against God's will. And our position is weaker by the day." My hands shook as I took a deep draught. "The Philistines have taken all the territory Father once ruled. Perhaps if Abner would unite with David, we can drive out our enemies and restore Israel."

"David?" Phalti glared at me. "He's the cause of our problems. If he hadn't allied with Achish, none of this would have happened. He's the usurper and a vassal of the Philistines."

I smacked the goblet down and stared at him. "No, he's God's anointed king. Many people are moving south to join him."

"What you're suggesting is treason. I'll have no part in it." He slammed the table so hard the wine goblet toppled and spilled over my robe.

"Look what you did." I swiped my hands over the darkening red spot. "I'm only worried about the boys."

"So am I. There's too much farm work, and servants depart every week." He put his head between his hands and pulled at his hair.

I touched his shoulder. "Perhaps we should ask David to grant us asylum."

Phalti forcefully removed my hand. He narrowed his eyes. "Who do you take me for? An idiot? All I do is work hard to provide for you and your sons, and you want to go back to your precious David. Go, and I'll have nothing to do with you."

He stomped out of the room and slammed the door.

I blew out fear and sucked in anxiety until my head spun light and my fingers tingled. The children screamed, and the babies cried. I worked with Naomi to feed and change them. A nagging twinge dug into my heart. I should have considered Phalti's feelings. He was a good man, too good for me. *What if I lost him too?*

* * *

I knocked on Phalti's door. He had retired for the night without speaking to me.

"What is it?" he grumbled.

"May I come in? I want to talk."

"If it's about David, I have nothing to say." The hurt crackled in his voice, gritty and tight.

"It's not about him." I opened the door and let myself in. He sat on his bed in his bedclothes and held his head between his hands.

"I'm sorry." I shook him gently. "Please, I'm so sorry."

"You don't need to coddle me. I know how you feel."

"How can you when I don't even know?" I laid my head on his shoulder. He had grown muscular from the hard labor on Adriel's farm. His presence comforted me, and his scent was clean like warm leather.

I stroked his beard. "Phalti, kiss me."

His head snapped back and one side of his face twitched. His lip curled in a tight line. "No. I won't touch you unless David puts you away. I made a vow."

"David will never grant me a divorce. He also made a vow."

"Then leave me alone." He ignored my roving hands, his voice tight and constricted, barely above a whisper.

My fingers tightened on his shoulders. "Tell me you hate me."

"I don't hate you."

"But you yelled at me. You said you didn't care."

"You want to leave and go to David, don't you?"

"We'll go as a family. It's only to seek asylum, not as his wife. It would be temporary until the civil war is over. It's not safe here, and I'm scared."

"Would you stay with me if David wanted you?" He crossed his arms and stared at me, his eyes hard as flint.

"He doesn't want me. He's forgotten me."

The edge of his jaw quivered. "That wasn't what I asked, and you know it."

"You used to care about me. You used to be my friend. Why are you so cold now?"

Phalti grunted and pulled my face to his. "Answer my question first." His voice deepened as he held my gaze.

I lowered my eyes, unable to feel anything but a hollow sense of loss. I wanted to love him, maybe even care for him, but my emotions were sealed like ointment in a fragile clay jar. David could come for me at any moment. Then what would I do?

He pulled away. "I thought so."

My body shook with the pain of his rejection. "Phalti, please. Don't turn your back on me. I need you."

"You need me like you need a mule. Don't worry. I'll take care of my children. I adopted them, and I'll provide for them. You've no love for me, and I've known it for a long time."

Not true. Definitely not true. My chest ached, and my nerves screamed for him. I wrapped my arms around his hardened body. "You're hurting my feelings."

"What are you trying to do?"

"Tell me you still care—that you're still my friend. I want you, Phalti, to want me. I need you." *To love me because I think I'm falling in love with you.*

"You don't want me."

I pulled his head and pressed my lips against his. He groaned and opened his mouth, and I tangled with him. A wall of heat rushed me, surprising me with its fury. We sunk onto the bed.

"I want you to take me now." I tore open my robe and moved my hands under his tunic.

"No." He jerked out of my grasp. "You want to seduce me, so I will take you to David. You care nothing for me. Witch."

His teeth clenched, he wrapped a blanket around me and shoved me out the door.

"That's not it. That's not it." Pain shot through my fists as I pounded on the door. "Phalti, talk to me."

An agonizing chill roiled my heart. He had misunderstood me and no longer loved me.

The babies cried in hunger. I fumbled with them. Everything was twice as hard without Phalti's help. I did not call out. Sobbing and exhausted, I sunk back into bed, a baby at each breast.

Sometime during the night, Phalti put the babies in their cradles and covered me with a blanket. His touch lingered, but when I opened my eyes, he was gone. An oppressive, suffocating pain sat like a stone on my chest.

I rose and lit an oil lamp. I found a scrap of parchment under my bed and scribbled a note, addressing it to Abigail, wife of Nabal, in Carmel. I couldn't write David's name with the civil war going on, but I hoped Abigail would pass my note to David. Phalti had rejected me, and I had no one I could trust.

I sent the note through a special courier, paying him with a precious gem that had belonged to my mother.

* * *

Naomi and I busied ourselves with the babies while Phalti went to town to deliver scrolls and letters. Joel and Gaddiel ran around the table in circles, fighting and squalling. Eliah tugged on my skirt to be picked up.

The front gate banged, and the gatekeeper's grandson ran into the kitchen. "Another bandit."

Naomi snapped her fingers. The three older boys hurried to their rooms and hid under their beds as we had practiced.

My heart thudding, I tucked the babies in their cradles and stepped into the courtyard. "What do you want?"

A rough voice yelled. "Open up. We're hungry."

"How many are there?" I pushed the boy to the wall to peek.

The old gatekeeper shuffled to the gate and yelled, "Be gone. There's no disturbing good folk with this noise."

"We're just hungry. We won't hurt anyone."

The boy returned. "One man and two women. The man has a knife, but the women are covered. I can't tell if they're armed."

"Get an omer of barley and a basket of raisins," I said. "That should be enough."

I yelled over the gate, "We'll lower food over the wall. Now, be gone."

"God bless you, lady." The man's voice softened as the boy tied the basket of grain and raisins and let it down over the wall.

Naomi tugged my sleeve. "Are we leaving soon?"

"I don't know. It depends if I can trust David or not. I've secretly sent a message with a courier to his wife Abigail telling him where we are."

"How is he going to come for us? We have five children, two of them babies. Shouldn't we go to your brother's house? I'm sure he has plenty of guards."

"They can't keep us safe. Ishby is king in name only. Abner's the one with the power, but he's fighting against the LORD. David promised me when he became king, he would fetch me and take care of me forever."

A scowl sharpened her face. "Well, he's not king around these parts. People here hate him, especially since he allies with foreign kings against Israel."

I sighed. "David does what he has to do."

The door opened. Phalti stomped across the room glaring at me. "You're still here? What happened to your savior? How many months has he been king already? Oh, that's right. You must still be waiting for him to remember you."

He stalked out the back door toward the fields. His shouting woke the babies and scared the three older boys. Their screams pealed through my nerves. By the end of the day, Naomi and I dragged our feet, utterly exhausted. She had flour in her hair, and my dress was stained with spilled juice, food particles and dripping milk.

"Naomi," I wheezed, "I've decided. Tomorrow, I'm sending a message to my brother to ask him to move us to Mahanaim. He should still have servants to help us with the work."

There was no sense waiting for David to send Ittai. We could all be killed before he arrived. I would leave a note with the gatekeeper directing him to Mahanaim.

She slumped over my shoulder with a dishrag. "I agree with you. Another day like this and we'll both be raving mad."

After I settled the babies and kissed the boys good night, I dug through Phalti's writing table to find a reed and parchment. I hadn't helped him with his business since my babies were born. I shoved aside a few scrolls in progress and could not find a single piece I could use. I wiped my forehead with the back of my hand and blinked back tears. I did not want to bother Phalti. He hated me and could barely stand the sight of me.

"Michal?" Phalti's pinched voice bent over my shoulder. "What are you doing in my things?"

"Looking for a piece of parchment and a reed."

He crossed his arms. "Look elsewhere."

I brushed past him and stumbled to my room. *Must he be so cruel?* I lit a lamp and rummaged through my things. Jonathan's blood encrusted leather sleeve held pieces of scripture he had hand copied. I untied the leather straps and pulled out the contents. I smoothed out a few scraps of parchment to find something usable. The script jumped at me. David's.

I held the scraps to the light.

My dearest Michal, I wonder if you're thinking of me. I'm sitting deep in a cave writing this by the light of a lamp. I will ask your brother to help you escape. I cannot wait to hold you in my arms again, your loving husband, David.

Pain flooded my soul. My breathing in spurts, I picked up another scrap.

My dearest Michal, why have you not written? Give me a sign. Let me know you still care for me. I despair of ever seeing you again. I miss you. Your David.

A choking sob screamed in my throat. "No. Why? Oh, God. Why?"

Michal, I'm leaving Israel. Remember me, always. David.

I flung through other scraps. David. I had broken his heart, and he'd given up on me. It had always been my fault. I crumpled to the ground and ripped at my hair, wishing my heart would die, that the pain would drain to the last drop of blood.

"Michal? Are you all right?" Phalti placed me on my bed. He picked up the scraps. His face white and his jaw slack, he put the pieces back into the sleeve.

He sat at my side. "Did you still want parchment? Do you want me to write a message for you?"

"Please." My mouth was so dry I could barely dictate. "Ask Ishbaal to send carts and fetch me, my maid and my sons. I need his protection."

He scribbled the message. "I'll deliver it myself. You don't want me to come?"

I took his large hand and rubbed his palms. "You're too good to me. It'll be better if you stayed away from me. You deserve someone better. I'm sorry it turned out this way."

I turned away from him and floated past pain into an expanse of numb emptiness.

In a week's time, Ishbaal sent men and carts. Phalti remained cold and distant, although he did come to see us off. He kissed the older boys. He didn't bother with the babies because it would mean getting too close to me, and they were too young to know him.

He stood in the middle of the road, his arms crossed, and stared at me until I was too far to see him. *What are you thinking, Phalti? Please don't hate me.* Each turn of the wheel took me farther and farther from him.

CHAPTER 20

Proverbs 30:18-19 There be three things which are too wonderful for me, yea, four which I know not: The way of an eagle in the air; the way of a serpent upon a rock; the way of a ship in the midst of the sea; and the way of a man with a maid.

>>><<<

The sound of hoof beats alerted me. I scooted to the edge of the ox-cart. A burly man with flowing black hair appeared in a cloud of dust on a black horse. His partner, slim and sandy-haired, drew a knife and jumped off a roan horse.

"Who goes there?" The two guards my brother sent stepped forward.

The black-haired man brandished his sword and dismounted. "Unhand the princess and nobody dies."

My pulse racing, I drew my shawl over my face. Two guards and the man who drove the ox-cart; the odds were about even. I didn't factor in the gatekeeper's grandson. He came along for the joy ride.

"There's no princess here. Just a couple of maids," the older guard said.

The black-haired man scanned us. I huddled with the boys, urging them to keep their heads down.

"Back off." The guard yelled and pointed his spear at the black-haired man.

The black-haired man swung his sword. The guard thrust his spear and missed. The attacker sliced the guard's arms with a down stroke and jerked his sword around, cutting open the man's abdomen. Blood and entrails gushed out of the guard, and he fell to the ground. Naomi whimpered, holding onto Eliah, who cried and threw up. The two older boys made exclamations of disgust.

The younger guard's spear wobbled in front of him as he stared at the black-haired man.

The second attacker booted the younger guard in the behind and threw him off balance. His spear tip grazed the ground, and the black-haired man sliced his neck open.

Acid shot into my throat. I covered my sleeping babies, one in each arm. The driver fled, and the gatekeeper's grandson cowered beneath the wagon.

The black-haired man wiped his sword on his accomplice's robe. Footsteps crackled on the leaf-strewn road. Around me, my boys blubbered and clung to me and Naomi.

My hair was yanked and my scarf pulled off.

"Is this she?"

The gatekeeper's boy crawled from under the wagon and nodded. The black-haired man threw him a coin, and the boy sprinted away. The man grabbed my face and stared. "Ah, just as they said. Green eyes with brown flecks. I got you now."

He swung me around by my waist while his partner pried my screaming babies out of my arms and handed them to Naomi.

"No, no! My babies, my babies." I kicked and struggled, but the big man's grip tightened like bands of iron. "Who are you? Where are you taking me?"

The black-haired man squeezed my cheeks and yanked me to his horse. "You either cooperate, and I'll let your babies live, or I can kill them now."

"Let me have my babies, then I'll cooperate."

"Do we look like nursemaids?" His young partner snorted. Naomi and my boys stared wide-eyed, stranded on the cart. My babies squealed and cried.

My attacker pushed me belly down onto the horse and jumped on behind me, pinning me with his strong hand.

I flailed and grabbed at his legs. "Please... I beg you."

His punch caught me between the shoulder blades and knocked the wind out of me. "Shut your mouth, or I'll kill all of them."

He pressed down harder while I struggled for breath. "You'll either ride on your belly like a sack of barley, or you can be nice and sit with me."

My hardened breasts, full of milk, screamed with pain. "I'll sit up and cooperate, but where are you taking me?" I crawled into a more comfortable position.

"I didn't say you could talk." He snapped the reins, and we galloped away

My babies' screams faded in the distance.

The man whistled as the miles rolled by. My stomach lurched to the beat of the horse's hooves, and my aching head jiggled against the man's shoulder. Who was he? Where was he taking me? He was heavily perfumed with myrrh and balsam, and his hair and beard were richly oiled. His clothing showed him a man of wealth.

One hand clamped around my waist, he fingered my temple and neck with the other hand. "Daughter of Saul, for years, men have sought you. They've scoured the known world looking for you. But you had disappeared. Some said you died in Philistia, others that you ran off to Egypt with the young Philistine prince. Who would have thought you a nurse to your sister's babies, married to a poor scribe in the countryside?"

"What do you want with me?" I said.

"You? You're the key to the kingdom of Israel. The man who has the daughter of Saul can take the crown."

"You're putting too much worth on me. As you said, I'm a backwater housewife."

He cupped my face and turned it. "Oh, no. You're still a beauty. And he'll make the trade and reward me handsomely."

"Who?"

He laughed so hard, his chest thundered into my back. "Your husband David, of course. Without you, he cannot unite the tribes. Eleven tribes back your brother. Only Judah rebelled. They're fighting because David wants your father's crown. All we have to do is get there before the other princess."

"What princess?"

He voice lowered to a growl. "The one I love, and the one your husband aims to marry."

Sweat broke across my brow, and a pincer of pain seized my heart. "What did you say?"

"David wants to marry my girl. Only you can stop him."

"So David did not send you?"

It took a moment before he jerked aware, his eyes cleared from their reverie. "Eh? I've got to stop them. The crown is mine and so is the princess."

He squeezed me tighter and urged his horse forward, his partner following close behind.

The man was probably a lunatic. Nothing he said made sense. Did my father have another daughter I didn't know about? And what would David want with her? David had not sent him. He would have sent Ittai, and he would never have so cruelly separated me from my babies. I had to escape.

At nightfall my captor tied me to a tree. He sharpened his knife while his partner went to the river to fish.

My breasts leaking milk, I prayed, "Oh, dear God, I have not been good. But please, look on me with mercy and bring me back to my sons. And, God, give me another chance with Phalti."

I woke with a start. A man's breath over my face chilled the little hairs on the back of my neck. He pawed my aching breasts and bent over to suckle. I lifted my knee and struggled to sit, my hands fastened to the tree. It was the slim, sandy-haired man, the accomplice.

He put a finger to his lips and whispered, "Don't cry out. He's asleep."

"What do you want?"

"I want to look at you." He ran his grubby fingers through my hair. "Will you kiss me?"

I glared at him. He didn't appear muscular, but rather thin. If I could disarm him…

I smiled and licked my lips. "Come closer."

He leaned toward me, and I kissed him, fighting the urge to retch. "Do you want me to touch you?"

He leered. "But you have to be quiet, promise?"

"Yes, yes. Now, cut my hands loose." I wiggled my shoulders.

He cut my bonds and dropped the knife to the ground.

While he untied his breeches, I kicked his groin, grabbed the knife and ran. He fell back, moaning in pain, his breeches tangled around his ankles. The black-haired man sat up and rubbed his eyes near the campfire.

I tucked the knife in my robe and grabbed the reins to mount the black horse. The monster pawed the ground and snorted, shaking off my feeble jumps. The other horse whinnied and tossed his head, spooked by the rustling in the bushes.

Not waiting for the black-haired man to discover me, I tripped toward the woods. Twigs snapped, and brush crackled. My captor shouted to his partner. "Get her, she's over there."

Shivering and whimpering, I crawled up the bank and ducked behind a rock pile.

A mounted man dropped to the forest floor and charged the black-haired man. Grunts and shouts punched the moon-slivered night. I steadied myself with a branch and peered over the rock pile. The black-haired man struggled with a large, square-shouldered man who held him around the waist and wrestled him to the ground.

"Aghh!" the man screamed. I covered my ears and turned to run.

"Michal." The strangled cry stopped me. Phalti?

I slid down the bank of rocks and sprinted toward them. The black-haired man squatted over Phalti and shook his neck. "Where is she?"

The knife in both hands, I sprang into the air and stabbed the black-haired man in the lower back. He lurched and swiped me with his elbow. I landed on my back. The man stepped toward me, his eye sockets hollow, his hands clutched in front of him. He reached to grab me, but crumpled and fell on his face. Blood spurted from the embedded knife, still quivering in his back.

Phalti's eyes were open but pinpointed in shock. I slapped his face, still warm. Blood seeped through his robe. I peeled back his bloodied clothes and found a puncture wound right below the collar bone. His mule nuzzled but could not rouse him.

"Someone, help me," I cried. "Phalti, don't die."

Emotions I didn't know I possessed flooded over me. My hands ached where I touched him. My mouth ached where I piled kisses on his cooling face. My chest ached as I tried to cover his bleeding heart with mine.

A tentative poke on my back distracted me. "Mistress?" It was the younger man. "There's a village close by. Shall I get a doctor?"

"Oh, yes, yes. Please go."

"Will you have me arrested for kidnapping you?"

"No, no… just help me."

He scrambled onto the mule and rode off.

Phalti's pulse weakened, and he grew cold. I yanked the robe off the dead man and stuffed the cloth over his wound to stem the flow of blood. He reached for me, and I grabbed his hand.

"Don't die. I love you, please don't leave me." A deluge of regret clouded my vision. I showered him with desperate kisses, tasting the sweet man who risked his life for me, the one who stood by me through my pregnancy, and took in all my children even as my husband had abandoned me.

I held Phalti's head in my lap, cried and prayed, and wondered why he had come after me. *Please, God, don't let him die. He's more noble and honorable than I.* Caressing his clammy face, I waited for the young man to return.

The dawn arrived with the village physician, a cart and a horse. They stuffed wool in Phalti's wound and lifted him on the cart.

My captor's accomplice wrung his hands and tapped my shoulder. "Mistress, will you forgive me?"

"Yes. I thank you for your help. Now go."

"I have nowhere to go." In the light of the day, his youth was even more evident. His big brown eyes moistened like a puppy's.

"What is your name?"

"Ammiel of Lo-debar. I was captured by that man and made a slave." He nodded toward the man I had killed.

"Who was he?"

"He's a Geshurite from the kingdom to the north. His brother is Talmai, the King of Geshur. They were on their way to deliver the princess Maacah to marry King David, but he decided to capture you instead. Then he'd get his brother killed in exchange for you. He told me you're more valuable than the princess because you are the daughter of Saul."

The loon was in love with his niece? Keeping control of my voice, I said, "You may come with us. I will ask my brother to restore you to your land."

Tears blinding my eyes, I excused myself to go to the river. The doctor tended to Phalti, and the villagers stepped aside to let me pass. I splashed water on my face. David was marrying again, this time to a princess. The Geshurites would pinch us from the north. We were surrounded, completely surrounded. My wounded heart clenched and clenched and clenched. I tore my clothes and spread myself in the shallow water. *David, David, why have you forgotten me? Why have you taken her and forsaken me? Why are you so far from helping me?*

* * *

Ammiel told the villagers I was King Ishbaal's sister, and they gave me a clean set of clothes and food for the journey. The physician accompanied us. I held Phalti's head in my lap as the cart lurched its way to Mahanaim.

His eyes closed, his skin clammy, he moaned and labored to breathe. "Michal, I go now."

I smoothed his hair. "No, no, you can't go. We have many more years together. We have the boys to raise and our grandchildren to play with. You can't leave me now that I've found you. Phalti, stay with me. I do love you so much."

Had he heard me, or understood what my heart told him? His head lolled, and his breathing steadied. I lay next to him. My prayers drifted into dreams—Phalti smiling at me, stroking my hair and kissing me.

I woke in a soft bed with my babies clinging to my breasts. Their tiny suckling sounds calmed my heart, lifted my gloom and worry. Rizpah, my father's concubine, sat at my bedside.

"How's Phalti?" The words croaked in my parched throat. I couldn't recall how I ended up in the bed with my sons.

"He's alive," she said. "I've missed you, can you believe that?" She wore widow's garb and a mourning veil.

"How are you? And my two brothers?"

"They're spunky little boys, always into mischief. Already friends with your boys. We caught them slinging stones into the well. You weren't here to paddle them, so Ishby did the honors." Her laughter trilled, melodious like a flute, and brought a smile to my face.

"Do you miss my father?"

"He's in a better place," she said. "He left me, you know?"

"He did? Where did he go?"

"Found an old lover. Someone he wished to marry but was forbidden to."

"Who?" I sat up, balancing the two babies.

She laughed in her throat. "I don't know. He took his gold and aimed to run away with her. Imagine my surprise when Abner told me he had died on Mt. Gilboa."

"Along with my brothers..." A sob choked me at the memory.

She wiped a corner of her eye. "Let's talk of happier things. Your husband most certainly loves you."

"He does?" My thoughts wobbled toward David and his betrayal.

"Why, of course. Your maid has told me all about him. Dashing and devoted, he tried to rescue you. Didn't I tell you he would be good to you?"

I looked down. "He's hurt because of me. I must see him."

"He's resting, but hot. I sat with him last night. He's very weak, and several times I thought he'd cross over. But I called him back. Here, let me take the babes when they're done feeding."

A crazy pang of resentment edged my gratitude. What was she doing sitting with Phalti? Did he see her in his delirium and dream of her? Milky white, blue-eyed beauty, she had bewitched my father and drove out my mother.

Phalti was asleep when I pulled a chair to his side. He labored to breathe, his face too pale. A sheen of sweat shimmered over his forehead hot with fever. I pulled his hands into mine.

Phalti tightened in my grip, and his eyes rolled. "Where am I?"

"You're still alive. You're with me."

"Michal... you're here?"

"Yes, I'll never leave your side."

"I thought I had died, and you were an angel." His breathing shallow and his eyes wet, he tried to sit up. "I saw angels. I wanted to leave and go with them. So peaceful, no pain. Only joy."

I rubbed his thick beard. "Rest, we'll talk later."

He closed his eyes. "But you said I couldn't go. That it wasn't time. That you needed me."

I grimaced. And I bet the angel had blue eyes, too.

"I do need you," I said.

"Yes, you told me there was no one else. That you're left alone, your husband deserted you." He babbled until he fell asleep. What else had Rizpah told him?

* * *

While he was feverish, Phalti basked in my care, a hazy smile on his face. But as he recovered and the fever left him, he became withdrawn and sullen. He watched me out of the side of his eye and avoided my direct gaze.

"Are you not happy with my care?" I broached the silence one warm evening.

He drew his mouth to a line and turned toward the wall. "You're a princess, daughter of Saul. You don't have to take care of me. There are maids."

"What if I told you I wanted to care for you?"

"I'd think you lied, like you lied about other things."

I straightened. "What other things?"

"Things you said when you thought I was dying. I wish you had let me die." He covered his face with his large hand.

"You're talking in riddles. A couple of days ago, you seemed happy to let me wipe your face, feed you and change your bed. Now you wish me gone?" I pulled his hand off his face and wiped his hair out of his eyes.

He closed his eyes and gritted his teeth so tightly his mouth twitched. "Ammiel said his master was taking you to David. If I hadn't interfered, you'd be back with him and happy."

My heart lurched at his words. I doubted I would have been happy to confront David at his wedding to the princess of Geshur. "Did Ammiel explain they kidnapped me, and I was trying to escape?"

Phalti didn't reply. Ammiel had obviously left this part out to protect himself.

"You don't believe me," I said.

"Please, I don't want to talk." His voice stiffened. "Send a maid or Rizpah to sit with me."

"No, I'm your wife, and it's my duty to sit with you."

Rizpah was the last person I wanted at his side. She had already shown too much interest in him.

"Then don't talk to me." He sounded like a stubborn boy refusing to go to bed.

"Fine. I wish you'd stop being a grouch."

I tuned David's harp and sang while Phalti sobbed into his pillow. After his breathing steadied into sleep, I put the harp down and held him. He shuddered with a residual sob but did not wake.

Tears slipped over my cheeks. I ached for answers. Phalti, why do you weep? Are you in love with Rizpah? And you can't tell me?

A few days later, Phalti was strong enough to hobble to the garden with the help of two guards. I sat with him in a spot near the wall under a green bay tree, shaded and cool. I left him several times to tend to my babies and returned to find Rizpah holding his hand.

A surge of bile erupted from my stomach, and I marched over. She dropped his hand and left without speaking to me.

"What is she doing here?" I shook him. "Is there something you're not telling me?"

"No, she was listening, that's all."

"Listening about what? What is it that you can tell her and not me?"

"Michal, you're not jealous, are you?" A boyish grin brightened his face.

"I'm not. I mean, she's my stepmother."

"Was. She's a widow now."

"Does that mean you're courting her, are you?"

"Why, you *are* jealous. Come here." He pulled me into a warm hug and kissed my temple.

Feeling suddenly tiny, I closed my eyes and whispered, "I don't want to lose you."

"I didn't know you cared."

I hugged him tighter. "I do care. I meant every word."

He kissed my forehead and stroked my hair. "Is it true you're alone? That your husband deserted you?"

"Yes. He's taken another wife, the princess of Geshur. Ammiel's master wanted to use me to stop the wedding."

"And you didn't want to stop it?"

"No. All I thought about was you and my sons."

"Do you still love him?"

Pain and regret tangled in my heart. My throat tightened. "He's gotten over me. I cannot love a mirage."

"And what about the other things you said? About needing me? I wanted it to be true. It kept me from slipping away." His voice was soft, barely above a whisper.

"It's all true," I said. "Do you still care about me?"

"I've always cared. But I wanted you to want me, too."

"Oh, Phalti, I do want you, very much." Beads of sweat broke on his nose and forehead, and I wiped his face with my sleeve. A chuckle rumbled from my throat. "Another thing, did Ammiel ever return your mule?"

"No, he didn't. But it was worth losing another mule to get you back." A wide grin split his face.

171

"I'm glad to know I'm worth more than a mule." I tapped his nose and kissed him. He returned my kisses lazily, swayed and almost swooned. The guards carried him back to our bedchamber.

I bathed him in cold water, savoring his sweet smile. The ugly scar on his chest quivered, jagged, hairless and pink as I passed the washcloth over it. "Phalti, the other day when I sang for you, why did you cry?"

"Because you sang of duty and not of love. You sounded so mournful, like part of your heart had died."

"I'm that obvious?"

"Only to me. Michal, let me show you how a man can love." He stroked my hand and brought it to his face. "Let me heal your heart and care for you as you deserve."

The intensity of his words and the fervor in his eyes shook me. "You're still weak. I'll dry you and help you to bed. Are you hungry?"

He climbed out and grabbed me around the waist, nudging me to the bed. Dripping wet, he propped himself over me. "I love you, Michal."

A supreme sense of fulfillment overwhelmed me. Emotions danced in my heart. This man, this loving, kind man loved me, and I loved him, too. The blessed ray of sunlight pierced through the fog of despair. "I love you, oh, how I love you, Phalti, son of Laish."

He cradled me in his arms and kissed me. His hot tongue left a path of fire everywhere he touched. My feelings blossomed to an entire new realm of happiness, a love not born of desperation, but of contentment and peace.

Phalti and I loved each other that day and for many more days and nights. As Abner sparred with David, we reveled in our love, our children, and the new life growing inside of me. The following year, I bore Phalti a daughter, Anna, a sweet, spritely, laughing baby, brown curls and hazel eyes. My life was perfect and complete.

CHAPTER 21

2nd Samuel 3:13 Thou shalt not see my face, except thou first bring Michal Saul's daughter when thou comest to see my face.

>>><<<

Anna, my little daughter, snuggled with her blanket on the stone floor, exhausted from her birthday celebration.

"Are you sure she should sleep here?" Phalti pulled a blanket over her shoulder.

I removed the blanket. "It's hot and steamy inside. And her brothers are all sleeping out here."

Phalti ran his fingers through my hair. "Three years old, can you believe it?"

"Oh, if we could only keep her this age." I patted my baby girl. All charm and dimples, her little curls would bounce and she'd chatter with anyone who'd listen.

"You say this on each of her birthdays. One of these days she'll be getting married. Then what would you do?"

I picked up the plates and toys strewn around the courtyard. "May that time never come."

My brother Ishbaal walked by, rubbing his back. "That was some party. They never tired of having Uncle Ishby be the donkey."

I chuckled. Ishby was a boy at heart. He usually played rough games with sticks and swords, but with Anna and her little girl friends, he'd loop them on his shoulders and jog through the garden, his club foot forcing him into a bouncing gait that delighted them all. Hard to believe he was king of Israel.

"Good night, Ishby," I called after him.

Phalti touched my elbow and nudged me toward the roof. "Let's sleep under the stars." A web of sparks followed his warm hands as he caressed my breasts, his gaze intent on me.

"Stop it, the children might see," I said.

He took my hand and led me up the steps to the rooftop. "Are you happy?"

"I am. I feel safe with you." I hugged him, his sultry male scent stimulating me. "How about you? Are you happy with me?"

"Always, my dear." He kissed me long and deep, bunching my hair around his fingers. "What do you think the future holds for us?"

I stretched and swayed in his arms. "I'm content as long as you're with me."

"Do you think about David?" His voice affected a casual tone.

"Why bring him up? I wish he and Abner would stop fighting. They're destroying everything my father and brothers fought for. Israel is in ruins."

"I also wish we'd have peace," he said. "Then I'd go back to Gallim, buy my house and land back, and raise our children there."

"Is that where you want us to live?" Right now, it was safer east of the Jordan River, away from the fighting.

"Yes, but the Philistines occupy the town. This civil war needs to end. When it does, would you come to Gallim with me? It won't be easy getting started again, but I'll work hard."

How could I not want to go with him? "I'll work at your side. Where you go, I will go; where you live, I will live; where you die, I will die."

"And if David were to come for you?" He walked to the edge of the roof and stared at the horizon.

A chill skittered up and down my spine. What bothered him? I pulled my arms around his waist. "Why are you worried?"

"I want you to be sure and never regret."

"I'll never regret choosing you." I touched his chest over his heart and raised my gaze to his. "At first, I was afraid to fall in love with you. I fought it as long as I had feelings for David, and I wouldn't have gotten close to you if I still thought about him."

"I don't ever want to lose you."

It hurt me that he needed reassurance. Hadn't I proven over the years how much I loved him? I squeezed him between my arms. "You won't ever lose me. Even if David were to keep his promise to fetch me, I shall not go. I am yours now, and we'll be together, always."

His eyes gleamed in the moonlight. "I knew I could trust you. We have a special bond, don't we?"

His excitement pressed into me, and I squirmed with anticipation. "Oh, yes, we do."

He ruffled my hair and nibbled behind my ear. "Now that Anna is weaned, think we'll make another baby?"

I pressed a hand to his chest. "What are you waiting for?"

Our lips touched, and we lost ourselves in a dance as ancient as time, yet uniquely ours.

* * *

Loud thumps woke me. I crept to the edge of the roofline. A man pounded on Rizpah's window.

"Open up, woman," the man shouted.

"Abner, I'm Saul's wife." Rizpah's voice warbled and took on a panicked tone.

"You fool, Saul is dead, and I'll have you as mine. Open up."

"The king has placed me under his protection." Her voice rose.

Abner guffawed. "He's only king because I say so. He will not deny me your hand." He drew his sword and flashed it in the moonlight.

"Go away," Rizpah said. "Men who would be king disgust me."

Abner beat the wooden window with his sword and broke the shutters open. He climbed in and moments later, Rizpah's muffled screams chilled my bones and set my teeth on edge.

I shook Phalti. "You have to do something."

"What's happening?" He rubbed his eyes.

The thud of crashing furniture jolted him fully awake. Rizpah's rhythmic cries of pain penetrated the muggy heat.

Phalti pulled on his clothes and hurried down the stairs with me. We ran around the courtyard, stepping over the sleeping children, and sprinted into the corridor.

The beating stopped, followed by a loud thump as Abner dropped himself out the window. The crunch of his footsteps retreated into the night.

Phalti's face paled. "He's left. I'm bringing Anna into our room."

"I'll comfort Rizpah. Tell Naomi to draw a bath for her."

Phalti went to rouse Naomi while I knocked on Rizpah's door.

"Rizpah, it's me, Michal. May I help you?"

"Go away. No one can help me now." She groaned behind the door.

"I'll tell Ishby to set a guard. Please, let me come in and comfort you."

"You can't." She clawed at the door for several moments before it opened. Her throat made small mewing sounds as she pulled her tattered dress in front of her breast.

I held her while she wept. My father would have wanted me to be kind to her.

Naomi prepared the bath, and we tended to Rizpah. I combed her straight black hair while she scrubbed herself vigorously with a sponge and dripped tears into the water.

"I was on the rooftop," I said. "He had a sword, and he broke your window. There was nothing you could have done."

Naomi hummed a sad tune. Rizpah's cries echoed. "I'm scared. I'm so scared and so alone."

* * *

Ishby came as soon as I summoned him. His eyes flashed when he looked at the broken window. He strode back to his audience chamber and called for Abner. Following a loud uproar, Abner stomped out of the palace, mounted a fast horse, and announced to everyone within earshot his intention to turn the kingdom over to David.

I went to Ishby. "What's this I hear? Will Abner betray a son of Saul?"

He frowned. "It appears so. What shall I do? I did not want to be king. All I ever wanted was to be a prince, to sit with my family and to laugh and play."

"There is only one thing to do. You must make a league with David before Abner does. Send a messenger today. Tell him you will turn over the kingdom to him as your brother Jonathan had sworn. It's the only way to save your life."

He called his scribe and dictated a letter. I took Jonathan's ring off my thumb. "Here, David will recognize this. Take this to David, and he will have mercy on us all. I know David. He is not unkind to forget his friendship with Jonathan."

* * *

In the beginning of winter, messengers arrived at the palace gate.

"King David requests Michal, his lawful wife, restored to him."

Phalti stepped in front of me. "What is the meaning of this?"

"Abner has gone over to David," I said, "so Ishby sued David for peace, and he promised us safe passage. All of us, including you."

He growled, "Why did you not tell me of this?"

"I didn't know what his answer would be." My face burned, and my throat constricted.

He turned to the messengers. "Why should we comply? David is not our king. We won't be leaving without our king's command."

Ishby's guards stood still. Not one man stepped forward to intervene.

One of the messengers spoke, "You may all stay. Only the king's wife is required. We have orders to take her to her husband."

The other messenger held out a scroll. "And you, Phalti. From now on, your name shall no longer be Phalti, the Deliverance, but Phaltiel, the

Deliverance of God. You are hereby rewarded. The king has deeded you this palace and the lands surrounding it."

He handed Phalti the scroll which he promptly threw in the dust. "No, you will not take my wife. I will die before you take her from me."

"Phalti, don't be foolish." I tried to hold him back, but he charged and drove the messengers back to the gate.

A sword flashed. Ittai rode up with a contingent of warriors. He dismounted in front of Phalti, grabbed him by the front of his robe and pushed him. Phalti staggered a few feet but did not fall.

Ittai turned and bowed to me, presenting his most winsome grin. "I have come, Michal, to fetch you as David promised. Now, pack your things and gather your little ones."

Phalti moved toward me, but Ittai's men corralled him and started to beat him.

"Stop!" Ittai commanded. "Restrain him, but do not hurt him. He has done King David a great service by guarding his wife while the king was in exile."

Lying on the ground with his arms tied, Phalti shot me a look that broke my heart, a look that accused me of betrayal. I bent to his side. "I didn't ask him to come."

He turned his face into the dust. I knelt in front him. "Honestly, ask Ishby. We only sued for peace."

Phalti's jaw tightened. "Go. It's what you wanted."

I turned to Ittai. "Please, don't make me go."

One side of his eyebrow snaked up. "Isn't this what you've been waiting for? Your husband wants you back. He sent for you as he promised. I came as I promised."

Tears streamed down my face. My heart wrenched itself from my chest. "I have a husband here. I love him, and I have children, a family, and a home."

Ittai took my hand and lifted me. "Your rightful place is with the king. You're sad right now, but you'll be fine as soon as you see his face. Phalti's not your real husband anyway."

I pounded Ittai on the chest, so distraught I didn't care about the onlookers. "No! Phalti's my husband, here, in my heart. He's only done good to me. How can I leave him? Please tell David to put me away. I've been unfaithful."

Ittai put his arms around me. "King David forgives you of everything, completely. Now, let's get your children and your things."

"I can't go. I won't." I pushed from his chest and kicked him in the shins.

"Sister." Ishby's voice spun me around. "I have a note from King David. It reads: Deliver me my wife Michal, whom I espoused to me for one hundred foreskins of the Philistines." He tapped my shoulder. "He paid for you in blood. I witnessed it myself. I command you to go. Now stop carrying on as one of the foolish women."

My feelings numb, I packed my things and gathered the children, Joel, Gaddiel, Eliah, Joshua, Beraiah, and Anna. They were ten, eight, seven, the twins five, and three.

"Eemah, where are we going?"

"Why's Abba on the floor? Are they going to kill him?"

"Eemah, where's my dolly?"

"Come," I said, "we have to get our things and go see Uncle David."

"Who's Uncle David? When will we be back?"

"My tunic is itchy. Why do I have to wear this?"

"Stop it. Eemah, Joel's hitting me."

I pinched Joel's shoulder. "Stop hitting your brother. Now, be a big boy and help Naomi with the bags."

Joshua and Beraiah ran circles around us, laughing and hitting with the wooden swords Ishby gave them. "We go fight Philly Peens."

They ran behind the horses, swatted at the tails, and scrambled underneath them, rolling among their hooves.

Ittai laughed. "You little rascals, now do what your mother says." He bent down and picked them up, one under each arm. "Which one of you wants to ride with me?"

"I do."

"No, I do."

"Me first, I'm older."

"No, I'm smarter."

"Well, if you both stay still, I'll ask your mother if you both can ride with me. But only if you sit still, or you'll have to ride in that thing like a little baby." He gestured to the covered litter and laughed again. Putting them down, he examined them with a stern look.

They stood stiff and straight, holding their breath and looking at me with eager eyes.

"All right," I said. "You may ride with the captain if you promise not to fight."

Ittai picked them up and swung them around until they squealed in glee.

With Anna over my hip, I bent to where Phalti sat on the ground. "Please understand. It's the only way. Abner has betrayed us."

"The only betrayal around here is yours. You lied so well."

"How can you not feel it in here?" I pointed to his heart. "And know that I love you. I know you feel it, and I know you know. You cannot deny what we have."

I took David's emerald off my neck and placed it around his. "Look into it when you miss me and know that I also will be thinking about you."

His face softened for a moment, but his eyes remained as flint. He jerked his shoulder and bounced the gem and would have torn it off his chest had his hands not been tied.

"Remember us." I placed my hand on his shoulder only to feel him stiffen and shrug it aside. Anna whimpered and squirmed.

Phalti tilted his head toward her. "Hold her close to me. Let me kiss her."

I held her, and she flung her little arms around his head. "Abba, hurry, come, we go now."

"Good bye, darling. Abba will see you soon." His voice collapsed into the dirt.

My throat closed and my eyes blurred. I picked up Anna and walked away as fast as I could.

"I want Abba," Anna cried when she realized Phalti wasn't coming. "I want Abba." She screamed and threw herself out of my arms. Eliah broke from Naomi, and Joel and Gaddiel clambered off their donkeys.

"Abba, Abba," they wailed. Joshua and Beraiah squirmed in Ittai's arms.

I entreated Ittai, my hands clasped at his chest.

He cleared his throat and signaled to his men. "Phaltiel may come along. King David will decide what to do with him."

He shoved Phalti, none too kindly, and growled at him. "You will walk with your hands tied to the mule. Don't try any tricks." He glanced at me and punched Phalti in the belly. "You were lucky to have her all these years."

I leaned at the opening of the litter and stared at Phalti. Pulled by the mule, he kept his head down. My heart cracked as a net of pain tightened over my body. How could this be? Long ago, I had prayed for this day, dreamt about it, and wished for David to keep his promise.

At twenty-six, I was no longer the young girl who let him down the window. My hands rough with child-rearing, my only concerns were domestic, and I was satisfied to be the wife of Phalti, the scribe. What did David expect from me? And why would he be so cruel to Phalti?

The miles dragged on, and Phalti jogged behind the mule, struggling to keep pace. The children calmed when they saw their father, only asking why they tied him up and whether Uncle David would put him in jail.

After we forded the Jordan, we set up camp. The men pitched tents for us. When Phalti tried to draw near, they flashed swords at him. Phalti stood with his head down, shivering from falling into the water. I begged

Ittai to tend to him. After taking him to the river to wash, Ittai lent him a cloak and tied him to a tree.

As the sun set, Phalti sat far from the fire, his figure forlorn and dejected. I handed Anna to Naomi and brought him a blanket. Soon, the boys, Naomi and Anna gathered around him and we formed a circle. I untied Phalti's hands and rubbed his shoulders. Joel fed him while Gaddiel and Eliah climbed on his back and the twins and Anna hugged his legs and pushed each other to get in his lap. Ittai sat across from us and chewed on a cinnamon stick but did not interfere.

* * *

They woke us early the following morning. As the men packed the tents, I found Phalti near the river and wiped my hand on his forehead. "You're feverish."

His large hand caressed my neck. "Please ask David to have pity on me, a poor man, and a commoner who loves you."

"I will ask David if he'll allow you to stay at the palace. Maybe he only wants me as a figurehead to unite the kingdom. And he can use you as a scribe."

We kissed and held each other until Ittai separated us and put me in the litter with Anna. Phalti sniffled and coughed, dragging further behind the mule. Ittai slowed the pace as a cold, light rain soaked the thirsty ground.

Uncle Abner met us at the city of Bahurim.

Ittai dismounted and saluted him. "I've brought the king's wife as he requested."

Abner said, "I'll take her from here." He scanned the anxious faces of my children. "Why have you brought them? David only wants his wife."

Ittai replied, "Certainly you can't separate the children from their mother."

Abner growled, "The Lady Michal is my cousin. You're only a captain of the guards. No one told you to make decisions. This is a diplomatic affair, not a family gathering. Now stand aside."

Abner sneered at Phalti. "And who is this, the prisoner?" He slapped him. "You fool. Go back to Mahanaim while you still have your head."

Phalti didn't answer. Tears filled his eyes, but he kept his gaze on me. The rain dripped off his beard, and despite his fever, he shivered.

I knelt before my father's cousin. "Please, Uncle Abner, let him come with us. I'll ask David for asylum. David is forgiving, and he will take all of us."

"The children he might countenance, but certainly not your substitute husband." He turned to Ittai and said, "Untie him. Send him back."

When Ittai failed to move, Abner cut Phalti loose. He pointed a sword at him. "Get lost, fool."

Phalti fell to his knees. Anna whimpered. I rushed to his side as he reached for me. "Michal, I can't live without you."

I stroked his beard. "I love you, Phalti. I don't want to leave you."

He wrapped his arms around Anna and me, his huge body wracked with sobs. When Abner pulled Phalti back, I pushed Anna into his arms. "My baby girl, don't forget me."

Phalti stared at me while I backed away, my heart rending into jagged pieces.

Ittai's gentle hands lifted me, an empty shell, into the litter. Phalti's voice caressed me. "Michal, you are the most magnificent woman I know, and I believe you."

He pressed his face into Anna's neck, looked at me, and walked out of my life holding the dearest part of me in his arms.

As we rounded the next bend, I lost sight of them. God had sent Phalti. He protected me when I was most vulnerable. He loved me when I was cold to him. He comforted me when my heart was broken, and he never asked me for anything I did not wish to give. He was the mighty Boaz whom I had asked God for.

CHAPTER 22

Song of Solomon 1:4 Draw me, we will run after thee: the king hath brought me into his chambers: we will be glad and rejoice in thee, we will remember thy love more than wine: the upright love thee.

>>><<<

I raised my eyes as we approached the gates of Hebron. A wintry breeze pricked my cheeks, and my teeth chattered. The towers ahead loomed menacing and bleak. David was the king. What could I have done? How could I live without Phalti and Anna? I closed my eyes and tilted my face to heaven. "I don't know what lies ahead for me. But, God, you have brought me so far. Please grant me courage to face him. Let me find grace in his eyes."

We passed through the palace gates. Joshua and Beraiah had fallen asleep in Ittai's arms, their heads lolling one on each shoulder. Eliah slept tucked in Naomi's arms. Joel and Gaddiel jumped from one leg to the other toward the bushes.

Menservants greeted us and unloaded our belongings. Ittai handed Joshua and Beraiah to me. "My princess, I will inform your king that you have arrived."

I gave him a half-hearted smile. "What am I going to do now? How will I face David when my heart hurts so much?"

"Build yourself a little box and put Phalti inside of it. When you're alone, take him out and look at him. But when you're with David, lock him up. It's the only way." His eyes softened, and he blinked twice before he kissed the sleeping boys.

"Can you check on Phalti and Anna? Send some food and a mule?"

He squeezed my shoulder. "Yes. I should have thought of it. I'll go to Bahurim right away and find them."

My older boys gathered around my legs.

"Eemah, I'm tired."

"I'm hungry."

"Where are we? Where's Abba?"

"Where's Anna? Eemah, did you lose her?"

Eliah held up his chubby arms. "Pick me up."

Joshua and Beraiah woke and squirmed to the ground. I hefted Eliah in my arms and kissed him, hugging him too tightly.

Naomi shushed the children. "Your mother is as tired as you are. Let's go with these nice men. Perhaps they have something for us to eat."

They brought us to a courtyard lined with trees. Several women with their children played in front of a large fountain. They stopped and stared at us.

Joshua and Beraiah ran up to a little boy. "Hi, want to throw rocks?"

The boy laughed, tapped Beraiah on the arm, and ran around the fountain. Before I could restrain them, Joshua jumped into the fountain while Gaddiel clambered up a tree.

Joel hung back. "I'm hungry."

Eliah clung to me when I tried to put him down to corral Joshua. "I want Abba."

Naomi took him, and he threw himself on the ground and screamed for Phalti.

I yanked Joshua out of the fountain. A servant chased Beraiah and collared him. Another managed to coax Gaddiel off the tree with promises of raisin cakes while Naomi wiped Eliah's tears.

Another boy ran by, and Joshua slipped out of my grasp. I stumbled and splashed into the pool of water.

Laughter pealed from the other women, and two of them rushed over, as one body, to my side.

"Oh, you must be the new queen." The long-haired one spoke.

"Somebody, get Joshua." I yelled.

"Oh, leave him. He's having fun. Here, let me help you." A slight, thin woman with chestnut-brown hair and a freckled face held out her hand. "I'm Abigail, David's third wife."

"And I'm Ahinoam, David's second wife," said the walnut-colored beauty with raven black hair. I recognized her as the one on David's sleeping mat.

They both twittered and smiled at me, conspiratorially, like old friends.

"You have probably surmised that I'm Michal." I twisted my lips in a self-deprecating smile which brought another round of soft laughter.

"We remember you from the tent." They giggled as I wrung water out of my robe.

"Don't worry, Michal, you'll get used to it. We all share the same husband." They laughed as if it was the funniest joke.

I mumbled my cordialities at meeting them and excused myself to tend to my children while suppressing another round of despair. I couldn't understand how gleeful they were about sharing a husband. They acted as if it was as natural as growing up in a house with many sisters.

Three more women sauntered around the yard. The haughty woman had to be the Princess of Geshur. Petite, she was a dark beauty, decked in jewelry, her lush, oiled hair flowing down to her waist. The second one sported a crown of flaming red hair. Exceedingly fair, the too-smart look on her face warned me to be wary. Behind her slunk a buxom beauty, blue-eyed and fair with straw colored hair. Young and shy, she blinked her doe-like eyes at me and smiled. *What a collection you have here, David.*

I entered the house they designated for me and found my children sitting on benches at a table. Naomi and the other servants fed them lamb wrapped in flatbread, slices of cheese, grapes and cakes.

I walked into the sitting room, my heart heavy with thoughts of Phalti and Anna. I dreaded my first meeting with David. Could I convince him to let Phalti stay? David was king now. Would he have changed? My heart teetered. I hadn't seen him since the morning I left Gath. He had stood under that olive tree and looked after me. He had loved me then. *Michal, don't forget me. Don't forget this moment, this night. Whatever happens.*

I inhaled sharply, my feelings in turmoil. I had forgotten him, and I had not believed his promise. Thankful that Naomi and the servants took charge of the children, I slumped on the couch. My chest tightened and a lump formed in my throat, making it hard to breathe. *Michal, no matter what, remember my promise.*

* * *

A servant woke me. "King David desires an audience with you, and you have not been prepared."

"But... I'm too tired, exhausted," I said, but the servant looked at me sternly, her matronly looks told me she was in charge.

"Bring your maid, and we'll prepare your bath."

Dazed and groggy, I followed her up a flight of stairs. Naomi trailed behind me.

The room exuded pure luxury with all the trappings of a queen's bedchamber. A new harp, inlayed with gold, stood in one corner. Jewelry, bracelets, necklaces, and earrings lay on a smooth teak table, along with a carved wooden box. Gowns and robes hung on the rack. I ran my fingers through the silks and fingered the furniture. *Oh, David, why did you wait so long?*

A bevy of maidservants descended on me. They twittered like a flock of birds, carrying silks, creams, perfumes, and face paints.

"O Queen, we are at your service." They bowed prettily, regarding me under downcast eyelids, and crowded around me, simpering and chattering with soft, delicate voices.

Gentle, but unfamiliar hands removed my clothes and led me to a warm bath filled with fragrant bubbles. I leaned back and relaxed, marveling at how easily I slipped back into allowing other hands to touch and cleanse me. While I dozed, they smoothed my feet and elbows, massaged my neck and face, and combed and oiled my hair.

One maid dried my hair, and the others paraded around with an orchestra of dazzling robes: vermillion, indigo, silky, brocaded with gold and blue patterns, embroidered with pomegranates, fig leaves and artichokes, trimmed with silver threads and beads. Once, long ago, I had loved clothes and enjoyed dressing and coordinating my apparel. But since my return from Philistia, I wore plain robes and paid little heed to my appearance.

Each maid swung a gown, vying for my attention.

"O Queen, eyes like a cat, how about this peacock silk to set them off?"

"O Queen, your hair as lush as a forest, with this Egyptian linen, more regal than the queen of the Nile you'll be."

"O Queen, your skin, smooth as silk, a dress of cream and honey, to taste of your beauty."

I chose the honey and cream colored outfit and kept my adornments as simple as they'd allow: a few ornaments in my hair, a pair of pearl earrings, golden bracelets, and a single anklet studded with jewels. Without my emerald, the nook between my breasts dangled as empty as my heart.

"O Queen, the royal artificer, Nefertira," said one of the dressing maids as she retreated from my chamber. A woman, painted in the Egyptian style, approached me with a cart of pots. Her eyelids lined with kohl, lashes caked with thick, chunky tar, and a garish green texture under her eyebrows, she swayed her ample hips. Her bright red lips etched over pasty, stretchy skin elongated to reveal long, yellowed teeth.

"I am Nefertira, the royal artificer. I am come to make you fit for a king." Her accent clipped the words around her tippling tongue.

Naomi slunk in the corner with a horrified expression. I shook my head. "With all respect, Nefertira, I would prefer that my handmaid, Naomi, put on my kohl, rouge, and carmine."

Nefertira shot a disdainful look. "But... I do up all the king's women, and you are the most special, for you are the queen." *So I've been informed by this swarm of maids, but not a word from the king.*

"Nefertira, if I'm the queen, you must respect my wishes in this matter. I will not have a face my king would not recognize if I looked exactly like all of his other women, now would I?" My logic rattled her. Mumbling about her art and her skill to spin beauty out of a rat's nest, she bowed and retreated, her servant pushing the cart away.

The sudden silence was a relief. Naomi jumped to my side, and I hugged her with appreciation, laughing at the departed sideshow. Naomi held up a silver mirror and showed me the spectacle of my hair, dress, and jewelry. Even my mother, as queen, had not the extravagance David had just showered upon me.

Naomi went to work on my makeup, a little cream to smooth my skin, some eyeliner, not obvious, a bit of rouge on my cheeks, and color to my lips. A dusting of jasmine powder in my hair completed my preparation.

* * *

My window faced away from the courtyard and gave me a glimpse of the street below. Soldiers marched around the compound, messengers scurried to finish their deliveries, and serving girls hoisted water jugs.

A young man strolled around the corner with a little girl on his shoulders. She tickled his nose with a bouquet of flowers. He sneezed right under my window, set her down on a wall and handed her a piece of candy, taking the flowers in exchange. Her mouth stuffed with candy, she squealed and pouted for the flowers. How could he resist? He gave her the flowers as they walked away. The lump grew in my throat, and I dabbed tears with a handkerchief.

Raising my eyes, I spied him immediately. David. My stomach jittered with the wings of a butterfly colony, and my heart scattered like a flock of startled birds. I grasped the edge of the windowsill, astounded at the effect he still had on me. David walked in a fast pace, straight and confident. He gestured and gave instructions to the men attending him.

An insistent knock later, a messenger uttered, "Behold, the king."

My hand clapped over my chest, and my breath snatched in my throat. I stepped back from the window, my pulse galloping off a cliff. How would he receive me? Would he still care?

Not a moment later, David crossed the threshold. Changed, unbearably handsome and regal, he strode in, a conqueror, and clasped me in his arms. His face broke with a warm smile. My head reeled even as my tearful cheeks simmered.

For several long moments, I stared at him, not believing this moment had finally arrived. No words came from my mouth, just a small choking gasp I quickly swallowed. I was struck by the lines on his face and his darkened beard. The scar beneath his left eye quivered when I whispered his name.

He covered my forehead with a kiss. "How was the journey? I hope you are well rested."

"It went well, my lord. Thank you." Breathlessly, I looked into his sensuous eyes, searching for my past. His touch invigorated and stirred me in a wonderful but forgotten way.

"And the children? How are they?"

"As well as can be, I suppose." I lowered my gaze, a twinge of guilt surfaced at the thought of Anna and Phalti.

He leaned forward and stroked my hair. "Ittai gave me a full report." He added in a soft voice, "It must have been hard for you."

I closed my eyes, took a deep breath, and suppressed the damp heaviness in my heart. I would not let David see me weak. When I looked up, his eyes were warm and sympathetic.

He hugged me while the servants set the table. The aroma of my favorite dish, sea bass steamed in a sauce blended with chopped cilantro, chili, garlic, lemon, and cumin permeated the room. They lit the candles and poured goblets of golden wine, laid out rows of fruit, cheese and cakes, and departed as silently as they arrived.

David offered me some wine.

I waved it away, feeling shy and homesick as a sob escaped my pressed lips. He lifted my chin and stroked my cheek, awakening a glow that fought the clouds inside of me. "I fetched you as soon as I could, as I promised."

His smile was sweet like a three-year-old's. "Do you see me, Michal, as I was from the window ledge?"

And I did. So many nights, I had fought to hold the image of him at the window I lowered him from. So many nights, I prayed for him and asked God to bring him back to me. So many nights, I lay awake in bed, desiring him. *Oh, David, how I waited.*

But, lately—instead of the window, there was the road—the road at Bahurim where Phalti looked back with Anna. *How could I forget him who had loved me in my distress, gave me safety in my sorrow?*

I lowered my face to the crock of David's neck, missing the warmth of Phalti's broad chest. "I can't do this."

We stood in silence many moments, his fingers stroking circles over my shoulders. "Michal, I missed you so much. I used to stand on top of a rock and gaze into the night sky and picture you at your window calling to me."

"I missed you, too." My voice quavered. "I found your notes in Jonathan's leather tube."

"Then you know I cared." He lifted my chin and kissed my cheeks. And when our lips met, anger, pain, and sorrow melted as tenderly as the embraces of a tiny child with kisses as gentle as the downy fuzz on a newborn's scalp.

"Your father can't keep us apart now," he whispered as he nibbled behind my ear. "I've waited so long."

I couldn't speak. My feelings tumbled as an avalanche down a steep slope. Each boulder echoed Phalti or Anna's name in my ear. What kind of mother was I? What kind of wife?

CHAPTER 23

Job 5:18 For he maketh sore, and bindeth up: he woundeth, and his
hands make whole.

>>><<<

Hazy sunlight filtered through the window. I reached for Phalti before remembering where I was and drew the cover over my head. The side David had slept on was still warm with the scent of sandalwood and musk. He'd held me all night, comforting me, but did not push.

I wiped a tear from my face. How had Anna and Phalti fared in the rain last night? Anna's chubby hands, Phalti's gentle smile, her sweet dimples, his loving arms. Would David let me see them?

Oh, God. A man after Your heart would have mercy, wouldn't he?

David returned in the afternoon and ruffled the sheets. "You still in bed? Are you ready to meet the rest of my family?"

I shut my eyes. "We left Phalti and Anna in the rain, and I'm worried about them."

"Ittai's taken a couple of guards to escort them. They'll be fine." He kissed my temple. "I'm just glad to have you again."

After waiting for the maids to dress me, he led me down a corridor to the courtyard. All chattering stopped as we approached.

"Women," David said, "this is Michal, my wife. I've brought her back as I vowed, and she will be my queen." A sudden chill stiffened the atmosphere.

One by one, he introduced them. "This is Ahinoam, the Jezreelitess, and our firstborn son, Amnon. Abigail, wife of Nabal the Carmelite, and our little Chileab, born only a few days after Amnon." The women waved with their fingers and smiled.

David wiggled his finger at a petite woman. "Maacah, will you come here?"

189

The sultry woman tilted her chin and swayed toward us, the bells on her skirt tinkling. My eyes narrowed. This was the princess and she looked like trouble.

David smiled indulgently. "This is Maacah, the daughter of Talmai, king of Geshur. Where's Absalom by the way?"

Maacah pointed a pouty lip at him, wiggled her shoulders and went off to look for him. David seemed too proud of himself. I ground my teeth as unobtrusively as I could, aware his other wives watched me.

Joshua chased a boy about three years old. The boy screamed at the top of his lungs, his long, wavy hair bouncing in the breeze.

David laughed. "Maacah, you should keep an eye on your son."

Maacah jutted her lower lip at him and shot me a nasty glare. She swept Absalom into her arms, as if Joshua bore a loathsome disease, and handed him to David.

David swung the child over his head and bounced him in the air. The boy squealed with delight, and I could not miss the proud, happy gleam in David's eyes. A lump pressed my throat. He would have loved Samuel as much, if not more. A sudden lack of air seized my lungs, and I squeezed my arms to keep from sighing.

David put the toddler down and gestured in back of me. "Here are Haggith and Abital. They're new here, gifts from my latest allies."

The redhead and the blonde smiled and nodded, both quite young and with child, one further along than the other.

I looked to David for reassurance as he led me from his troop of wives, but my heart sank when he told me he had a meeting with his generals. "Make yourself at home. I'll expect you at dinner in two hours."

He conferred me with a kiss that hung in the air.

As he turned to leave, all the women's gazes clung to him, faces full of adoration. Maacah crossed paths with him purposely, dangling Absalom across her hips. David's glance darted to her, bringing a seductive smile to her heavily made-up face. When he passed the threshold, Ahinoam ran her hand over the sleeve of his robe and whispered in his ear. He gave her a throaty chuckle and pecked her on the cheek. Pressing Abigail's hand, he kissed her and fluffed her hair. She giggled; a flush of pleasure pinked her face.

So, this was how it would be. He'd have women fawning over him, praying for a wink or a nod, perhaps a word, maybe a smile, hoping in the evening there'd be a knock on their door, and David would deign to spend a few minutes with the fortunate one.

A chill closed over my heart. I disdained his wives and their obsequiousness. I would never be caught looking after David with such pathetic longing and desire. I marched back to my bedchamber alone.

An intricately carved sandalwood box sat on the table, a gift from David. An eight-armed pregnant goddess, surrounded by vines intertwined with peacocks, beckoned from the lid. I opened the box. A pungent scent reminiscent of cedar wood mixed with spices and earth greeted me. Strong like Phalti. Warm like his heart. I kissed the box. A tear dropped in and wet the wood. *Phalti, when I think of you, I'll catch my tears in here. And someday, I will bring this box with me and be your wife again. Anna, my darling little girl, forgive me for leaving you, but I shall be back soon.* I put my head on the table, oblivious of the time, not caring if I missed David and dinner with his bevy of delightful wives.

* * *

I dreamed of Phalti and woke with a heavy, monstrous millstone on my chest. I wheezed and coughed at the side of the bed. I should've thrown myself on the ground and refused to leave. I should've escaped with Phalti, risked death, maybe gone to Egypt or beyond. My heart and arms ached for Anna.

What kind of mother was I to give her up?

Naomi brought my boys for breakfast. I dried my tears and spent the rest of the morning playing with them, but I refused to unpack my belongings. Once David had no more need of me, I'd ask him to send me back to Mahanaim.

David visited with stick ponies, leather balls and wooden swords for my sons. They jumped in delight with their new toys and ran to the courtyard with a pair of manservants.

"What nice boys." David looked after them. "I missed you last night." He kissed my cheek. "Were you not hungry?"

I bowed my head. "No, not hungry, my lord."

"You miss your daughter, don't you?"

"Yes. I'm sorry. I can't talk about this." I studied the brocaded border on his robe and wished he would go away.

"You did a brave and noble thing. I'm not sure I could have let Phaltiel stay. Well, I'm sure he made it back to Mahanaim just fine."

He mentioned Phalti's name so casually, as if he were a pet mule and not the sweet, wonderful man I loved. I gripped my elbows and took a deep breath. "I have a headache."

David lifted my chin and caressed the side of my head. "Would you like some willow tea?"

I shook my head, and he led me to the couch.

"I missed you so much. Are you happy to be here?" A smile beamed on his charming face.

191

My lips trembled. I could not lie. David wrapped his arms around me and kissed my cheek. He held me for a long moment, tracing a finger over my face from my temple to my cheekbone, around my ear and down my jaw and back again. His amber eyes solemn and glistening, he kissed each tear that trailed down my face. "I never forgot you. When Abner sent me a message, I refused to meet him until you were restored to me."

My chest tightened. "Why did you take so long? You asked me to wait in Israel, yet you took more wives instead of coming for me."

His eyes dipped beneath golden-tipped brown lashes. "I only took them as political gifts and to make alliances. Besides, your uncle and brother sought to kill me."

"And me? Am I also a political gift?"

A pained look crossed his brow. "No, you're my wife."

One among many. "What do you want from me? Is it the kingdom? Allegiance from the eleven tribes?"

He tightened his grip. "I want you restored to me. Don't you want to be back?"

"I don't know. I had a family, and you've torn it apart. I had—"

"Michal, look at me. I'm your family, your husband."

My heart clenched. If only Samuel had lived and he'd kept me instead of taking those other women. "You have your wives and your sons. Once you are anointed king over all of Israel, please send me and my boys back to Mahanaim. We don't belong here."

"You're going to be my queen. It's what we dreamed about."

"I don't want to be queen. I just want to…" A torrent of grief and pain tossed my heart and slammed it against my ribcage. I hid my face in my hands. How I missed Phalti, my gentle husband who loved only me.

"You'll have to put him behind you." David raised his voice. "He agreed with Jonathan and Elihu to look after you without defiling you. But he took advantage of you. Joab told me to kill him—"

Raw fear congealed in my gut. "No. Don't. Please don't." I grabbed his robe. "If you hurt Phalti, I'll never forgive you. Never."

He pried my fingers off him. "If I wanted to kill him, he'd be dead already. But as for your daughter, I'll send Ittai to fetch her."

"Can't you let Phalti live here, too? Can't you take him as a scribe?"

David's face turned red. "No. I've rewarded him well for taking care of you. Did you ever wonder why he married you? Jonathan paid him to act as your husband, so your father wouldn't marry you to Doeg. How do you think he obtained that house, the livestock and vineyard? He, whose ink-stained hands didn't have two pieces of silver to rub together."

"Stop it. Stop talking." I screamed. My chest heaved with pain. Each sob drove needles deeper into my heart. "He loved me. He wasn't paid to do that."

"And did you love him? Did you?"

"Yes." I covered my face. "Yes, I did. And you broke my heart when you ripped me from his side."

David threw the table over, knocking the water jugs and breaking the plates. "Why do you have to ruin everything for me?"

I gripped my knees and rocked on the couch, pangs of grief stabbing my insides. Ruin everything for him? What about Phalti, and Anna, and my family? "Do you not understand how I feel?"

He gaped at me, clenching and unclenching his fists. "How could you lose your heart like this? Why didn't you wait for me?"

"I did wait. But now it's too late."

David ran toward the door, then turned and returned to my side. "I'll give you time, Michal. I promise you. You'll love me again. You will. You have to."

* * *

David invited me and my sons to dine with him that evening. Not wanting to embarrass him, I allowed Nefertira and her crew to prepare me. Ittai returned with my excited sons who tugged and bounced around him. He winked at me and departed after prying Joshua and Beraiah from his legs.

"Eemah, Uncle Ittai gave me a real knife." Joel grinned as he pointed to the sheathed knife on his belt.

"I want one, too." Gaddiel whined.

Joshua and Beraiah ran circles around me, kicking a leather ball. "Eemah, play ball."

Eliah wanted to be picked up. He hugged me with his chubby arms. "Where's Anna? Where's Abba?"

David entered after a servant announced him. He handed candy to the boys and rubbed their heads. "Are you going to introduce these fine boys?"

I clapped my hands and ordered them to be still. Joel and Gaddiel stood at attention, but Eliah clung to me, and Joshua ran to David and stared at him. Beraiah tucked a thumb in his mouth and hid his face in my skirt.

"Joel is the eldest. He's ten about to turn eleven." Joel bowed to David.

"Ah, I remember you at our wedding. You were just a tiny baby." Recalling Merab and Adriel, so young and alive, with baby Joel tightened my throat.

"And this is Gaddiel, he's eight. He was just a toddler when I escaped from Gath. And next is Eliah, who's seven."

Gaddiel bowed obediently, but Eliah grabbed my skirts when I put him down and picked up Beraiah.

David bent down and handed Eliah a honey cake. "Don't be frightened of me. I don't bite." He turned to the twins. "And you two. How old are you?"

Joshua stuck his hand out. "More candy, Uncle David. Candy."

A servant handed Joshua a honeyed sesame stick. David looked confused when Joshua gave him a hug and grabbed his crown, tilting it to the side. Joshua giggled and squealed.

"You're a little rascal. How old are you?" David asked.

Joshua held up five fingers. "We born the same day, but he the baby." He pointed at Beraiah who hid his face in my breast.

David tweaked his cheek and rubbed his hair. "You're a handsome boy, Joshua. You must have gotten your dark looks from your grandfather Saul."

David took Beraiah from my arms. "You are so cute." Beraiah stuck a thumb in his mouth and stared at him wide-eyed. "You and me are going to be best friends. I was also the youngest son of my family, and my hair was just like yours." He looked at Beraiah and back at me.

A smile crept onto his face as he kissed Beraiah and rubbed his head. "Were you pregnant when I saw you in Gath?"

I swallowed, thinking about Samuel, our baby. "No. No, I wasn't pregnant, at least not when I first arrived."

He set Beraiah down, who promptly ran off with Joshua. "Are you saying I got you pregnant?" He took my hand.

I nodded and cringed inside, taking a deep breath to tell him about Samuel.

Before I could speak, David kissed me full on the mouth. "Oh, Michal. You don't know how I wished to have sons with you."

"I… uh… They're…" I couldn't speak. How I had wished the same thing. My heart twisted and turned as the ever-present void left by Samuel throbbed in my chest.

His smile lit his entire face. "They are so precious. Joshua looks like your father, and Beraiah looks like mine. And they're my eldest sons. You've made me so happy."

* * *

When it was time for dinner, David asked Naomi to bring the twins to his side, seating Joshua on his right hand and Beraiah at his left. With one arm around Joshua and the other around Beraiah, David bent his head to pray. "Dear LORD, thank You for bringing my wife back to me. You've blessed us with this fine set of boys and have given me two sons, Joshua and Beraiah. You've loved me and favored me, LORD, and delivered me from my enemies. I praise You for remembering Your servant. In Your name from whom all blessings flow, LORD."

David's words brought tears to my eyes, yet my heart skittered. How could I live this lie and not let David know his son had died? He was overjoyed, laughing and making jokes with the boys. I couldn't help but smile as I pictured him as the sweet, rambunctious boy he must have been.

One by one, the boys fell asleep. Naomi picked them up, and I tucked them to bed. David stood at the door of my bedchamber, waiting.

He took my arm. "You're a wonderful mother. I love seeing you with your children. And I'm sorry about Anna, I truly am."

"You don't have to be sorry. You're the king."

He hugged me. "But I'm still a man—a man who loves you very much."

My heart agonized with a sour weight. How could I let him believe this lie?

"I'm not sure how to explain…" I began.

He kissed me before I could finish. "Then let me. Now that you've given me sons, there is nothing in the world that'll stop me from loving you, ever."

He swung me in his arms and pulled me to the bed. "You've made me the happiest man in the world. I'm your David, always yours, and you're mine, always mine."

"You want me again? As your wife?"

"Yes." He moved forward imperceptibly, waiting for me to close the gap. Something drew me, a faint stirring of affection, memories, the thread of a song. And the realization embedded itself into my heart. I had never stopped loving him.

His gaze fastened on me. I sank willingly into his embrace and kissed him. He responded slowly, almost languidly, crumbling the clods of my despair, replacing them with a sweet, comforting sensation. My tongue danced with his; the deepening kiss loosened the constricting bands from my heart, muting the ache.

"Touch me." He held my hands as I became reacquainted with the contours of his sculpted body. His hands wandered over my belly and hips and peeled the silks and linen off me before cupping my breasts. Tingles ignited and heat pooled between my thighs as my body churned with the memory of our marriage bed.

Instinct replaced restraint, and I tasted him, licking the slightly salty skin, nibbling his chest, and nuzzling my face to the velvety skin below his waist. His scent enticed and aroused me. My hands traced remembered pathways, and my fingers closed and gripped him, stoking the fires of desire that singed me from head to toe. And I suddenly had a deep longing, a maddening need to have him fill me and love me, until I had forgotten my very name.

In a single motion, David swung me on top of him and impaled the secret spot deep inside of me, causing me to shiver in fountains of pure delight. My entire body tightened and clenched, not letting go, not ever wanting to release him.

"Keep your eyes open," he said, "I want to look into your soul."

He caressed between my legs and brought me to such heights of bliss that I struggled to open my eyes. An eruption of sparks rose deep within and showered over my shoulders and chest. As I fell from the heights, his eyes darkened first, sharpened intensely, and relaxed as he exhaled in satisfaction.

We lay there in the moonlight, our fingers entwined, our damp bodies enveloped in the silken embrace of the bed sheets. David pulled a coverlet over my shoulders and kissed the back of my neck. "Where's the emerald I gave you?"

"I left it with my daughter. I couldn't leave Phalti bereft." My voice choked.

He cradled my head and caressed my shoulders.

"For a long time that pendant gave me hope, faith that we'd be together again." I tried to explain, but his mouth pressed on mine, nibbling, sucking, and then jockeying with my tongue.

Heat built again, this time slower and more gradually. I tasted him, salty and tangy, the edgy scent of his loving and the memory of what he could do to me tugged me into the pleasure of his hands. They explored me, fingering and arousing me until he completed me again with joy unspeakable, cascading over and above the cries of my renewal.

CHAPTER 24

Isaiah 40:2 Speak ye comfortably to Jerusalem, and cry unto her, that her warfare is accomplished, that her iniquity is pardoned: for she hath received of the LORD's hand double for all her sins.

>>><<<

A few weeks later Uncle Abner returned in triumph after conferring with the elders of the eleven remaining tribes of Israel. David prepared a feast to celebrate the union of Israel and the ending of the civil war.

He seated me in a position of honor at his right hand. Uncle Abner sat on the other side of him. I was uncomfortable and hot under layers of clothing and jewelry and makeup and decorum. A jewel encrusted crown encircled my head, a little too tightly, but I acted my part. My father would have been proud.

David raised his goblet for a toast. "Today, the house of David and the house of Saul are united. We will have peace between brethren. Together we shall defeat all of our enemies, starting with the Philistines."

The crowd cheered and stomped their feet in approbation.

David waited until they quieted. His face glowed as he presented me to his court. "Michal, my queen, my wife and daughter of Saul."

He held my hand and lifted it, accepting the cheers and accolades of his people. He wore Jonathan's ring.

After many toasts and speeches by various dignitaries, Abner proclaimed to David, "I will arise and gather all Israel unto my lord, the king."

He bowed low, and David sent him in peace, then took my arm and walked with me out of the hall. I kept my gaze averted from the women's table where his five other wives sat.

"My queen." David swung me over the threshold and kicked the door shut. He laid me on a gilded bed, soft with wool, laden with silks, perfumed with sandalwood and dusted with myrrh.

He removed my crown and fluffed out my hair. "Are you happy?"

I hesitated, yet he looked so expectant that I mumbled, "Yes, I am." Visions of Anna bouncing and giggling blurred my eyes with tears.

"I'm glad." He leaned in and kissed me tenderly. "Because today, our dreams came true. I will be king of all Israel, and you, my dear, are my queen. Didn't I say I would keep my promise?"

I opened my lips to reply, but he captured me with his mouth. I took in his musky, sandalwood fragrance and blinked back tears. The image of Abner and my betrayal of Phalti saddened my heart. *I* was the price to be paid for a united Israel.

David's eyes were closed, but he drew back at my lack of response. He stroked my temple. "You did well this evening, and you made me proud. You can relax now."

I squirmed out of his arms. "Then help me get out of these heavy robes and clean my face."

Closing my eyes, I let David's gentle hands remove the layers of powder, kohl, malachite, carmine and rouge that Nefertira had caked on me. He stopped at the top of my left eye. "Did you know you have a little scar? A cut? I can see it only when you close your eyes."

"Then I shall keep my eyes closed for you. So you can see how scarred my heart is."

"Are you still thinking about them?" His voice scratched with irritation.

I covered my face. "How can I not? Do you know what it's like to be torn from your daughter?" I didn't remind him of Phalti, although I still ached for him.

David was silent for a moment. "I know what it's like to be torn from you. I know what it's like to have my heart ripped from my chest when I thought you'd forgotten me. And right now, I know what it's like to have a wife who loves another man."

He shoved the basin of water onto the floor.

Hot anger flushed my chest. "You did all these to me. And not with one woman, but five."

"Do you know who I am?" he shouted. "I am the king of Israel. Is a king to be treated with disdain from his queen?"

"I don't want to be your queen. You have five other wives. Why me?"

He gripped my shoulders. "Because you're the wife of my covenant. And you're mine. Mine!"

"No, I'm not yours. You're so arrogant. You think you can order me around because you're the king?"

"You have my sons. You will stay and be my queen."

Guilt and frustration battled. I pushed him and jutted my chin. "They're not your sons. I lied to you." My voice jabbed to hurt him.

His face blanched before reddening. "You're lying right now. You can't hide anything from me. I read your face when you told me I had gotten you pregnant. That was real."

His words tore the scar on my heart, and the familiar, lingering pain cut through my chest. My false bravado turned into real sobs. I crumbled on the bed and hid my face on the pillow. Yes, Samuel was real, too, too real.

David pulled on a cloak and slammed the door.

* * *

I wasn't prepared for the events that closely followed David's coronation. The curse struck the house of Saul again. David's treacherous nephew Joab ambushed and murdered my uncle Abner by pretending to deliver a message from David. They buried him with much fanfare, yet Joab walked free.

A week later, while I played with my boys in the yard, Haggith ran by screaming.

"I saw them at the courthouse." Her grey eyes bulged, and her breathing was ragged.

"Saw what? Haggith, calm down." Abigail patted her shoulder. "And what were you doing near the courthouse?"

Haggith collapsed on the floor, her eyes turned back in their sockets, and saliva dribbled from her mouth. She writhed so hard I thought she'd go into labor. I bent over her to check her womb. Still soft. Not labor pains.

Abigail yelled for Ahinoam to bring a spindle. "She's having another seizure."

They forced open her mouth and shoved in the spindle. Haggith gagged, and in a few minutes she sat up, dazed. Little bits of dirt and twigs entangled her red hair. She lowered her head and cried.

David stepped into the courtyard with a grim expression. He stared at me in a way that selected me for bad news. "Come with me."

Naomi and Abigail gathered the boys while Ahinoam helped Haggith back to her apartment.

"What is it?" I tugged his sleeve. "What has happened?"

He put a finger on my lips. "Just come with me."

"Is it Phalti? Anna? Are they all right?"

"They're fine." He led me up the spiral stairs and sat with me on the couch. "It's your brother, Ishbaal. He's dead."

"Ishby! No… no-o! How can it be? I thought you protected him." My teeth chattered and grief welled in my eyes.

David held me tightly. "I did. But I didn't count on two men plotting to ingratiate themselves to me by killing the last son of Saul."

"You mean your guards killed him?" I pushed him hard. "David!"

"They were Ishby's men. I've executed them already. They're hanging over the pool near the courtroom."

I recoiled at the horror of my brother's death following so close to Abner's. Even though Abner and I did not get along, he was still a member of my family and my father's chief commander.

"But, David, if they're hanging, why does Joab walk free? Joab ambushed Abner under false pretenses."

David rubbed his hair and clasped his face. "Michal, alas, the sons of Zeruiah are too hard for me. Although I'm anointed king, I'm weak. The LORD shall reward the doer of evil according to his wickedness."

"What do you mean they're too hard for you? Since when is murder winked at? My father executed all murderers. Do you allow your nephew to commit murder, yet you execute two strangers?"

David's eyes narrowed. "Wife, I thought to comfort you concerning your brother. But I see you care more to meddle in the affairs of my kingdom. My word is law here."

"Wrong. God's Word is Law."

"A law you obviously didn't follow when you lay with Phaltiel."

"I? I? What about you and all your wives?"

"It's not the same," he said. "A man is allowed more than a single wife. What woman in Israel has more than one husband?"

I put my hands on my hips and pushed up against him. "I am that woman. Because of your neglect, I now have two husbands."

"You talk like a crazy woman. I have a busy afternoon. Grieve for your brother, but don't expect me tonight." He strode out the door and slammed it.

Oh, Ishby, my dear brother, my brother, the happy prince. Why hadn't you come with me and stayed under David's protection? Panic clutched my throat. Phalti and Anna must have been in the palace when Ishbaal was killed.

I glanced at the courtyard from my window. Ittai played with Joshua and Beraiah. I willed him to look at me, but he continued to play, fetching a small rawhide ball and rolling it back to them. Ishby used to play with my boys. Ishby, who only wanted to be a boy and stay a boy—Ishby, my sweet, simple brother, born with a club foot and a big heart.

I sank on the windowsill and wept.

* * *

The door opened with a knock, and a servant set a platter of food on the table. I muttered my appreciation and was about to shut the door when a bronzed hand grabbed the frame.

Ittai slipped in. "David just told me. I see you're mourning."

"I'm in a perpetual state of mourning."

Ittai cradled me in his arms and rocked me, whispering sweet words in my ears. "Is there anything I can do for you? Ask me anything."

"Can you see that Phalti, Anna, Rizpah and her two sons are protected? Go there and assure me they are safe."

"Yes, I'll go right away and take a contingent of my hand-picked guards and place them there. Is there anything else?" His eyes glinted, and he kissed my hand before moving to my lips.

I pushed him sharply. "No, Ittai. No more. I have vowed to keep myself for David alone."

David was right. I was his wife, and even though he infuriated me, I still owed him loyalty and allegiance.

Ittai closed his eyes and placed my hand on his bearded cheek. He turned his lips and grazed them across my palm, open mouthed with a hint of his tongue. I withdrew my hand from his grasp and rubbed it as if it contained a coiled snake.

"I shall do as you request." His lips tightened to a thin line, and he tilted his head markedly to the left and then the right, his joints popping. With lowered eyelids, he went to the door. He turned for one last look before he shut the door quietly.

* * *

David did not return to our bedchamber until the end of the middle watch, deep in the night, smelling like bergamot. I made room in the bed for him and turned my back. Bitter to swallow, but at least he crawled back to me every night and kept me company.

"Did I wake you?" He cradled me from the back, wafting the citrusy scent over me.

"No. I couldn't sleep thinking about my losses. My father, mother, Jonathan, Merab, Melchishua, Ishui, Ishbaal, Abner, Elihu, Adriel. All I've been doing is mourning. And when I finally get over mourning one set of people, another set die, and I mourn all over again."

Samuel, centered in my heart, remained unspoken.

"I'm sorry, darling." He rubbed my shoulders. "Half of my family has died, too. When I came to my kingdom, the first thing I did was go to Moab to fetch my parents." His voice caught in his throat.

I shivered and shut my eyes. Poor David.

"They would have been proud of me. Michal, if your father hadn't driven them away. They were so old…" He sobbed. "I never found their bones. I… never… found… their… bones."

My heart pinched, and chills sprinkled my scalp. David's sweet mother and father were buried in unmarked graves, far from home. I turned and clasped his hands. "Oh, David. It's all my fault. If you hadn't married me. If you had only stayed away, they'd be here now."

"Don't blame yourself. I desired you the moment I laid eyes on you."

I kissed the tears off his face. "And I wanted nothing but to love you and be the wife you should have."

He met my eyes. "Then you don't hate me?"

I stroked his cropped beard. "I could never hate you."

His smile was as sweet as a child with a honey-cake. "If your father hadn't hated me, we could have been happy together—the way God intended—a man to cleave to his wife and the two shall be one." He put my hand on his heart. "My heart for yours, Michal."

"And mine for yours." I embraced him, the bergamot scent mingled with my jasmine.

"Flesh of my flesh."

"Bone of my bone."

"Two in body."

"One in spirit."

CHAPTER 25

Psalm 127:3 Lo, children are an heritage of the LORD: and the fruit of the womb is his reward.

>>><<<

"Found another one." I laughed. Dust motes danced in the morning light streaming through our window.

"Ouch," David yelped. "Do you have to pull them all out?" He shoved a goat-hair pillow at me.

I thumped it back at him. "Did you know I used one of these to fool my father?"

"No joking?" He laid his head back on it and kicked up his knees.

"Its hair was as scruffy as yours. I placed it on top of the cedar Asherah pole, put a blanket over it, and they thought you were sleeping in the bed, dead as a log."

"You mean the idol your father's mysterious woman friend gave us?"

Veiled from head to toe, the woman had attended our wedding and greeted me with only a squeeze of a hand. "I wonder who she was."

"Perhaps she was a war captive he fell in love with, or maybe the witch of Endor." David wriggled his fingers in a spooky manner.

I didn't like the direction of the conversation. "I wonder what happened to the idol after my father stabbed it."

"Firewood?" David laid his head in my lap. "Try and find another one."

My fingers filtered through his thick hair, sun burnished copper, mixed with cedar and chestnut hues.

"Here's another one." I held it out to him.

He slapped my hand playfully. "It's golden, Michal. See how it's tinted?"

"It's hard to tell with the sun shining so brightly. It looked white to me."

"You're cheating. I won't count it. Seven kisses and not a strand more." He cupped my face in both hands and kissed me seven times.

* * *

I sat with Jehiel, my sons' tutor, in the scroll room and went over their lessons.

Jehiel handed me a parchment. "Joel is a bright lad. Here's a copy of the Ten Commandments written in his own hand."

The writing was smooth and precise. I smiled faintly even as my chest rose in pride. Merab would be gratified.

"And Gaddiel, he's just starting. Sometimes he daydreams. He's frustrated that he can't keep up with Joel."

"I'll speak to him about paying attention. He's a good boy, but sensitive. Perhaps we can find something he'll excel in over Joel. Maybe music. Can you arrange for someone to teach him how to play the harp? I can even play duets with him."

"That's an excellent idea," Jehiel said. "And Eliah. He's still young. We're reading stories to him. His favorite is David and Goliath."

We both laughed.

"Now the twins…" A loud clap on the table startled me. Ittai flopped down next to me.

"Go ahead," he said, "I wish to hear about my two most favorite boys."

"Ittai," I said, "are Phalti and Anna well?"

Jehiel cleared his throat. "O Queen. I will find you another day. Joshua and Beraiah are simply delightful boys." He bowed and departed.

Ittai clasped my hands and grinned. "I'm glad to be back. I missed you and your boys."

"I missed you, too. You never fail to make me laugh. So how are Phalti and Anna?"

"They are doing well. They miss you, of course, but I told them you were being well cared for. Phaltiel let me hug Anna and ride her on top of my shoulders. She's so rambunctious, calling for more, more, more. She tired me out. She was so cute. I imagined you must have been a lot like her."

My eyes moistened, and a scratch caught in my throat. "Did she ask for me?"

"Phaltiel tells me she cried for you every night for the first week. But he would dangle the gem and swing it back and forth and she'd stop. Now I think she's happier. Rizpah…" His voice snagged, and he coughed.

"What about Rizpah?" My heart squeezed, alerted.

204

"She watches over Anna. I hope you don't mind. Rizpah claims she always wanted a daughter, but sadly your father died before she could bear one."

"Is she…" I stopped. What right did I have to question Phalti's personal life?

Ittai shifted on the bench. "She seems jumpy around men in general. One time, I came around the corner and almost bumped into her. She must have jumped fifty feet and shook like she saw the devil."

I pinched Ittai's cheekbone. "I can see the resemblance. But does she seem apprehensive around Phalti?"

"No, they're good friends. Phalti would never hurt even a grasshopper. Perhaps it's only men of war she's afraid of."

"Yes. Perhaps." I remarked drily. Inside, my stomach lurched, and a dull ache settled under my ribcage.

Ittai lifted my hand and pressed it to his lips. "Anything else you wish me to do?"

"What would I do without you? Can you give me regular reports?"

"You'll never be without me. I'll keep you apprised, and don't you worry. They will be safe."

* * *

David and I walked hand in hand through the budding forests surrounding Hebron. "I will be gone the next month to prepare my troops. It is time to push the Philistines out of our territory."

I stroked his beard and hugged him. "I agree, but will you be safe?"

"Isha, don't spend all your time worrying about me."

"I'll miss you too much."

We walked around the base of a huge oak; the trunk must have been two and a half cubits in diameter and the canopy spread as wide as a shrine.

David put his arm around my waist. "Abraham met angels under this tree. Let's kneel and pray."

The soft spongy litter of leaves and nut caps cushioned our knees. "Oh, LORD God," he prayed, "our land has been at war, divided and invaded. Grant us this day the fortitude to reclaim it from the Philistines. Let me start in the land of Benjamin, in Gibeah, where the Ark of the Covenant lies. Grant us victory to restore this land to Your glory and reclaim the Ark. Bless us with Your presence in a united Israel. And bless my union with my wife, Michal, daughter of Saul. Give me, I pray, another son, an heir who will join the house of Saul and the house of David in perpetual and undivided peace. In Your name, LORD."

I stood, and he remained kneeling at my side, his arms around my hips and his face pressed to my belly. A reverential silence descended amongst the heavy multi-tiered branches. Save for the slight rustling of the leaves, no birds chirped and no animals scuttled. Tears streamed down my face and anointed his hair. David's prayer touched me deeply. I would never grieve him and tell him about Samuel.

We returned to our bedchamber, and David asked me to trim his hair and beard to prepare him for war. He lay in a tub of warm water and closed his eyes. His hair had grown long over the winter, hanging down to his shoulders. I cut it all off, pulling and clipping to one finger's width. The beard proved to be trickier. Whereas the Philistines simply shaved with a razor, our men believed it an abomination to appear shaven: like men wearing women's clothing. I lay the shears on its side and clipped small patches until his entire beard stood like a shadow the width of a blade of the shears. I hummed a Philistine love song. David had fallen asleep with his head in my arms. Wet, his hair appeared browner than red; his beard and eyebrows were definitely darker than the copper curls lying on the floor.

I propped him up and took a washcloth and a piece of soap. Sponging the cloth over his body, I ran my fingers over his hard chest and the muscles that strung his shoulders. David opened his eyes and focused intently on me. "Maybe God will answer my prayer tonight. Take off your clothes."

My gown and robe pooled at my feet as I stepped into the tub. Our bodies slid together, slippery with soap. We joined in perfect harmony and tempo, mounting a crescendo of chords to a summit of pleasure, erupting in tremors and blessed release.

* * *

I settled with my harp under an olive tree. Young Abital, David's sixth wife, fluttered, birdlike to my side. Her pregnant belly appeared halfway to term, and her usually pale face glowed bright pink. She smiled through straw-colored eyelashes.

"May I touch it?" she asked.

"Certainly." I handed the harp to her and helped her balance it in her lap. She plucked a few strings. Her girlish smile dimpled her cheeks on both sides.

"My mother had a stringed instrument. It laid flat on her lap and she pushed the strings over little quills to make it sound differently. I wish she had taught me to play before she died."

"I'm sorry to hear that. Where are you from and how old are you?"

She handed the harp back to me. "When my half-brother was born, my father traded me for a side of beef. The trader brought me here. I come from a land where ice covers the earth for half a year, and the other half of the year, the sun never goes down."

"Is that possible? Why would the sun never set?"

"I don't know, but that is how it was in our land. I don't know how old I am. The trader didn't ask my father, and the man who bought me kept me several years as a daughter. When he thought I was old enough, he gave me to your husband and guaranteed my virginity, the only thing that mattered."

"Well, that must have made my husband happy," I said.

"He's a nice man." She blushed becomingly. "He only touched me once. And after that, he told me I was too young and has left me alone. He doesn't beat me like my father beat my mother, and he gives me lots of goodies to eat. He even gave me a white bird. Would you like to see?"

"Sure." I put my harp down. Joshua ran by chasing Absalom.

"Joshua." I called and ran after him. "Joshua."

Absalom tackled his mother's legs and squirted around her so fast that Joshua ran into her. Maacah, Absalom's mother, grabbed Joshua by the hair and threw him to the floor. "You little bastard."

Joshua started to cry. I gathered him in my arms. Maacah tossed her hair over her shoulders and curled her lip in a contemptuous sneer.

After I dried Joshua's tears, he ran off with Beraiah. I marched to Maacah's side of the courtyard and stood in front of her. She shot a seething glare at me.

I glared right back. "Whatever you have against me, do not take it out on my son. He's a child."

She leaned back on the stone bench and crossed her arms. "How dare you bring five bastard sons into David's family." She kept her voice even, almost as if reciting lines from a book.

"I'm the queen," I snapped. "And if I were you, I'd be careful what you say around here."

"Not for long, my dear. David will tire of you. He needed your Uncle Abner's help to get all of Israel behind him. Being seen with you was part of the deal." She flicked her fingernails and regarded me under half-closed eyelids.

"It doesn't matter what you think. But touch my children, you'll answer to me."

She feigned a yawn. "I have my own children, David's heirs, to worry about." She patted her belly. "In fact, he impregnated me shortly after your arrival."

Abital bustled back into the courtyard. "O Queen!" she chirped, gaily. "Here's my little Beulah."

A giant white bird perched on her shoulder. A pale yellow crest on the bird's head extended and contracted like a unicorn's horn.

"My, she's cute," I exclaimed loudly and turned my back to Maacah. I held out my hand and Beulah peered at me. Rolling her eyes, big and round, a black dot completely surrounded by the whites, she put one foot out tentatively, and upon Abital's urging, she stepped onto my hand, her feathery crest raising and lowering.

"Helll…oooo?" she said.

I glanced at Abital. "Did she just say hello?"

Abital nodded. "Yes, she talks. Say 'King David.'"

Beulah said, "King Daaa-vieee."

We both laughed. Abigail and Ahinoam wandered over to our side.

"Hi, Beulah."

"Oh, you pretty bird."

All the bird talk must have sickened Maacah. She put her hand over her mouth and walked back to her chamber.

"She likes to have her head scratched," Abital said. "Fluff her feathers like this, backward." Beulah bent her head at Abital, and she fluffed her feathers up.

"Up? Not down?" I said. "Wow, she likes this. Look, she's scratching the air with one foot while you're tickling her."

"Isn't she sweet?"

"May I?"

I handed Beulah to Abigail and thanked Abital. Maacah's words had upset me, although I didn't want to show it. I glanced at the other women. Ahinoam sported a tiny bump on her otherwise slim frame. Haggith was as big as a boat and ready for delivery at any moment. Only Abigail remained frail and slender. But she, too, had a son of David to her claim. While it was true I hadn't bled, I had just weaned Anna and couldn't expect to be pregnant so soon.

I sauntered back to my room and tortured myself by recalling the times David spent with his other wives. What if it were true that David put on an act with me to win the hearts of Israel? If he truly loved me, would he visit them so often?

* * *

Day by day, Maacah continued to aggravate me. I appeared calm and collected, but my body wouldn't cooperate. My nerves upset my stomach, and I became nauseous whenever I spied her.

Ittai met me on the way to pick up my sons from their tutor. "What's wrong? You look so pale."

He held his arm for me, but I refused to take it. Out of the corner of my eye, Maacah studied me, one eyebrow arched, the other one tilted. One hand rubbed her chin and the other one hung over her flat belly.

"Let's get the boys and have lunch." I looked away from Ittai, my voice clipped and brisk.

"Why so cold?" Ittai asked.

"You're David's servant. Is he asking after me?"

"He'll be back in two days. I'm riding out to meet him. I'd like to know what to tell him if he asks." He tried to catch my eye, but I turned my face.

"Tell him I'm fine. There's nothing to worry about." My voice barely edged out through my clenched lips.

"Knowing you, there's precisely much to worry about. What's wrong?".

We walked side by side. I held my face straight ahead and my hands folded over my chest, walking with as much stiffness and formality as I could muster.

"It is not your concern. I can no longer be friends with you."

Ittai's steps fell back. "So long, Princess."

* * *

David returned with hundreds of new recruits. He devoted his time to their training. All around the palace, men hastened to polish their new iron weapons and set their houses in order.

Waves of queasiness engulfed me. I missed Ittai, but the break was inevitable. I could not devote myself to David if I allowed Ittai to flirt with me. The trouble with Maacah had taken a toll. My back ached constantly, and I felt drained and miserable.

Ittai bowed low before me. "The king requests your presence."

A pang tripped my heart at the coldness of his tone. I straightened my shoulders and turned away from him. After I put on my jewelry and picked up my sandalwood box, I followed him to David's tower.

David opened his arms and hugged me tightly. "Isha, I missed you so much." He swung me on the couch, showering me with kisses. "Are you happy to see me?"

A flush of warmth embraced my vindicated heart. "Yes, yes. I've missed you, too."

David put his hand in his robe and took out a present wrapped in a piece of silk brocade. "I hope you like it."

I leaned over and kissed him full on the lips. "David, I like everything about you."

"Go ahead. Open it."

I pulled out an exquisitely tooled silver box. Engraved filigrees and curlicues spun around a sunflower's flowing rays. Leaves curled in spirals and waves, surrounded by a border of silver dots and rectangles. The box curved elegantly, with not a single straight side, almost like an animal with four graceful feet.

"I love it." For the first time in weeks, a smile tickled my cheeks.

"Put it next to your sandalwood box. I noticed you're always looking at it. This one is shinier, and I hope you'll love it too."

"It's perfect." I closed my eyes to shut out images of Ittai's sad face. A tremor of uneasiness rumbled my stomach, and I stiffened myself to hide it.

David removed my hair ornaments, letting my hair fall down over my shoulders. I laid back as a wave of dizziness washed over me, and I swallowed to keep my stomach settled.

"Isha," David said, grazing my cheek with his fingers. "You look pale. Are you feeling ill?"

A cold sweat broke over my forehead. "Phalti, the bowl." I muttered and put my hands over my mouth. David handed me a bowl. I put my head between my knees and threw up.

He helped me to the bed and slammed the bowl, splattering the table. "You are ill. I'm calling the doctor."

"No, I'm fine. I'm sorry. I'm so sorry."

"Are you pregnant? When was the last time you were unclean?"

"I-I don't know. I don't remember." A flood of dread chilled the back of my head as pinpricks crawled over my scalp.

"What kind of answer is that? A woman always knows. In fact, I know. You haven't had it the entire time I've been with you. Michal, look me in the eye."

I buried my face in the bed covers, and he yanked them off. "When did you last bleed? Was it at Phalti's house?"

"I was nursing. I didn't know you were coming to take me." My voice quavered and dried to a rustle.

David froze as if stunned. Only the rapid blinking of his eyes and the slight flaring of his nostrils showed his inner turmoil.

"What are you going to do now?" I asked.

"I'll need time. I should have stayed away from you, kept the rules concerning war captives. Then there'd be no confusion." His voice was soft. He closed his eyes and exhaled.

"So, I'm a war captive now?"

David thinned his lips and went slowly for the door. His head down, he shut the door with a dull thud.

CHAPTER 26

Psalm 27:9 Hide not thy face far from me; put not thy servant away in anger: thou hast been my help; leave me not, neither forsake me, O God of my salvation.

>><<<

David and his men stood on a cliff overlooking the Philistine host spread from one end of the valley to the other. The enemy stood shoulder to shoulder, their weapons glinting in the sunlight, their voices rumbling like a earthquake. The heavy breathing and whispers of the men behind him quickened his heartbeat. How could so few go up against so many?

His hand sweaty over his sword, David lowered to his knees and prayed, "Dear LORD, my God. Deliver me from the hand of the Philistines and let me drive them from your land. Let me take back Gibeah where your Holy Ark lies. Let not my hand be slack. In your name, LORD."

His nephews eyed him, waiting for his command.

"The LORD is with us, do not worry." David strengthened his voice and puffed out his chest despite the rumbling in his stomach. "We now have iron, too."

He took a stick of kohl and rubbed black patches under his eyes to keep the glare of the sun from blinding him. The acrid sweat of nervous men mixed with the charred odor left by the brushfires the Philistines had set to clear the valley of obstacles for their chariots and horsemen.

David reviewed the battle plans while praying nonstop in his heart. With Joab in command of the highly trained archers and spearmen, Abishai would lead the experienced light infantry to outflank the enemy. David planned to hold the center with the raw recruits and fend off the brunt of the Philistine charge. The key was to lure the Philistines into the rocky hills.

Abiathar, David's priest, led the morning prayers and asked for the blessing. The Israelites lined up on the north end where the terrain was rough and uneven. The priests blew the shofar, and the men beat their shields and cheered.

David's men stood their ground, refusing to charge into the valley. At first the Philistines jeered and bellowed. After a quarter hour of standing down, they marched forward. Their horses reared and bucked, unused to traversing around the large piles of rocks studded with burnt thorn bushes.

"Shields up." The first volley of arrows whizzed over their heads. David glanced at the line. The Philistine host had seemingly grown larger as they advanced. Sweat stung his eyes and he gulped, mouthing another prayer.

The first clash resounded above the battlefield. Angry grunts met the clang of iron on iron. David raised his weapon and pushed with his shield. The howls of the dying met a volley of curses as each man struggled to survive.

David yelled, "Hold the line. Hold them. You. Step back up. Hold them."

Another line of arrows whistled above. Several men hollered and fell, breaking the line. David charged into the gap, slashing his sword. Blood sprayed his face as he sliced the Philistines who broke through the ranks. Grunts and screams alternated with the clanking of weapons. Joab's troop emerged from the canyon walls. They shot at the Philistine flank with a barrage of arrows.

Breathing hard, David pushed the men forward, even as they fell and died.

"Hold them. Do not retreat. Hold them. God will deliver." His voice hoarse and his throat raw, he coughed as sweat burned his eyes. Cries and screams surrounded him. The line crumbled. The Philistines roared and surged forward.

David ran to meet them. He dispatched one Philistine, then another, and another. Covered with blood, he screamed, "The battle is the LORD's. He shall repay."

The Israelites responded with a loud clamoring shout and the blowing of the shofar. From the left, Abishai and the mighty men, experienced fighters, cut through the Philistine flank. Joab's group blocked the Philistine retreat while David rallied the men with renewed vigor. "Kill them. Kill all of them. Leave none alive."

David swung right, then left, then up, and down, spearheading the attack through the broken line. He stared a Philistine in the eye and howled at the top of his voice before slicing his throat. He charged the next man in a burst of fury, his sword gutting him. The next man dropped his sword and turned. David cut his back open, and he fell into the row behind.

The remaining Philistines stared at him wide-eyed. David waved his bloody sword above his head. "For the Glory of the LORD. Charge! For Israel! Charge!"

The Philistines cried with confusion. A hot, blasting wind blew from the east and whipped dust and grit in their faces. Panic broke the Philistine host. They crowded their ranks to flee. Joab cut them off, and David's recruits pushed through the opening. Hollering with the taste of victory, they mowed down every man in their path.

The birds of carrion circled overhead as the sun lowered in the west, the sky as crimson as the surrounding soil. David wiped his sticky, sweaty face. His lungs screamed for mercy, and every muscle ached as he staggered to the top of a rock.

"Blow the horn. We have victory." David held up his fist and fell on his face to thank the LORD of Israel.

That night the Israelites celebrated and praised the LORD. Boys from the villages looted the enemy camps and stacked up piles of armor, iron weapons, helmets, shields and clothes. David ordered all the images and idols of the Philistines destroyed in a huge bonfire.

David raised his hands and thanked the LORD God above.

"The LORD hath broken forth upon mine enemies before me, as the breach of waters. To God be the glory. Great things he has done. Praise the LORD. Praise the LORD. Let the earth hear his voice. Let the people rejoice. Tomorrow, we retake the villages of Benjamin for the LORD. For Israel."

* * *

The wagons circled with the bodies of the fallen. David wiped his brow and grunted. Men and boys lay stiff legged, each with a linen tag tied to his wrist. Swarms of flies buzzed amidst the sour, pungent stench of death. Tears seeped into David's eyes, and he turned away from his generals.

"How many were lost?" David asked.

"Nine hundred sixty-five. We still haven't combed the woods and separated all the Philistine dead."

"See that they are identified and taken to their hometowns. List them for me so they can be honored." How many widows, mothers, sisters, and daughters must he comfort? The price was so high. Yet they had died in full glory, liberating the land of Israel from the Philistine overlords.

The stalwart faces of his new recruits flashed through his mind. Young boys, some who held the sword for the first time. Had he pushed them too far? Should he have trained them more? Rekem from Hebron, Naam from Ziklag, Uzzi from Gilead, Jerimoth from Mt. Ephraim.

David hiked to the top of a cliff. His shoulders sagged. A boy lay broken over the jagged cleft, his sun-bright curls gelled with dried blood. David bent over him. "My son, who's your father?"

The boy's ashen face quivered, and he struggled to open his eyes. David brushed the dirt from his downy cheek.

"My king." His breath uneven, the boy cried, "'Tis an honor to die for you. For I am dying, am I?"

"Yes," David grasped his hand. "God has you in His hand." His tears dripped on the boy's lips.

"My father is…" the boy choked. The last ray of sunlight reflected over his stilled eye.

David lowered the young warrior's eyelids. *You could have been a mighty man. You could have had many sons and daughters. You died too young.*

* * *

A dull cloud settled over me with David's departure. My heart churned and my stomach roiled with nausea. I busied myself with my sons. They remained the only blessings God allowed me to keep.

Ittai appeared at the door with a deliberate blank face to escort me to my sons. He said nothing and I said nothing. When we entered the women's courtyard, he bowed and left. After I breakfasted with my boys, Ittai walked them to their tutor.

I settled under a large tree to read a scroll David had left on his desk. Maacah walked by with Haggith. She stopped two cubits in front of me and cast me a disdainful glance. "Haggith, I say. When is your babe due to be born?"

"Any day now. I know it'll be a boy."

"Of that I'm sure. Our husband has so many sons. I can't see why he'd let five sons of Saul move into our family and contend for our husband's throne." Maacah's voice rose with emphasis on the last word.

"I agree," Haggith replied, twirling her hair with a finger. "Joab said to kill them. I don't know why our husband is so stubborn. He usually listens to anything Joab has to say."

I gritted my teeth but would not give them the satisfaction of removing myself. With studied nonchalance, I rolled and unrolled the scroll to the next section. Interesting, why would Haggith have such intimate knowledge of Joab's thoughts?

"That's what my father would have done. You know my father is King of Geshur. My father helped David squeeze out the sons of Saul. Her father." Maacah stopped and sneered. "Her father was mad King Saul. And she's just as crazy as he was."

Haggith fluttered her idle hand over her breast. "How do you know?"

Maacah squirmed and bobbed her head as if she possessed the biggest secret. She leaned forward and whispered loudly, "David told me when we were in bed. He complained that she talked like a crazy woman."

"Oh, that is so funny," Haggith said with a rolling titter. "But why didn't he tell me?"

Maacah patted her arm. "Oh, dear Haggith, you must not be doing something right. But don't worry, David will soon tire of her and send her back to her husband, the scribe. He won't have any need for her once his kingdom is established."

Unwilling to be driven off, I seethed in silence. Perhaps they were right. David had already tired of me and suspected I carried Phalti's child. Perhaps I should go back to Mahanaim before it was too late. The thought of Rizpah befriending Phalti sickened me, and my heart drummed that familiar aching beat as I picked up the scroll. Another wave of nausea struck, but I held it back so Maacah would not get the satisfaction of affecting me.

* * *

I spied Ittai taking lunch with my sons. He escorted them back to their tutor and returned to pick up his cloak.

I cornered him behind a wall. "You must help me."

He walked away, ignoring me.

I ran after him. "Ittai, you're my only friend."

To keep out of view of Maacah, I ducked behind a clump of junipers and cut across the courthouse garden. Ittai headed for the guards' quarters. I climbed over a low hedge and waylaid him before he could enter the gate.

"What are you doing outside of the women's compound?" His voice was firm with a hint of annoyance.

I braced my hands on my hips and glared at him. "I didn't know I was a prisoner."

Ittai looked around. "The king wants you confined to his tower and the women's courtyard."

"I'm not going back there." I stomped my foot. "Now that David's gone to war, you can take me to Mahanaim."

Ittai grabbed my elbow. "I'm walking you back to David's tower where you'll stay. You'll either cooperate, or I'll truss you like a goat and haul you back."

I jerked my elbow from his grasp. "You men are so overbearing. I dare you."

His eyes glinted. "Oh, and I'd dare a lot more too."

Before I could raise my arm to slap him, he had it twisted behind my back. He clamped his other elbow around my neck and pressed the side of his face against mine. "Won't we make quite a spectacle?"

"I could have your head for this." I dug my fingernails into his forearm.

The strength of his arousal pressed against my back sent shivers up and down my spine. I sucked in a breath and huffed, "Unhand me, guard."

"Not until you're back in the king's bedchamber. Let's go."

He unclamped me and steered me up the stairs to David's bedchamber. His dark eyes hard, he led me into the room and turned to leave.

"Wait." I pulled him into the chamber and hugged him. "You're not angry, are you?"

He glanced around and shut the door. "I thought we weren't friends anymore."

I blinked and put on a face of contrition. "Oh, Ittai. I can't let David suspect anything, that's all."

He wrapped his arms around me. "I understand. People were watching. I had to be gruff with you too."

"That means you'll take me away from here?"

He set his chin on the top of my head. "And how will I get away with it? David would catch me, torture me and cut off my head."

I tickled his ribs. "You'll manage. You're very clever."

A one-sided grin wavered on his handsome face. "Nice try. And how exactly am I to steal the pregnant queen from the bedchamber of her king?"

"What? How did you know?"

Ittai lifted my chin with his thumb. "I know everything about you. It's my job."

"No, really. Who told you?"

"Your husband. He told me to make sure you're comfortable and have all your needs met."

I poked his chest. "Then why have you been ignoring me?"

"Ah, so there's a need I haven't met?" He tightened his embrace and chuckled.

A cold sweat broke on my nose, and my stomach rumbled.

Ittai loosened his hold immediately. "Sorry. I don't want to hurt the baby. Maybe you'll have twins again." He added with a cheerful chirp.

I backed away and put a hand on my mouth. Ittai grabbed the bowl and held it for me as I sunk into the couch.

"You'll feel better after you retch." He offered helpfully.

I put my head down. "No. I'm better now." I wiped my face with my sleeve and took a deep breath. Tears pooled in my eyes. "David thinks this baby is Phalti's."

"Well, is it?" Ittai rubbed my back.

"It might be. It all depends on when the baby is born. But I can't stand to wait here and watch David hate me. Phalti would accept the baby no matter who the father is."

"Yes, I've heard Phalti is very loving." His voice dipped to a soothing tone.

"He is the manifestation of love, the perfect husband." I wailed and bemoaned my fate. "But you and David stole me away from him, and now I'm sure he's going to fall in love with Rizpah, if he hasn't already."

Ittai's lips were upon mine before I could take another breath. Warmth washed over me as his mouth comforted me, his tongue, like living water, nourished and refreshed me. Heat anointed my chest, and confidence sprang in my heart. Ittai would always help me and be my friend.

Several moments transpired before my tears quenched. I lifted my head and stared into his concerned eyes. "I will face David, no matter what. I am his covenanted wife, and if he executes judgment on me, I shall go to the grave willingly, but only after my baby is born. Will you promise to rescue my baby if it should come to that?"

Ittai ruffled my hair. "He won't execute you. He could accept the baby. He's done it before." He stiffened and grimaced. "I've said too much."

Curiosity sparked in my heart. "No, tell me."

"It's not certain, so I should not say. And if it happened, it was forced on them." He kissed my cheek. "I'll have dinner sent up. Would you like company?"

"Yes, but chaste company only."

"Then let's eat with your sons. I love those boys."

* * *

The mid-summer afternoon burned hot and sultry, and sleep buzzed behind my eyelids. I languished in its steam. David had been gone for months. Alone in the tower, I sat by the window plucking his harp, balancing it across my pregnant belly. The nausea had passed and the baby kicked vigorously. Naomi had gone to the water tunnel to find news. The door thumped. "Naomi? Have you…"

David shuffled in, slouching, his body covered with grime and sweat, his footsteps heavy. Fingers of trepidation gripped my sides, and my heart tumbled to my knees. I clutched the harp as if it were a shield.

"David?"

He rubbed his brow with the back of his hand and dropped his bag at the foot of the bed. Grunting with a neutral sound that meant nothing, he yelled through the door for the servants to draw water for his bath.

I shoved the harp to the floor and sat at the table, my hands under my thighs, my stomach feeling like a stone, heavy and dull.

Naomi appeared as David came out of the bathroom. "Oh!" she exclaimed, lowered her head and retreated.

David pulled up a chair and stared at me. An earthy odor emanated from his blood-stained garments. I drew deep breaths unobtrusively, daring not to speak. The babe sensed my agitation and launched a volley of kicks.

A manservant filled the tub. "O King, shall I bring a maid to tend to your bath?"

David glared at me. "No, that'll be all."

The servant retreated, and David stepped into the bathroom with audible groans. The urge to comfort him overcame me. I would rub his shoulders and he'd melt in my arms, just like before.

I walked to the table and took out the shears. Silently, I entered the bathroom and knelt on the floor in the same spot where I had cradled his head and cut his hair the night he asked God to bless us with a child.

I raised the shears to his head. In a single motion, he knocked them to the stone floor and locked his arm around my neck. I gagged and sputtered. He swung himself out of the tub and threw me against the wall. I slumped in the corner, gasping for breath.

He poked my face with his finger. "What were you trying to do? Don't you know I'm a warrior?"

"I wanted to cut your hair. Please, David." I touched his hand.

The air whooshed out of his lungs, and he shook his head in a jerking fashion. "You tried to kill me."

"No, no, David. Never. These shears aren't sharp enough." My heart in a panic, I cowered in a corner as David ran to the bedroom with a shout.

He came back and pointed his sword at my neck. "I have returned from killing thousands of Philistines. I have cleansed the villages of Gibeah, Ramah, Mizpah, Geba, Laish, Nob, Gallim, Hazer and Elon. I've left none alive, not a soul. You, daughter of Saul, should be thankful. I have shed blood to take back what your precious father lost."

I sat terrified in the corner, shaking so hard that my breath came in small gasps. "Don't kill me. I'm your wife, Michal."

"I know who you are and what you've done." He moved the sword down to my belly, ripping the fabric of my dress. The babe felt the pressure and kicked hard. The sword nicked me, and a small patch of crimson stained my dress.

I clamped my hand over my belly and trembled.

The sword clattered to the floor, and David crouched to my side. He brushed back a strand of my hair, his gaze flickering from my face to the spot of blood on my abdomen. "Eglah, my Eglah. Are you hurt?"

"No, it's just a scratch." I stared at him, not knowing what to believe. "Who's Eglah?" Did he confuse me with a concubine or a wife I had not met?

He shuddered and closed his eyes, gripped my shoulders and leaned his forehead on mine. "You're mine, Eglah."

Cold chills poured over my scalp, freezing the back of my neck and digging into my sides. I shook and chattered so hard I thought I would black out. Either he was out of his mind, or Eglah resembled me. When he opened his eyes, they stared as vacant pinpoints.

I reached for a pitcher and poured cold water on his head. He didn't move, so I waited while the water dripped off his hair and beard. His jaw opened and shut in cycles like a broken heartbeat.

After a few minutes, he grabbed my shoulders. "I'm sorry, Eglah."

"I'm Michal, not Eglah."

"You're Eglah, and you will bear me a son. From now on, you are no longer Michal, but Eglah, my precious heifer." He picked up his sword, sheathed it, and stepped back into the tub.

"Cut my hair and trim my beard. I like it when you do that. And when you're finished, take off your clothes and join me."

* * *

When I woke, David was gone. I had no idea what had happened last night. Other than the spell when he attacked me, he had been warm and loving, calling me Eglah through the night. I rolled to his side of the bed and soaked up his lingering warmth. The baby rumbled contently, and I smiled. After I washed my face and cleaned my teeth, I put on a sheer green dress and went to the window. The dawn broke hot and heat shimmered in the distance. David whistled below. He led a horse and a mule.

"David." I yelled and waved. He looked up and flashed a wide grin. A delighted tingle wrapped my waist, and my heart fluttered. He was still so handsome.

He bounded up the stairs and burst into the room. "You're up." Folding me into his arms, he kissed me deeply. "I want to feel him kick again." He pressed his hand over my belly.

"There, did you feel it?" I moved his hand. His eyes widened, and he leaned over to kiss the top of my abdomen.

"You are all mine," he said, "and so is the little one. I prayed and asked the LORD. He assured me I should keep both you and the child."

"Did he tell you the babe is yours?"

"No, he didn't, but it's the right thing to do. As the LORD espoused Israel to Himself, remaining faithful, so should I forgive you and receive both good and bad from your hand." He grasped my hand and kissed it.

"Oh, David." My eyes watered. "I mean to always do you good. I promise it."

"I know you mean to," he replied. "Now pack a few clothes, and let's get something to eat. I'm taking you on a trip."

"A trip? You mean outside of the palace?"

"Yes, trips or journeys usually take place outdoors." He ruffled my hair. "Arik, my bodyguard, and two others will follow us. Do you want Ittai to come?"

"No, there is no need of Ittai. Whichever guards you're comfortable with will be fine."

The guards met us outside the courtyard. David hoisted me on his horse and jumped on behind me. "Are you comfortable? You're not too big yet, are you?"

"I feel like a cow," I laughed and leaned back on him.

"Which is why I call you Eglah," he said. "I had a red heifer when I was a boy, and she followed me around wherever I went. She bore our family many big, strong bulls."

"So I'm named after your pet cow?" I flicked my hair in his face.

"You said it." He tilted my head to the side and kissed me, long, hard, and deep.

CHAPTER 27

Song of Solomon 1:14 My beloved is unto me as a cluster of camphire in the vineyards of Engedi.

>>><<<

We headed east from Hebron past green pastures and lush vineyards. The pastured countryside soon gave way to spindly trees and thorny shrubs scattered in arid, rocky soil. Majestic rock formations decorated the landscape with streaks of brown, red and tan. As the sun set, David pointed toward a ridge of shimmering bands. "Tonight we shall stay in the hills of Hachilah where I once met your father in a ravine."

It was a dark hill, a peak extending from a long plateau. Finger-like valleys cut between the cliffs. Arik and David dismounted and stood at the edge of a ridge.

"Do you think this is the place?" Arik shielded his eyes with his hand.

"No, maybe over there." David pointed to a trench. "It's now overgrown, but I remember it like yesterday."

The men hiked down a steep path to make camp. David led me to the top of a rock overlooking the ravine. He hugged me and planted a warm kiss on my cheek. "I want you to see the sunset, as I saw it all those years ago." The vermillion sky, lined with purple and orange clouds, shone with a red glow. "I imagined you looking at the same sunset."

The sun slipped slowly beyond the horizon. I swallowed a lump in my throat and snuggled closer into David's arms. Right as the last ray edged into the darkness, he turned my face to his, stared in my eyes and pressed his lips to mine. David's hair burnished golden-red, and the sight of him was more beautiful than any sunset imaginable.

From the valley below, the smell of wood smoke and roasted meat watered my mouth. David tugged my arm and rubbed my rumbling stomach. "Is the little one hungry?"

The five of us sat in front of the campfire as it petered out to glowing embers. David played his harp and sang of the glories of God, His creation, His mighty works, and His power. I leaned against his side, listening to his heart, awash in a sea of calm contentment. This was the David that I treasured, the man after God's heart, the man of my dreams.

The men rolled sheepskins and blankets on the floor of a cave. David carried me and placed me on the bedding. He cradled me until we both fell asleep.

In the dark of the night, he nudged me.

"What? Uh…" I yawned.

"I want you to see the sunrise." He tickled my scalp. "Wake up."

My limbs heavy, I fought to stay asleep, turning and snuggling back on the skin mats. David lay behind me and placed his hand on my belly. "It's fine if you don't want to wake up."

"You couldn't sleep?" My words were slurred.

His hand clutched me, and my womb hardened. "I woke up, that's all."

"David, what were you thinking about?"

"Nothing. It's gone now." His voice wavered, and I drew his face onto my breast.

"Did you have a bad dream?" I stroked his hair and wiped the sheen of sweat off his forehead.

"No, don't worry. Just go back to sleep." He softened against me and blew out a deep breath. I kissed the top of his head and closed my eyes.

* * *

When I woke, David was shuffling outside of the cave. He showed me an old sycamore tree. A carving at the base read *Michal, David's wife*. The bark had healed leathery and grey. A warm flutter bubbled in my chest, and the baby squirmed. I smiled and clasped his hand to my womb. He hadn't forgotten me while hiding from my father. I kissed him. "What a wonderful way to start the day."

"This is the place where Abner camped," he said. "Do you want to hear the story?"

"Yes, but after I eat." My stomach growled, and the baby kicked in agreement. David smiled as he felt the kicks, then he handed me bread, grapes and cheese.

"See here." He pointed to a ravine. "Here is where your father lay asleep. All the camp of men slept about him. No one stood watch. Even Abner was asleep. Abishai urged me to strike your father dead."

"What made you stop?"

"My belief in God and that I should repay evil with good. Who am I to kill the LORD's anointed and be guiltless? Instead I took your father's spear. It was the one he threw at me while I sat in his chamber and played the harp. I also took a skin of water."

He pointed to the top of a hill across a ravine. "I climbed up there with the spear and water skin. When your father woke, I called to him. I asked him why he hunted me and to tell me what I had done to deserve it. I waved the spear and water and showed how I could have harmed him. Do you know what your father said?"

"Was he angry?"

"No. He said he had played the fool and had sinned. He actually called me his son and asked me to return. Then he blessed me and wept."

"So why did you not return with him?"

He kissed my forehead and sighed. "This wasn't the first time I let him go. I will show you En-gedi where I had him trapped in a cave. Your father was sorry then, but he continued to pursue me."

"I wish he had been truly sorry. Oh, David, what he put you through. I'm sorry, so sorry." I rubbed my face against his shoulder.

"Eglah, it was never your fault. You were always my beloved wife. But I couldn't come for you as I promised. Abigail's brothers tracked us, and Ahinoam had a miscarriage shortly after this confrontation. That's why I went to the Philistines."

I stared at him. "You stole Abigail from her family?"

"It wasn't like that. I'll tell you another day. You made both of them happy by giving them your gowns. You're a wonderful and generous soul. I used your gold to buy supplies for my men and their families." He pulled a golden bracelet set with large gobs of garnet from his robe.

"I saved this piece for you. It reminded me of the drops of blood I shed on our wedding night." He slipped the garnet bracelet on my wrist. It matched the necklace I had given Ittai's mother. My heart warmed. David had never stopped caring for me. He had remembered me even while in the wilderness.

I studied the deep red of the garnet. "My friend Jada gave me all the jewelry and gold. Please remember her generosity, and deal kindly with her if you should meet her. Jada of Jezreel." I hoped David would not someday order the killing of witches like my father had done.

He clasped my hand. "I will."

While the men packed the camp, David wandered back to the tree with his knife. When he finished, he pulled me over to show me his handiwork in fresh, green letters. *Eglah, David's wife.*

Laughing and a bit giddy, I tapped his chest. "I get a double portion?"

"Yes, only you."

* * *

We descended in elevation through drier and drier land. The sun beat hot, and my head throbbed. David noticed my discomfort and carried me to a cave. The cool, dank air comforted me. I rested my head on the cold stone and surveyed the vast emptiness and the waves of heat shimmering in the distance. "It's a desert out there. I can't imagine you traveled on foot."

"A lot of the men had wives and children. I only had Ahinoam. I don't think Abigail could have made the trip."

The cool interior of the cave relaxed me. "What was Ahinoam like back then? She's so quiet now."

He stroked his chin and looked out the mouth of the cave. "I found her in a haystack. The Amalekites slaughtered her entire village, including the man she was betrothed to. She's carried that grief to the present. Sometimes she doesn't understand why God kept her alive. I wish I could do something for her. She had another miscarriage while I was gone."

"I'm sorry." I pressed his hand. "No wonder she seems so sad all the time."

"She's suffered the most hardship." He rubbed his lips in my hair. "I tried to find her a home in a village, but she insisted on staying with me, even when I had warned her of the dangers. I'll need to check on Abital when we return. Haggith already had a son. I named him Adonijah, but I missed his circumcision. We had to finish the job of reclaiming our land and burying the dead."

David laid my head in his lap and sprinkled water on my temple. "Are you feeling better?"

I studied his serious face, lined from the hardship he'd endured. "You're a busy man." I pushed away twinges of jealousy. "And I love you." There was no point trying to change the fact he had married them. Soon we'd have a son together.

David played his harp until the heat subsided. I napped with my head on his thigh, the sweet chords and his presence washing away the clenching in my abdomen.

We resumed our journey in the late afternoon. The barren landscape led directly to an overlook of the Salt Sea. It lay vast and shimmering, blue, surrounded by stark red cliffs. Jagged, white pillars of salt poked dimply heads and shoulders from spires and ridges near the shoreline.

The path narrowed at the edge of a sheer cliff. David dismounted and unpacked the mule. "I want you to ride the mule. She's the most surefooted." He packed the supplies on his horse and put me on the mule. "I'll walk in front and lead the animals.

I hardly dared to look down from the back of the mule's neck. The drop was so steep I would plunge and not hit anything until I landed in the ravine far below. Sweat stung my eyes, and my heart pounded as the throbbing in my head rushed louder. I took a drink of water from the skin and fanned myself.

David looked back. "Trust the mule, Eglah. Don't lean. Sit straight up to help her."

My heart palpitating, I squeezed my thighs around the mule's back. "But the path is sloped toward the edge."

"Close your eyes. The mule is wise. She'll pick the best path. Do not pull or push her." He picked his way carefully with a stick, holding onto his horse. Each step they took was more of a controlled slip, kicking up clouds of dust and scattering pebbles into the ravine.

I gasped and looked up at the sound of a grunt and scraping steps. David stumbled and fell off the edge of the cliff while his horse squealed. I jerked upright and choked on my breath, and my womb tightened immediately.

"David!" I screamed. His feet dangling off the side, he held onto his horse's halter. The frightened animal tossed his head and trampled his hooves, causing a tumble of rocks to slide over David's head. Thankfully David was able to prop his elbow above the edge and pull himself to safety.

I cried and bawled like a baby, and it was several moments before David could convince me to continue. He patted my thigh and grinned sideways. "It'll be something to tell our grandchildren and a good reason to use braided leather halters."

At the edge of the mountain-top that overlooked the Salt Sea, the path became too steep for riding. David asked two guards to take the animals to a cave to rest. Arik accompanied us, carrying the bed rolls and supplies on his back.

An oasis, a shock of green, lay below the edge of the cliff. Swaying palm trees lined a river cut into the canyon. Farther out, the shoreline of the Salt Sea stretched for miles on either side, brown and arid. The mountain-top split into two with a narrow crevice on either side. A steep, rocky path over rugged boulders led to the oasis below. I held onto David tightly. Some of the steps were up to a cubit deep, and I found it difficult to pivot and hike while wearing a long dress. My skin prickled with sweat, and my chest swelled with heat.

David tore a slit up the side of my dress and squirted water on my face. Slowly and carefully, we picked our way down the side of the boulders. As the cliffs behind us rose and darkened, we rested in a shady nook.

225

"Drink. There are fresh water springs to refill." He squirted more water on my face and laughed. Coneys sunned themselves on the rocks and nibbled on the bushes. Wild goats and ibex scaled the sheer cliffs to the side of us. Above us, birds of every type and color tweeted and screeched, darting from their nests in the cliffs to the giant reeds and thicket of trees below.

We descended the last stretch of rocks in the shade of the cliffs. Sure enough, springs trickled from between the rocks seemingly from nowhere. Tiny waterfalls refreshed the landscape, and trees grew in a crack where the hidden river disappeared into the thirsty sand.

A lush grove of palm trees welcomed us with a curtain of fronds. David pulled me under its cool, damp canopy. A balmy, briny scent softened the sultry heat. My feet sunk on a mossy mat, soft as a bed, and the rushing sound of the cascading waterfall drowned out the bird calls above.

Arik dropped the supplies on a flat rock. "My king, I will hunt wild goat." He bowed and trampled down toward a stand of balsam trees.

David's face split into a wide grin. "Time for a swim." He pulled me into his arms and removed the sweaty rags from my body. "You look so good." He rubbed my womb. "So round, so perfect. I'm thirsty, let's jump in."

A trickle of excitement rejuvenated my spirits, despite my headache and flushed face.

"Are you sure we're private?" I glanced around.

"Who'd be so crazy to hike down here on a hot summer day?"

A veil of water showered the jeweled pool, set amidst the towers of red and yellow sandstone cliffs. David nudged me behind the curtain of the waterfall and kissed me while water cascaded over my head and shoulders. Laughing and sputtering, we splashed under the falls and waded to a shallow area. He climbed up stone steps and dived into the center of the pool. He shook his head as he surfaced and lay on his back. I couldn't swim so I contented myself with sitting on a flat rock under the falls.

"If I believed in goddesses," he yelled, "you'd be the goddess of the pool, the one who pulls a man in and never lets him take another breath."

"And if I believed in gods, you'd be a marble statue standing over a pool, your gaze farseeing, and a bird perched on your fig leaf."

He wrapped his fingers around my hair and pulled me into the water, kissing me. I pressed my hands over his powerful chest and traced between each muscular ridge on his abdomen, admiring the angles and planes, and imagining a sculptor chiseling each delectable detail.

David's sides shook, and he chuckled, "Enough tickling. Now it's your turn." He lowered himself to his knees and hugged my belly, kissing the entire expanse, his beard fanning over my skin like butterflies as I tried to suppress my giggling. The baby squirmed and tumbled in response.

"That's my boy." He patted my belly and carried me back to the palm canopy. "Time for a nap."

Refreshed from our swim, we lay on a heap of lambskins. David held my womb possessively. "And you're mine. My marvelous wife." He kissed the back of my neck. Content, I closed my eyes and snuggled into his inviting chest. Dreams of a perfect family danced in back of my eyelids.

I woke to the delectable aroma of roasting meat. Arik had bagged a wild goat. I pulled on a simple linen dress and joined David in front of the open fire pit. Arik handed us strips of meat, a loaf of bread and a skin of wine. David fed me, and I fed him. We laughed and played like newlyweds.

After we finished eating, David held out his hand. "I'll show you where I met your father inside a cave. I cut off the hem of his garment. He was, shall we say, indisposed at the time."

I put a hand over my mouth to keep from laughing. This would be one story my father never told at the banquet hall.

We climbed over rocks above a meadow of reeds. The travertine marble walls of the canyon swirled and dipped above us. Scrambling behind a grove of acacia trees, we discovered a domed cave, hidden above the river. After my eyes adjusted to the dark, David pointed to a stone with a natural hole in the center. "Your father sat here with his pants down." The corner of his mouth tilted up and quivered with suppressed laughter.

"And we were hiding over there." He pointed to the shadows within where the air smelled dank and moldy. "He didn't see us, and he sat alone because of his modesty. My men urged me to strike him dead. But how could I do such a heinous thing? He left his robe on a rock, so I sneaked up behind him and cut a piece off."

I giggled. "And what did my father do?"

"He didn't know how close I was. After he finished his business, he left the cave. I followed him and bowed to the ground before him. I showed him the piece of his robe and assured him I meant him no harm. I asked him why he hunted me as if I were his enemy." Tears pooled in his eyes.

David had just shown me how noble he was. I hugged him and kissed his beard. "You did the right thing. That's why I love you so much."

"He told me I would be king someday and made me promise I would not cut off his seed." He stroked my face. "How is it possible that someone as marvelous, as loving, as kind and generous as you could come from someone like him?"

I blinked back tears of happiness at his sweet words. "You returned his evil with good. You spared me, my sons, Rizpah and her sons and Anna. We were the last of the house of Saul. Jonathan had a wife and son, but no one knows where they've gone."

I fingered Jonathan's ring. David wore it on his third finger. "I wore his ring five years," I said. "On my left thumb."

He slipped it on my thumb. "If I find them, I will bring them to my house and care for them. Oh, Jonathan, my friend, my brother. How I loved him."

"And he loved you, too. His ring proves he believed in you."

His face broke, and he kissed the ring. We held each other and wept, deep in the En-gedi cave, where David had prevailed over my father.

* * *

In the evening, the sand on the beach cooled enough for us to walk barefoot. David led me to the edge of the Salt Sea. The thick, slimy water lapped against my ankles, quite unlike the fresh water pool we bathed in earlier.

"Eglah, even if you don't know how to swim, you won't sink here. Do you want to try?"

"Let's wait until after sundown. I wouldn't want anyone to see me."

"Modest, aren't we?" David chuckled and drew me into his arms. "I can think of better things to do while waiting."

He found a flat expanse of cool sand and pulled me down next to him. We kissed and cuddled until the sky darkened. He undressed me and carried me into the water. "Keep your eyes closed, or they'll sting. Now lay back."

I leaned back in his arms, and he held me in the oily bath of salt. The tiny cuts and scrapes I got from the hike through the cliffs stung. He removed his arms, and I popped to the surface. My hips would not stay down, and my belly bobbed high above the water, round and clear like the full moon, my breasts peaking like mountain tops above the clouds. Embarrassed, I folded my body and could not find my footing. I flopped to keep my head above water until David pulled me into a standing position.

"Don't hide yourself. You're beautiful." David took my hands. "Relax and close your eyes. Put your arms out straight to the side."

He tilted me back until I was floating again, my eyes closed. I felt him at my feet, the full moon above me. He walked backwards, holding my feet level, as I floated on water as primordial as the fluid in my mother's womb.

Our skin slimy with salt, we headed into the mouth of an enormous fissure in the mountains. A large spout of water flew over the lip and cascaded over a ledge of rock ending in a wide, shallow pool. The salt washed off our bodies as we embraced and dipped in the pool with the water gushing over us.

After bathing, we hiked to a flat rock overlooking the Salt Sea. David pointed to the round moon. "I used to look at the moon and imagine I could bounce messages to you."

He cupped his hands and yelled. "Hello, Michal!" Turning his face, he cupped his hand to his ear. "Well, Michal... at least that's what I used to call you... Your turn."

"Hello, David," I said.

He pushed me lightly. "That didn't even carry to the thin reed over there. Louder."

"Hello, David!" I yelled and heard a faint echo in the distance.

"Better." He stood and cupped his hands. "Come back to me, Michal!"

A bouncing echo called to me.

I stood behind him. "You come back to me, David!"

"I love you, Michal!" The yipping of the jackals carried the echo back to us.

"I love you, David!"

David... David... David... clamored back.

David clapped his hands over his ears. "My, you are a loudmouth."

He tucked me into his chest. The warmth of his love spread over me, protective and comforting. We kissed until my eyes dropped like lamb's wool. David carried me to the palm grotto and laid me on the bedding and caressed my entire body. We made love slowly in an almost hypnotized state until every nerve ending I possessed was satiated.

I lay curled with my back against his chest. As our breathing slowed, he said, "I will wake you for the sunrise. Sleep."

* * *

David nuzzled me with his beard. "Wake up." I struggled to hold onto the blankets, but he kissed my eyes. "Open up."

Sounds of the night soaked through the last remnants of sleep, the flush of an owl's wings and the distant barking of a jackal. Night bugs chirped a steady cadence. I stretched and yawned, squeezing my eyes tightly before opening them.

David's warm lips were soon on mine to arouse me to full wakefulness. I pulled on a robe and followed him to the top of a large rock. Below us the Salt Sea lay black; her waters shimmered in the moonlight to the rhythm of her lapping waves.

David surveyed the expansive view. I admired his profile, so solid and strong. I recalled the crazed twist in his face when he had held the sword to my abdomen. Just as suddenly he had clung to me and called me Eglah and mooned over my unborn baby and promised to cherish him. And now, he held me as if I were his treasure. What had happened to change him?

"David, why did you take me on this trip?"

He squeezed my shoulders and kissed my hair. "I wanted to show you the part of my life you missed."

"And I wanted to be with you." A lump rose in my throat. "It's beautiful out here, so peaceful now. But what it must have been like back then."

He held me tighter. "Yes, I try not to think of those days. It was pretty frightening, always at the edge of death."

A slow shudder rumbled my back. "I'm scared." I stroked his forearm.

"What are you afraid of?"

My throat tightened and tears burst forth. I had missed being David's wife through his wilderness trek. I had not comforted him, aided him, loved him while he suffered my father's wrath.

"What's wrong?" David cuddled me, kissing me with bearded lips. "Why are you crying?"

Burying my face into his chest, I tried to get the words out. Everything was too perfect, too intense, and he was too loving. It wouldn't last.

"Did I hurt you? I should have let you sleep." He sounded disappointed.

"No, no." I wiped my face. "I want to see the sun rise. I-I want... want..."

"What do you want?" he whispered and kissed my ear.

"Happy... I want..."

"Are you happy?"

"Yes... but." I took a deep breath and caught another sob. "It never stays."

David rocked me in his arms. "My love, I mean to make you most happy."

"Do you believe happiness and love are the same?"

"No. The person you love the most can make you most miserable." He squeezed me. "But if I had to choose, I'd rather have love."

I shivered and clung to his tenderness, wrapping this moment around my heart. "I want both."

The fuzzy morning star winked from the horizon to herald the beginning of the dawn. Moments later reddish tinges rimmed the mountains across the Salt Sea. The haze above the sea took on an orange tint as the rays of the unseen sun brightened the scant clouds a dark pink hue mixed with purple linings. The hint of a ghostly crimson fan spread into the sky above the purple hills, the colors growing more intense as the bright spot greeted us.

"Good morning, Isha." David wet my lips with a kiss.

"Good morning, Ishi." I licked his lips and folded him into my embrace.

Below us, the waters reflected the orange-purple patterns and the vibrant colors above. Red, orange, purple and blue gave way slowly to the white light of the sun, wrapped in a conical robe of its red glow as it took its place in the sky, driving away the departing dark.

Angelic choruses sang praises to the majestic glory of the LORD. David's face glowed as bright as a seraph, and he sang:

Bless the LORD, O my soul.

O LORD my God, thou art very great; thou art clothed with honor and majesty.

Who coverest thyself with light as with a garment:

who stretchest out the heavens like a curtain:

Who layeth the beams of his chambers in the waters:

who maketh the clouds his chariot:

who walked upon the wings of the wind.

* * *

Early the next morning, we packed our camp to trek back up the steep rock wall. The air was still cool, so we hurried to tackle the most strenuous parts. I tired easily and needed help. Arik and David pushed and pulled me up the boulders and over the rocky steps. Around mid-morning, we finally emerged at the top of the cliff. Arik whistled to signal the two guards with the animals.

I didn't want to worry David, but my womb had hardened while I climbed. Thankfully it had softened once I was seated on the surefooted mule. David led the horse up the difficult switchbacks we traversed on the way over. This time we crossed without incident.

David waved to his guards and said, "We'll go back by way of Ziph and Keilah."

He placed me back on his horse and held me between his forearms. "I fought the Philistines on their behalf, but the ungrateful rogues betrayed me to your father. We can stop at Abigail's estate in Carmel and take a break."

"Will you tell me Abigail's story now?" My head lolled contently on his chest.

He held me closer and kissed my temple. "Your father gave me no rest back then. He sought me every day. One time, we were trapped inside Keilah, a town that had gates and bars. Your father planned to besiege us. I sought the LORD and He commanded me to flee right away. So we went, six hundred men and their families, and escaped to the wilderness of Ziph. Your father pursued us from Ziph to Maon, and surrounded us on the side of a mountain."

"How did you get away?"

"The LORD delivered us. Just as your father came for the slaughter, a messenger reported the Philistines had invaded the land. While he fought the Philistines, we escaped to En-gedi. After En-gedi, he returned home for the winter. It was a cold, hard winter, and we were hungry and tired. We came upon the farm of a wealthy man in Carmel. He owned over three thousand sheep and a thousand goats. We made friends with his hired shepherds and protected them from bandits and wolves. We were so hungry we begged him for food."

I shuddered to think how David had suffered. "You were hungry? I didn't know."

"Yes, I was crazed with hunger. The man refused us, and I planned to kill every man on the farm and rob it. I was on my way to attack when Abigail appeared before me. She led donkeys loaded with bread, wine, sheep, and corn, clusters of raisins and cakes of figs. She fell at my feet and told me her husband was a fool and entreated me to spare their lives. I can still see her…" His breath seized, and he stopped talking.

When he caught me gazing at him, he kissed me and pressed me to his chest. My heart lurched, and I fought pangs of jealousy. She had helped him and possibly saved his life, and I could not begrudge her his affection.

A jolt in my abdomen sharpened into pain that tightened around my womb. I leaned forward and clutched my side. Sweat popped over my face, and my head buzzed like hundreds of bees swarming at a hive.

David tightened his grip on me, which only caused my womb to contract again. "What is it?" he said. "You don't look well. Relax."

I lurched forward, and my eyes watered. "I can't. Get a midwife."

CHAPTER 28

Psalm 139:14 I will praise thee; for I am fearfully and wonderfully made: marvellous are thy works; and that my soul knoweth right well.

>>><<<

David carried me to the shade of a large sycamore tree. He sent the guards to find help and procure a cart to take me back to Hebron.

I drank water and lay on my left side, my head in David's lap, waiting for the pain to subside. *It can't be happening now. It's too early, unless it's Phalti's baby.*

About an hour later, a guard returned with a flagon of wine. The pangs had subsided, and I rested comfortably on David's knees. "I like it when you rub my head," I murmured. "It calms me."

"That's how I used to get my little cow to behave," David said. "She was so stubborn. Her mother died, and I fed her milk from a skin. She'd follow me around, but when I wanted her to go back to her pen, she'd stick her legs out and resist until I rubbed her head. Like this."

He rubbed my head a little rougher, and it didn't calm me anymore. I held his hand until he relaxed and lightened his touch.

Arik came back and reported, "We're not far from Carmel. Abigail's brother is following with a cart, and the servants are preparing a room. I've also asked for a midwife to meet us."

After a slow ride, we arrived at the estate Abigail inherited from her former husband. Servants greeted us and brought me to her bed after a relaxing bath. The midwives gave me some medicine, and my womb stopped tightening. David left my bedside to let me rest.

When he returned later in the afternoon, he asked, "How are you feeling?"

"Better." I smiled. "I missed you."

"Are you up for any visitors?" he asked. "They came as soon as they heard."

"Is Naomi with them?"

"Yes, and so are Abigail and Ittai."

"Why would Ittai want to see me?" My voice squeaked, and I hiccupped with sour wine.

"He feels responsible since he's your bodyguard." David patted my hand. "But it's fine if you don't want to see him. How about Abigail?" He kissed me and touched my face. "She wants to be your friend."

"I'll see Abigail now. Later, after I'm rested, I'll assure Ittai I'm fine." I didn't want David to suspect I had any reason for avoiding him.

David called for Abigail to enter. His affection for her shone in the manner he greeted her and the tender way he touched her. She had always deferred to me and treated me kindly, but I couldn't help thinking of the years I missed with him.

After scanning him with adoration, she bowed her head. "My queen, I'm honored to have you at my home. I'm here to serve you with whatever you need."

"Thank you. You may call me Michal."

David watched us with interest, sending me a smile of encouragement.

Abigail sat at my bedside and took my hand. "Are you still having contractions?"

A clammy sweat broke over my brow as she rubbed my hand with her cold, wet, nose-of-a-dog fingers.

"They come every now and then," I said. "But they don't hurt."

"That's great. The wine and yam root must be working. The midwives are conferring. They've asked me to count your contractions and time them. You're still too early, about three months, and the baby is too small to be born." She glanced at David, and a look of worried understanding passed between them.

"When you have a contraction, squeeze my hand, and watch the mark on the candle." She held up a wooden stick with notches against the top of the candle and noted the number. "David, do you want to get a servant to help watch the mark?"

He nodded and returned with Ittai.

"Eglah, I have some business in Hebron, but I'll be back tonight." David pecked my cheek. His lips curving, he pinched my behind and departed.

Ittai suppressed a snort. My womb tightened immediately, and I squeezed Abigail's hand.

"Lady Abigail," Ittai said. "I don't know how to mark the count." He held up the reed and parchment. "Perhaps I should hold her hand, and you can measure the candle and write it down."

Abigail agreed and held the stick to the candle, dipped the reed into the inkwell and made a mark.

Ittai clasped my hands with his large, firm hands and stroked my palm softly. My breath hitched, and I squeezed his hand to signal another contraction.

"Mark it." His deep, throaty voice sent shivers down my spine.

"Abigail," I said under my breath, "I'm hot. Can we count contractions later? Ugh, another one."

"They seem to be coming more frequently all of a sudden." Her eyes wide, she ran out the door and called, "David. Has he left? David."

Ittai stroked the side of my face. "I feel so bad that this has happened to you, Michal." He caressed my name with his voice.

"It's not your fault." My breathing quickened when he tried to kiss me. "Please let go."

"Just tell me you still care," he whispered.

"I can't do this." I mouthed the words, barely sounding them, as a stronger contraction tumbled me to the side. I buried my head in the pillow and peered at him with one eye.

He let go my hand just as David and Abigail rushed into the room.

"How is she?" David said.

"How many contractions?" Abigail asked.

Ittai threw his hands up. "Too many, I lost count." He ran from the room.

The two midwives hurried in and looked at each other. David hugged me too tightly. I raised my hand to signal another contraction.

"Calm, my lord. Sit." Abigail commanded. "If you're going to get her excited, king or no king, you will have to leave."

"What happened?" David said. "She was calm when I left. Give her more wine."

He grabbed my hand, kissed it and rubbed it, causing another contraction. "Stay calm, darling, stay calm."

I signaled to Abigail. "They're starting to hurt."

She tapped David on the shoulder. "My lord, you're exciting her. Please, you must leave. I and the midwives will watch over her."

David smoothed my brow. "I'll be back tonight." He looked like he wanted to kiss me. My womb hardened again, and I clutched my side.

"David, don't go." I panted.

"My lord. You have to leave." Abigail's voice was tight and firm. "I've never seen her so agitated."

One of the midwives felt my womb. "It's hardened since the last time we were here. If she doesn't calm down immediately, she'll lose the baby. I checked her size, and it is too young to survive."

I put my arm over my face and gulped back tears. "Oh, David. I don't want to lose our baby."

He bent over me. "I won't leave your side. Everything will be fine."

235

How would he know? Everything wasn't fine with Samuel. An ache curled my heart just above my belly, and I prayed silently.

"My lord." Abigail gripped his arm. "You must leave."

"You'll let me know?" He gave her a tender look and let her lead him out the door.

Abigail came back and asked Naomi to bring me chamomile tea. She then took out a loom and sat back to weave. The clack, clack of the shuttle and her gentle humming soon lulled me to sleep.

By evening, the effects of the wine, yam root and chamomile tea had calmed my contractions. My little inhabitant wriggled cheerfully, bringing a smile to my face. Abigail put out the oil lamp and tucked me in. I imagined she hovered over me like a mother, and even kissed me, patting my head and smoothing my hair from my face.

When I woke, David sat at my side, holding my hand. "I've brought your things. The midwives say you must stay in bed until the baby is born."

"I don't want to lose your baby." I brought his hand to my cheek. "Do you love me?"

"I love you, Eglah."

"Say my real name." My voice surprised me with its vehemence.

He stood and walked to the end of the room. "I've given you a new name, one that Phalti never used."

"Phalti's not here with me, you are."

"I'm sure you still think about him." His left eye twitching, he fiddled with the things on the table—combs, a mirror, and my two boxes: sandalwood and silver.

I reached to him, gesturing with my fingers. "Don't torture yourself. We're going to have a baby, our baby. Come, lay next to me and hold me."

"You sure it won't hurt the baby?"

I wiggled my fingers and smiled. "Come."

He peeled off his robe and crept into the bed beside me and carefully placed his hand on my hipbone. "Michal, I love you. I do love you."

* * *

A month and a half passed in peace. During that time, Abital delivered a healthy baby boy. David named him Shephatiah, a judge of the LORD. Abigail sat with me daily and told me about her life in the wilderness. After she helped David, my father sought her head, and her own brothers hunted her, ostensibly to rescue her from the outlaw David. Surprisingly, David was Nabal's near kinsmen, and hence she was able to keep the estate and land after marrying him.

One night, after she had gone to her room, a dull pain prodded me out of my dreamless sleep. I sat up and a gush of warm fluid collected between my legs. My screams brought Naomi and Ittai. Naomi ran to fetch Abigail and a midwife.

Ittai smoothed my hair from my face. "Are you afraid?"

I clutched my abdomen. "I'm going to lose David's baby," I cried. "I can't believe this is happening."

"You won't lose the baby. I won't let you." He held me as another contraction pushed its way through my womb. "It's my fault for not going with you on the trip. I would have carried you over the cliffs."

His eyebrows lowered over serious eyes. "Why didn't you want me to come along? I'm your personal bodyguard."

"Aaahhh…" Another contraction sent me to my side. "I think the baby is coming. Something moved down. Ittai! Help me."

He threw his hands over his head and skipped around the room, going to the door and looking up and down the corridor. "Where are they? I don't know what to do."

"When the baby comes, cut the cord with a clean knife. Heat it in the flame." I gestured to the oil lamp.

"But, where's the baby?" He fumbled with the lamp, almost spilling oil over the blankets and starting a fire. "I don't see it."

Panting and out of breath, I propped on my elbows. "It's burning down there. The baby's coming. Do something."

His arms flapped like the wings of a beheaded chicken, and his eyes circled wider than an owl's. His panicked breathing scraped my nerve endings raw.

Forgetting his uselessness, I pulled off my blankets and untied my robe. As the next contraction rolled around, everything shifted and a heavy surge of fluid propelled a mass through my birth canal. I had not pushed, and there was no excruciating pain, only a dull numbness as the tiny form shot out in deadly silence.

My throat filled with dread. "Is he dead?"

Ittai cut the cord with the hot knife. "He's trying to breathe. His mouth is open."

"Then do something! Turn him upside down and pat his back."

I had never seen a baby so tiny. He fit the span of Ittai's large hand and wrist. Ittai turned him on the stomach and patted his back. Nothing. *This can't be happening. Oh, God, please don't let me lose this baby.*

As a raw, primal howl of anguish collected in the back of my throat, Abigail and the midwife swarmed in. The midwife grabbed my baby by the feet and slapped his bottom with her fingers. No sound. She laid him on his back and pressed his chest.

After many panicked heartbeats, a gurgling cough followed by a tiny whimpering cry swaddled my heart with relief. Black flitting stars circled my head, and I collapsed in a heap on the bed. The warm stickiness of the afterbirth passed between my legs. I held my hands for my baby, but Abigail wrapped him with a towel and held onto him. She asked Naomi to find a milk-nurse.

The midwife massaged my womb and spoke to Abigail. "She's still bleeding too much. Send for a doctor and a priest."

They looked around and stepped over Ittai. He had fainted.

My body floated as if on a barley seed pillow. My head burned, and my mouth and throat scratched with dry sand. A dull pain suffused me from head to toe. Voices drifted between my dreams. Naomi sang, her song tinkled like the trail of a smoky caravan, the camel feet plodding, the bells on their harnesses jangling wearily, the scent of sulfurous tea spiraling up.

* * *

Time passed slowly in the white desert. Alone, in the shifting dunes, I padded on feet of wool. My neck ached, and my head bloated to the size of a mill stone. A thudding noise pounded my aching joints, my bruised womb throbbed and clamped, and fire seeped like anointing oil through every pore of my body.

Abigail's voice flitted like the wings of a butterfly. "David, you're here. You must pray for her."

"How's the baby? Where is he?"

"He's very small. I'm sure he's yours."

"How can you be sure? Nine months ago she was still at Mahanaim."

The moving of furniture and shuffling of feet followed.

"David? Where are you going?"

I struggled to wade through the slogging swamp of fog. *David, come back. David.*

"He's with the nurse. He's as small as a kitten. David!" Her voice floated down the corridor after departing footsteps.

My arms ached, and my head pounded with a deep throbbing. A warm hand caressed my shoulder, and a man's beard tickled my cheek. "Michal, wake up." A soft, wet kiss painted my lips. "The king is here. Wake up."

A dark form hovered above me, and I squinted in the streaming sunlight, wondering if I floated on clouds. I opened my mouth and my jaw cracked. Ittai brought a wineskin to my lips. His white teeth glistened inside a grin as wide as the Great Sea.

He wet a cloth and swabbed my face. "I rode all night to find the king. He was way up north, beyond the land of Issachar, up near Mt. Tabor. He couldn't come right away. They were fighting the Syrians, but I dragged him back as soon as I could."

"Where…" I parted my parched lips and mumbled, "my son?"

"He's alive." His image faded between sultry, black clouds.

"He's alive?" I tried to focus.

A gentle kiss closed my eyes. "Yes, he is. And he looks just like David." The kiss moved to my lips. "And he's as precious as you."

"Where's?" Dizziness engulfed me. "David?"

Footsteps and commotion disturbed my aimless wandering through feverish fog.

"My king, we did everything we could. The baby came too early, and her insides were torn by the sudden delivery." The midwife's voice dripped like a warm honeycomb.

A rough hand touched my cheek. "I will fast and pray for her. Interrupt me if she wakes." David's disembodied voice drifted away.

My dream body grasped for him but missed. Instead of David in my arms, a rough boulder bounced off a cliff and pressed on my chest. *David! Don't you believe the baby is yours? What about your promise?*

"What are you doing here?" Abigail's pinched voice squeaked with tension.

"I'm her bodyguard," Ittai replied. "My job is to watch over her."

"Not while I'm here. Out. I saw you kiss her. Shall I tell the king?" The door slammed, and Abigail brushed the tear from my cheek.

* * *

I rubbed my eyes as Abigail kissed me good morning.

"David is here," she said.

"David?" I blinked, dazed. "Where?"

Abigail dropped my hand and led David in. She hugged him around his waist before tucking and straightening his tunic and brushing his beard. "Have you slept? You haven't cleaned your beard." She crinkled her nose and flicked ashes off his shoulders and sleeves. "You should at least wash your hair."

David appeared not to hear her. He held my gaze, his look not quite benign, almost resentful. I steeled myself. Abigail had talked to me while I lay delirious. I'd been sick more than a month. During that time, David had taken my son with his nurse to the palace in Hebron and left me with Abigail.

He crossed the room in two strides and lowered himself onto the bed. His unruly hair poked in disheveled spikes, a fine grey dust clouding the

239

russet tint. He reached for me with shaky hands and collapsed on my pillow, his unkempt face inches from mine.

"I want my baby." I glared at him. "Where is he?"

"Is that all you have to say to me?"

We stared at each other for several long moments, our breathing uneven, his stale breath fanned my face and mine blew back through my fuzzy mouth. I'd had plenty of time to think, to remember. He had argued with Abigail and suspected the baby was Phalti's. He hadn't kissed me nor comforted me. Ittai had. And now, Ittai was gone. Abigail told me David had made him his armor bearer, that Ittai had requested the change.

He drew closer and pressed his nose against mine. "I prayed and fasted until the LORD granted me your life. I don't know what I would have done… had you d-died."

My heart softened, and I reached for him. "My baby."

His palm covered my cheek. "Our baby. He's small, but perfect. I named him Ithream, in honor of your father."

"My father?" Ithream meant 'exalted by the people.'

A shy smile crinkled his face. "Yes. The people loved your father. He stood head and shoulders above all men and was rumored to be the most handsome man in Israel when he was young. Now is the house of Saul joined to my house by our son Ithream."

"But…" A cold shiver trailed down my spine. My father was David's enemy and had been rejected by God. David meant to do him honor, but I feared the name described my father too well. He regarded the people more than the LORD.

David squeezed my hand. "Ithream may be small now, but he'll grow to be a tall, strapping man." He kissed my forehead and yawned. "He and his nurse should be arriving later this evening. I've already sent a messenger to the palace."

I rubbed his beard and tried to untangle his hair as he fell asleep. "Thank you, David. I love you."

Abigail stepped in, followed by Naomi with a tray of food. They helped me from the bed. My legs bent like willow branches, and my arms flopped like numb vines. After they bathed me, washed my hair and cleaned my mouth with mint and myrrh, my head cleared and my stomach growled with hunger. I bowed my head on the table and gave thanks to the LORD for my deliverance, my baby's life and David's care. The flatbread, lentils and toasted grain never tasted better. Even the sour goat's milk brought life back to my limbs.

"Abigail, how can I thank you?" I said.

She bowed her head. "I am honored to serve you, my queen."

I waved my hand. "My friend, do not call me queen. Call me friend."

Tears shone in her eyes. "Friend." She clasped my hands. "We both worried for you." She looked at David who snored in the bed. "He stayed with you every night, and I stayed with you during the daytime."

"Then why didn't he speak to me?"

Abigail laughed. "Men. Strong and silent, that's our David. Do you remember Chileab playing his harp for you?"

Her words brought a smile to my face. "It was all like a dream. I dreamt of harps, and deserts, camels, smoke, and angels, fluttering wings, and soft voices. And I smelled David, a lot." A bubble of laughter tickled my chest, and both of us fell to giggling.

"That must have been when you dreamed of the camels."

"Oh, and the snore—troops of disgruntled horses, blowing their lips and shaking their manes, saliva dripping."

We laughed again. "And how about grunting lions, you talked about giant cats purring, golden eyes and tawny manes." She patted my back. "I am so glad you're well. When you started coming around last evening I went to get David, but he insisted on praying at the altar until the morning."

She and Naomi helped me to the garden to walk and exercise.

That evening the milk nurse brought Ithream to me. His head barely larger than a pomegranate, he nursed sufficiently and was alert, although he breathed with a persistent wheeze. Billows of love flooded my chest as I gazed into his honey-sweet eyes and stroked the soft, reddish down on his head.

David had washed himself and broken his fast. He looped an arm around me. "See, didn't I tell you he's perfect?"

"Yes, he looks a lot like you."

"Unlucky boy," he said and tickled Ithream with his beard. Ithream gurgled and kicked his feet with delight.

Alone with David and Ithream, I finally felt a sense of belonging and accomplishment. And I hoped David would always be as pleased with me as he was this moment. *Oh, thank you, LORD, for bestowing upon me my own son of David.*

* * *

My older sons embraced their baby brother. I reminded them to be careful with him because of his weakness in breathing. They marveled over him and missed their sister, Anna.

Eliah cried most pitifully, "I want my sister back, Eemah. Where is she?"

"Where's Abba?" Gaddiel whined. "Uncle Ittai said we can visit him, is that true?"

"Children, we'll just have to be happy here. Uncle David has given you a wonderful home in his palace. You will grow up as princes. Abba and Anna have to stay in the Eastern Palace. Maybe he'll let you visit someday, but right now, there's a war going on and it would not be safe." I neglected to mention that there would always be war going on.

I drafted a message to Phalti to let him know about my son's birth, requesting him to bring Anna to see her new brother.

Daily, I waited for a reply, and when I saw Ittai practicing with my boys, I pestered him. He grimaced. "Didn't David tell you?"

"Tell me what?"

Ittai took a deep breath. "Phalti is not allowed to visit or correspond with you. He is fortunate he is still alive. He has taken Rizpah to wife, and David is deeply offended."

My stomach clenched with a pang in my ribs, but I sat still. By custom, David, being Saul's successor, should have all of his women.

Ittai squeezed my hand. "Be glad David is merciful and has not put Phalti to death."

By taking Saul's widow, Phalti made himself my father's kinsman redeemer, entitled to raise seed for my father. Phalti also made himself the stepfather of Saul's two young sons and a danger to David should he make a claim for the throne. But Phalti had no such intentions, unlike Abner. And I couldn't begrudge him happiness, especially since I could no longer be his.

Shortly after I returned to Hebron, Maacah delivered a baby girl named Tamar. And even though David delighted in his sons, there was an extra spark in his eyes when he talked about his new daughter. I rejoiced for his happiness, but was miserable with missing my own daughter.

If only I alone had his children, he'd cherish me and we could be our own little family. Would we ever be happy like David's parents were? I cradled Ithream to my breast and kissed him. A tear dropped on his tiny nose.

CHAPTER 29

Job 32:1 So these three men ceased to answer Job, because he was righteous in his own eyes.

>>><<<

David jogged at a fast pace with a troop of recruits. He led them through a grove and scaled a wall without breaking a sweat, his battle-hardened muscles propelling him easily as he urged the men forward. Coming to a clearing, he raced across the meadow and scattered a herd of goats. The grunts and huffs of the boys lagged behind him.

He pushed them harder, lengthening his stride, and shouted, "Move, move. Faster, knees up." He charged to the foot of a pile of boulders. "Scale to the top and down twenty times." The walls of Jerusalem would be steeper, higher and better defended.

Arms and legs burned as he climbed the rock wall. Joab and Abishai cracked whips at the laggards. The pain in his limbs invigorated him, and stinging sweat washed away domestic conflicts. Unburdened by wives, his nephews rode all day, slept in the fields, and devoted themselves to warfare.

Blessed, yes, with six women, four infants, and three older boys, actually five if he counted Michal's twins. He wiped away Maacah's strident voice. She begged and whined for him to sleep with her each time he visited Absalom and Tamar. His head hurt just thinking about her.

And Michal. She had been unusually quiet, almost fearful that her happiness could not last. His heart tightened for her, yet he had to pay attention to his other wives and children too. She'd have to learn her place. David gripped the handholds and scraped his body over the ledge, ignoring the bruises and cuts. A warrior should not be burdened by the desires of women. Especially not a king, God's king.

He scaled to the top of the boulders and yelled at the struggling recruits. Uriah the Hittite, a rugged young man, leapt to the top after him.

A veteran of David's exile in the caves, he nevertheless trained with enthusiasm, even while his companions sat around polishing their weapons. He had once saved David's life in the craggy cliffs of the Judean wilderness when Saul's men had him trapped.

David waved to him. "When do you think these boys will be ready for Jerusalem?"

Uriah wiped his brow. His face flushed bright pink, and sweat dripped off the ends of his straw-colored hair. He pulled on his light brown beard. "Another month at least. Jerusalem will be tough. It is a fortress, well-guarded, perched above natural valleys. I've scouted it. The walls are at least five cubits thick."

"I will take it from the Jebusites. It will be the City of God, where I can rule Israel in peace. It is my destiny." David surveyed the meadow below, his gaze stopping at his palace. "My palace on Mt. Zion will overshadow this provincial one. I shall bring the Ark of the Covenant and place it on the highest hill in Jerusalem."

He called for the men to line up. "In a month, we march on Jerusalem. The man who opens the city gates to me shall be my commander-in-chief. Now train long and hard."

David dismissed the men and walked back to the palace with Uriah at his side.

"My king," Uriah said. "I have given thought on what you told me about your God. I am ready to disavow the Hittite gods and goddesses and believe only in the God of Israel."

David clasped his shoulder. "You have gladdened my heart."

"Will you attend my circumcision? It would be an honor, my king."

"I will." David was proud of the young man. How many nights had they spent at his fire talking about God while Uriah clung stubbornly to the Hittite pantheon? David kissed him on both cheeks. "When will you take a wife?"

* * *

Abigail found me in the nursery with Ithream. "The LORD has delivered Jerusalem into David's hands."

She gave me the details as I rocked Ithream to sleep while he wheezed, his breathing sounding like tiny whistles. He was a little over a year and a half and not walking yet. I worried he would always be weak because of his early birth.

"Did you hear that?" I tickled his red curls. "Your father's coming home."

Abigail sat to tell me the details. The bloody siege had lasted all winter, a long and gruesome campaign. The defenders on the wall shot arrows and threw rocks. Occasionally they had sallied in the fields. But at the end, Joab had diverted the water sluices and crawled through the tunnels. He had marched the men triumphantly through the city and opened the gates for David.

I stared at her. "And now that murderer is his commander? What about Ittai?"

"Ittai only cared about stopping the slaughter of the inhabitants," she said. "They were given a chance to leave with the clothes on their backs or stay and become loyal subjects."

"How did Ittai accomplish that?"

"You don't know? David swore a blood oath when Ittai saved him from the men of Gath. They would have hung him for killing Goliath and murdering the two hundred men, um… well…" She blushed. "Anyway, I shall let the other women know. David plans on making Jerusalem the city centered on worshipping God."

David? Blood brothers with Ittai? How come neither of them ever told me?

Talk at the women's compound revolved around the type of palace David would build and who would have the rooms of pre-eminence. Maacah boldly proclaimed she should have the largest accommodations because she would be the mother of all the rest of David's children.

"David should kill the whole lot of them, sons of Saul, that's who they are," she said loudly, strutting all three cubits of her tiny body and flipping her long hair with a toss of her head. My face hot, I ignored her as I handed Ithream to his nurse.

"David is not like other kings," Abigail said. "He is a true follower of Jehovah. Each man is responsible for his own sins and not for those of his fathers."

Maacah pouted. "Well, my father would have killed all of them, starting with the lunatic daughter of Saul. No one in the house of Saul should draw another breath."

I balled my fists. "We are not threats to David. We do not desire his kingdom. If anything, I'd be suspicious of you and your son. How do I know your loyalty isn't to Geshur?"

"At least I have David's flesh and blood son. You keep delivering bastards. I counted your months, Michal. All of us know Ithream is Phalti's son."

"He was born prematurely."

Maacah looked at her fingernails and licked her lips. "You know, I've a thought. Girls?" She looked around to make sure all of David's wives were in hearing range. "It just occurred to me that Michal has borne a son to David's servant, the dirty Philistine captain of the guard."

"I don't have to listen to this." I fumed and turned to leave.

"She has cuckolded not only our husband but her sainted scribe, Phaltiel." Maacah's laughter screeched to the skies.

"You take your lies back."

"I can't take back the truth. I've seen that guard look after you. What did he do? Get in your dress? Is that why you sent him away? Guilty. Guilty."

I gritted my teeth. "What about the way you tried to corner him? You lascivious wench."

She flung her fluffy hair with a smirk. "Ah, jealous, aren't we?"

"I've nothing to be jealous over you, concubine."

She drew her lips back in a thin sneer. "Try, queen mother. When my son Absalom becomes the next king, you shall be consigned to the dirtiest dungeon."

"David has two sons ahead of yours, Amnon, and Chileab."

Maacah lifted her chin. "Shows how little you know." She blew a smirk and swiveled her hips. "My father protects David's northern trade routes, and my son shall be king."

* * *

"Eglah." David led me by the hand. "I've captured the palace and had it cleaned. Now it is time to move in. I want you to be the first to see it. I will, of course, extend it as my family grows." He kissed me. "We will have many more children, won't we?"

To Maacah's chagrin, David placed my sons in the area closest to his—a set of rooms to house the boys, a dining area, and a kitchen. Ithream and his nurse had their own room. He selected a tower which overlooked the palace wall and moved me into his bedchamber.

Abigail was next to Ahinoam with Abital close on the other side. Since David gave me authority to assign the rest of the rooms, I placed Maacah and Haggith in the nether sections closest to the scullery. But when he asked me to manage the harem activities, I begged off, and he turned to Ahinoam and Abigail, his next two senior wives.

David showed me the throne room. "You and I will be together presiding over the court."

Behind the canopy were two golden chairs: one in the center, large and ornate, and a smaller one at the side. I understood my duty, to sit with dignity and respect, portray a royal demeanor, define a subdued and elegant beauty, and intimidate the petitioners by glaring at them when they angered my husband, or look at my husband in admiration when he rendered judgment. My presence would grace his throne, giving it glory like the two golden carved lions that lay at his feet. Perhaps he would ask my opinion, but I would never offer it in public.

"You, my queen, will be the glory of Israel. There will never be a queen as glorious as you, daughter of Saul. Oh, and from now on, you are to let Nefertira do your hair and face. You will surpass the beauties of Egypt, Babylon, and Assyria."

I flashed him a smile but groaned inside. While in Hebron, I had successfully eluded Nefertira. David hadn't minded then, but now, the stakes were higher. He intended to become an international power, but being an international power meant treaty brides. My heart froze at the prospect. Suddenly, none of this seemed very glorious. A darksome cloud filled me with gnawing dread.

* * *

David grappled the ropes, hoisted himself over the wall and dropped outside the palace. He pulled a cloak over his head and headed for the lane of foreigners.

He was tired of being a hero. Being everyone's hero meant he was expected to be heroic all of the time. Right now, he wanted to forget. Forget the men whose bloody faces lay stone cold and fish-eyed stiff. Forget the women crying in the streets and the children's wide-eyed stares. Forget the old men prostrate in the ground, their clothes torn and ashes in their beards. Forget the piercing arrow wounds, the spear-cut gashes and sword-cleaved limbs of his companions while he walked unscathed, with not a scratch, not even a broken toenail.

And forget the contentions of his wives and their petty, inconsequential demands. Was he not the king? Was he not to have peace? David pounded a fist into his hand and walked toward the tent of purification. He could do what he wanted.

Captured women, gifted to him by God, paraded in front of him. His commanders chose the fairest ones and presented them to him, purified, cleansed and made beautiful. He would shame them if he refused. And he didn't wish to refuse. Unknown women took the edge off his pain, sparked his numbness and dissipated his guilt. No expectations, no demands, and definitely no promises. So quick, easy, and pleasurable. He ached for that oblivion, no matter how short-lived. He would forget their names, not bother to ask.

He refused to look in their eyes. But the facelessness never lasted. And the oblivion he sought never quite removed the stares of resignation, grief, and death. No, there was no satisfaction, no escape, no respite. He longed to crawl out of his skin and vaporize as a puff of dew.

God, did you know this when you anointed me? Did you know I'd be so weak? Oh, God, did you know?

* * *

David stumbled through the door of our bedchamber, reeking of perfume and wine. I turned on the bed and rubbed my eyes. "You're back late."

"So?" He flopped onto the bed and grabbed my neck to kiss me, slobbering over my lips.

I shoved him aside. "I don't want to taste another woman. Where did you go tonight?"

"I don't have to answer to you." He swung his legs into the bed and pushed me toward the wall.

"David." I tapped his back. "Why am I not enough? Why are you still adding women?" My emotions edged in desperation, I should not have spoken, but I couldn't keep my tongue still.

"Can you stop bothering me?" he said.

"Don't you love me?"

He ran both hands through his hair. "This has nothing to do with love. You're a king's daughter. Your father took concubines. Did your mother ever bother him?"

"But you're not like my father. You're God's man, and I thought we loved each other."

He blew out of his mouth. "We do, but there are areas in my life I don't want you to intrude."

"But it hurts me. It's a knife in my heart."

He looked at the ceiling. "Just don't think about it. Now go to sleep."

"How can I sleep when I wait for you, wondering where you were, imagining you with somebody else, worried you'd forget me, not love me anymore."

"You have nothing to worry about. But I do need to have a large family of heirs. Ithream is not the most robust son I have, and you have not borne me another child, even though I spend more time with you than the others." The look of frustration that crossed his face stabbed me where I was most vulnerable.

"But you already have many sons. And God alone anoints the next king. What good did all my father's sons do for him?"

"Michal, stop it!"

I recoiled, shocked when he resorted to my birth name with anger.

He pounded a fist on the bed. "I bring you back after you lived with Phaltiel, and you think you can tell me how many wives to take, how many children to father?"

I was defeated. Of course, I had no right. He was the king, the LORD's anointed. Who was I to chide him? I lowered my face. "I wish you wouldn't take more women."

"Do you want me to stop coming to you? I don't need this aggravation." He sat to pull on a robe.

I tugged at his sleeve. "Please, don't leave."

"You can't tell me what to do. Maybe I've given you too much, spoiled you. None of my other wives pester me."

"Oh, David," I sobbed. "Why am I not enough for you?" I buried my head on his chest. "Do you know how badly it hurts?"

"You're a woman. You should accept it. Not be jealous like a man."

I could have slapped him. "I feel as intensely as you do. I love you so much I want to die." My eyes ached behind their sockets, and I squeezed them as tears spilled from the corners.

His voice softened. "Maybe you *are* too much for me." He lifted my chin. "I'll never forget you betrayed your father and saved my life. Did you ever think what would have happened if you hadn't let me go?"

My throat ached, and I stared at him through blurry eyes, recalling the moment he dropped out of my window and out of my life. How I had believed him then. Would it have been better if he'd died?

"What are you thinking?" He wiped a tear from my face.

"That I wouldn't have let you go, if I knew I'd lose you."

He gasped and pulled my face to his. "You haven't lost me."

"But you're not my David anymore." My chest heaved, heavy with sorrow. My innocent David had left that night, taking my hope, my dreams, and my living heart.

"Then I should have stayed and been yours forever. Would you have liked that?"

I couldn't answer for several moments. The loss overwhelmed me, and I clung to him. "Of course I'd rather you lived than died."

He drew me closer, his amber eyes smoldering. "We both died that night." His fingers tightened around my shoulders. "I want it all back. The way it was. The way it was meant to be."

He ripped my nightgown and plunged into my flesh. Love and pain, pain and love, entwined and mated, inseparable. I wrapped my arms and legs around him. "I want you back. All of you."

"Someday, it'll be the two of us. I mean it."

A chill constricted my voice. "Why someday? Why not now?"

"I'm the king and it's difficult. Can you please understand?"

"I can try." I closed my eyes, and a corner of my heart hardened into black pitch. *But it might kill my love for you. Poison it. One day I might not care.*

He sniffled and wiped his eyes on my chest. "Can you accept me?"

I bit the inside of my lips. He was right. Although a part of me disintegrated, I'd accept him, and I'd still care for him, and I'd always love him to the end of eternity and back. No matter what.

* * *

Standing in front of a pile of bodies, David's stomach knotted. His breath clung to the back of his throat. He felt as if he hung on the edge of a crumbling cliff. The clamor of voices made his head ache. Why was he so weak? Was this what happened to Saul?

Abishai and Joab stood at attention. They collected the tally and ordered the bodies burned. Their backs were straight as poles, and their chins were lifted up and strong.

Did they have nightmares? Or was he the only one. He dared not let them see him flinch. He was the king. He led the charge. He ordered the killing.

Joab's face reflected bloodlust. Abishai's mouth snarled with glee. The rusty, salty tang of blood mingled in the air with the pungent stench of bowel contents and decaying flesh. David's stomach turned and toppled.

Why did the killing bother him? He should be used to it by now. These were his enemies, the enemies of God. He carried out God's will to slaughter them. And God protected him. Other than the scar Saul inflicted on his wedding night, David bore no marks, no wounds of the flesh. And yet he hurt, and he wept inside. Far easier to bear a flesh wound than the one that bruised and battered his soul. The bloody face of the lad lying on the mat in front of him mocked him.

He'd gone weak.

Most days it took all the strength he could marshal to lift his sword and push it through another body, someone's husband, someone's father, someone's son. Images of wailing widows, slack-jawed orphans, and hunched mothers meandered under his eyelids.

"My king, the war captives." Abishai stood at his face. He leered at the women as he licked his teeth. "Will you grace me with a virgin?"

David wanted to let them go. He imagined his wives captured and humbled. Or his daughter, precious Tamar. He gritted his teeth. "Take them back to Jerusalem and prepare them." He turned toward his tent to shut out the sound of weeping women.

"Kill all women with children, spare only the virgins." Joab's throaty voice rang.

Weakling. Be a man. Look at your nephews. They are proud and strong. They live in the field. You live in a palace, weak with women and catering to their desires, especially Michal.

Cries turned into shrieks of terror as the men moved to separate mothers from their daughters. He shut his eyes, but a compulsion to look overcame him. A woman, eyes like Michal, blood trailing from her beseeching lips stared at him. The icy chill spread from his neck to the back of his scalp.

"No!" His eyes widened as a sword sliced her throat. Her crying baby fell from her arms, splattered in her blood.

David drew his sword. "Let them go. There will be no captives."

Joab jutted his chest. "Uncle. The men deserve reward. They fought hard for you."

David sheathed his sword and picked up the squalling infant. "There shall be no killing. Take the virgins and let the rest go."

Abishai glared at him and cast a disdainful glance that seemed to shout, 'Weakling.'

David washed the baby's face and changed her bloody clothes. She was a tiny girl with light brown curls. Honey brown eyes blinked. She cooed and sucked his finger. He kissed her and smiled for the first time in days. He'd give her to Ahinoam who had miscarried again. He tucked the baby into his robe, willing his jaw to stay still. He had to focus, stay in control: most of all in front of his men, his mighty men.

They would not follow a weakling.

* * *

I lingered at my window and watched for David's horse. He had been busy. There were tribes to subdue, nations to conquer, allies to be won and enemies to punish. He needed to consolidate his power, expand our borders, and create a buffer of allies.

I waited anyway.

When he finally arrived, he brought a train of war captives. They seemed younger than before.

I didn't want to argue—I didn't. But when he came to me that night, he was looking for a fight.

"Michal, are you happy I'm back?"

I tugged his neck for a kiss. "Of course I am. Am I not always happy to see you?"

"I've brought war captives. I don't need them all. What would you think if I were to reward them to my loyal subjects?"

"Do whatever you want. Aren't you the king?"

He grinned. "Yes, but my queen should give me advice."

"Free them."

"What would be the point of capturing them?"

"My point exactly. You don't need them."

"Look, I'm being generous today. Come, why don't we go take a look? I want you to pick one for Ittai. He has served me loyally, and he has no woman."

I clenched my teeth. *Why would David want to disturb Ittai, who seemed perfectly happy?* "Perhaps you should ask Ittai to select one himself."

"No, I want your help. Didn't you always say you wanted nothing but to help me?" He turned my cheek to face him. "Or is there some reason you don't want to pick one for Ittai?"

"No reason at all." My voice squeaked and betrayed me. "He should select one himself. I'm not his mother, you know."

"No, you are definitely not his mother. I can tell by the way he looks at you. That's why I want you to select one for him."

"He doesn't look at me at all. He's not even my guard anymore."

"Maacah says you've been carrying on with him."

"Oh, and suddenly Maacah's so believable? Ask her if she gets hot for him herself. Anyway, I haven't spoken to him since he became your armor bearer."

"Well, he's a horrible armor bearer. I had to save his sorry self. I'm assigning him back to your duty, and I'll be watching you two carefully."

I crossed my arms. "Do what you want. Ittai is not my concern."

He grabbed my elbow. "Oh, really? I get the feeling he holds a large chunk of your heart. You know, now that Maacah's pointed it out, it really was quite obvious."

My nerves shot fire over my scalp. "What's obvious?"

"He loves you. And he's smug about it. Despite your coolness and protestations, he holds a fancy for you."

I bit my lip. "I can't help it if one of your servants takes a liking to me."

"Ah, it's more than a liking. He manipulated me to give him your guardianship. When he brought his skills in iron smithing, I asked him what he wanted in return. Do you know what his answer was?"

Without waiting for me to respond, he continued. "His pick of position. And he chose to be your bodyguard. I thought it funny at the time because I did not imagine you'd reciprocate."

"Well, I haven't." I turned my back on him to control myself. "Why are you torturing me? Can't you see I'm desperate for you? You're the one who lances my heart every time you go to another woman."

He grabbed me tightly, bruising my arms. "I will not be desperate for you, like you are for me."

"Why, David? Why not?"

"I need to stay in control, put you in a box. I was almost killed had Joab not saved me. I was thinking about you, Michal, you and Ittai." He shook me. "Tell me nothing happened, or I'll die. And don't lie because I will beat him and rake him with whips."

"Maacah's been lying to you. I have not as much touched Ittai's hand since he became your armor bearer."

"You must want only me," he said. "Otherwise, I'm putting you in a box and shutting you away. I need to stay in control for the kingdom, for Israel."

His twisted visage showed he was already out of control, so I lied. "David, you are in absolute control. See? I only want you."

Grappling him with all my might, I fought him with my tongue, my fingers and my legs. We wrestled all night, excruciating love, the kind that bordered on hatred, too anguished to comprehend, fearful and ultimately thrilling.

He pounded his head on the bed. "Don't make me love you the way you love me. I cannot allow it. I cannot allow you to have that kind of power over me."

I straddled him and grabbed his neck. "It's too late. You told me on our wedding night that you intended to possess me wholly, and now you want to draw back? I won't let you."

"You don't give me peace, only turmoil. I'm the king. I have responsibilities. If I make a mistake, the entire country suffers. I have enough wives to keep me happy."

I raked his chest with all ten fingers. "I don't think so. If you did, you wouldn't incessantly add more."

"They don't talk back to me. They don't make demands. They don't expect anything of me." He grumbled like a boy resisting his chores.

I pressed my thumbs over his throat and spoke slowly and clearly, "But they don't truly love you the way I do. I want to possess you. Are you afraid of me? Would you rather have the white-hot stiletto of a single dagger or the hollow of a thousand lukewarm reeds?"

David dragged a long, shaky breath. "I want peace in my wives," he whispered, "and you don't give me peace."

"You're right." I encircled his head with the silken threads of my sash. "I am anything but peaceful." My voice oiled cloyingly, I slid over his body. "But you need me, like you need no other."

My arms slithered around him, and I dug my nails into his back. His eyes half-closed, his breathing ragged, I reeled him into my web, my taut, sticky, tangled web. As a woman with eight arms, I trapped David, subduing him with sensual pleasure, until he lay exhausted at my feet.

He murmured, "Eglah, oh Eglah, love me." And I had succeeded in putting his demons back into a box.

For now.

CHAPTER 30

Lamentations 2:1 How hath the LORD covered the daughter of Zion with a cloud in his anger, and cast down from heaven unto the earth the beauty of Israel, and remembered not his footstool in the day of his anger!

>>><<<

Ithream, my four-year-old son, clung to my knees while David gathered his wives and children in a circle and announced, "It is time to bring the Ark of God to Jerusalem. We have subdued our enemies. Why do we leave the Ark of God out in Gibeah when it should be with us in Jerusalem?"

Abigail shook her fist and cheered. "Hear, hear. It is what we've all been waiting for."

I did not have Abigail's zeal. Ithream's breathing problems left me little time to help with worship services. I was forever slipping potions down his throat or staying up late to watch him sleep.

The other women gave various signals of approbation and left to tend to their children.

David patted Ithream. "How's my boy doing?"

Ithream raised his arms and gave his father a gapped toothed smile.

I handed him to David. "His breathing seems to get worse when it's cold."

David kissed him and ruffled his hair. "You've got to stop making your mother worried."

He lifted him on top of his shoulders and turned around in circles while Ithream squealed and coughed. "You're too little to go, but I'm going to ask your mother to come with me to retrieve the Ark of God."

My stomach gurgled with acid, and I wrung my hands, not wanting to leave Ithream's side.

"What is it?" David eyed me. "Don't you want to come with me? Lead the procession with me?"

254

"It would be an honor, but I'm afraid." My voice scratched through my dry throat.

"Why is that? The LORD sits in the mercy seat between the cherubim, and His blessings will be upon us."

"But the Ark did great harm to the Philistines. And when it came back to Israel, God cut down many people who did not treat it reverently."

"Do not worry. It will be a good thing to have God's presence in Jerusalem." He jogged out of the courtyard with Ithream on his shoulders.

The next day, we set off on mules alongside a newly constructed ox-cart drawn by two white, virgin heifers. I almost asked where the Levites were to bear the Ark as Moses instructed, but David waved me away with a quick kiss and trotted off to give instructions to the musicians.

The people played on harps, psalteries, flutes, trumpets, cornets, and drums. They danced and sang the entire four miles. We approached my hometown, and my throat tightened. Where had my father's glory departed?

Joel trotted to my side. Fifteen years old, he'd already joined the palace guards under Ittai's command. "Mother, did you used to live here?"

Gaddiel and Eliah, at thirteen and twelve, followed him. "Where is Grandfather Saul's house?"

I squinted in the direction where our palace had stood. Part of a wall jutted where the guard tower would have been, the place where I met David. Memories of the soft spring breeze, the scent of night jasmine, and the warmth of his chest and arms flooded me. I pulled my mule toward the direction where the gate would have been, but new dwelling places blocked my path.

"Do you see that rock pile? Your uncle Jonathan used to stand there and practice shooting arrows. And over beyond that hillock is where the gate used to be. My chamber was above where you see that house, the one built with jagged rocks."

David trotted toward me and called, "Eglah, boys, come on. You'll miss the loading of the Ark."

He raced off to the front of the line without looking back.

My heart tugged for one more look. *Over there, above the broken walls, I fell in love with you.* I glanced at the place where my wedding tent had been placed and pointed my mule toward the departing procession.

By the time I approached Abinadab's house, the main procession had already turned around. The golden Ark of the Covenant sat on the ox-cart. I averted my gaze and backed to the side of the road. Its brilliance overwhelmed me, and my stomach gurgled again. Jada had told me of the calamities the Ark caused while in the cities of the Philistines.

We turned near Nashon's threshing floor. The cart lurched and the Ark slid. My heart skipped a beat. One of the young men on the cart grabbed the Ark and kept it from falling. An unearthly shriek turned my breath of relief into horror as the man clutched his throat and tumbled to the ground.

David dismounted and ran toward the cart.

"He's dead, he's dead," the other man on the cart shouted.

"Who, what?" Confused voices clamored for answers.

David raised his hand. "My people, return to Jerusalem. We will leave the Ark here. The LORD has struck Uzzah dead."

Anxious silence descended on the people. They put their instruments away and backed slowly away from the Ark.

David beat his chest and fell on his knees. "Why, LORD? Why have you made this breach against Uzzah? From henceforth, this place will be called Perezuzzah."

My nerves froze. *How dare he reproach God? Oh, God, we have displeased you. Have mercy on us all.* I rode with my head down. We should not have played the music and acted so gleefully. God demanded respect, and we should have behaved with more decorum and formality.

* * *

Wails greeted us at the palace. I peeked at David. His face had been in a marked scowl the entire journey back.

After I dismounted, Naomi rushed toward me, her mouth agape, and tears running down her cheeks. "Come quickly, my lady."

Behind her, Ithream's nurse wrung her hands. A dull pounding noise invaded my head, and I screamed, "Ithream, where's Ithream?"

Gentle hands restrained me. Ithream's physician met me at the door. "I'm sorry. Prince Ithream has gone the way of his fathers."

"It can't be. He was fine when we left. What happened?" I raced to his bed with David's ragged breathing behind me.

"No, no! My baby." I grabbed the limp, lifeless body of my son. He'd had a cough, but no fever, and David had assured me he'd be fine. This morning, he had smiled at me and banged on his drum as I kissed him goodbye. I squeezed tighter. "Ithream! My baby. Why did God have to take you too?"

David gently removed Ithream from me. "Come with me to the altar. Let me make a sacrifice and entreat of the LORD. I have sinned in the matter of the Ark."

I pushed away. "What good will it do? Will you bring my baby back?"

Without looking at him, I ran to the top of the wall and stared over the shrouded city. The low hanging clouds and grey skies mourned with my empty arms, bereft of both Ithream and Samuel, sons of David, my sons.

David returned covered in ashes, his clothes ripped in shreds. He sat at my side. His golden-brown eyes drooped heavily. We sat until the sun went down, speechless, somber, separate.

The next day, we buried Ithream. The maids had dressed his body in a purple brocaded robe trimmed with golden figs. Sunlight streamed through the window, highlighting his reddish curls. His thin, pale face slept peacefully, the light playing on the golden tips of his tawny eyelashes. His tiny, bow-shaped mouth, puckered with a bluish tint, would never kiss me again. The small, thin hands tucked over his chest would never bounce a ball nor latch onto my hand. I caressed his sweet, little head and wished the LORD had struck me instead.

* * *

I kicked off the blankets, my body bathed in cold sweat. The slicing pain in my chest raged like a feral beast trapped in a pit. *Oh LORD, why have you taken him? Why punish a four-year-old for his father's sin? Why didn't you kill me? Oh, why am I cursed? Always cursed.*

I pounded on David's back and pulled his robe. "Why did you sin with the Ark? You were disrespectful, so noisy, heathen, and Ithream is dead."

"Go back to sleep," he grumbled.

"Monster! It's your fault. You sinned, and Ithream died."

He grabbed my wrists, gritting his teeth. "Don't you think I feel bad already without you finding reasons to blame me?"

"You have many other sons. And many wives and concubines."

"You still have your other children. Let them be a comfort to you. God has not left you entirely bereft."

I put my hands over my face. "God has taken so many people I love. Every time I have a bit of happiness, he dashes me on the rocks of judgment. Why does He hate me so much? I wish I had died."

David sighed and held me to his chest. "You still have me, and you're still my queen. Is that not enough?"

"What good is being queen when my son is dead?"

Why did God put me and David through so much? We lost each other for so long, and now He'd taken our child, our only child.

David kissed my forehead. "I'd do anything to make you happy again."

"You can't make me happy, ever. I'll never ever be happy. Just let me die."

He rocked me and caressed my back. "I'll do anything for you. It won't make up for Ithream, but if there's anything I can do, I would."

I shook my head and rested against him for several long moments. "There's nothing you can do." I had nothing left with which to hold onto David. Nothing. I had not been able to conceive after Ithream. Why would he want me when I had no sons for him?

David squeezed me tighter. "Ask me anything."

Could he care for my sons as his own? Perhaps he would formally acknowledge Joshua and Beraiah as his sons and assure me a place at his side. Would he really do anything?

I took a deep breath, my face in his neck. "Can you adopt my sons and acknowledge them as yours?"

He stiffened and pushed me back. His eyes widened and then narrowed.

"David? There's no law against it, is there?"

He hid his face in the pillow. "I can't have Merab's oldest sons supplant mine for the throne."

"I only ask you to acknowledge them, not replace your sons. No one can replace Ithream." The familiar ripping pain clawed through the core of my heart. I flung the pillow from the bed. "You didn't mean it, did you? You don't care if I'm happy or not."

His amber eyes wavered slightly before hardening. He gripped my arm and exhaled through his teeth. "Did Phaltiel father your twins? Did he?"

"I already told you he didn't."

"But you also told me they weren't mine. So which is it?"

I squeezed his shoulders. "They're not Phalti's because I didn't sleep with him until you married Maacah."

He recoiled. "How did you know when I married Maacah?"

"Talmai's brother kidnapped me to stop your marriage. But I got away. I killed him."

He wiped a lock of hair off his forehead. "You killed a man?"

"He ripped me away from my nursing babies. He was cruel, and he almost killed Phalti when he came to rescue me." I covered my eyes with my fingers. "I stabbed him in the back."

"Why didn't you tell me this before?"

"There was no point. You married another princess—one whose father was useful to you."

David slapped the pillow. "I'm not that kind of man. I cared about you even when your father hunted me."

"No, you forgot about me. You left me with Phalti until such time when it was convenient for you to take me back—when you wanted the throne of Israel."

His eyebrows lowered. "If that's how you think about me, why do you stay? The kingdom is mine now."

The coldness in his voice filled my wounded heart with fresh pain. What happened to the love? The promises? The dreams?

"So you won't acknowledge my sons?" My voice rattled in my parched throat.

"I'll love them as my own, but I won't acknowledge them. I'll not bring shame into my household. I have plenty of sons. I don't need sons of Saul."

Was Ithream a son of Saul to you? Are you glad he's dead? I threw myself into the bed and crawled under the blankets. *Ithream, my son, my son, why couldn't I have died for you?*

David pulled on a robe and went to the door. "Never mention this again. Even if I had fathered Joshua and Beraiah, I cannot acknowledge them. You were married to Phalti at the time of their birth. I suggest you see Nefertira and get yourself fixed up. I have a busy day today, and I need you back in the throne room. I will not put up with any more excuses. You're still the queen. Don't ruin it."

* * *

The door swung open with a bang, and I looked up from David's prayer scroll.

David stepped into our bedchamber with a fervent gleam in his eye. "It's been three months, and this time I will succeed in bringing the Ark back."

A servant followed and peeled off David's ceremonial robe before slipping a dressing robe over his linen underclothes. Another servant handed him a goblet of wine.

David leaned over me. "It will bless us when it lies in Jerusalem. I'm going to build the LORD a temple, a golden temple for his Ark."

"But the Ark is a fearful thing. Remember what happened last time?"

David's head bobbed as he waved his hands. "I've searched the book of the Law, and this time the Levites will carry the Ark as God has prescribed. I need you to gather the women to come with me."

"Oh, I'm so weary and have a headache. Please forgive me and excuse me this time." I did not wish to witness to another disaster.

He had seemingly forgotten about Ithream. Of course, he had many other sons and daughters, whereas Ithream, my only connection to him, had been snuffed out because of his sin. I slumped on the couch.

David's mouth turned down. "Promise me, Eglah, when you hear the music, you'll come to the window and watch. It's important for me, for us, for our kingdom, that we have the blessing of Almighty God."

He gave me a perfunctory kiss on the forehead and left. A cloud of depression blanketed my soul, and I curled into a ball of tears on my couch.

Ching, chang, plink, tinkle. The jangling noise and the people's cheers roused me. I put on my queenly face and walked stiffly to the window, chin up, expecting to see nothing, but to grace the window with my ceremonial presence in case David should look up.

"Ahhh... eehhhh... Aaooohhh!" Squeals rose from the serving girls and women of the street. I opened my eyes wider. What could those silly creatures be swooning for? Weren't we expecting the Holy Ark of the Covenant of the LORD? Why were the people dancing in the streets like some heathen procession, whooping and jumping around like monkeys at a Philistine circus?

As the parade drew closer, the source of their enthusiasm leapt to my sight. David trailed the Ark, springing and prancing hysterically. He was stripped to his linen underclothes and exposed his shoulders and thighs. He threw his head back like a wild man, swinging his arms in the air, turning and whirling and skipping, whooping at the top of his lungs.

I leaned out the window. My glance traveled to the maidens leering at his display, and the bile came up my throat. *Does David not respect the Holy One of Israel? Is he causing more shame and judgment to fall on our house? Hadn't he done enough damage? And worse, which of those maidens would soon appear in his bed?*

He had ripped my heart, exposed it cruelly to every slave girl in the kingdom and shattered the image I had of a man loved by God. The clanging cymbals, hoots, and whistles paraded past my window. So ecstatic was David in his crazed dance, he did not give me a passing glance. The horrid girls threw themselves in his path as he high-stepped over them, no doubt giving them a close-up glimpse of his crudity.

The train of wives, sons and daughters followed, waving palm branches. Abigail passed below my window and looked up. Chileab waved, and I waved back, forcing a smile on my face. Tamar followed Maacah and Absalom. Her long fiery hair burnished gold in the afternoon sun. I gazed after her, longing for my daughter, for my lost innocence and cherished love, all washed away by David's indifference.

"Mother!" My five remaining sons saluted me. So handsome and strong, they reminded me of my brothers—hearty and hale, in the prime of their youth. Ittai stopped his horse under my window. Our sad eyes held each other for a long moment before he hastened off at the sound of the trumpets.

Late in the evening, David trampled toward the palace with a coterie of vain fellows, laughing and singing lustily. A gaggle of serving maids frolicked around them, weaving and staggering with their tabrets and mincing steps.

David called to me, "Eglah, did you see me? Did you see the Ark?"

Squeals of approbation from the drunken contingent swirled up to the window.

I saw him all right. I rushed down the stairs, threw open the door and collared him like one of my grown sons.

I slapped his face. "How glorious was the King of Israel today, who uncovered himself today in the eyes of the handmaids of his servants, as one of the vain fellows shamelessly uncovers himself!"

David's eyes blazed. The crowd silenced. He grabbed my wrist. "God chose me over your father and your father's house to rule Israel. I'll dance and shout all I want for the LORD's glory."

He clamped my arms as his voice lowered. "And I will uncover myself and be yet viler and abase myself further. And the women you're so worried about? They shall honor me, even if you won't."

He pushed me into the house and slammed the door. What an indecent spectacle I had made! I sunk to my knees, but David threw me over his shoulder and marched up the stairs. He flung me over the window ledge and screamed. "What do you see?"

"Nuh-nothing."

The street glistened with the blood of the sacrifices. Every six steps they had killed oxen and sheep. Trampled palm branches and discarded garments littered the lanes.

He pushed me out further. "What do you see?"

"Nothing."

He lifted my legs and thrust my torso out the window until I hung partway down. My gown flipped, exposing my legs. "David, stop. You're scaring me."

"What do you see?"

"I see you, David. You and the women dancing."

"And you despised me, didn't you?"

"No. I didn't. I didn't."

He pushed me further and leaned his weight on me. "And what else did you see?"

"The Ark. The Ark of the LORD."

"And you were jealous, weren't you?"

"No. You disrespected the LORD. You disrobed in front of him."

"I humbled myself before the LORD. But you were jealous of my zeal. And you hated it."

"No, I didn't."

He pulled me back and shook me. "Why are you denying it? Don't you know I can tell by looking in your eyes?"

Bitter herbs prickled my chest, and I pounded on him. "You're right. I am jealous. I'm jealous of all your wives and your sons. I'm jealous because you're the LORD's anointed, and you're favored by God. And I'm jealous because... Ithream's dead, and I'm nothing but the cursed daughter of Saul."

David shook his fist. "You want to be favored by the LORD, then you should have come and celebrated the homecoming of his Ark. Your father let it languish all these years. The least you could have done was honor me with your presence. You're the one who's despicable."

He pushed me back into the room. A blinding white light flashed and black dots swirled as an excruciating pain pierced my soul.

I lunged for the open window.

PART III

CHAPTER 31

Psalm 2:12 Kiss the Son, lest he be angry, and ye perish from the way, when his wrath is kindled but a little. Blessed are all they that put their trust in him.

>>><<<

David's heart broke. He expected it to be some momentous feeling, some tremendous agony of thundering pain, a cracking and splitting asunder as the earth in a quake cleaves the ground. Yet, it clicked like the snap of a chicken bone.

He sat at his wife's bedside. He shouldn't have been so cruel. They'd had fights before. Nothing had changed, had it? He punched his knotted thigh. Yet this time was different. The breach was momentous, irreparable. She had shamed him in front of his kingdom—despised him and rejected the Ark of the Covenant, the visible presence of God on earth.

He brushed a tendril of hair from her clammy forehead. He had drugged her after she tried to throw herself out of the window. His fingers ached as he touched her. It wasn't a matter of his forgiveness. No, she needed a pardon from God Almighty.

The dawn broke pale and dreary, a mist hung over the city. It was supposed to have been a day of joy, a day for praising the LORD God of Israel. His city, Jerusalem, the city of God, a holy city. The presence of the Ark would mean peace for Jerusalem. With God's Almighty power at his side, who could defeat him? Who indeed but a jealous woman?

He had given her no reason to be jealous. He had brought her back from exile, made her queen, given her his bedchamber. He had favored her above his other wives. So why was she so possessive, so intense? He curled her hair around his finger and kissed her. Her breathing shallow, she lay where he had tucked her.

He walked into the sleeping city. Street sweepers cleaned the debris. Rubbing his eyes, he headed to the temporary tent that housed the Ark of

God. He removed his robe and sandals, entered, and bowed before the Ark. He waited, meditating on the Word of God.

His mind cleared and refreshed, he prayed, "O LORD, Holy are You who sit between the cherubim, over Your seat of mercy. Have mercy on my wife, Michal. She is a woman void of understanding and full of feeling. Spare Your wrath and take not her life."

I will spare her life for your sake. Her crown will you give to another. And your heir will issue from another. However, you shall not give her bed to another, for she is bone of your bone and flesh of your flesh, the wife of your covenant. You shall veil her and keep her hidden until her heart is pure for you.

* * *

My body woke to the sudden firing of a thousand flames. Sweat prickled my skin, and my muscles quivered involuntarily. My head throbbed as angry claws dug pincers into my limbs.

David rubbed my arms and hands. "Are you getting your feeling back?"

My fingers twitched violently. I could barely catch my breath. The scream of irritated nerves stabbed every surface of my skin, and those parts that could move writhed in agony. Pain coursed rapidly into waves of nausea.

"What is happening? Am I dying?"

"No, you're waking from the drug." David carried me to the bathroom and lowered me into the tub with my clothes on. "Maybe cold water would help."

"Is this how hell is?"

"I don't know what else to do." He kissed my forehead, concern written in his face.

Burning shivers raced through my body, the agony too much to bear. My body howled, and I screamed. David held me as feeling returned in my limbs, each nerve firing with renewed intensity. The long night rolled on.

Morning came with the slant rays of sun. My body had chilled, and the echoing of pain had ebbed to a dull heaviness. David's face drooped. He laid my head on the pillow and stared at me with sad eyes. A chill squeezed my throat as his fingers slipped from mine.

"Are you leaving me now?" I asked.

The left side of his face twitched. "Things have to change. You're no longer my queen."

"It's over?"

He nodded.

"Oh, David." My leaden arms wouldn't move. "I still love you."

"Don't." He cupped my face with both hands, his thumbs rubbing my cheeks. "Don't say that."

"But I do, David." My voice faded with my hope. *I'll always love you.*

"You tried to kill yourself." He rubbed the lump on my aching head and pulled back my hair. "I tackled you before you jumped, and you hit your head on the window ledge."

Even through my blurred vision, he appeared as radiant as the day I met him. Older, yes. But still handsome. The fine lines etched in the corners of his eyes made him look distinguished, a man of character. His masculine lips stretched beneath whiskers, red and brown, with a sprinkling of silver.

He stroked the back of my neck. "I still remember the first time I saw you in your father's room. You were a pretty girl, curious and mysterious. I wondered if you were betrothed or had a line of suitors. And I despaired that I, a poor man, could never have your hand."

Tears swam in my eyes. I held onto his image, memorizing it, and cherishing the proximity I would soon lose.

"You were friendly to me," he said. "Remember when you helped me with the weapons and armor?"

"Yes."

"You must know I cared for you back then. I didn't want to admit it, but I dreamed of you, and when you said I should have a wife who loves me, well, then, I figured you would be the one."

"Am I still?" A thousand bees stung the inside of my chest. I could not let him go.

"You have affronted God. You'll be taken care of. Don't worry."

"But, David, I can't live without you. Please forgive me?"

He pulled me up and held me. "You should worry more about God's forgiveness. Do you trust Him?"

I rubbed my face in his neck. "How can I, when He's against me?"

David lowered his mouth to my ear. "He's not against you. He wants you to love, trust, and obey Him with all your heart."

"He'll never forgive me, no matter how many lambs I sacrifice. I'm too much of a sinner."

"He will, Michal. He'll forgive you if you believe His Word and ask Him to save you from your sins. Will you do that?"

Could I really believe? Would God then favor me also? My glance inquired of David, and the look he gave me was one of pure love and devotion. Would David also favor me again? Maybe love me again if I trusted in the LORD?

"Will He really forgive me? Would He shine his face upon me?"

David squeezed my hand. "If you ask. All you have to do is believe and ask."

"David?"

He hugged me, almost as if he adored me. "Go ahead. Will you believe?"

I nodded. "I do believe."

He took both of my hands. "Let's pray. Ask Him now."

I bowed my head. "Dear LORD, I'm a sinner. Please save me from my sins. I'm putting my trust in You and want to make peace with You. In Your name, LORD."

David's face lit with a wide smile. "He's forgiven you. Do you feel better? Relieved?"

Peace and comfort floated over my head and shoulders, and a giant knot disintegrated. My chest warmed as if oil anointed my heart. I took a deep breath. "Yes. He's accepted me. Now I know how you felt when Samuel anointed you."

I looked hopefully at David. "Do you forgive me also?"

He palmed my face and kissed me, too tenderly. "I have to go."

My heart broke into tiny splinters. "David..."

"Goodbye, Michal." He turned quickly and was gone.

* * *

"The Philistines are back." Abishai's face contorted with rage. "You'd think after we decimated their forces they'd stay home and lick their wounds."

David stroked his beard. "I know Achish, their king. Although he's old, he is still fierce and ruthless. I suppose he thinks we'd slacken off and send our troops home to tend to their fields."

"But isn't that exactly what we've done?" Joab said. "The barley harvest draws near, and none but your mighty men are ready for war. Shall we conscript more men?"

Abishai glowered. "The real problem is you harboring the sons of Saul. God will not bless. Let me, my lord, take care of them for you."

Joab cracked his knuckles. "And the daughter of Saul. I will relish getting my hands around her neck."

David thumped his scepter on his throne. "Nephews or not. You are not to touch them. I will go to the LORD and inquire."

"Why inquire when you know what you must do?" Abishai drew his sword. A murderous gleam sparkled in his eyes.

Joab shook a strident finger. "Uncle, it is the LORD's will. None that pertains to Saul shall live."

"I will speak to the LORD, and he will answer me. Do not touch them, or their blood will be on your head."

Joab sauntered off in a manner that showed he was neither cowed nor repentant. David's hands shook while he paced the chamber. *Oh God, help me, help me.*

He summoned Ittai who had proven worthless as an armor bearer. Was he capable of defending Michal against Joab and Abishai?

Ittai bowed low to the ground.

"Michal and her boys are in danger," David said. "Joab and Abishai have advised me to execute them."

Ittai drew in a sharpened breath. "O King, what will you do?" His tone wavered and sweat popped over his brow.

"We need to protect them. Where do you suggest we hide them? Will they be safe at Phaltiel's? How many guards do you have there?"

"I have ten Cherethites. I can increase the guards to fifty. All Philistine. They will not follow Joab or Abishai."

"How old are the boys?"

"The youngest two are ten. I can keep them safe."

"What about Michal?" David stroked his chin. "What do you recommend?"

"She's your wife, O King." His face appeared unchanged.

"That she is. I will keep her in Jerusalem. She will hate me more when I remove her sons from her side, but I will not allow her to go back to Phaltiel."

"It is as you say, my king."

David pounded a fist to his cupped hand. "Take the children to Phaltiel. Increase the guard to fifty. Take them in secret during the night."

"I shall do as you say." Ittai bowed.

"And guard Michal with your life. I'm sure you will give it your best." David drew his sword. A sudden surge of bile roiled his chest. "But first, I need to try you. See if you're capable. To the training ring. Now!"

Ittai's eyes widened, but he followed David to the armory. David tapped the hard-packed earth with the end of his spear. It would be so swift. Images of Michal's father, his spear pinned to the wall inches from his head, flitted through his memory.

Ittai approached slowly, his dark face guarded.

"Sword or spear?" David growled.

Ittai tied his long hair with a leather thong. "Your choice, O King."

"Spears first, then swords. Yell 'Yield' or lose your weapon."

David circled his spear and attacked. Ittai parried the blow and jumped to the side. David swung around and jumped toward Ittai's back. Ittai pivoted, as lithe as a jaguar. David poked at his heart. Ittai faltered and stepped back but recovered. He brought the shaft down on David's shoulder. The bone-cracking pain kicked David's anger up a notch.

David whipped at Ittai, but he dodged, sliding his feet low on the ground. He surprised David by arcing his spear up at the last second, catching the tip of David's spear. David stumbled and almost lost his weapon. Ittai attacked, hit the side of David's neck with the shaft and knocked him down. Ittai's foot landed on David's spear hand, and he clamped David's neck with one hand, dripping sweat on his face.

"Not bad, Ittai. Not bad." David conceded. "Now the sword."

David swung before Ittai's sword was halfway out of its sheath. Ittai jumped back quickly. He flashed white teeth and blocked with the hilt. Clash and retreat. Thrust and parry. Iron pounded on iron. Ittai danced like a crazed leopard. Swing, block, turn, thrust. David could not find an opening. The clanging rang like a blacksmith's hammer amidst their grunts and huffs.

"Yield, Ittai."

"Never, King."

David's muscles burned like hot cords, his shoulders heavy. Ittai kept coming with amazing endurance. David backed up, blocking in defense. It was all he could do to hold off Ittai's attacks. *I will not be defeated by an uncircumcised Philistine, especially one who loves my wife.* With a surge of strength, his last ounce, David swung at Ittai's head.

Ittai blocked but not solidly enough. His wrist twisted. That had to have hurt. David focused his strength and feinted to the left. Ittai stumbled to block the nonexistent blow.

"Michal is mine." David yelled and thrust the point of his sword into Ittai's chest.

Ittai clutched his chest and said, "You don't love her like I do."

David punched his face. "How dare you? She's my wife."

"You don't care about her." Ittai gasped for breath. "You have no idea. What. She. Needs."

David left Ittai passed out in a pool of blood.

Every muscle sore, he dragged himself to his bedchamber. She wasn't there. Of course. He'd thrown her out. His weakness, his wife, his Michal.

CHAPTER 32

Psalm 13:1 How long wilt thou forget me, O LORD? for ever? how long wilt thou hide thy face from me?

>>><<<

The Philistines crossed the border and spread themselves in the Valley of Rephaim.

David bowed before the Ark of the Covenant and prayed, "Dear LORD, God of Israel, the entire nation of the Philistines has gathered against Your people. Grant us the victory for Your name's sake."

The LORD answered, *Do not go out against them head on. Turn aside behind them and wait near the mulberry trees. When you hear a sound as of going in the treetops, move into battle—for I will have gone before you to smite the host of the Philistines.*

David led his troops to the rear of the valley and camped against the mulberry trees. The mighty hosts of the Philistines spanned as far as the eye could see. They had gathered from Gibeon to Gaza, from Askelon to Ashdod, intent on reclaiming the lands they lost.

Joab approached, stomping his feet. "What exactly is the sound of a going?"

David surveyed the valley below. "I will know when I hear it. Wait until I give the signal."

Abishai's gaze darkened with his lowered brows. "It's getting toward dusk. Are we expecting to fight in the night?"

"Patience, nephews. I've gone to the LORD, and He has assured us victory. We must obey Him exactly." David walked away and knelt on the ground.

He closed his eyes to pray. "LORD God, Almighty God, who sits between the cherubim. Grant us the faith and confidence to wait on You and bestir ourselves on Your behalf. Smite the Philistines and grant us the victory. In Your name, LORD."

The chirping of crickets and subdued night sounds soothed him. He recalled the trip he took with Michal to En-gedi and the badlands of Judah. She had been pregnant with their son Ithream. He wiped his eyes with the back of his hand. Ithream was Michal's hope and joy, her only link to him in the flesh. His son. Their heir no more. And the LORD promised no other. David closed his fist. His knees ached, and yet he knelt, waiting until his legs were as numb as his heart.

There was no sound except for the coming and going in the camp of the Philistines. David's men walked around eyeing him. Joab and Abishai tossed stones at the trees and glanced over every few minutes. David lowered his head to listen more intently.

The wind shrilled with a faint whistle. A woman's sob, her voice lilting, curling and twirling—a long, throaty moan—stirred the leaves above. Michal's voice, rich in overtones, rose amongst the tops of the trees. The Philistine love song weaved between the branches, drawing the pain of his heart into his throat. David gasped; the twin strands of yearning and regret mated in the caressing breeze.

Michal, my love, my lost love.

An icy fingernail tickled his ears. A whisper, faintly moving sounds. A ghostly march. At the tops of the trees. Marching feet, a woman's sigh. Michal singing, her words moving, aching, drawing his soul. Marching, marching, marching. The footfalls approached and shook the canopy of leaves—the marching of a hundred thousand spirits.

David raised his hand. "Attack!"

In the dark of the moonlight, the Israelites swarmed. Hordes of Philistines stood as clay soldiers, frozen. Their eyes gaped, silently pleading. But there was no mercy. David's men gusted through the camp, cutting and thrusting and killing, killing, killing. On and on the Philistines fell as Michal's voice soared, and the heartbeat of spirits marched through the tops of the trees.

* * *

Arik, David's guard, stood at my door. I had moved with my sons to a tiny house outside the palace a few days ago.

"I've come to remove your sons," Arik said.

"No. You can't do that." I tried to slam the door, but he wedged his shoulder against the frame.

"King David has given the order. They must leave now. There are men in the highest positions that aim to kill them."

A sinking curl of fear twisted my gut. "Joab and Abishai?"

"I do not have the authority to reveal this. We have no time to lose."

I stood against his chest, refusing to back down. "Unless I hear from the king himself, I will not let you touch my sons."

He pushed past me and gestured to his men. "Take them by force. You may question the king when he returns."

Arik held me against the wall while his men marched into my sons' rooms, roused them, and dragged them to the door.

Confused faces streamed past me. "Eemah, Ee-mah!" Their cries rent the air until cut off by heavy gags. They were herded out of the house and thrown onto horses.

I struggled to shout, but Arik clamped a big hand over my mouth until the hoof beats had receded in the distance.

He loosened his grip and bent over me. "It is better this way, my lady. They will be safe in Mahanaim. They will be with their father."

I grabbed him. "Let me go with them. Please."

He pried me loose. "The king says you are to stay here."

Sobs racked my chest, and I clawed at the floor. "Where's Ittai? Does he know?"

"He knows."

"Why isn't he here? He wouldn't have let you take them. He wouldn't have."

"He is in prison awaiting execution."

I lifted my head. "Prison? What has he done?"

"It might not matter, he may die before trial. Good night, my lady." Arik shut the door.

* * *

The LORD had utterly defeated the Philistines. With their best troops frozen and slaughtered, the Philistine villages and towns were defenseless. Thousands of Israelites joined in the massacre and pillaging that followed. Entire villages were razed, large amounts of loot taken, and war captives, both male and female, were taken as slaves.

The victory celebrations lasted through the dark hours of the night into the next day. David returned to Jerusalem in high spirits. Large crowds turned out to welcome him. Women danced in the streets with tabrets and bells. "David has slain ten thousands. David has slain ten thousands."

David visited the jewelry merchants to buy presents for his wives. Vendors swarmed around him with their wares. His servants grabbed handfuls of necklaces, bracelets and hair combs. David wandered the stalls and came across a carved jade box. It consisted of two pieces of solid jade, mated to fit together. A carved dragon swirled around a phoenix whose tail curled behind the dragons legs, entwined in a loving, yet ferocious standoff, snout to beak. Alive and tense.

The merchant bowed. "Honored King, take this box and bestow it on your queen. The dragon and phoenix symbolize marriage unity between a king and a queen. It is yours."

David stared at the box; his heart ached and twisted to the point of bursting. Marriage unity, one man and one woman. How had it gone so wrong? Flustered, he shoved some gold coins at the merchant who refused. "It is an honor for my treasure to be bestowed by my king for the elegant Queen Michal."

Leaving the gold on the table, David pocketed the box. His head servant paid for the rest of the jewelry. Joab and Abishai sauntered over, sardonic grins pasted on their faces.

"Uncle, buying presents for your many wives?" Joab laughed.

"We don't have that pleasure, now do we?" Abishai punched his brother's shoulder.

David wasn't in the mood for joking. He mounted his horse and headed for the palace. Once he entered his bedchamber, he took the box out of his pocket and set it on the table where Michal's two other boxes would have been.

Arik knocked on the door. "O King, the sons of Saul have been secured."

"How is she?" David's voice choked more than he wished.

"She is well." Arik bowed and retreated.

David bathed without the help of a maid servant and put on a common cloak to shield his face. His heart beating at a furious pace and his nerves tight in his stomach, he sneaked out of the palace by a back gate and headed for Michal's house.

She opened the door and started to close it, but he lodged his shoulder between the door and its frame and stepped in. Her eyes were red and swollen.

"Eglah." He expected an onslaught of bitter words, but her jaw shook silently, and she ran for her room.

Pain pummeled his ribs, and his heart wrenched lower. He caught her and hugged her. "I wanted to tell you myself, but I had to fight the Philistines."

She shook silently in his arms. He laid her down on her couch and dipped a cloth into water. Although the evening was warm, she shivered, and her eyes were unfocused, dull and lifeless. David wiped her face and pulled back her hair. "Your sons will be safe with Phaltiel. I've increased their guards to fifty men, Philistine mercenaries."

She closed her eyes, seeming somewhat settled. Gently he wiped the dirt and ashes from her face and flicked them off her robe. He asked Naomi to draw water.

Stepping over a large rolled up rug, David placed the jade box on her table next to her two other boxes. He picked up an ebony comb and went to Michal's side. She lay on the couch with her eyes closed, breathing hard, an occasional lingering sob tightening her chest with a wheeze.

"I had to protect your sons," he said. Her silence filled him with foreboding, as if she stored her anger and bitterness for a giant blast, much like a whirlwind's final gust.

Naomi filled the bathtub, and he carried Michal to the bathroom. She offered no resistance. She allowed him to peel off her clothes and place her into the tub. She allowed him to wash her and comb her hair. He did all his motions, slowly, gently, almost reverently. And when he finished, she allowed him to tuck her into bed. He took off his robe and climbed in. He couldn't leave her alone to suffer, to mourn. He held her and closed his eyes.

When David woke the next morning, Michal was already awake. Her eyes froze his attempted smile. Emotionless as solid malachite, they stared at him.

He leaned to kiss her but met her palm.

She backed away. "Why did you take my sons? And what have you done to Ittai?"

David raked his hair. "I will find you another guard. Probably Arik."

Her chest fluttered and color rushed to her face. "Arik tells me Ittai is in prison and might die."

He tucked in his tunic and tightened the sash of his robe. "He'll live. Why do you care?"

The tone in her voice changed to pleading. "He's a friend, and if he's hurt, I want to see him."

He turned to leave. "I cannot allow it."

"David, please. I beg you." She grabbed his arm. "If you even care for me a tiny bit, please release him. He couldn't possibly have done anything."

An irrational ache seized his heart. *He loves you, that's a crime enough.* "I'll send him to Mahanaim to guard your sons. Now stop worrying about him."

"But, how did he get hurt? How serious is it?"

His gut wrenched. Concern was written across her face. Would she worry about him as much if he were hurt?

"The doctor says he'll live."

She covered her mouth and trembled. "You… you did it? You tried to kill him?"

David's pulse swished in a haze of red behind his eyelids. He clenched his jaw and dug his thumb and fingers into her shoulder. "I fought him in the training ground."

Her lips twisted with a snarl. "Go away. How could you? Ittai didn't do anything wrong."

David punched the wall next to her head. "Am I not enough for you? Does my love mean nothing?"

Michal's glare sharpened like daggers. "If this is being loved by you, I wonder what it's like to be hated."

"Do you know who you're dealing with? I'm the king. I come here and show you favor, and you repay me with disdain? It's always the same. You never change." He turned toward the door and pointed a finger at her. "Arik will be your guard. I'll not be responsible for your safety if you disobey him."

Michal picked up the jade box and threw it.

It hit his forehead. He fell and knocked the back of his head on the edge of the table. He sunk into a pained darkness.

When David opened his eyes, Michal and Naomi were staring at him with fear etched on their faces. He groaned and his head throbbed. He tried to stand, and the floor rolled.

Michal grasped his elbow. "I could have killed you. Let me help you."

David crawled on her bed and hung his head between his knees, a clump of nausea churning in his stomach. Naomi discreetly retreated.

"I didn't mean to hurt you." She touched the lump on his temple. "Why do I always do the wrong thing?"

David waited for the floor to stop spinning. Her hands felt good on him as she rubbed his back. His mind wandered. The young princess looked up from behind her fascinating hair, multi-colored like wild burled rosewood. She held his harp in her lap, and his heart in her hands. He bent her head back and kissed her softly, tenderly.

He opened his eyes. "Do you still want me?"

"I…" She stopped and bit her lips. "No. Not anymore. You're no good for me. You've been hurting me since the first day I met you. Always hot and cold."

"Am I that bad?"

"You make me most miserable." A scowl blanketed her face.

David stroked her cheek and kissed her, opening her lips with his tongue. "Do I make you miserable now?"

She sighed and squirmed while he rubbed his beard over the hollow of her neck. "How about when I do this?"

Her breath hitched, but she did not stop him.

He twirled his thumb over her breast. "And this? Does this make you feel miserable?"

A moan escaped her, and she pushed out of his grasp. "Don't touch me. Do you think that's all I want?"

David stopped, not used to being refused. He stood and pulled his robe together. "I have to go. Is there anything else you need?"

"Yes, let me go to Mahanaim with my children. They're the only reason for me to live."

David clenched his teeth. What would the people say if he lost his wife to Phaltiel? He took a deep breath. "No. I need you here, near me. They'll be safe, I promise."

"I don't want to see you again," she said through gritted teeth. "Leave me alone to trust God and find peace with Him."

"But…" He would never divorce her, nor allow her to live away from him. He bit the insides of his cheeks, swallowing the bitter pang of loss. If she didn't want him, then he didn't want her either. She could rot in this dingy house for all he cared.

He picked the jade box from the floor and pressed it into her hand. "Remember me."

One corner on the lid had chipped off, right over the head of the dragon.

"How could I ever forget?" Her voice turned to ice and chilled his blood.

David stared at her for several moments. His throat swelled, and he choked, unable to get any words out. Why did she have to look so glorious, almost shining, her face serene like still waters, her eyes glittering gemstones, her mouth, a perfect rose. Why did she have to be the daughter of Saul? And why had everything he dreamed of gone so wrong?

Her hand slipped from his grasp and dropped to her side. "Goodbye, David."

David could not speak. He went to the door without looking back. He couldn't, even if he wanted to, and he didn't.

It was over, no song, no dream, only pain.

CHAPTER 33

Job 30:15 Terrors are turned upon me: they pursue my soul as the wind: and my welfare passeth away as a cloud.

>>><<<

"Come Naomi, let me show you something." I led her down a narrow alley through streets filled with foreigners. David brought in mercenaries, legions of Gittites, Cherethites, and Pelethites, all Philistine. He also numbered among his friends, Ammonites, Gibeonites, Jebusites and Hittites. All these people brought their families to Jerusalem.

We stopped in front of a white-washed mud-brick home, sheltered by a myrtle tree, its sweet fragrance welcoming. "A priestess of Asherah lives here. You remember Jada, don't you?"

"Oh, yes, I do. Jada was ever so kind to us and took care of all our problems."

Before I could knock, Jada stepped out and invited us in. "Michal, my dear, how have you been?"

I bounced on my toes and hugged her. "I've been great. How about you? Where did you go after we left each other?"

"Oh, I went to a cave where my mother had stayed before the Prophet Samuel drove her away."

She raised her voice. "Zina, come out and say hello to my friends."

A pretty girl around ten years old stepped toward us. She bowed. "I'm Zina. Are you a real princess?"

"Yes, I was the daughter of King Saul, but that was a long time ago. Now, I'm sort of a free spirit."

I stared at Zina as if looking into a mirror of my younger self. She had my olive-toned skin, my straight nose, and hair that waved like curls of strikingly grained mahogany. But her eyes were amber, and she had twin dimples when she smiled.

"Whose daughter are you?" I asked.

She shrugged and looked at Jada sideways. "Ask Mother."

Jada put a hand on her hip and shook her head.

I slid a look at Jada. "Perhaps he's a king, or a prince, or a hero?"

She laughed and shooed Zina to the kitchen.

We sat at the table while Zina placed some dried fruit, vegetables, and bread in front of us.

"So, what brings you here today?" Jada patted my hand. "I was under the impression David kept his wives under lock and key."

"Well, apparently he let me out of the cage."

Her brow arched in a frown. "Did he tire of you, my dear?"

"Oh, no. He'll never tire of me. But he has decreed that I'm to be removed as queen. Apparently I angered him the night he brought the Ark of the Covenant to town."

"Ah yes, I remember that parade." Jada picked at a pomegranate. "All the yelling and jeering, the chanting and noise. It was enough to embarrass the gods. Dagon would never have put up with it."

"You wouldn't have recalled seeing David?"

She tilted head. "No, I'm not sure I saw him. There were quite a few maidservants dancing after the Ark, and a whole lot of priests making sacrifices, bloodying the streets."

I shuddered at the memory of the lowing and squealing of the sacrificial animals.

Her eyes lit. "Ah, one of them made a big commotion. A handsome one with flaming red-brown hair, I thought he had too much to drink." She laughed melodiously.

"That was David."

Her mouth pursed into a tiny circle, and she placed her hand on my shoulder. "So what's troubling you? I know you too well, my dear."

I pressed my lips into a smug smile. "Nothing. Nothing at all."

* * *

I waited patiently for the LORD; and he inclined unto me, and heard my cry.

With Abigail standing at my side, I unrolled David's prayer book and smoothed it on the table.

He brought me up also out of a horrible pit, out of the miry clay, and set my feet upon a rock, and established my goings.

Abigail held one side of the scroll. "David asked if you could make copies. He has many scribes, but he would like you to make his personal copy and one for each of his sons."

I set a stone on the corner of the scroll and wiped my hands on my robe. "So this job is in place of raising my children? Does he think to ease my imprisonment with busy work?"

Abigail blinked. "He can explain if you'd let him."

My heart squeezed and closed. "There's nothing for him to say. He's destroyed me already."

"What message should I deliver to him?"

I clenched and unclenched the sleeve of my robe. The bitterness at the edge of my heart crawled to my throat. "It's useless. Thank you for your help, Abi. Will you come back on the Sabbath?"

"I will. David's going to war again, so we can stay out later." She kissed me on both cheeks and departed with her servant. Her vanilla fragrance lingered wistfully.

The throb of loneliness returned as soon as the door closed. I yearned to visit my children, but David disallowed it during wartime. And these days, we were continually at war. David's campaign of reconquering the land God promised to Abraham kept him away from Jerusalem—which was just as well, since I had no desire whatsoever to see him.

And he hath put a new song in my mouth, even praise unto our God.

Beautiful words. But how hateful he'd been to me. A dark grey mist blurred my mind, and tears welled in my eyes. I idly unrolled his scroll and perused his unruly script.

For the enemy hath persecuted my soul; he hath smitten my life down to the ground; he hath made me to dwell in darkness, as those that have been long dead.

David, are you my enemy? How could you be the man after God's heart and hate me so? My father had persecuted you. Maybe that's why.

Therefore is my spirit overwhelmed within me; my heart within me is desolate.

Desolate. An abandoned, desolate woman. Oh, David. You've left me so alone.

Cause me to hear thy loving-kindness in the morning; for in thee do I trust.

My lips trembled. Loving-kindness. I wrote the words from David's heart and memorized them as they flowed onto the parchment.

Thou wilt shew me the path of life: in thy presence is fulness of joy; at thy right hand there are pleasures for evermore.

If I couldn't have David's presence, at least I had his prayers at my right hand.

* * *

Seven years passed. David had tucked Michal into a secure corner of his heart. Every morning he made a vow to not think about her. He stayed away from Jerusalem by going on campaigns. He subjugated the Moabites, contained the Philistines, and pushed the Syrians all the way to the Euphrates. He plundered the King of Zobah and stripped him of his golden shields. He put garrisons from Damascus to the Gulf of Aqaba.

He subdued the Ammonites, Edomites, and Amalekites, and completed everything Michal's father failed to do in God's sight.

David returned to Jerusalem with a burning desire to build a temple for the LORD. He sought Abigail, his third wife. She updated him on the collection of building materials and the preparation of the songbooks. After a long and enjoyable evening of reviewing plans and outlining worship services, he relaxed on her bed.

"Abi, come. Put the diagrams away." He rubbed his eyes and patted the bed.

Abigail lifted her head from the table and blushed. She walked over to the side of the bed and sat down stiffly. "Shall I deliver your latest psalms to Michal for her to copy?"

"Yes, yes. But come closer. I don't bite." He had kept his word and not approached Michal, only spying her at a distance when she worshipped at the tabernacle or went to the market. Cantankerous and unruly woman. He had many wives, he didn't need her. She ought to know her place and stop intruding into his thoughts.

David beckoned at Abigail.

She shifted an inch, maybe two. "My lord."

He pulled her down to his side. She gasped and fluttered her eyelids.

He chuckled. "Abi, we've been married how many years? More than ten?" And yet she blushed like a virgin. So unlike that seductive witch he had married when he was young and stupid. His loins tightened despite his thoughts.

He kissed Abigail behind her neck. "You don't have to do anything you're not comfortable with."

He touched her gently and smoothed her thin brown hair, so soft and silky. David suppressed images of Michal, her neck open, her back arched toward him, and her hips tilted, so invitingly. Abigail's tiny whimper reminded him to cool his ardor. He exhaled through pursed lips and cursed Michal silently.

He kissed Abigail's cheeks. Brushing her lips lightly, he stroked her temple and planted another kiss, eliciting a miniscule indrawn breath. Remembering to keep his touch light, he put out the oil lamps and undressed her in the dark.

David fell asleep and dreamed. His head pounded, and his eyelids spasmed.

A man clawed her body and pressed between her legs.

David lunged and throttled him. My wife, my wife. You shall not touch my wife.

Michal scratched his face.

Michal. Love me, Michal.

He forced her lips open, grappled and held her hands above her head.

She bit his tongue and kicked him. I hate you, David. I despise you.

He grabbed her neck and shook the life out of her.

Shafts of sunlight speared his throbbing eyeballs.

"Michal, how you hurt me." David covered his face. "Come back to me, Michal."

He heard a sob, a soft sob, and opened his eyes. "Michal?"

Soft brown hair cascaded to her waist. Red marks encircled her neck. Abigail stared at him, her jaw quivered. She covered her throat. "You had a nightmare. You thought I was Michal."

"I didn't mean to." He kissed her, but she deflated and withdrew. He recalled the ease and humor of the night before. He recalled what her first husband had done to her. And he recalled and tasted her fear.

"Abi, don't be frightened of me. Don't. Not after all we've been through." It had taken him years to gain her trust. What had he done? Abigail shrank from his touch. Had he forced her? Treated her roughly? His head spun, and he moaned, "Abi, I'm sorry."

Abigail pulled on her robe and ran out the chamber.

* * *

I opened the door and smiled. My seventeen-year-old sons Joshua and Beraiah stood there, one dark and muscular, the other slim and red-headed. They clambered in with their luggage and weapons. David had finally relented and allowed them to come back to Jerusalem to join the palace guards. I craned my neck to see if anyone was behind them. Butterfly wings tickled my heart.

Had Ittai also returned?

Joshua set his things down and looked around the small house. He immediately spied the rolled-up rug I had purchased before my exile and crouched beside it. "Mother, that's a huge rug."

"Can I open it?" Beraiah asked.

"Yes, make sure you roll it back. I don't want it to get dirty."

Naomi flipped her eyes back. "It's a present for someone special."

Beraiah smoothed his hand over the threads. "It's beautiful, crimson red, the tree of life, a pomegranate border with partridges. I bet King David will like it."

Joshua traced the outline of the tree. "Would you like us to deliver it?"

"Hold on, boys. Who said anything about it being for David?" I grimaced as Naomi suppressed a twitter. "Actually, I was wondering about Ittai. Is he coming back to Jerusalem?"

A shadow with the scent of fresh bay leaves fell over me. "Did I hear my name?"

Naomi quickly excused herself to buy food.

Joshua and Beraiah jumped to attention. "Commander."

Ittai handed them silver coins. "You boys run along and get something to eat."

They thanked him and scurried out the door.

"So, what's this I hear about a gift for your king?" he said.

Fanning myself, I turned from his cheeky grin. "Let me gift this rug to you as a welcome back present."

He turned me to face him. "Forget the rug. I want you."

My lips quivered. His dreamy eyes made me soft and syrupy inside. He could not have been more handsome. His strong jaw rugged, his face chiseled and masculine, the curl of his upper lip suggested wicked pleasures. His warm male scent permeated my resolve, and I let him draw close and kiss me.

My heart responded like flower petals in a light breeze. How long had it been since a man kissed me? I shuddered to count. Warm tingles traversed my shoulders and down my belly.

But when he touched my breast, I pushed back. "I can't commit sins."

He let me go a little too abruptly and covered a scowl with a grin. "Deny me now, but you can't stop me from loving you, or trying again."

"You tempt me." My voice lowered. "So, has your wish come true yet? The one you made on the wishing tree?"

His eyes twinkled. "Has yours?"

"It was long ago." I gave him a sidelong glance. "You tell me."

He crossed his arms. "How am I to tell you if you haven't told me what your wish was?"

"I'm thinking you might have some information."

"I've not a clue unless you tell me."

I tapped his shoulder. "No, you first. Go ahead."

His amused smirk infuriated me. "I can already tell it hasn't come true. So sorry. You'll get no more information from me."

"You stinker." I punched his bicep.

"Call me whatever names you want. I'm still not telling you. But perhaps…" He licked his lips suggestively.

"No."

He wagged his tongue. "Not even a chaste kiss?"

A bubble of amusement tickled my throat, and I sputtered, "Chaste kiss? Is there such a thing?"

He palmed my face with both hands. "Try me and decide." He lowered his face to mine. His minty breath and palpable heat allured and aroused me, raising the hair on the back of my scalp and dampening my inner thighs dangerously.

"Just keep it chaste," I murmured. And our lips touched, like a thread of a whisper, a single silk of a spider's web, and the tiny prickles of a tart persimmon. The hairs of his mustache brushed my upper lip, and the puffs of my breath panted on his beard. A kiss as soft as the belly of a newborn babe, as light as the fur of a baby bunny, as pious as the flurry of angel wings awakened every deep sense and emotion I had dammed behind the wall of righteousness.

"Was that good?" Ittai asked when the long moment faded.

"Oh, yes." Tears sprinkled my eyelashes. "Why are you so good to me? Sometimes I don't think you're real, but someone I conjured."

He stroked my face. "Oh, I'm real. But I've learned not to have expectations."

"Why is that?" I peered into his deep, dark eyes.

"Expectations cause disappointment."

"Do I disappoint you?"

"No, because I have no expectations."

I fingered his beard. "How sad."

"No, not sad. Just realistic. Do you think I can stand loving you all these years if I expected anything of you?" His voice caught and stumbled with obvious disappointment.

I tapped the tip of his nose. "No, but something is missing when you don't expect anything."

"Yes, what's missing is disappointment."

"No, not just disappointment." I paused, trying to frame my thoughts. "What's missing is something deeper, more intense."

"More fearful, yes. But intolerable. So I take what life gives me and try to be satisfied." He forced a smile, but his eyebrows lowered.

I flicked a burr off his shoulder. "You're aiming too low. If I were like you, I'd forget about David, while away my hours painting my fingernails and sunning myself on the roof."

"Haven't you been doing just that?" Ittai's gaze swept the room. "Or have you also become one of the scribes?"

"I've been doing both. Sunning myself makes me feel peaceful and calm." I held out my arm and showed him my tan. "And copying scripture makes me feel one with the LORD." I patted Jonathan's leather sleeve, the one he had always worn at his side when going to war. It contained the scripture he used to read to me.

I stepped toward the door. "Come. Let's sun ourselves on the roof. There's a nice breeze up there, and when I close my eyes, I can almost hear Delilah sing."

* * *

Ittai and Michal lay on leather couches on top of her roof, unaware that King David watched them. They joined their voices and sang the songs of Samson and Delilah. They touched not the hand, nor gazed with the eye. The threads of their song rose, twined and wove together, mating in the air like smoky traces through a desert sunset.

* * *

The chill of the evening descended, but my smile did not fade. My youngest sons were back, and Ittai had gone with them to find lodging. A soft knocking on the door drew my attention. I looked up from my writing desk and rubbed my wrist. Ittai had left his cloak. I put down my reed and picked up his cloak, bringing it to my nose before opening the door.

Abigail stepped through the threshold with a manservant. I clasped my throat, then recovered and kissed her on both cheeks. "What a surprise. Come in."

She kissed me. "I heard your twins are back. What great news."

"Yes, nothing could make me happier. So, what brings you here?"

"David has written another series of worship psalms for the temple." She motioned for the servant to set down a stack of parchment. "Of course, he only trusts you to transcribe them and copy them with your pretty script."

"I'm the only one who can read his scribbles." I waved my hand. "How's Chileab? You should bring him more often. I love his harp playing."

She dismissed her servant after he loaded the stack of completed scrolls into a cart. Her eyes flickered, and she trembled. Naomi took her sandals to wash her feet while I placed fruit, bread and wine on the table. She clutched her shawl over her breast and stared at the top of Naomi's head.

"Abi? Are you well?" Usually, she exuded cheer and had many uplifting stories to tell.

"Give me a few minutes." She hugged her elbows and took several deep breaths. When Naomi dried her feet, she thanked her with a kiss and turned to me. "How do you like it outside the palace?"

I swirled the wine goblet and sipped. "It's peaceful, and I definitely don't miss all the tension. Now that my youngest two are back, things couldn't be better."

She fiddled with an almond date roll. "I'm wondering if David will let me and Chileab leave the palace?"

"You mean to your estate in Carmel?"

"No, he won't allow it. But perhaps I can get the house next to you. I'm tired of judging the disputes in his harem."

I winced. The harem remained a sore spot even though I had long ago disavowed any claim to David's time or affection. "Does it bother you... to share him with so many?"

"Why, no." She stared at me. "I've always known he had other wives. It honestly lightens the load. What I meant is the bickering amongst them. Maacah can be a real pain, and the new ones each pride themselves on their fathers' prestige. Ahinoam tears her hair out trying to find suitable accoutrements for each new princess or... excuse me... I know you don't care to hear."

She pursed her lips, looking as if she were about to cry.

"Something else is bothering you," I said.

She lifted her head, and her shawl dropped. She tried to cover the red marks on her neck, but I was faster.

I grabbed her wrist. "What's happened? Who did this to you?"

Tears bubbled from her eyes.

"David? He hurt you?"

"He didn't mean to. He was having a nightmare."

"That's no excuse. Has he hurt anyone else?"

"I don't know, although I've sensed a chill among the other women. It started after he returned from the wars."

A sense of dread pinched my throat. "You told me he was excited about building the LORD a temple. What went wrong?"

She wiped her eyes. "I don't know. He's obsessed with the temple. I'm afraid he's headed for a fall. Michal, what if the LORD will not allow it?"

I pressed her hand. "For his sake I hope this will not be so. You're trembling."

"I was so afraid, and he was so strong. Maybe you can help him. It seems as if he were reaching for you."

My heart flipped. "Me?"

"Yes, he called your name." She gripped my arm. "He said you had hurt him. And... he cried for you."

David. An avalanche rumbled through my soul and threatened the barrier I had built during my years of solitude. I slumped forward and rubbed my eyes. "No, Abigail. Don't bring this back to me."

Her lips thinned. "You cannot stand by and do nothing. The king needs to be strong and in control at all times. He is ruler of Israel. If he needs you, you must go to him. Would you want Israel weakened?"

She left me with my head in my hands, the pulse rushing through my ears, and my heart squeezing sludge through my veins. I unrolled David's prayer book with heavy hands.

I am weary with my groaning; all the night make I my bed to swim: I water my couch with my tears. A powerful fist punched my heart, releasing an enormous flood of anguish and yearning. How alike we two were. Me and David. David and I.

I stretch forth my hands unto thee: my soul thirsteth after thee, as a thirsty land. Selah. Shooting pains traveled from my heart to my fingertips. I collapsed on my bed. I needed David as much as he needed me.

* * *

David beheld his beautiful eleven-year-old daughter as she walked around the room with a tray of sweets. Her adorable smile warmed his heart. "Tamar, that was delicious."

She put another tart in his mouth. "I made it myself. I milked the goat, took the honey out of the comb, milled the wheat and gathered the nuts."

Today was her birthday. Ithream would have been eleven, too, had he lived. David's heart clenched at the memory, and he hugged Tamar a little longer than usual. "Happy birthday, daughter. I love you."

Her mother, Maacah, handed her an embroidered sack. "Open it."

Tamar revealed the gift, a bridal veil. David shot up in his seat. "Wait, I have no intention of marrying off my jewel so early. This will have to wait at least five more years."

Maacah slipped an arm around his neck. "My thoughts exactly. You are ever so wise, my lord."

After all the presents were opened, Chileab strummed his harp and sang a psalm he had composed. David couldn't help but be amused at Absalom's impatience. He tossed his hair and rolled his eyes about at every chord. Adonijah and Shephatiah traded elbows and pinches while Abital, his sixth wife, played with her white bird, Beulah.

His first born son, Amnon, sat sullenly next to his mother, the equally sullen Ahinoam. Her adopted daughter, Sarah, played on the floor with Maacah's kitten, a grey with brown patches. The kitten's ears were sharp and pointy, and she swatted playfully at a skein of wool. She rolled onto her back under David's legs. Large green eyes stared at him. David's heart twisted, and he turned away.

Chileab tilted his head back and sang loudly of God's glories. Beulah, the white bird, did not want to be upstaged. She screeched even louder, bobbed her head, and flapped her wings, her saucer eyes rolling as she flopped her yellow-crested head upside down from one side to the other. Everyone laughed except for Abigail. Her gaze was trained on her son.

David peeled Maacah's arms from his neck and put a hand on Abigail's shoulder. "You should be so proud. Chileab sang marvelously." She flinched but covered it with a warm smile.

A high-pitched shriek followed by laughter drew his attention back to Maacah. Abital's bird had landed in Maacah's puffed-up hair, and her talons were hopelessly entangled. The bird flapped her wings, shaking feather dust and white down all over Maacah. She swatted at the bird while Abital tried to extricate her.

Beulah screamed with a deafening shriek, "Bad Maacah. Bad Maacah." She was a jungle bird, extremely expensive and extremely loud, from the isles in the eastern seas past India.

David roared with laughter.

The bird safely back in Abital's hands, Maacah clutched her robe and glared at Beulah. She shrieked back, "It's supposed to be 'Bad Michal,' you stupid bird." She ran her fingers through her hair, tangled with a mess of feathers and bits of fluff, and huffed from the room.

David shook his head at the departing circus and went across the room to Ahinoam. A distant look in her eyes, she appeared not to have witnessed the scene. He took her hand and pressed it. "I shall see you later this evening."

* * *

Ahinoam welcomed David at her door. She was his second wife, earthy, solid and voluptuous—a quiet one, not given to words. She led him straight into her bedchamber. Amnon stayed in his room, and her little girl had already gone to sleep.

Without a word she cupped both hands around his face and pulled him in for a kiss. David ran his fingers straight through her hair, smooth and silky. He pulled her dress off, and she undressed him. They tumbled on the bed, and she received him immediately.

David dreamed.

He stepped over piles of sticky wetness. To his left, a figure stumbled. The sword clattered. A head rolled, glistening red. A wild squirrel lodged in his stomach, clawing fervently for an exit. Red, crimson, a river. The Nile turned to blood.

Shammah. Blood spouted from his chest, a gaping hole. His legs heavy as iron, he fell on piles of empty eyes and gaping mouths. Squish. Crawl. Shammah, hold on.

David cradled his head. Shammah, brother, mighty man. He tried to talk. Blood oozed through his teeth. He stared into the wind, the long, distant stare.

Come back, brother, come back. David shook him. Wake up. Wake up, don't die. David slapped his face.

Ahinoam cried, "David, stop, stop, stop."

CHAPTER 34

Proverbs 13:12 Hope deferred maketh the heart sick: but when the desire cometh, it is a tree of life.

>>><<<

All winter, David's wives peeked at him with guarded eyes and whispered among themselves. His nightmares had thundered in tune with the winter storms, and his temper raged at anyone who crossed his path. One courtier had dared suggest a harpist! As if that would cure him.

The balmy spring weather did little to relieve the tightness in his chest. Ittai had been back since summer, making it difficult for David to concentrate on his duties. He had assigned Ittai to train the young guards, and he spied on Michal incessantly, donning commoner's clothing and following her. As far as he could tell, other than the first day Ittai visited her, they had stayed away from each other. Abigail spent more nights sleeping at Michal's house than in the palace, and he didn't mind it the least. She was as good a guard as any when it came to deterring Ittai.

He prowled the women's courtyard looking for his five oldest sons. It was about time to make them men, maybe select a few to take on the upcoming campaigns.

Absalom and Adonijah walked up first. They were dressed in their tunics and breeches, spears in hand, sporting hair too long for battle. Absalom's brown locks gleamed long and silky; Adonijah's coppery mop was a tangled mass.

Abital held Shephatiah's hand and stepped forward. Large for his age, his golden-brown hair was cut short. David acknowledged his youngest wife. "Abital, you're always so fresh and clean."

She bowed. "My lord, please keep Sheppy close to you and don't let his brothers abuse him."

"Rest easy, dear. He has learned to ride quite well. I will not let him joust just yet. That will be for the three eldest."

He pounded on Abigail's door. "Chileab?"

"Here, Father." Chileab's thin face peered out the doorframe. He pulled at his sash and rushed out. The bull-headed Amnon lurked at his side with a scowl. These boys were nothing like Michal's sons. Their mothers had spoiled them.

They trotted to the training field outside of Jerusalem where the ground rolled level. A small brook traversed the meadow, scattered with a few rock formations. The sun shone brightly, and a hint of a breeze made it a perfect day. A few recruits trained near the willows, but the field stretched open before them.

The boys took off on his signal. Absalom took the lead. His hair flying in the wind, he whooped at the top of his lungs, his spear in hand. Adonijah, always eager to keep up with his older brother, charged after him. Chileab dropped his spear and stopped to look at his fingernails while Amnon cantered in a slow and meandering pace. Sheppy's horse had trotted the opposite direction.

David turned his horse after Sheppy. "Boys, race around that hill while I find your brother."

Sheppy's horse jumped the brook and splashed to the other bank where it found a patch of green grass near the reeds. David cantered in the direction of the brook.

He saw her almost immediately. Michal stood under a willow tree with Ittai watching Beraiah and Joshua ride. She turned her head and whispered in Ittai's ear, then laughed when he playfully pushed her.

A green blast of bile erupting with the surge of his pulse, David yanked his horse around. He thundered toward them, but Beraiah reached her first and threw his mother onto his prancing chestnut horse.

Michal screamed, "No jumping, no jumping."

Beraiah laughed and tossed his rusty-brown hair, an impish curve on his lips. He kicked his horse and tore across the field with Michal bouncing across the withers.

Joshua raced his white horse after Beraiah. Both horses jumped a hedge while Michal let out a continual scream. David's blood pounded in his ears as he recalled Michal's screams of passion, and he kicked to join the chase.

Beraiah launched into another jump, cleared a creek and splashed to the other side. Ittai pounced on his black war horse and galloped after them.

David spurred his horse harder. *Michal is mine.* Crazy inside, fury boiling, screaming. Mine! Mine! Mine! He flew at them with the speed of an avenging angel.

"Hey, pass your mother to me," Ittai shouted. "I'll show her what riding's all about."

Beraiah spurred his horse harder. "Never."

Joshua crowded in from the other side and drove his horse right into Beraiah's. With a lunge, he ripped his mother off her mount and spun her face-down on his lap. She had barely righted herself when his horse reared. The animal's front hooves landed with a thud, and Michal's mouth hit the horse's neck. She let out a howling scream that ended in shrill laughter.

David raised his spear while Ittai charged Joshua with a heavy stick. Joshua dodged by spinning his horse. Ittai reared around and caught Joshua in the small of his back. "Unhand your mother, you ruffian. Ha, ha, ha."

"Never," Joshua shouted, but he did not see David crowd him from the other side.

David lunged for his wife just as Ittai wrapped his arm around Michal's waist and whipped her over his mount.

"Ha, ha, I have you now, Princess." Roaring in triumph, Ittai tore away.

A nest of wasps exploded inside David's chest, and he pounded after them. *My wife, my wife, my wife.*

Ittai spun around. Shock registered in his eyes as David rammed him with the blunt end of the training spear. He fell off the horse and tumbled over a rock. Michal reined the horse to a stop. She jumped off, ran to Ittai and threw herself over him.

David dismounted and pulled his wife up. She beat against his chest, screaming hysterically. Joshua and Beraiah helped Ittai to a sitting position. Ittai groaned and held his head between his knees.

"Mother," Joshua said, "he's not hurt. Just his wind knocked out."

Michal ignored them. She flailed in David's arms, so he did the only thing he could. He pushed her face down to the ground, stabilized her with a knee, pushed the golden garnet bracelet up her arm, and tied her wrists with a cord.

By now, an audience had gathered. David's sons, Michal's sons, the recruits, and Ittai stood in a row, their faces impassive, their mouths gaped slightly open. David slipped a cloak over Michal's head and put her on his horse. "Ittai, take the boys back to the stable. Riding lessons are over for the day."

He led his wife away. His war captive.

* * *

"Are you sure you still want this spell?" Jada flashed her teeth and ushered me into her house. "He sounds dangerous to me."

"David needs me. He won't admit it, but he needs me."

"I have to warn you, this is strong magic. He will become obsessed with you, insatiable and wild for your love. He will be tortured when you're not around. Are you sure you want to go through with this?"

A large cat reclined on the hearth, his copper hair like David's. Golden-brown eyes flickered at me as if amused. He yawned, his tail twitching at my indecision. I twisted my fingers. "Yes, I'm sure. I love him so much, and I miss him."

Jada waved a finger. "In that case, I'm not sure I should grant you the spell."

"Please, I want to be back in his life. I've been shut out for eight years." I paced the room, my good intentions tossed to the east wind.

"When he touched me." I closed my eyes, savoring the memory. He had brought me to his tower. He had slipped a black hood over my head and tied my hands. And he did unbelievable things, things I had never imagined possible. But while the red-hot glow suffused my body, he wrapped me in a veil and cloak and carried me back to my house. He spoke not a word. It had been anonymous, impersonal, but oh, so exciting.

That had been over a week ago.

"I'm ready." I removed my clothes and stepped into the bath. After toweling me off, Jada took out the perfumes, paint and makeup. She rubbed my palms and the soles of my feet with henna. She dusted my hair with jasmine powder and oiled my neck, elbows and knees with lotus oil.

Jada dipped a brush in dark brown paste. Painstakingly, she painted my body as if I were a living canvas. I closed my eyes as the stiff brush scratched while she chanted incantations. She sprinkled vinegar over her artwork and left it to stand until everything dried.

"Now, Michal," she said, putting her brush away, "though the paste will wash off, the stain will remain on your skin for a few weeks. So go ahead and scrape off the paste while I entreat Asherah for you: that David will be bewitched and his heart will be cut so only you can satisfy him."

Jada lit incense and sat cross-legged on the floor, the middle finger and thumb of each hand making a circle. She droned a humming sound until the incense sticks were consumed. "The goddess has heard. The spell has been set. All that remains is for you to appear naked in front of him. Now put your clothes on so no other man spies you, lest he, too, become crazed with lust for you."

Jada kissed me. "May all your dreams come true, may David's heart and body be tied to yours, and may he never escape your charm." We walked back to my house and she took leave, looking back with a knit of worry on her brow.

I waited for Ittai to deliver me. *What if David does not accept the gift? What if I smother? What if I don't have a chance to undress before he throws me out?*

Ittai showed up with an ox-cart. "Okay, Princess. Ready?"

"Yes. Are you sure David is available?"

"Of course. You mean to sneak into the palace, past the guards, and into his bedchamber. Clever, very clever." He chuckled. "You are the most interesting person I know."

Ittai approved of my every scheme, always ready for a practical joke. I poked his belly. "Yes, and won't he be surprised when he sees me."

Ittai unrolled the rug. "It is beautiful. Red, I like red. And the tree of life in the center. Pomegranates and partridges, so pregnant. Ha, ha, ha."

"Make sure David doesn't leave me there too long, lest I smother."

"Don't worry. I won't leave his door until he's found you."

"Now, turn around. I have to undress."

His eyebrows shot up. "You're going in there naked?"

"Of course not. I'll be enclosed in the rug. And besides, I want the full effect of Jada's artwork to hit his eyes as soon as he unrolls me."

Ittai turned around. "Okay, let me know when you're ready."

I peeled off the linen robe and lay down with my arms outstretched over my head so that my hands would dangle near the border of the rug to form a breathing hole. "I'm ready."

Ittai's gaze roved over the painted designs. "Does this rub off?"

Our eyes met. A large wolfish grin spread over his face, and he lowered himself. "Let me taste and see if David should drink out of this cup or not."

I inhaled sharply and pushed him. "Stop it. You're not supposed to touch."

Ittai raised both hands. "I was only going to warm you up for him. He's having dinner and will be ready for a mighty fine refreshment."

The ox lowed in the setting sun. Ittai wrapped me in the rug and set me on the cart.

* * *

David perused the documents, his neck stiff from the late hour. The treaties had to be reviewed. He would extract a heavy tribute from the Edomites. He wiped his forehead, a long, tiresome day behind him. He dreaded the night when the headaches and bad dreams would consume him. Nothing could alleviate them as they tossed him night after night as helpless as a rudderless ship. His dinner grew cold on the table.

A hurried knock distracted him. "O King, we have brought you a gift."

"Bring it in," he replied. "Is it from the Syrian ambassador?"

The door swung open, and Ittai bowed to the ground. "A gift from the Queen of the South."

Three guards lifted a large, heavy rug into the room and lowered it gently. They promptly turned around and left Ittai standing there with a huge grin slashed across his face.

Ittai flourished his hand over the rug. "O King, your gift. Please unroll it right away."

David kicked the rug. "I've never heard of this Queen of the South. Why has she not sent messengers first?"

"Search me," Ittai replied. "I was coming back from my duties and found this ox-cart with a messenger asking me to deliver this to you. They said the Queen of the South wishes to make an alliance by sending this gift."

"Bring me the messenger so I might question him." David's tone indicated irritation. He had no time for jokes and this sounded like a huge distraction.

"O King, I'm so sorry. I dismissed him. He seemed nervous, so I told him I'd take the gift to you myself." Ittai peered from under dark, long eyebrows, like a puppy dog pleading for a bone.

David stomped his foot and crossed his arms. "I do not take gifts from anyone without knowing who they are and what they are requesting. Take this back to the Queen of the South. I'm sorry, but I must have more information."

"O King, I would if I could, but this rug is extremely valuable and very heavy. It is starting to rain, and I would not want it ruined. Why don't you open it now and see if you like it, then I'll search for the messenger and bring him to you." Ittai ran his hand across the rug, caressing it as if it held a live tiger.

David laughed. If Ittai fondled it with any more vigor, the rug would purr, perhaps even roar.

"I'm tired and had a long day. The rug can wait."

Ittai patted the rug right over the lump in the middle. "O King, the messenger said there is a message in the center of the rug. How can I convey your response, if you have not read it?"

The rug wiggled ever so slightly.

"Very well," David said in a tone designed to show his displeasure at having his already cold dinner interrupted. "Go ahead and unroll it."

Ittai's face showed agitation. "O King, do not be displeased, the messenger said the Queen of the South requested you open it personally." He waved his hands palm up and hunched his shoulders up and down at the same time.

"There is no Queen of the South. For some reason, you want me to open this rug. Well then, I won't open it until you tell me what the hurry is." David put on his firm king's voice. *Let her wait longer, this Queen of the South.*

Without a word, Ittai ran out the door and shut it. David snickered at his barely concealed stupidity.

"Well, well, well, the rug is alive," he said to the creature inside. He unrolled it slowly.

Michal rolled out, naked, painted with serpents and not breathing, her face tinted blue. David jumped over her and blew into her mouth. He was rewarded with a flutter of her hands, a sharp gasp and a cough.

"Michal, didn't you know you're not welcome in the palace?" David said with a stern voice. "You are the naughtiest girl I know."

A chuckle snuck out of his decidedly gruff tone. He threw her a robe and turned his back so she couldn't see his smile. His chest tightened with a web of heat. The last time he touched her, he had not called her name, nor seen her face. It had been too much to handle.

Michal wrapped her arms across his chest and nibbled the back of his neck. "I wished to deliver you a gift and some refreshment, make an alliance with you."

A tantalizing chill tickled the back of his head and traveled down his spine. It had been so long since a woman wanted him, really wanted him, as a man, not as the king.

She pulled him down onto the rug. "Feel this rug, so soft."

Holding his hand, she rubbed it across the nubby woolen fibers. Slowly, she removed every article of his clothing, handling every part of his body, awakening a deep, smoky, burning desire. She turned him facedown and massaged his shoulders and the back of his neck. His arousal pressed hard onto the rug.

Completely energized, David fought for control, resisting the urge to move his hips on the rug. He unseated her and turned on his back. "Michal, let me look at you."

She stood and the robe slithered to the floor. "Behold, the Queen of the South."

He lost his breath. A real goddess stood above him. Her legs and arms were golden pillars climbing with vines. Twin serpents wrapped around her round breasts, and a girdle of flowers swirled around her waist. Curlicues twirled up her legs and entwined her arms.

The room spun, and he feathered his fingers up her legs, tracing the vines to the poppy girdle. He knelt in front of her and pulled her down, licking the snakes' heads circling her full and pendulous breasts, delighting in the way she pulled his hair and thrust her hips into his chest.

Her body so very perfect, David slid a hand between her thighs, trying to control the tremors that tickled his belly as he stroked her slippery flesh. Heartened by her moans of pleasure, he laid her on the rug and arranged her hair so that it framed her hot, flushed face. "I'm going to impale you now. How do you want it, hard or soft?"

"Both."

Greedy girl. She'd get more than she bargained for.

"Good, because I'm going to make you feel absolutely and utterly miserable."

He wrapped a hand around her neck and turned her on top of him. Her body, soft and firm at the same time, he ached to enter her.

"Does this make you miserable?" He licked and sucked her lips, so luscious, tender and wet. Then he gave her the edge of his teeth and scraped her lower lip, tugging and shaking before pushing his tongue to the corners of her mouth. Her tongue yielded to his pressure, and he thrust it in rhythm to the movement of his hips and the hard length pressed on her belly.

Abruptly stopping, he grinned. "And how about this? Does this make you miserable?" He grasped both of her breasts and rolled them in slow, smooth circles, then craned his neck to lick and suck them. Michal's head flailed, and she gripped his shoulders, unable to answer coherently. His mouth increased the pressure on her breasts while his hands moved further down, eliciting hurried pants and moans.

He broke contact with a slurping sound, gritted his teeth and said, "And now, to make you truly miserable..."

He raised two fingers and waved them in front of her eyes, then plugged them between her legs, while his thumb danced in circular motions outside her soaked entrance. Her body jerked and wiggled under his ministrations, and she made short, choppy, desperate sounds. As her breathing became more frantic, a massive surge of heat flashed to his loins, and the ache became more than he could bear.

"Miserable and wretched," he shouted and plunged into her wet heat rocking her hips, and moving her with a tight frenzy. She clenched and fought as her eyes went through their cycles, hazy with lust, then flashed into sharp points before flooding a lustrous pool of jade. The trembling of her contractions spurred a mighty, hot wind that whipped over his shoulders, driving everything he possessed deep inside of her.

Holding onto the glow, David caressed her cheek and kissed her gently, followed by downy tickles that hovered just over the hairs of her skin. Barely able to breathe, he pulled her into his arms and leaned against the wall in a sitting position. He grabbed her waist and cradled her limp body between his open legs, her back to his chest. Spreading her legs, he lightly wiped his fingers over her skin. She writhed and rolled, but he held back, lazily fingering her with faint, rolling circles, one hand at her breasts and the other between her legs. "Hold still, and I'll make you most wretched."

294

He maintained a steady circular motion, bringing her closer and then further. The longer he sustained her to higher and higher plateaus of excitement, the more pleasurable her final ascent would be. So he waited and watched her quivering body, waiting for her to tighten against his fingers, and even as she clutched and moaned, he slowed his touch, nudging her ever so slightly, a bit at a time, up and down the rail of intensity. She straightened and stiffened, trying every way to exert pressure against his relaxed hands. Her body arched and jackal-like yelps bobbled from her throat. Her fingernails dug into his forearms, but David held back.

"Stay still and let it surprise you," he whispered and stroked her lightly, as if she were a soft piece of silk.

While he played her at a slow and steady tempo, he whispered all the things he'd like to do to her. She was close, oh, so close. At the last second, he captured her mouth and inhaled the frenzied screams, his fingers twitching to her never-ending pulses. Her body convulsed and lifted him off the rug with her before falling back. The tremors fading slowly into the dark, she buried her face into his chest and sobbed. His heart bathed in a swoon of contentment, he kissed the tears off her until her breathing steadied.

CHAPTER 35

Hosea 4:16 For Israel slideth back as a backsliding heifer: now the LORD will feed them as a lamb in a large place.

>>><<<

David donned a common cloak and veiled Michal before walking to her house. "It has to be this way. I can't be seen with you lest there be a rebellion. God may have forgiven you, but I'm not sure about my men."

"The daughter of Saul has become somewhat of a legend, hasn't she?" Michal smirked and stepped in front of him.

David turned her to face him. "Some men have long memories. Ittai will move all your things back to my bedchamber. I'll see you in the evening."

He kissed her in front of her door and gave her a tiny shove on the behind. He hadn't felt so lighthearted for years. Last night he had slept peacefully, undisturbed by gory images, flashbacks, and screaming headaches for the first time in years. He had never thought Michal, his most boisterous wife, would bring him peace.

He strolled by the jasmine patch in his garden and breathed deeply. By the time he entered the throne room, he was ready for the petitioners.

* * *

Ittai rushed through my door. "I have a note from Phaltiel. The messenger from Mahanaim was delayed, but here it is."

"What does it say?" I tore it from his hands.

My dear Michal, time has flown by, hasn't it? Our daughter, Anna, has been betrothed to Machir, the son of Ammiel of Lo-debar. Please ask King David if he can spare you a few days to attend her wedding this summer on the day of Tammuz. Rizpah and I look forward to seeing you. Yours, Phalti

My eyes watered with pride. "Did you hear that? My baby's getting married."

296

"Will David let you go? I can escort you and keep you safe."

"Of course I have to go. I haven't been out of Jerusalem since David allowed me to attend Eliah's wedding. I'll ask him tonight. Oh, won't it be such a great time? I can't wait to see Anna." I twirled around and flung my shawl in a circle above my head.

"When I last saw her, she was already a pretty rosebud, just starting to bloom." Ittai's eyes took on a dreamlike quality. "Now she must be positively gorgeous, like you must have been on your wedding day."

I flung a kiss on his cheek. "You've been a good uncle to all my children and a good friend to me."

Ittai and I walked into the yard and waved to the new neighbors, a burly man and his mother, equally large-boned. I greeted the older woman. "My daughter is getting married."

She cracked a large smile, revealing gapped teeth. "My son also. Next week, he takes his bride."

"What a coincidence. My daughter is marrying next week, too. Tammuz is a lucky time to marry. It's the summer solstice."

"Come meet my son's bride when you return." She called as we took leave.

"Delightful people, what's her son's name?" I asked Ittai.

"Uriah. Uriah, the Hittite."

* * *

David drummed his fingers on his throne. The Ammonites were making trouble again. His ally, Nahash, the Ammonite king, had passed away. David had sent ambassadors with condolences to his son, Hanun. Instead of taking comfort, Hanun accused them of being spies. He drove them away in shame by cutting off half their beard and exposing their buttocks. An Israelite man without a beard was an abomination, so the ambassadors waited in Jericho until their beards grew back. That had been several months ago, and now trouble brewed again.

"O King," Joab said. "Hanun has hired Syrian troops to meet us in the field. We must move against them immediately while they are still far from Jerusalem. We beat the first wave, but they have recruited more Syrians from beyond Lake Chinnereth. We must attack now."

"Take the mighty men and have Abishai lead the troops," David commanded. "I will meet you with the Philistine mercenaries."

A steady stream of petitioners approached the throne awaiting judgment. David settled business disputes, domestic disputes, boundary claims and other disagreements. By evening, his head throbbed and his eyes ached.

He returned to his bedchamber drenched in sweat and worry. Michal was not present. He sent a messenger to fetch her and asked a servant to draw his bath. He flopped down on the couch to wait for her. At least she would be a comfort to him.

She appeared, cloaked and veiled. David lifted her veil and sniffed her fragrance. She hugged him, her cheeks rosy, with a faint smile on her face.

He handed her the shears. "I'm going to war again. Can you trim my beard and cut my hair?"

She nodded. He stripped off his clothes and lay in the tub, his muscles tight and his neck cramped. She raked through his hair and beard, singing her Philistine song. When she finished, she took off her clothes and covered him in the tub. They made love until dinner time.

Servants set the table and departed. Michal clasped his hand across the table while they gave thanks for the food.

"I hate to leave you so soon." David dipped a piece of bread into the lamb stew. "But the Ammonites are stirring trouble up north. When I return, I want to take you on a trip. Maybe we'll go to the coast near Mt. Carmel."

She picked at a date cake. "Actually I received some good news today."

"Good news? I could use some. Tell me."

"Phalti wrote me. Here, see for yourself."

He winced and glanced at the note. "My, this is good news. It looks like the wedding is only a week away."

"Will you let Ittai take me?"

"Ittai? Don't you want me to attend?"

"Oh." Her mouth rounded. "I thought you're going to war."

David's stomach clenched as a worm of jealousy squirmed inside. "I am. And that means you're not going anywhere." He threw the note back at her.

"She's my daughter, my only daughter." Michal's voice rose to a whine.

He wiped his mouth. "I'll let you visit her after we defeat the Ammonites."

"But that could take forever."

"Michal, don't argue with me." He turned back to his food.

When he looked up, two large tears rolled down her face. "Can't you send a guard with me?"

David slapped the table. "No. I cannot spare any troops to escort you. I'm leaving tomorrow with the Philistine mercenaries. I may even require Arik."

Michal pouted and turned her face. "Go ahead and take him. He hates me anyway."

"You mean he keeps you safe. Arik is solid and reliable. Quite unlike that gadfly Ittai."

She closed her eyes and pushed from the table. "May I go back to my house?"

David caught her at the door. "If we defeat the Ammonites before next week, I'll come back and take you myself."

"You want me to wait?" She curled a hand around his arm. "Are you happy for me? Happy my daughter is grown? And sad for me that I wasn't there to be her mother, that I missed her every day? Anna and Ithream are two darts in my heart."

He buried his face in her hair. "I wish Ithream had lived. But nothing has turned out the way I wished."

* * *

Three days passed. I tapped my fingers against the wall and paced my room. If David did not return in another day, I would have to go by myself. It would take at least two days to make it to Lo-debar, in the country of Gilead.

Ittai stepped into my house. "There is no sign of David or any messenger about the war. What do you want to do?"

I looked out the window. Uriah was setting up for his wedding already. "We'll have to take the chance. I can't let a little war stop me from attending my daughter's wedding. Take me back to David's tower to pack."

Ittai, ever so efficient, had moved all my belongings back to David's place. We walked back to the palace and ascended the stairs to the tower.

He opened the door. "I'm sure we can avoid the hot zones. I'm a skilled scout. I used to spy and scout for your brother, Jonathan. What are you bringing in terms of presents?"

"I've woven a few fringes Anna can use for circumcision gowns. Of course there's the gold and jewelry." I opened my trunk and selected several pieces.

"We should spread them out. Let me wear a few pieces. This way if we get into a fight, we don't lose everything."

"Good thinking," I said. "Always well to take precautions."

We divvied up the jewelry and gold between us. Ittai ran ahead to the stables while I packed a few gowns and several pairs of sandals and went back to the house to wait.

After Ittai brought two horses, we waved to Uriah and set off.

* * *

David wiped his brow. The LORD had wrought a great victory. The Syrians fled after his forces killed forty thousand horsemen and captured seven hundred chariots. Two days before Tammuz. If he hurried and rode all night, he could fetch Michal and take her to Lo-debar.

"Joab, you and Abishai clean up. I have to go back to Jerusalem. I've a wedding to attend."

David returned late in the evening and went straight to Michal's house. Naomi opened the door. She stepped back and bowed. "My king, she's not here."

David stepped over the threshold and stomped his foot. "Where did she go?"

"My lady and Ittai went to Lo-debar. They left two days ago."

David's stomach clenched, and he bruised his knuckles on the wall. He returned to his bedchamber and ripped his clothes. After a bath, he headed to Maacah's house.

His son Absalom came to the door. Fifteen years old, he was almost as tall as his father. David punched him on the shoulder in greeting.

His daughter Tamar curtseyed and bowed her head. "Father, my lord."

David took a green jade necklace from his robe. It was to be a present for his disobedient first wife, but now he took pleasure in giving it to his daughter. "For you, darling."

"Oh, Father, thank you. It's beautiful." Her face shone, and little dimples appeared at each corner of her smile.

Maacah approached from behind and slinked her arms around his waist. "My lord, no doubt you've come from a great victory."

"Yes, the LORD has given us the victory. We've beaten the Syrians, so they will no longer help the Ammonites. I came back early to celebrate."

She pressed his chest. "You came at the right time. I've fixed a meal of wild partridge and greens. Tamar made pistachio cakes for dessert."

David broke into a grin. "Let's eat. I'm famished."

He kissed his fourth wife, and she eyed him with a suggestive smile.

After dinner, he played a board game with Absalom and Tamar. Maacah went to her room to wait, but David took her hand and led her out the door. Absalom's glare had unsettled him as he looked back and forth between his father and mother. Ever since Michal was disposed as queen, Maacah had been pestering him for the position. But David would never elevate the daughter of one of his allies over that of another.

Maacah followed David up the stairs and stepped into the tower. She glanced around furtively, as if she expected Michal to jump out. He lit the oil lamps and pulled her in his lap. "Have I been a stranger?"

She batted her eyelashes. "No, my lord, you're never a stranger."

"Then why haven't you kissed me yet?"

She perched her petite body on his knees. He cupped her around the back of her head and touched his mouth to hers. She responded tentatively.

He tapped her nose, smiling to reassure her. "You can do better than that."

She took a deep breath and opened her mouth. He kissed her deeper, but did not feel her response. Everything he did, she complied. When he laid her down on the bed, she did as he indicated. When he took off her clothes, she helped him. Wherever he touched, it was the same. She yielded. There was nothing to push against. No fight, no excitement—Maacah, the beautiful, desert rose, was prettier to look at than to touch.

CHAPTER 36

Jeremiah 5:8 They were as fed horses in the morning: every one neighed after his neighbor's wife.

>>><<<

A month went by, then two. Michal did not return. Neither did Ittai. Every day, David looked out the window and waited. Other than her maid, no one went in or came out of her house. He walked down the stairs and headed for the throne room but bypassed it, stopping in front of the court house to stare at the pool. His nephews spotted him and brought him back.

"Uncle," Joab said, "we must fight the Ammonites in their capitol city. We've defeated their Syrian allies, but unless we vanquish them in their home territory, they will continue to challenge us."

"I agree," Abishai said. "Why have we delayed two months instead of moving in while they were disorganized from the last battle? Now it will be much harder to dislodge them."

"Haven't the mighty men been out there since Tammuz?" David asked.

"Yes, but to what purpose? We need reinforcements."

David slammed a fist on the petitioner's table. "Don't question me. Take whatever troops you need and go."

"You mean you're not coming?" Joab asked.

"How can that be?" Abishai said.

David turned away from them. "I've a few things to do here before I can go."

Joab and Abishai exchanged looks.

"Uncle, you're distracted because of her," Joab said.

"You're worried about that witch, the daughter of Saul," Abishai said.

"And you will risk your kingdom for her?" Joab pointed a finger. "I tell you. If you hadn't been pining for her, we could have destroyed the host of the Ammonites in the field."

"We wouldn't have to resort to a siege," Abishai said.

"If she has run away with your Philistine guard, then I say good riddance."

"And if you're worried about her, send a bounty hunter to kill both of them, bring their heads back to you. But right now, you need to worry about the Ammonites."

"People won't follow a weak king who is the lapdog of a scornful woman."

"You're henpecked, Uncle."

David toppled the heavy table. "Enough!"

* * *

David rolled and turned in his bed. The miserable drizzle did nothing to cool the oppressive heat. He wiped the sweat off his brow. He could send for a concubine. But what would that do? His women bored him. Only Michal loved him. And she didn't fear him. She'd love him all night without tiring. He clenched his fist. He would not allow a woman to torment him.

He stared at her house. The air hung hot, like the night he returned from battle and hurt her with his sword. What had happened to him? The battlefield had seemed so real. And the blood, all the blood. *God, You said I was a bloody man, that I'd shed too much blood, and You won't allow me to build the temple. Am I forsaken?*

David took off his robe and lay on the floor. The hours passed with his thudding heartbeat, and his eyes stayed open. *Just one more look. Maybe she's back.*

He walked to the window. *She's there! A goddess bathing in the rain. Oh, God, you've answered my prayers.*

He peered through the drizzle. She was definitely there. He leaned out the window and shouted, "Hello, Michal!"

She didn't look up. Perhaps she couldn't hear him through the rain. He cupped his hands and shouted louder, "Hello, Michal!"

She must have heard me. She's deliberately ignoring me.

"Michal! Over here!" He waved both arms. She stretched in the tub, her curvaceous body shone in the moonlight. Her hands circled her breasts and slipped down her sides. She rubbed her belly and one hand slid between her legs.

David's eyes widened. Her hips undulated and splashed water over the sides of the tub. A hot poker pointed straight from his loins, and his groin ached. *Michal, you witch. What have you done to me? Why are you writhing like a serpent knowing that I'm watching you? Oh, Michal, I want you right now.*

David ran to the door. "Arik. Arik."

"Yes, O King."

"Fetch Michal right away. And arrest Ittai. They're back."

"Yes, O King." He ran down the stairs, calling for the other guards.

David stepped back to the window, but Michal had disappeared. The tub glistened in the moonlight, the water still lapping at the edges.

The minutes slogged by. Footsteps bounded up the stairs. David opened the door.

Arik and another guard stood there, wet from the rain. "O King, she is not there."

"How can that be? She was bathing on the rooftop."

They looked at each other before answering. "O King, we checked with the maid. There was no one there but her."

"Impossible, the maid is hiding her. Bring her to me, and I will whip her until she talks."

Again they exchanged looks.

"Now!"

"Yes, O King."

"Arik, I want my wife back tonight. Or your head will be on a platter. Do you understand?"

"Yes, O King."

David sat at his table and fingered the chipped side of Michal's jade box. The phoenix's sharp beak pointed at the dragon's snout. The dragon's claws grabbed her breast. And her tail wrapped around his hind legs. But his tail entrapped her wings. The dragon bared his teeth. The phoenix's stare pierced through him.

A knock on the door roused him. When he opened it, Naomi bowed to the ground.

"Naomi, where is your mistress? And if you lie, I will beat you myself."

She trembled on the floor. "O King. I lie not. My mistress has been gone a little more than two months. I have not seen or heard from her."

"Then what was she doing bathing on the roof? I saw her with my own eyes."

"O King, that was not her. That was our neighbor's wife. I helped her maids drag the tub to the roof and fetch the water. It was too hot inside the house."

"Neighbor's wife?" Anger drained down to David's toes, and a white chill crawled up his back. "Who's your neighbor?"

"Uriah, my lord, Uriah the Hittite."

David stood. "You may go. When Michal returns, you're to let me know. Go to the gate and call for Arik."

Neighbor's wife. Thou shalt not covet thy neighbor's wife. Neighbor's wife. David's head spun, and he fell on the floor. Images of the bathing lady taunted him.

She was so beautiful, so much like Michal. Shapely, her breasts full and heavy. And the way she moved. His body heated like an iron, hot and hard. David unrolled Michal's rug and lay on it, taking deep, slow breaths. No use. He imagined her rolling and moaning under him. How did such a beauty exist without his notice? Why was she not his concubine?

He called out the door. "Arik, come here. Your head is spared. Look out my window. You see that house? The one with the empty tub on the roof. Go now and get the woman and bring her to me. I wish to talk to her."

"Yes, O King."

David returned to the window. Her husband would have been gone two months already. He was one of the mighty men, a big bear of a man.

He would talk to her and console her, perhaps praise her husband. There could be no harm in a little friendly conversation. He put all thoughts of undressing her out of his mind. He was the king, and he took interest in his subjects. He cared about their families.

The guards walked her into the street. She clutched a cloak tightly around her face. Curiosity stirred his loins. He rubbed sweaty palms against his robe.

Minutes later, they were at the door. The woman stepped in, her head bent low. She half-bowed, but settled for a nod under her hood. Arik shut the door and left them alone.

"Come, sit. Tell me your name and whose daughter you are." David kept his voice smooth and level.

She sat at the edge of the couch, her hands clasped.

He moved next to her and removed her cloak. She averted her gaze, but he tilted her face and lost his breath. Her skin shone as smooth as alabaster, and her eyes, dark blue as a moonlit lake. Her mouth, a perfect rose, lush, shaped like Michal's. He touched her hair. A mass of curls wrapped themselves around his fingers, trapping him. David throbbed like never before and leaned closer. She trembled and shut her eyes.

Her neck moved. "I am a man's wife."

"I am the king."

"My lord." She waited, her eyes downcast.

"Are you afraid of me? Have you seen me before?"

A faint smile curved her lips. "Yes, you danced with me in front of the Ark of the Covenant."

"So you remember me?"

She looked down at her lap. "My lord, king. What do you want with me?"

"To behold you, up close. When I saw you move in the bathtub, you moved my heart." A bright red blush rose from her cheeks to her temple. She stroked her neck with three long, elegant fingers.

David gestured to the table. "Hungry? Some fruit and wine?"

"My lord, I've dined already." She glanced at the table, her gaze settling on Michal's boxes.

David picked up the sandalwood box and placed it in her hands. "Have you ever seen anything like this?"

The carved pregnant goddess with eight serpentine arms stared from the lid.

The woman drew her breath in. A tinge of a smile crossed her face, and her eyes flicked a you're-a-naughty-boy look before going back to the box.

"Go ahead, open it," David said.

She opened it. Scraps of parchment peeked out. "Oh."

She shut the box quickly. David's face heated, and his fists tightened. Love notes. His.

She handed the box to David. "It's quite lovely. Where did it come from?"

"A place far to the east called India."

"Do women have eight arms there? Might be useful. Think of all the weaving and embroidery they could do." She fanned herself, and her lips parted slightly.

David put the sandalwood box back on the table and followed her gaze.

"What about that one? The silver one?" She pointed to it, exposing her wrist.

He handed Michal's silver box to her, and she examined it, turning it every which way. The way she ran her fingers along the curves made David's mouth water.

"It's lovely, so intricate: the sunflower in the center, the curling leaves and vines, and the border of circles and squares. Ah, see here the rays curve from the petals like that of the sun. Not a straight edge. Like a wild beast, crouched." Her tongue darted over her upper lip. "Ready to leap."

David could have pounced on her, but he cleared his throat and said, "You're an artist, I see. Do you like it?"

She blushed again, flicked her hair off her shoulder and opened it. "Arrowheads? Oh."

She set the box on the table. Dried blood flaked off the arrowheads. A chilling sensation, silent like a panther, stalked David's shoulder blades.

He poured wine into a pair of goblets and placed one in her hand, lightly brushing it with his fingertip. While she sipped, he took his harp from the corner. "Do you like music?"

She bobbed her head. "I hear you're one of the best."

Her eyes sparkled with interest, and she touched the harp, caressing its wooden frame.

"Surely you exaggerate." He coughed. "I don't know if I can play or sing with you staring at me like that."

She lowered her face, and her breath quickened. "Oh, my king, I apologize."

David put the harp down and took her arm. "No apologies needed."

He tipped her chin and stared into her eyes, deep, lustrous and oh, so blue. He could swim in them forever. "You're beautiful."

She closed her eyes, drew in her breath, but did not back away. Her lips trembled slightly, and her cheeks glowed.

David composed himself and led her to the wardrobe. He took out a sky-blue gown with dancing bell sleeves trimmed with silver threads. He dug through Michal's jewelry and found a blue star sapphire set in silver.

"A gift from your king. Stand up."

She gulped a mouthful of wine and stood for him. David held the gown in front of her. It enhanced her creamy skin, blue eyes, and black lustrous hair. Perfect. "Hold it up to your chest."

She held it while he placed the sapphire around her neck. She squirmed at his touch, and a smile lit her face.

"Would you like to try the dress?" David moved her hair from under the necklace and touched her smooth white neck.

"Doesn't it belong to your wife?"

"It doesn't suit her. Go ahead. There's a screen, or you can step into the bathroom. I promise I won't peek."

Her hips swayed as she walked toward the bathroom. She looked over her shoulder with a flutter of her eyelids and a sidelong smile before stepping in. His groin tightened in a flash, and he took a sip of wine to cool the heat in his chest.

Moments later, she emerged, a dream in blue. David stepped up and held her softly in his arms. She looked radiant and felt so inviting. His head swirled in a haze of desire, and he bent down and touched his forehead to hers. She stroked his jaw, and her breath shortened. He inhaled her sweet fragrance and opened his mouth.

Their lips met, and he kissed her softly, savoring the freshness of her tender touch. Her tongue danced between his lips, and his hands crept down her shoulders to fondle her breasts. Small, mewing pants encouraged him, and he lifted her and placed her on the bed.

He trailed kisses down her neck and over the fabric of her dress, heartened by her faint moans. Her back arched to meet his firm arousal, and a tiny cry escaped her lips as his hands explored her delicious body.

"Do you want the dress off?" he asked.

She nodded and raised her arms. The dress slipped off easily. She was gorgeous, so smooth and supple. She had never had a child, her skin soft, her belly tight with no marks and sags. There was so much to kiss and handle. David moved her to the bed, rueing he had only one mouth and two hands.

He placed her hand between her legs and kissed her breasts. "I want to see you do that again."

She stiffened and flushed, a cloud of embarrassment tinted her face.

He had no intention of defiling her. He just wanted to watch her up close. "Go ahead, I saw you on the roof. Show me what you did in your tub."

She withdrew her hand as if she touched the flame of an oil lamp. "No, I can't."

Her lips quivered so deliciously, he immediately pressed himself to her. She writhed and moaned again. Her hands clawed his back and removed his robe. As it fell to the floor, she moved her hands under his tunic and tugged.

David's arousal responded immediately. He raised his arms, and she pulled his tunic off. Her fingers pressed the muscles of his chest and slid down to his belly. Her hands around his waist, she grabbed his sides while he rolled her breasts, their mouths and tongues entangled. She removed his breeches, and David could no longer control himself.

With an anguished cry, he possessed his neighbor's wife. She rocked and moved under him like a bucking horse. Her cries of delight punctuated the air joined by the groans of his release.

As David held her in his arms, she told him her name. "Bathsheba, daughter of Eliam."

CHAPTER 37

Job 6:4 For the arrows of the Almighty are within me, the poison whereof drinketh up my spirit: the terrors of God do set themselves in array against me.

>>><<<

The day buzzed hot, and David sweltered under his robes. A throng of petitioners filed into the throne room with their petty disputes. They droned and droned. He turned most of them over to Hushai, his chief counselor.

A messenger brought a report from the battlefield. "The Ammonites have withdrawn to Rabbah. We were forced to lay down a siege."

David banged a fist on the side of his throne. "Send five hundred men. Arm them with shields and pikes."

Only a few more messengers, and he could go back. To what? Certainly not Bathsheba. She was another man's wife, Uriah's wife. David tightened his lips against clenched teeth. His throat soured. He should never have touched her.

"O King, a message from your servant Phaltiel of Mahanaim."

"What does he want?"

"He begs you to travel to his son-in-law's house in Lo-debar to pray at your wife's bedside."

David blinked, suddenly alert. "What happened?"

"She was shot by an arrow," the messenger said. "He thinks she's dying."

Michal? Dying? An ice cold spear shafted his heart. He raised his crown and slammed it on the throne. "Why has no one come to tell me? What is wrong with all of you? Where's Ittai?"

"Ittai is guarding her, my king."

David turned to Arik. "Bring my horse. You and Uri are coming with me. Hushai, find the best healer in the land and send him to Lo-debar."

David lowered his head while waiting for his horse. *O LORD God, I have sinned. Forgive my sin and have mercy on me. Let Michal be healed, so I can love her again. O LORD, correct me with your judgment, not in anger, but with mercy.*

* * *

David prayed the entire way to Lo-debar. He wore out several horses, exchanging them along the way. Without waiting to be announced, he pounded on the door. Machir and his wife, Anna, ushered him in. He rushed to Michal's bedside, pushing past the people gathered around.

She was pale, her breathing labored, and she burned with fever.

David knelt, grabbing her hands. "Eglah, I'm here. Why didn't you wait for me?"

Her eyes fluttered and rolled in his direction.

He brought her clammy hand to his lips. All he could hear was the rasping of her breath and the sobs of those around. David bent his head down and prayed for the mercy he did not deserve.

"David," she said, her voice so weak it wasn't even a whisper. "The scarlet cord. The window."

"What scarlet cord? What window?"

"The City of God. Look for me. I'm going." She stared far away. A smile came to her face. "Ithream, Merab, Jonathan, Mother, Sam—"

"No!" David grabbed her hands. "Eglah, don't go."

His screams brought a rush of people to her bed. Phaltiel fell at her side. Ittai hugged her feet and legs. Anna whimpered and fell at her chest. Michal's five sons and other relatives crowded in. They cried and entreated, competing with the ghosts, a tug-of-war between the living and the dead.

"O Living God," David said, "Grant me a miracle. O God, don't forsake me, Your servant, David. Let my wife live."

"O LORD God," Phaltiel said. "Take me, your worthless servant, and let me die in her place."

"O God of Israel," Ittai said, holding Michal's legs. "No one loves her like I do. Dear God of Israel, I can't bear it if she died. You know how much I love her." His wail rent the room.

David's fingers tightened around Michal's hand. Ittai had no right to say the things he did, and in front of everyone. David breathed into her ear. "Eglah, come back. Come back to me, only to me."

He kept one hand on her chest to feel for her breathing. The rasping shuddered into a sob. He could barely hear her over the din. Her head burned hot, too hot.

"Cool her with water," David ordered and looked into her glassy eyes. "Don't leave me. Don't."

"Come, my lord, David," she muttered as her breathing labored and her fingers tightened around his. David hid his face next to her ear and thanked the LORD in his heart.

Rizpah stepped in. "The healer is here."

Phaltiel rose and rubbed his eyes. Ittai remained slumped at the foot of her bed, his hair spread on her feet, seemingly unable to lift his head.

A woman approached. She was past middle-aged, but strikingly beautiful. Her copper-bronze hair shone in the lamplight like little glistening snakes. Blue-green eyes, as calm as the sea, stared at David.

"My king." She bowed. After David acknowledged her, she hurried to the bedside.

She placed her fingers at the side of Michal's neck. "Bring melons, cool melons and cucumbers. There is too much heat inside of her. It needs to be cooled. Open the windows and let the breeze in. Bring me a candle and oil."

Servants scurried off to do her bidding.

The healer took out three cups and laid them on the table next to the bed. "I will balance her humors. Have the maid fetch boiling water. I've brought chrysanthemums and camellia with a little rhino horn powder."

She surveyed the room, her hands on her hips. "All men must leave. You embody fire and heat. The women may stay. I need you to sing and chant."

Her severe tone raised spines over David's back. He yanked Ittai off the end of the bed and pulled him out of the room. The healer's assistant, a young woman brushed past him. David blinked at her image, a vision of Michal as a young princess.

He took a deep breath and marched Ittai out of the house. "I heard what you said, and it's not true."

Ittai's jaws shook, and he blubbered, tears and snot mixed in his beard. "You know nothing about her."

"How dare you? I ought to cut your tongue out right here."

Ittai's eyes remained steadfast. "You don't accept her. You want her to be a certain way that only exists in your mind. You treat her as a possession, not a woman."

David slapped him. "And you? What's your story?"

"I accept everything about her and never ask anything in return. And I'll always love her no matter what you do to me."

"Then that'll be all you'll have, a memory. You're banished from my kingdom. I give you two days." David pulled out a dagger and cut a line over Ittai's left cheekbone. "Now you have a mark just like I have for the same woman. Now go."

David called to Arik, "Escort this renegade to the border. He's not welcome in my kingdom. In two days, I will have a bounty on his head."

"Yes, my king," Arik saluted and grabbed Ittai by the elbow, leading him away.

Marching back toward the house, David turned a corner and bumped into a young man in a chair set on wheels.

The man bent his head. "My king, I'm sorry I was in the way."

David stopped and stared. The young Jonathan's face—chestnut hair, a square jaw, and light brown eyes.

He grasped the young man's hand. "What is your name and whose son are you?"

"Meribbaal, son of Jonathan of Gibeah."

"I am King David. See here?" David held up his third finger. "I wear your father's ring."

Meribbaal blinked and opened his mouth.

David pushed his chair to the parlor. "Do not be afraid of me. Your father was my best friend. How long have you been here? Where is your mother? Do you have any other brothers or sisters?"

"It is I only," Meribbaal said. "My mother passed away shortly after my father died on Mt. Gilboa."

"Do you have anyone else? Would you like to come and live with me in Jerusalem?"

"I have a young son, Micah. My wife died giving birth. I like living here in the country."

"Meribbaal, I swore an oath to your father to preserve his seed forever. You must come and live with me, eat at my table. I'll have the best tutors for your son. He will grow up like a prince. You will be a blessing to my house."

"But I'm of the cursed house of Saul." His gaze shifted to his crippled feet.

"I will show you kindness for your father's sake. I will restore to you all the land of your grandfather. And you shall eat bread at my table continually." David patted Meribbaal's shoulder.

Meribbaal bowed his head and thanked him.

The hours crawled by. David paced the garden and punched the wall. Around mid-afternoon, Rizpah set a tray of food in front of him. "My king, have some refreshment."

"Send Phaltiel to me."

She nodded and swept her skirts back into the house.

Minutes later Phaltiel arrived and bowed to the ground. "O King. Your servant is present."

"Get up off the ground and sit with me," David said. Phaltiel looked like such a lumbering idiot. How could Michal possibly have cared about him?

Phaltiel gripped the table as if it were a shield. He wouldn't meet David's eye.

"Tell me what happened," David said. "Did Michal make it to the wedding?"

"They had not shown up yet. I wanted to hold up the wedding, but Machir's parents insisted it take place on Tammuz, the summer solstice."

"If only I had been there…" David wiped his forehead. "Go ahead."

"Two days later, Ittai appears with Michal. She had been wounded. He tried his best to extract the arrowhead but was unable to cut deeper. The village healer closed the wound and assured us it would not harm her. The arrow was lodged in her left shoulder, in the joint."

David gripped the side of the table and winced. "Ittai is incompetent. I should never have let him back. You should have sent for me immediately."

"We thought she'd recover," Phaltiel said.

"Well obviously she hasn't. What's wrong with you? Why did you wait two months to tell me where she was?" David swept the water pitcher from the table, smashing it on the stone floor.

Phaltiel lowered his face. "My king, I apologize. We thought you knew."

David grimaced. Of course, he should have inquired, but that would have shown too much concern for a disobedient woman. He would have lost face, been the target of gossip. As if he wasn't already.

"What kind of woman is Rizpah?" David said.

Phaltiel jerked his head and blinked. His mouth opened and closed and opened again.

"By right, she should be my wife. Why did you take her?"

Phaltiel's brow creased, and he opened his mouth again, but no words came out.

"You have taken two of my wives." David pounded the table with both hands. "Tell me why I shouldn't have you executed. Give me one reason."

Phaltiel's shoulders quivered, and he wrung his hands. Beads of sweat popped on his forehead. He stared at the table. "Anna, Michal's daughter."

"So you admit to adultery? You stupid oaf. Didn't you know she was my wife?"

Phaltiel remained silent, but his face flushed and the tips of his ears reddened.

"Tell me about Rizpah. Go ahead. I have all day." David leaned back and trotted his fingers on the table.

"She… she's… a good woman. She's had a hard life as Saul's youngest concubine. After Saul's death, men abused her, and she's easily

313

frightened. I love her, and I'm gentle to her. She's happy with me." He recited in a flat tone.

"Why isn't she my concubine?" David's fingers skittered back and forth across the table.

Phaltiel kept his eyes down. "We have a family and many children. When Michal's sons came back, she loved them as her own. She also raised Anna. She's a good wife, and I love her very much."

Phaltiel's confession filled David with guilt. Would Michal have been happier if he had left her with him? Why did he feel as if he had to exert his dominance? What kind of man was he compared to Phaltiel?

"You may keep her. I have no intentions of breaking your family again." He turned away so Phaltiel wouldn't see the wetness in his eyes. Why couldn't he have lived peacefully in the countryside with Michal and had many children with her?

His mouth dry, he stalked back to the house and looked through the window. Michal lay on her stomach, her back exposed. An ugly wound glistened on the top of her shoulder blade, raw and bright red, swollen with a black center. The healer's assistant heated the tiny cups in the flame of the candle. She handed the hot cup to the healer who pushed it down onto Michal's wound. Michal stiffened and cried out.

Smoky trails of incense swirled in the room. Four young maidens, including Anna, chanted an atonic mantra. The healer applied oil to Michal's back and moved the cup over her skin while the assistant cleaned the pus that oozed from the irritated wound.

The healer lit a candle in front of wooden goddess that stood on the table. War drums thumped in David's chest. God would not be pleased and could take his mercy away.

He stormed through the door, grabbed the idol and threw it in the firepot. "You shall not have this abomination anywhere near my wife. She is a daughter of the Law."

The chanting halted, and the healer pushed herself into David's chest, her arms crossed low over her waist. "Michal is my daughter. My name is Jada of Jezreel."

David took a large step backward. Her mother? The woman who provided the gold that Michal gave him was Michal's mother?

Michal raised her head. "Jada, be kind to my David. No more idols. Let him pray for me."

David knelt at his wife's side. Her sweet smile melted him, and he held her hand. "Oh, Eglah. You're going to be healed. I know it. I will take you back to Jerusalem and take care of you. You shall stay in my tower and never leave it again. You are my precious wife."

She lowered her head to the pillow. "Am I really?"

* * *

"I have to go away." Voices dripped over me like tiny raindrops. Who? I struggled in my sleep.

"Michal, I shall never forget you." Gentle hands tucked me into the blankets I had tossed. I caught a sob, then another, like drops of blood on my face.

The woman leaned over and kissed me. Wet drops of rain washed her face. I raised her hand. She flickered in my sight like the flame of a smoky candle.

"I know why you did it," I said.

Blue-green eyes. Veiled with tears. My father's vision.

"I've broken the spell. The goddess is angry at me. I shall never see you again." She cut a long braid of my hair.

"Call on Jehovah," I said, "the name of God. Call on Him and don't leave me."

Her sobs turned into gasps. "Remember me. Always remember me."

"I shall never forget you, Jada." I couldn't make myself say the word, not yet. "Believe He will save you, call on Him, and I shall meet you by the brook, the brook where you gave me life, the brook where you named me, and the brook where you gave me up."

"I am so sorry, so very, very sorry." She wept in my arms. "I have to go."

"You loved him. You were the only one who really loved my father."

Blue-green eyes framed in copper.

"My mother."

The wind and rain howled like a thousand dying women.

The door shut.

CHAPTER 38

Numbers 32:23 ...behold, ye have sinned against the LORD: and be sure your sin will find you out.

>>><<<

David sat at the side of his wife's bed. "Eglah, I have to go back to Jerusalem. You are still too weak to travel." He smoothed her hair as she opened her eyes.

"I'm comfortable here. Go ahead and don't worry about me." Her forehead shone from the fever. "Why did Jada leave?"

He shrugged. "She left the medicine and the herbs. You didn't tell me she was your mother."

"I didn't know. Where has she gone?"

"I don't know. She told me to put all the gold I was going to pay her in your father's name and to dedicate it to the Temple building fund."

"I miss her." Michal said.

"Why didn't you wait for me? I hurried back, but you had already left."

She took his hand and stared at it. "I'm sorry I disobeyed you. I should have waited."

"I was angry, but now that I almost lost you..." His voice crumbled. "Look, we'll be happy again. I promise. I mean it."

She rubbed his hand on her face and shook her head.

"What's wrong?" he said. "You don't believe we can be happy together?"

She pressed her fingers on his. "I thought being God's anointed meant you would be like God, but now, I've learned to temper my expectations."

Her words struck him like a branding iron, searing his conscience. "I have disappointed you."

"Don't make promises you can't keep. No expectations, no disappointments." She let go his hand and turned to the wall.

* * *

David stared at the parchment.

The message was clear. *I am with child. Your neighbor's wife.*

She had to be lying. She came to him. She could have gone to others. Her husband was away, and she lived by herself with her maids.

"Arik, bring the maids of Bathsheba to the palace for questioning. Meet me at Abigail's house."

"Yes, O King." Arik bowed and walked off in a fast clip.

David rushed to Abigail's house with a queasy feeling in his stomach. He waved off Ahinoam and Maacah as he pounded on Abigail's door.

She opened the door.

"I need your help," he said.

"My lord, what is happening?"

"Arik is bringing a few maids to you for questioning. I need to know if their mistress has been seeing men."

Abigail's cheeks reddened. "You want me to interview concubines for you?"

"Ah… forget it. When they show up, ask them to go to Maacah's." David ran out of her room.

"Maacah. Maacah."

She turned and smiled at him.

"Can you do me a favor?"

"Anything, my lord." She touched his sleeve.

"I need you to interview Lady Bathsheba's maids. Be thorough and don't let them evade. I know you can do it."

Maacah's mouth dropped into a little circle.

He bent down and planted a kiss. "Will you do this for me, my sweet?"

She nodded and made a small squeak when he pinched her behind.

"Give me a full report," he said. "Uh… and ask about any possible pregnancies and whether she'd seen other men and the timing of her husband's leave-taking."

"My lord, I shall do as you say. I'll leave no stone unturned, no hedge untrimmed, no leaf dangling." She smiled seductively and pinched his thigh. After a deep, long kiss, she swayed her hips back to her house.

David hid behind a large bay tree. Arik appeared with the two maids. Abigail pointed them to Maacah's house and slammed the door. He rubbed his sweaty palms and tapped his feet. How could this be? He'd only seen the woman once. Perhaps her husband had been back. But then why would she write him the note? How much gold would silence her?

After the maids left Maacah's house, David sprinted to her door. Ahinoam and Abital stared after him as they came around the corner with their looms.

"What did they say?" David didn't bother to remove his sandals. He plopped down on her couch and waved his hands. "Tell me, now."

Maacah smiled and wound her way to his side. She placed his hands on her waist and smoothed out his lap. Taking her time, she arranged herself across his legs and wrapped her arms around his neck. She kissed him and smiled. "My lord, do you want the long version or the short version?"

"Both, but give me the short first." David's lips trembled when he kissed her again. Maacah would extract a kiss for every sentence.

"Mmmm, you haven't kissed me like that for ages." She twirled his moustache. "The short story is that she has been with a man who is not her husband. Her husband left home more than two months ago, shortly after their wedding."

She puckered her mouth, and David rewarded her with another kiss, this time deeper.

"More details. How many men has she been with?"

She leaned in for another kiss. "She has only seen one man since her husband left."

"Did they tell you who?" He rewarded Maacah with another wet, languorous kiss.

A little breathless, she continued. "On a hot, mid-summer night, muggy with a slight shower, she decided to take a refreshing bath on the rooftop. She stayed up there for a little while. After she had cooled down, men from the palace came and fetched her."

David stiffened. "Who?"

Maacah pointed to her lips to remind him she expected another kiss.

His stomach turned and churned, and he delivered the kiss with much difficulty.

Maacah perked one eyebrow and ran her fingernail down his cheek. "Oh, my lord, you can do better than that. Try again?"

David kissed her with more effort.

She wet her lips and stared so close she appeared cross-eyed. "They asked her to have a visit with a certain king who wanted to talk to her." She lingered on the word 'talk.' "Is it possible she talked to the King of Israel?"

David waved her away. "That's not important. Did she see or talk to any other men after this conversation?"

Maacah slithered into his arms. "No, she has not talked to anybody else. And wonder of wonders, she is with child. How does that happen with talking?" Maacah lowered her voice to a whisper. "I'd like some of that talking right about now."

A slow chill rolled in David's belly. Maacah took his hand and led him to her bed. He lay down, bathed in cold sweat. Could he even perform?

Stalling for time, he asked, "And how does she know this man she talked to impregnated her? Perhaps she was already with child?"

Maacah touched the tip of his nose. "I left no trail unmarked." She wiggled with the anticipation of a terrier growling down a rabbit hole. "By the way, I had to use some of my own silver to gain this information."

"I'll pay you every bit and with a bonus too. Tell me."

Maacah ran her tongue across her teeth and demanded a kiss.

Satisfied, she continued. "She had her monthly blood shortly before her husband left home."

She leaned forward, and David bestowed another wet kiss on her quivering lips.

"I deserve a big bonus," Maacah said as she slid her hands down to his crotch. "There was crying, begging, and pleading on Bathsheba's part to fill her womb. But Uriah refused to touch her. Seems he's quite the fundamentalist. Joab's orders came, and Uriah purified himself and refused to sleep with her. Can you imagine what that does to a woman's feelings?"

A cold chill scratched David's shoulders, and he removed Maacah's hands. "You are the goods, Maacah. And I will pay up, eventually."

He pressed his lips to hers and held it for a couple of heartbeats.

"I'm good, aren't I?" she said. "You owe me quite a few nights. Now where was I?"

"Is there more?" He kissed her between her breasts, not really wanting to hear but unable to resist.

"Oh, yes." She moaned and made soft clutching sounds before continuing. "She went to a fortune teller who told her Uriah would come home unexpectedly."

"So, what does that mean?" David stopped what he was doing.

"She took a preparation of mandrake root and rhino horn powder." Maacah giggled and tugged his robe open. "It means she was preparing to conceive after her uncleanness. The bath was to purify her for a child."

David gasped. A hive of bumblebees took up residence in his bowels.

Maacah arched an eyebrow. "Don't tell me the king is worried." She wormed her fingers down his abdomen. "You're quite a good talker. Are you, by chance, the lucky man?"

David's heart jittered and sweat drenched his forehead. "What should I do?"

"I know where to get the herbs that cleanse the womb. There is a—"

"No, definitely not," he said. "This is not allowed in my kingdom."

"Very well then, looks like you'll be a father again."

David groaned as nausea kicked his belly. "Will you keep this a secret for me?"

"You can always trust Maacah. Am I not your fourth wife and a princess?" She rubbed his shoulders with her tiny hands and leaned her face on his chest.

"I have no choice. What should I do now? I don't want to take her for wife. I can't anyway, she's Uriah's wife." Obliged, he gave her another peck on the mouth.

"Things do look bleak for you, my lord."

David closed his eyes. "What if he kills me?"

"He wouldn't dare." Maacah chuckled, seeming to enjoy all the attention he lavished on her. "Well, there may be something you can do."

"What is it? Tell me." He planted an urgent kiss on her lips and fondled her breasts for good measure.

"Uriah is one of the mighty men, right? And he is under your command?"

"Yes, yes." He nodded. "He is out fighting near the walls of Rabbah."

"Ask him to come back to you with a report of the war. Naturally he'll go home to his wife, so when he returns a year later, he'll have a baby to greet him."

"Maacah, you're brilliant." That idea cost David a roll in the bed and a couple more to be paid at a later date.

* * *

Uriah clicked his heels and bowed.

David clapped him on the shoulder. "My good fellow, go home to your new wife and enjoy dinner on behalf of your king."

After bidding Uriah farewell, David sat in his tower to enjoy a meal. His thoughts turned to Michal. Once he straightened out this nasty situation, he'd bring her back to be his favorite wife.

He spent the evening strumming on his harp and praying. But God did not answer. He seemed to be far away. Around midnight, David woke covered in sweat. He should check on Maacah. She could have gossiped to Haggith. Then the entire kingdom would know.

He pulled on a cloak and opened the door. A huge body blocked his doorway.

"Ughh, who goes there?" David called.

The man sat up. "O King, it is your servant, Uriah."

A sinking feeling settled between David's thighs. "Why aren't you with your wife?"

"My lord, how can I go to my wife when the Ark of the LORD and the king's commander, Joab, are out in the fields under a tent? I took a vow to remain chaste and purified so the LORD will bless me and preserve my life."

David fled across the courtyard to Maacah's house.

She flung the door open. "My lord, what a wonderful surprise! Come in, the children are asleep."

He stepped in her room, and Maacah tore off her clothes and lay on her bed.

"Maacah, let me talk first," he said.

"My lord, a little talk and then…"

"Yes, yes, I promise." David's hands shook. "He did not go to his wife. The dumb log is asleep outside my door. What will I do?"

"Is he not a man? I've gone and taken a look at this Bathsheba. She's not bad, my lord, although a little on the plump side."

"It's because she's pregnant." David thumped his hands on the bed.

"Now don't get your manhood all knotted up about this. Think, think. Was Uriah so drunk he passed out?" Her hand went to his groin to do some untangling.

"No, actually he wasn't. Tomorrow I will give him some drink, and he'll be sure to go to her." His heart skipped lighter, even giddy at the thought.

"That is a good plan, my lord. And since you're here, you can give me a few lessons." She tilted her head back and tittered with laughter. "Do me, like you do Michal."

David pressed his fingers over her little bird bones. "Then do not be so compliant."

He pushed her. She took a deep breath, her eyes flashing, and pushed him back.

"Harder, Maacah, pretend like you hate me."

She hit him over the head with a pillow. "Are you telling me Michal hates you?"

"I'm not telling you anything." He lunged and wrestled her to the bed.

* * *

Uriah became drunk but did not go home. He slumped in front of David's door and refused to leave. David considered having his guards lug him over, but Uriah was so stone drunk he would not be able to credibly perform the act. He would only remember the struggle with the guards and wonder why David forced him to go to his wife.

David threw up his hands and paced the room. His nerves tingled at every sound, and his heart beat in a strange rhythm. He passed by his window. She sat on her roof fanning herself. She looked so sad and forlorn. She had set the table with the food he had sent. There, she walked to the edge of the roof, looking at the street below. She put her hands over her eyes, and her shoulders shook with weeping. His heart thumped and threatened to burst from his chest. How could that lump abandon her, make her feel so worthless?

Bathsheba caught him staring. Her gaze pierced his already swollen heart. He pulled on a cloak with a large hood and stepped over the slumbering man.

She opened the door before he raised his hand to knock. All the fear and anxiety of the day served as a catalyst to fuel his lust. The heat between them flared like an oil lamp. She fought with the fury of a scorned lover and clasped him like a prisoner between her legs. David could have died in the hot rush of pressure that swallowed him deep inside of her.

Fever spent, David pulled his clothes back on for the long, slow walk to his empty bedchamber. How had such a beauty been kept from him? Uriah must have hidden her. He'd have a word with her father. She deserved a better life than to be neglected and hurt by such an insensitive man.

He sighed. Bathsheba had kissed him, long and lingering. "I think I'm falling in love." Her words echoed in his ear.

Skirting the sleeping form, David climbed the stairs to his tower: each step a thump, a hammer, a thud, a prison door, a coffin lid, the stone on the sepulcher. He slipped into his room and lit the lamp. *Oh, Bathsheba, I think I'm falling in love, too.*

David took out his writing instruments and penned a short note to Joab. *Set Uriah in the forefront of the hottest battle and withdraw from him so he may be killed.*

At dawn, he wrapped the note in a piece of cloth, tied it and handed it to Uriah to take to Joab.

David set his jaw as Uriah rode away.

CHAPTER 39

Malachi 2:14 Yet ye say, Wherefore? Because the LORD hath been witness between thee and the wife of thy youth, against whom thou hast dealt treacherously: yet is she thy companion, and the wife of thy covenant.

>>><<<

Red, yellow, and orange leaves fluttered from the oaks and birches. The days turned chilly, and David had no word from the front. Perhaps Uriah had lost the note. Uriah was such a brave and valiant man, perhaps he survived. Or maybe Joab ignored the directive.

He should never have visited Bathsheba that night. He should have dragged that man into her bed and let her work her skills on him.

O God, let the note be lost and preserve Uriah's life.

David saddled a horse and told Hushai he would not be holding court for a week or two. His mind all a jumble, he packed some of Michal's gowns along with a tent and camping supplies.

He set his horse on the two day journey to Lo-debar. He rode alone and anonymously, dressed as a commoner.

If Uriah returns, pay him to divorce Bathsheba. It's simple.

No, he won't divorce her. He might ask questions.

Then order him to raise the baby as his own.

No, the baby is mine, and I want Bathsheba.

You have enough wives and sons. Uriah has only the one.

I can get him another wife. I need Bathsheba. He obviously does not love her like I do.

You have Michal and the others. You love them all.

But I love Bathsheba more. She does something to me.

It's only lust. You promised Michal she'd be your favorite wife.

I promised her she'd be my only wife, but I've already messed that up. What's one more?

Michal will be disappointed.

Then that is her problem. Maacah seems to approve.

It's only because she's getting all this attention from you.

I can't let Michal know. How can I keep her from finding out?

Keep her away from Maacah. Keep her isolated in your tower.

Can I trust Maacah?

Only if you satisfy her. You'll have to spread yourself out and give her what she wants.

What does Abigail think about me? I wonder if she suspects.

Abigail is loyal. She will pray for you. Do not worry about Abigail.

Oh my, I miss Ahinoam. She's been so quiet. I need to go see her.

You are in a world of trouble. How did you expect to keep one wife happy, much less a multitude?

I keep Abital happy. I buy her birds.

Yes, she's the only one. What about Haggith?

What about Haggith? Will Joab tell her?

No, she'll do and say anything Joab wants. She loves Joab, you knew about that.

No one must know.

Yes, no one must know.

* * *

I sat under a palm tree with my nephew, Meribbaal. A balmy breeze blew with the last heat of summer. Machir, Anna's husband, prepared for the grape harvest, a time when the entire family would stay overnight in watchtowers amongst the vines to guard against thieves. The green olive harvest followed, and after that would be the black olives.

Meribbaal rolled his wheelchair to my side. Crippled in both feet from an accident, he played a reed flute and whiled away the lazy afternoons with me. Our family had believed him lost, but Machir's father, Ammiel, had taken him in and given him a home where he'd be safe from the assassins who killed my brother Ishbaal.

A lone rider trotted up the dusty lane. I shielded my eyes from the evening sun. He wore a dark green cloak. His hair was cropped too short to be Ittai. Machir gripped his pitchfork and motioned us to the house.

I lingered, unable to keep my gaze off the solitary figure.

The rider dismounted. "Eglah," he said.

"David?" No matter how long we'd been apart, he still had the ability to stop my heart and still my breath.

Machir and Anna bowed at the sight of the king. Meribbaal lowered his head to his knees.

David grabbed my hand. "You look radiant and well. I've come to take you home."

"But you came alone," I said. "Is it seemly for a king to travel alone?"

Machir and Anna remained prostrated on the ground. David cleared his throat. "Tell your daughter and son-in-law they may stand. I came not as king, but as their father-in-law."

They brushed off their clothing and stammered with pleasure at having the king's company.

He bent and kissed Meribbaal. "The offer is still open. Come and live with me at the palace as my son. I swore an oath to your father to protect his seed."

Meribbaal bowed his head. "Who am I that the King of Israel shall take notice of me?"

"You are the son of my best friend." David squeezed his shoulder and pushed his wheelchair into Machir's modest home.

After an enjoyable dinner and evening of conversation, David followed me to my bedchamber. I arranged and rearranged my hair ornaments and jewelry on the table, afraid to meet his eye. Crickets chirped, and leaves rustled in the breeze. The sweet fragrance of the night jasmine wafted through the window, but I remained at the table while David took off his robe and sat on the bed.

Why was I so reticent? Could I not fall into his arms and forget the past? He had come for me, yet he seemed stiff and foreign, overly solicitous and polite. Something was not quite right.

He patted the bed. "You should get some rest since we'll leave before dawn."

I twisted the edge of my robe and tightened my knuckles. "There's something you're not telling me."

David stood and placed his hands on my shoulders. He looked at my reflection in the bronze mirror. "You're not happy to see me?"

"Why are you here?"

He pulled me to the bed. "Don't worry. I won't violate you since you seem so inclined to be cold to me."

Where did my David go? The man staring at me wore a mask. Something ate at him. I'd seen that haunted look in my father's face.

"You don't have to take me back if you don't want," I said.

"I know." He scrutinized my face for a long period of time. "Now, sleep. Tomorrow, we'll go on a trip, and we'll talk."

He put out the oil lamps and peeled my robe off. I lay awake a long time after his breathing steadied into deep sleep. What could I tell him? These last few months had been peaceful, and I had healed. But not quite. Ittai had disappeared. And my sons left without a word. Jada was also gone. My daughter and her husband loved me, as did Meribbaal. *I may not be entirely happy, but neither was I miserable.*

David snored.

325

I stared into nothingness.

* * *

David waited for his wife to say goodbye to Anna, Machir, and Meribbaal. He put her on the horse with him, and they rode west toward the Jordan River. The land immediately around Lo-debar was well cultivated and rolling, but as soon as they left the valley, the terrain became rockier. The earlier chill had given way to a pleasant temperature with a slight breeze.

"Is it dangerous for us to be out here alone?" Michal asked after a few miles. She seemed more relaxed than the night before.

"No, maybe we'll keep going north and never return. I hear there is a sea way to the north called the Black Sea."

"Yes, let's disappear and let the legends take us," she agreed. "The Black Sea. Sounds like a place with dragons and bats, and high lonely castles, and brooding dark-haired men."

"Brooding you'll get, but no dark-haired men while I'm around," he said.

She shivered, and he pulled her closer.

They ascended a trail lined with oaks and wild olives. Below them lay a narrow valley with a fast flowing brook, the banks lush with trees and shrubs. David hitched the horse near the water and pitched a tent under a shaded ledge.

As long as he could pretend this trip was about her homecoming, he could stay away from the edge of the nightmare back in Jerusalem. They stepped down a fissure in the rock. A waterfall tumbled over a precipice; the sunlight divided the spray into multi-colored points. A blue-green pool carved from the falling water shimmered below.

David stripped his garments and jumped into the water. Michal looped her legs on an overhanging branch and sat above him.

"Come, Eglah." He beckoned. "Aren't you hot? And need a bath?"

She shook her head. "I'll enjoy the breeze and the view from here."

David flipped his naked body into a dive allowing her to catch sight of his backside and surfaced with a shake of his head. "Come on in."

When she didn't respond, he leaned back on the water, showing her his entire front side.

"You're a vile man. Do you enjoy exposing yourself to everyone around?" Michal poked him with a long, slender willow branch. "Oh, how glorious you are, King David, naked David."

David swiped the branch out of her hands. But she grabbed another branch with leaves attached and swished it over his loins. He flipped onto his stomach. When she lunged to poke his backside, he yanked the branch. She lost her balance and plunged belly first into the pool.

Michal splashed, unable to gain a foothold. David grabbed her hair and dragged her into his arms. "Who's the glorious one now?"

He pressed his mouth over hers and swept her lips open with a wet kiss while his hands moved to strip her wet clothes.

Michal turned her head and pushed his chest. "Don't. I can't give in."

"What can't you give in to?" David nuzzled her neck. "I'm your husband, aren't I?"

She swallowed and leaned back. "Doing this isn't going to change anything."

"Who came to me rolled in a rug? You know you want me." He caressed her breasts.

She nudged his hands aside. "What I don't want is the gnawing pain—the pain I had buried."

"So, you'd rather have empty peace? No expectations, no disappointments? Is that it?"

Michal clutched her throat and blinked. "Why do we have to talk?"

He clasped her neck. "I waited eight years for you to come to me, and all the while, I sent you notes."

"You did not." She pouted. "I checked every scroll, unrolled it."

David chuckled at the blush that flushed her face. "Oh, but I did. Every psalm, prayer and hymn, I wrote to God, but also to you. Think I didn't have an army of scribes?"

He took her hand and entwined his fingers around hers. "I wanted you to know my heart, and I wanted you to have peace with God. Did you have peace?"

"Yes, I did. I buried you deep in the jade box, and I survived. But now… it's like we opened the box and let out a storm of pain."

He trailed a kiss behind her ear. "I can make you feel better."

"Not now, please." She tugged his arm. "Let's put some dry clothes on and get something to eat."

She pulled out of his arms. The lump grew in David's throat until it pressed over his chest. She was afraid. Michal, who never feared, now feared him. What had he done to her?

That evening, David sat at the fireside by himself and watched the embers die. Michal had eaten and crawled into the tent. He threw the last stick into the fire and joined her.

She lay stiff on her side, facing the far side. David crept behind her and cradled her. He struggled for the words that wouldn't come. The last eight years had been a tortuous journey of nightmares and anxiety. He closed his eyes and prayed for sleep, for rest, for peace.

He dreamed.

Sweat beaded into his eyes. He was on a cart flaked with dried blood. A bloated face, covered with flies, stared at him. Another arm dangled, the flesh hanging in strings over pale bone. The rolling of the cart sickened his stomach. Was he dead?

David clawed his face and peeled off flesh. The cart stopped. Women wept and wailed. A sonorous voice called the names. *David, son of Jesse.* Michal stepped forward, wrapped in a black veil. They threw his body at her feet. She dropped her veil, her face a skull. *I hate you, David. Now, be gone.* Her laughter cackled, wild as the whirlwind.

David sat and clutched his throat, gulping for breath. Fresh air. He crawled to the flap and snatched it open.

The night bugs chirped, and all was peaceful in the forest. But his mind raged. "You can't hate me. You can't."

"David?" Her hand found his. "Did you have a nightmare?"

He buried his face in her arms. "Don't hate me, Michal. I can't bear it."

She held him. "I don't hate you."

"But I've been horrid to you. I tore apart your family because I wanted you for myself."

She pulled him to the bedding beside her.

"And I drove Ittai away and cut his face. And then your sons followed him into exile."

She cuddled herself against him.

"I've killed innocent villagers. Leveled entire towns. Did it all in God's name."

She caressed his shoulders and kissed his neck.

"And I allowed women to be killed while taken captive. I turned away from their pleading cries."

She swallowed and stiffened but did not push him away.

"And I've hurt you the most. You were my bride. My virgin bride, the one I wanted to build my life around. And I destroyed your life."

She rubbed his head and kissed his hair. "I don't hate you, David."

He squeezed his eyes shut. *Oh, you would hate me if you knew what I'd done.*

"What if I'm a madman? Would you still care for me?" His entire body shook as angry stones pummeled his heart and wracked his body with sobs.

Michal enveloped him, her long arms and legs around him, and pressed him to the sleeping mat. She stroked his temple and stared in his eyes. "You're not a madman. You're troubled, very troubled. But you're not like my father was."

"You believe that?"

"Yes, God's Spirit abides in you."

"I cannot sleep more than an hour. And when I sleep, I fall into a chasm, and my soul is sucked into darkness. A thousand claws tear at me, and the shrieks rip my eardrums. Why?"

"I don't know." She ran her fingernail down the scar her father gave him. "It is so hard to be the king. God expects so much from a king."

Sweat popped over David's face. "I don't ever want to sleep again."

"Then don't sleep. I'll stay with you. I'll keep you awake."

He clutched onto her as a babe would to his mother.

"Relax and I'll sing for you." She held his head between her breasts and sang. Her lilting voice blew through the tops of the trees and carried the sound of marching feet, steady as the primordial heartbeat that calmed him in the womb of her love.

* * *

The next morning dawned misty and cool. David stretched and yawned. He had slept the rest of the night without disturbance. He propped over Michal and kissed her, but she yawned and pulled the blankets over her head.

David left her to go fishing. Would she still love her if she knew how evil he had become? How could he tell her? He pulled a fish out of the water and watched it flop to its death.

He returned to find her sitting on a rock. Silently, he roasted the fish, then handed her a fish and a piece of bread. Today, he'd show her his kingdom and convince her of his love.

They ascended a mountainous trail. The last peak was too steep for the horse. David tied the horse to a juniper tree and helped Michal climb over boulders and rock faces. She clung to him, sweat staining her dress and dampening her hair.

The silence of the summit drew his breath away. He held her, his heart to her back, and he waited, letting the grandeur of the view impress her. Down below, the sparkling ribbon of the Jordan River traced itself from the azure highlands of the Sea of Chinnereth to the vague, distant cliffs of the Salt Sea.

To the west, the tops of Mt. Tabor and Mt. Gilboa rose like shoulders above the clouds. He pointed. "The mount where your father and your brothers went to meet the LORD."

She shielded her eyes and said nothing. To the left, Mt. Ebal and Mt. Gerizim poked their heads above scarred and wrinkled foothills.

David swept his hand northward. The Sea of Chinnereth gleamed dark-blue and placid, framed by fertile valleys and rich plains, dotted by towns and settlements. "Do you see that white mount way up there, to the right? Mt. Hermon."

She sucked in her breath. "It looks like the Prophet Samuel: white hair, beard, and mantle of glistening snow. I remember being scared of him. Have you been there?"

"We conquered all the way to Damascus, but I've never climbed it. I rule the land from the River Euphrates to the Salt Sea and beyond."

He tilted her head back. "I would give it all to be back in your heart again. I would."

His lips hovered over hers. So close. She averted her face. "You're God's anointed. You have a mission."

David's fists clenched, and he bit the insides of his cheeks. So, she didn't want his heart. What was left? He stepped forward to the edge. Michal shivered and backed against him.

"What if we walked over the edge?" he whispered. "Oh, that we had wings like a dove! For then we would fly away and be at rest."

"You're scaring me," she said. "This place is so remote."

He tucked her back in his arms and squeezed. "Let's fly over the white mountain to the Black Sea and live in a castle of jade, up in the pines where the scent is fresh, high above all clamor, pain, and trouble."

Her voice dropped, suddenly sad. "I wish it could be."

David tilted her chin and kissed her, so achingly sweet. She held her breath, and he brushed her satiny lips again, encouraged that she hadn't pulled away. Afraid to deepen the kiss, he relished the feeling, soft and full, mingled with the taste of mint and the scent of jasmine. He moistened the kiss, and she exhaled with a soft hum, filling him with a whiff of hope as he slowly nibbled and tugged her lower lip, deliberately pausing after letting her have a taste of his tongue.

Her sharp intake of breath heartened him, and he pressed his advantage. His hands roamed down her spine and around her lower back. Her body softened, and she wobbled.

Her half-open eyes moistened, and her heart seemingly teetered on the verge of opening. Would she trust him again? Pebbles fell off the edge of the cliff. A twisted sensation prodded him. He had only to push. Would she know he had done it, or would she think she had lost her balance? Would those eyes reproach him all the way down?

Oh God, what is happening to me? Am I a murderer? David closed his fist and pulled back from the edge, sending a stream of pebbles clattering into the precipice.

Michal's jaw quivered, and she didn't look him in the eye. His heart smote. *Fly away and be free. Wander far off and never return. Oh, to escape the windy storm, the tempest, the siren of the seductress.* A dry and dusty wind whipped his face. He ground his teeth to shut out the howls of guilt, of regret, of despair. *Oh, what have I done? Oh, God, if I could only take back that note, I would. Oh, God, don't let Uriah die for my sins.*

The sun lowered in the west. Picking their way down in the dark would be treacherous. David took her hand. "I'll help you climb down. I won't let you fall."

She threaded her fingers between his and leaned on his arm. His heart expanded and warm relief swelled his chest. She still trusted him. *But what about Uriah? If she knew…*

Once they were below the tree-line, he pitched the tent beneath fragrant pine trees. After a meal of fish and wild berries, they sat in front of the fire. Michal hummed to herself as David threw twigs into the fire.

"Eglah, I wasn't always mean and horrible."

Michal stopped humming and stared at him. "Why are we talking about mean and horrible?"

Still staring at the fire, David said, "When I was a boy I dreamed great things. I wasn't satisfied to be a farmer or a shepherd or even a scribe. I wanted to reform Israel, to make it glorious and grand: greater than the Philistines, greater than the Syrians, even greater than all of Egypt. I listened to the tales of the caravans. And I dreamed of traveling to faraway places and bringing back horses, chariots, and weapons."

"It seems you are doing exactly what you dreamed of. You've conquered much of the known territories, the land God granted to Father Abraham."

"I never dreamed it would be so bloody." David covered his face.

Michal put her hands on his shoulders. "It has to be, Ishi. God is a consuming fire."

"I pursued them, overtook them and utterly consumed them. It sounds easy, but when you're actually there: the body parts, the stench of blood and guts, the flesh-picking birds. When you're covered with their blood—you don't want to look in their eyes. Never look in their eyes."

She rubbed his neck. "You didn't know all this the day you set out to be a hero."

"Ambition is a strange thing, isn't it?" He laughed and his throat constricted.

"But you've done a lot of good. And God is with you."

"What use is the good if it's all wiped out by evil?"

She touched his lip with one finger. "You overcome evil by good. It's what you've always done. Especially with my father, and with me."

What if I were the evil one? How do I overcome that? David covered his face and hunched his shoulders. A blanket of heaviness covered him, and he was tired, so very, very tired.

The fire crackled, dying into the glow of tiny orange embers.

Michal dropped her hand. "What's bothering you?"

He rubbed his eyes. If she knew, she would run screaming from him.

"You can't hide from me," she said. "You've done something, haven't you?"

"Like you said, being king is hard, and I'm tired. Let's move into the tent." David would not look at her. He couldn't tell her. Would to God he'd have peace. He let the darkness envelope him.

He dreamed.

The young princess held his hand. *You should have a wife who loves you.*

He smiled. *Yes, and that would be you.*

She shook her head. *If it were me, why are you still looking? Perhaps you should have a wife whom you love.*

A wife who loves me.

Nay, a wife whom you love.

David woke. *A wife whom I love. But do I know how?*

* * *

The morning mist evaporated with scents of honeysuckle and wild jasmine. Splashes of color highlighted the valley below. Dense spots of red poppy stained the meadows of silken grasses: a trail of blood leading toward the deep green riverbank, pierced in the center with a silver sword of water.

David and Michal descended from the ridges. The stands of oaks and walnut trees that flourished in the vicinity of the streams gave way to fields cultivated with wheat or lush green meadows full of sheep and cattle. These were the rolling hills the children of Gad and Manasseh had begged of Moses to allow them to settle: east of the Jordan, much fairer and more fertile than the severe hills of Judah and Benjamin.

A walnut tree with a dense canopy shaded them. David picked vines of yellow honeysuckle and twined them around Michal's head. She threw them off and wrapped them around his neck. "David, David, the Philistines be upon you."

Her laughter cheered his heart, and he allowed her to entangle him. "And I am willingly joined to you, my wife. Whatever God has joined together, let no man pull asunder."

"No man, David. Not even you." She reeled him in, and they kissed for a long moment.

They wound their way toward the Sea of Chinnereth. The fields, watered by full streams, were green with wheat and barley. Abundant balsam trees and thorn bushes grew along the path hedged by stands of pistachios and almonds. Gazelles sprang and bounded their way along tiny brooks where the grass grew thick and lush, and tall weeds and trailing vines covered the flowing water.

David took Michal to the edge of a brook. He'd pretend they were young again, with not a care in their hearts. Young and free. He drew five smooth stones and placed them in her hand. "You are my living brook, and with these five stones I wed you again. Will you marry me?"

She picked a single small stone, a green moss-colored one, and handed the other four back to him. "I will marry you again." She touched the stone to his heart and kissed it. "And I'll never throw this one away."

David lifted her and swung her around. They laughed until they were breathless, and they kissed until they wept.

Late in the afternoon, they crossed a dozen murmuring streams crowned with the rosy bloom of giant stands of oleanders and came to a stone basin where a spring gushed from the hillside. Villagers gathered there to fill their pitchers and water skins.

David let the horse drink, and they chatted with the villagers, buying strips of beef, cheese and bread. An old man pointed to a cairn of rocks. "Long ago, the Canaanites sacrificed there. You can still hear them cry. Cursed."

The village women ignored him, and a small knot of boys threw stones at him. He shook his walking stick at them. "One of these nights…"

David chuckled and gave him a silver coin. He pointed his horse toward the deserted rock structure. Small shrubs poked their heads above the cracks of the rocks.

Michal flipped her hair over her shoulder. "Don't tell me you're thinking of camping there tonight."

"How did you guess?" David found a flat area sheltered beneath a domed table. The wind off the lake kicked, but the rock face shielded them. He pitched the tent, made a fire and roasted the beef.

After dinner, he snuck up behind her and jumped.

She started with a yelp and punched his arm. "You brought me here to scare me."

He turned her on top of him. "I want you trembling in my arms when I fill your soul."

The wind whistled through the cairn, raising the hairs on the back of his neck. Her skin dotted with goose bumps as David slowly brought her mouth down to his. His fingers wove into her hair. "You are the wife I love. Will you stay with me?"

Michal stroked his beard. "I thought we wouldn't talk."

"But I have to know, before we… I don't want to ever hurt you again. I promise."

She traced his lips with her little finger. "Don't. You're all about vows and promises, glory and pride. You will hurt me again. I know it."

Her words cut him, and pain encircled his waist.

"So, you won't come back with me?" He kissed her fingers.

She blinked and regarded him with moist eyes. "I'm your wife. I will follow you wherever you lead, and I will care for you."

"Why do you care for a monster?" He covered his eyes with his forearm.

"You're not a monster."

"But what if I were?"

"You'd still be you, David. The boy who wanted to be better."

He gulped and hugged her tightly. "I do want to be better. I do."

CHAPTER 40

Proverbs 6:16-17 These six things doth the LORD hate: yea, seven are an abomination unto him: A proud look, a lying tongue, and hands that shed innocent blood,

>>><<<

David knelt on the top of his palace wall, turning his face toward the east. He bowed his head, but he had no words for the LORD. He tried a song of praise. His lips felt dry. He gave thanks, but his stomach growled. At least Michal had returned. He could be thankful for that. And the nightmares had ceased.

After a hectic day in the throne room, David returned to find Michal at her writing table. Her hair shone with amber highlights from their week in the sun.

She greeted him with a warm kiss, and he handed her a bouquet of lilies. The smile on her face melted his heart. He knelt in front of her lap.

"David, what are you doing?" She fondled his hair and raised his face.

"I'm so grateful you've returned with me." Tears blurred his vision as he slipped a necklace out of his pocket. "Put this on."

She drew in a sharp breath. "It's exquisite." Diamonds encircled the necklace and eighteen pear-shaped emeralds dangled off in intervals between diamond flowers set in white gold. While she put on the necklace, David fumbled for the matching earrings. Michal laughed and expertly looped them into the tiny holes in her earlobes.

David backed up to admire her. "Eglah, can you trust me again? Believe me?"

She paused and pierced him with narrowed eyes. "Why are you showering me with jewelry? Why shouldn't I trust you?"

Sweat moistened his palms. He should let her know about Uriah, his fears and his failings. He licked his lips. "I... have... Can I trust you to... care? If I tell you..."

"Tell me what? Is it Ittai? My sons? What have you done?"

He set his jaw. "They're fine. Why are you asking?"

She lowered her brows. "I was afraid to ask. But you seem to have something on your mind."

"I wouldn't hurt them. Trust me."

She grimaced and removed the necklace. "Because if this is blood money, I don't want it."

"It's not. I swear to you." His hands trembled. "Oh, Eglah, believe me."

Rough pounding on the door startled them. His advisor Hushai stood with a drawn face. A man behind him wrung his hands. David's stomach clenched.

"I have a messenger from Joab," Hushai said without preamble.

The blood drained from David's head, and his hands grew cold. The messenger bowed low. "O King, do not be distressed. We gained ground on the Ammonites. They came out to fight us, and some of your mighty men rushed them, forcing them back to their gate. Archers killed a few of them."

"How can that be? Didn't they know not to go close to the wall?" David asked.

"They thought to bust through the gate. They were the most valiant of men. Particularly Uriah. Uriah, the Hittite, is among the dead."

A chill like a nest of hatching spiders crawled over his skull and tightened around his head. Michal held him around his waist from behind.

David stiffened his lip. "Say to Joab not to be distressed. It is the vagaries of war. Make the battle stronger against the city and overthrow it. Encourage him with my words."

The messenger bowed and took leave. Hushai waited behind. "My king. Do you require me?"

"Yes, a moment." David kissed his wife. "I must give my condolences to Uriah's widow."

Michal squeezed his hand. "Of course. I'm sorry."

A guard ran ahead to announce his arrival. Bathsheba stood at the door, her head bent down.

"Behold, the king and his counselor." They stepped into her house. She kept her face trained on their sandals. Her belly was fuller and rounder than before.

"Lady Bathsheba," Hushai said. "We have come to bring you our condolences."

Bathsheba caught her breath and glanced at David. Her eyes rolled back, and she collapsed into the arms of her maids.

David waited for her to revive, sitting on the chair next to her couch. "Lady Bathsheba, your husband was a brave and valiant man."

He raised her hand to his lips and kissed it. She recoiled at his touch. David tried to catch her eye, but she kept them studiously trained on the ground. Fat teardrops rolled down her cheeks. Her maid bent over her and handed her a linen kerchief.

Hushai cleared his throat. "Ask us anything you need. We will see to it that Uriah gets a funeral befitting his valor. The king will take care of you. He will make you a settlement as a reward for your husband's loyalty and years of service."

Bathsheba nodded. They backed out of her house and departed.

* * *

By the time David returned to his chamber, Michal lay in the bed in her nightgown.

"I'm so sorry about Uriah," she said.

"He was a brave man. We will honor him with a grand funeral."

"Did he come to you while you were in the caves?"

"Yes." David's lips quivered, recalling Uriah's youthful face, so full of life and enthusiasm.

"How did his wife take it? I never did meet her."

"She is so young, and now she's bereft. I feel I should do something for her."

"Of course, did you offer her a settlement?"

"Not only that, but she's pregnant," he said.

"Oh, the poor thing. And a newlywed too."

"I don't know how she'll handle all this by herself."

Michal gripped his forearm. "Then we must help her."

He shut his eyes and lowered his voice. "I should marry her and give her a home here."

"Marry her?" Michal's voice raised an octave. "You can't marry all the widows of your men. You were not responsible for Uriah's death."

David raked his hair. "Uriah was like a brother. He saved my life once. Your father's men had me trapped in a rock pile. They shot arrows at me, and I fell. Uriah fought off the men and carried me back to the cave. I would have been dead."

"But that still doesn't mean you have to marry his widow. Unless I'm guessing she's extremely beautiful!" She shouted the last words.

He covered his ears. "I have to. I can't leave his widow bereft, especially since she is with child."

"So, will you adopt her child?"

"Uriah would have wanted it. He was like a brother."

Michal threw her hands into the air. "David, you horrible man. You adopt her child and not my sons. I can't believe I almost started to trust you again. I. Am. So. Stupid."

"Eglah, you're still my favorite wife."

"I don't want to be your favorite wife. I want to be your only wife. And don't call me Eglah!"

She removed both earrings and threw them at him. Her face twisting in pain, she ripped her clothes and rocked on the bed hugging her knees.

David rubbed her shoulders. "I will adopt your sons and acknowledge Joshua and Beraiah."

"My sons don't need you." Her voice choked through her tears. "Phalti has already adopted them, and he loves them."

"But you need me. You do." He pressed her, but she didn't answer. "Say you need me."

She pulled the coverlet over her head.

* * *

The air hung heavy in the room. David ran down the stairs and out the gate to clear his head. The horror of it all. Had Uriah delivered the note to Joab? He dared not ask. Where was the note? Maybe Uriah never delivered it. Others died, it wasn't just Uriah. Bathsheba must not find it. He had to meet Uriah's body and supervise the burial.

David wandered, unmindful of where his steps took him. He might have bumped into half a dozen people, but they stepped out of his way.

Uriah was a convert, but he could not have him buried. Not if the note remained in his clothes. The embalmers would find the evidence. But the Hittites, did they bury or cremate? These thoughts flitted through his head. His feet took him down the lane of the foreigners. Campfires lit the dark as families gathered around storytellers and relaxed after the evening meal.

David stopped in front of the tent of two Hittites who called to him, "Dear sir, what is it you're looking for?"

David addressed the older man. "My friend, a Hittite, has been killed. Pray tell me what the burial customs are. I wish him to have the most elaborate funeral."

"You've come to the right place. You will want a large golden urn and lots of wine. And wood, tinder, and kindling for a giant funeral pyre. We can build one. We also sell dogs."

"Dogs? What are they used for?"

"Companionship—we sacrifice the dog and put it on the pyre— honey, oil, and servants, too, if your friend had any. Did he have wives?"

"Yes, he did." David replied. "I'm sure she'll want to pick the golden urn."

"No, that wouldn't be necessary." The older man said.

"She'll be going into the fire. He'll want to have his wife." The younger one added.

"Yes, definitely," the older man said. "How many wives did he have? We'll have to consider the size of the pyre and the amount of additional wood and oil."

"Wait, wait," David exclaimed. "His wife is not dead. He, only, has died and he had no children."

"Yes, yes, she is not dead. But she would wish to honor him by joining him on his pyre and serve him in the afterlife." Both men waved their hands, pantomiming the tying of the wife.

"Some women are so eager they don't have to be tied." The younger man put his hand over his heart. "Ah, such great love."

"Stop, stop," David said. "I will be marrying his widow."

The men looked at each other, raised their eyebrows and stared at David. "We shall do as you say. Pray tell us where the body is, and we will prepare him."

"Do you dress him in anything special? Or does he go in the bloody clothes he wore in battle?"

"If he's a warrior," the younger man said, "he goes in the bloody clothes, as an honor to him."

"He is a warrior," David said. "See to it no one disturbs his clothing. No one is to remove anything from his body, not a sword, not a dagger, not a sash, not a belt, not a purse or pouch. Understood?"

David showed them his ring. "I am King David. And you are in charge of the funeral of Uriah the Hittite. I will personally supervise the preparation of the body."

The men fell to the ground. "O King, we are honored. We will provide dogs and an effigy for the wife."

With that piece of business taken care of, David visited Bathsheba and told her he had found the men who would perform Uriah's funeral in the custom of the Hittites.

He then asked her to be his wife. She bowed at his feet and said, "My lord, the king, I will."

David made his way back to his bedchamber. Scraps of thoughts, of forgetfulness drifted in his mind. But he could not catch a single one. What had he done? Where could that note be? Oh, bloody, bloody hands. Blood gushed from his fingertips as from a burst wineskin. He slapped himself and threw up in the bathroom.

CHAPTER 41

Psalm 13:3 Consider and hear me, O LORD my God: lighten mine eyes,
lest I sleep the sleep of death

>>><<<

A constricting pressure in my chest kept me confined in David's bedchamber. He would disappear for days and then appear in the middle of the night, sometimes agitated, other times stone-faced. I wandered from one end of the room to the other with a continued ache in the center of my belly. Tears lurked in my eyes, and the gloom of the world weighed over me like a soggy blanket.

I met Bathsheba shortly after Uriah's funeral. They didn't have a wedding. David just brought her into the harem. She was exceedingly beautiful. The bluest eyes, as placid as a desert pool, peered from her delicate face. Her black hair, curled in ringlets, framed white skin of pure alabaster. She was shorter than me, and plumper, a figure full of curves, delightful to a man's hands.

I propped on the bed and greeted her. Her hand felt clammy and cold, soft, no spine. I squeezed it hard. She winced, but did not meet my eyes. Her other hand rested on her pregnant belly.

David gestured toward me as if I were a curious antique. "Bathsheba, this is Michal, my first wife. I will return to her at night, after I've come to you. She keeps me from having nightmares."

Bathsheba accepted this without question. She bowed her head slightly, appearing lukewarm and aloof. Surveying the room, she stepped over the rug and ran her hand over my mahogany table. She picked up my jade box and arched an eyebrow.

David took her hand, his face full of indulgence. He whispered in her ear. She pointed to the broken corner and shook her head. After glancing at the closed door of the wardrobe, she looked over her shoulder at David and headed for the door. She had been here before, and David had lied to me. How many other lies had he told me? My heart closed as clammy and cold as Bathsheba's hand.

* * *

As time went by, I grew accustomed to David's routine. After a few weeks of infatuation with the voluminous Bathsheba, he went back to his usual rotation, although the petite Maacah seemed to claim more attention than before.

The ache eased in my chest, and Naomi helped me down the stairs to the garden for exercise. I shivered, unaccustomed to the outdoor air. Tiny flurries of snow swirled, melting on contact with the earth. After a brisk walk, I stopped at the women's quarters, in front of the house where I used to stay. It was time to break my isolation.

Abigail and Abital came around the corner, followed by Ahinoam, Haggith and Maacah. They rushed to my side and welcomed me with many hugs. Everyone looked older. I supposed I did too.

"So, has David brought you back?" Ahinoam said.

"He has allowed me to come back to the palace," I said. "So much has changed since I've been gone."

"We've missed you. Come sit with us." Abigail extended her hand. Ahinoam smiled and Abital bounced up and down on her feet. Haggith gave me a begrudged hand and an amused grin peeked from behind Maacah's shawl.

Abital tapped my shoulder. "David gave me another bird. Do you want to see him?"

"We're having a party for Amnon," Ahinoam said. "It's his seventeenth birthday."

Abigail took my arm. "Yes, Michal, you must attend."

Talk turned to David's new wife, Bathsheba.

"You know she's staying in your sons' old quarters?"

"She'll bring great trouble. Mark my words."

"She seems so young. Why would our husband marry the widow of one of his men?"

"She stays to herself. Thinks she's better than us."

"He seems to like her a little too much to be just the widow of his best friend."

"You know her pregnancy is quite advanced, considering he just married her."

"We shouldn't gossip," Abigail said. "He's done a noble deed for a good friend. Our husband has a kind heart for strays."

I knew better, but I kept my mouth shut. I had never hated any of David's wives, not even Haggith. I had been taught about kings and royal courts. But taking Bathsheba after promising me his undying love was unforgiveable. The pit in my stomach grew, and I closed my eyes to shut in the threatened tears.

* * *

Iron clashed on iron, shields broke, grunts and groans, the cry of the dying. The man in front fell, pierced by a spear. David turned toward the wall. Spears flew at him. His shield up, he stepped over the man. The man next to him was cut down. David charged forward. Arrows rained down on him. All around him, men died, screaming for their mothers.

Why wasn't he hit?

A slimy hand grabbed is ankle. Jonathan, with blood gushing from his chest, cried, "David, my brother." Uriah lay across from him. "Friend, friend, save me, friend." His eyes dimmed, then opened wide. "Betrayer, murderer, fiend." David dropped his sword and ran. Jonathan's voice trailed him. "Coward, usurper, traitor."

* * *

"David, David." I shook him. "You're having a nightmare."

A flash of lightning illuminated him. He flailed with sweat across his brow.

"No, no. Jonathan, don't say that. Uriah, my friend, my friend." His voice gurgled in his sobs. "Jonathan, don't hate me." Thunder accompanied the word 'hate.'

"David." I covered him with my body. "I'm here."

He shook like a bruised reed. I pressed my weight on him, rooting him to the bed. I kissed the sour smell of panic from his upper lip. "Jonathan loves you. See? You have his ring."

"Why did they die? Why am I still here?" He bucked and heaved underneath me, the shakes threatening to toss me off. I squeezed him in my arms, as if I could squeeze the distress from the core of his being.

"They deserved to live," he said. "They were nobler than I, a worm."

"Oh, David. I, too, am a worm left to grovel in the dirt. A withered, worthless worm."

"But you're not guilty like I am." The spasms contracted and tore David's sobs. "I'm so guilty."

"Guilty? What are you guilty of? It's Bathsheba, isn't it?"

He didn't answer, but shuddered and gripped me tighter.

"You had her, didn't you, while she was another man's wife. You took her, didn't you?" No longer eager to calm his distress, I tried to push out of his arms, but he held me like a chain of iron. "The baby is yours, isn't it?"

"You hate me," he said.

A slow boil of anger pulsated through my body. "Let me go."

"No."

"I defy you. Usurper." I twisted my knuckles into his ribcage, forcing him to release me.

"Saul's daughter." He clamped me from behind and slammed me down on the bed. The air expelled out of my lungs and pinpoints of light swirled around my head. He tore my gown off. "My enemy's daughter, do you hate me, too?"

"You lied to me."

"You left me. You went with Ittai." He pressed his thumb and fingers into the hollows of my cheeks.

"I wanted to see my daughter married. Don't you dare blame me for this." I dug my fingernails into the back of his hands.

"You betrayed me."

"No, I did nothing with Ittai."

His face glistened in a flash of lightning. "I don't believe you."

"It doesn't matter what you believe." Thunder rumbled behind my ribs.

For the space of a minute, neither of us spoke. Rain pelted the roof.

David broke first. "What has happened to us?" His hands trembled as he wrapped my hair around his fingers.

I closed my eyes. David kissed me, and I clung to him. And I wondered how I could still love him, despite the betrayal and lies.

"Michal," he whispered, "I need you to love me."

And I need to love you. It's the only reason I live.

I clave to this need, and it resonated as hope in my bruised heart, and I lied to myself, and I succumbed amidst the blistering ache and numbing agony, hovering on the tightrope between love and pain.

* * *

Bathsheba's baby fell ill shortly after being born. David spent seven days praying and entreating the LORD, as he had done for Ithream. However, the baby weakened and died and joined the other departed young ones in the grotto behind the women's courtyard. I was numb. I had wished ill on Bathsheba, but not this way—never this way—her first child, David's son.

David stumbled into my arms. "The babe is dead. Wash me, anoint me with oil, and change my clothes."

"You did all you could." I peeled off the sackcloth and shook the ashes.

He lay in the water and moaned. "O LORD, I repent of my iniquities. My soul is sore vexed. Return, O LORD, deliver my soul. Save me for thy mercies' sake."

He fell silent and wept. I hummed and worked the bath cloth over his forehead, around his sunken eyes, smoothed his nose, and scrubbed his beard.

His body, stiff and hard, shuddered with grief. I kneaded his shoulders and pressed the back of his neck. My fingers massaged his scalp. My palms rubbed off the ashes. They clumped into the water, swirled like powdered tea in a bowl of divination.

I picked up a sandalwood comb, honed smooth, darkened with oil and plowed his hair like a spring field, breaking the tangled clods of mourning.

I sheared his beard leaving stubble, dusted it with myrrh, as rough and prickly as the pins in his heart. I filed his nails, smoothed his elbows and feet. I spread oil of cassia over his body, as sweet smelling as the day we wed.

I led him to bed, wrapped in a heavy woolen blanket. "David, sleep well."

Humming a Philistine lullaby, I waited for his breathing to steady, and when he could no longer comprehend, I told him, "David, I love you. I love you so much, more than you know." And I kissed him in his delirium and held onto him.

He woke and kicked off his blankets, his naked body covered in sweat. "The baby, the baby. He's dead because of me."

He threw himself on his back, his hands grappling his face. "I am so feeble and broken. I'll never be happy again. There is no more strength in me. Just let me die."

"David, you're flesh of my flesh, bone of my bone, blood of my blood. Take from me, take all of me, take and live." I rubbed his head and pulled his face into my neck.

Small gagging sounds emitted from his throat. His stiffened fingers clutched my shoulders, my arms, and my breasts. I took his one hand, and then the other. One by one, I caressed the base of his thumb, then his index finger, working my way to the little finger, softening the agonizing ache that radiated from the caverns of his heart.

Slipping out of my gown, I swam against him, around him, on top of him. I dragged my face over his chest and belly, my hands down his sides. I pressed my lips against his hair, forehead, temples, kissed his eyelids and the side his nose. I inhaled his sobs, swallowed his grief, and tasted the bitter fruit, the sting of sin. Hand to hand, mouth to mouth, and eye to eye, I stared into the muddy depths of his misery, consumed his sorrow, absorbing his pain. His anguish pumped deep inside of me, filling and flooding me with a blossoming flush that cried out to the other side of paradise. And I received from David, the ebb and the flow of his heart, love and pain, love and loss, love and hope.

CHAPTER 42

Song of Solomon 5:16 His mouth is most sweet: yea, he is altogether lovely. This is my beloved, and this is my friend, O daughters of Jerusalem.

>>><<<

The thunderstorm broke, and the day dawned bright and promising. I rubbed my eyes while David rolled out of bed. The child would be buried today. I could hardly believe his demeanor when he took his meals. He consumed his food with alacrity and washed down the cakes and bread with wine.

I had drowned in my dreams. A childhood friend I barely remembered ran with me through a yellow field of fennel. I swung around and Merab handed Samuel to me. His face was bright and pink, and Ithream rode on a pony all cheery and light. Then it was all gone, and a sour curl drilled my stomach. I had woken bathed in sweat, a heat wave spread across my chest to meet the chill in the base of my spine.

My heart pounded with a dull thud. A sniffle escaped, and David drew my veil back. "Why are you weeping? While the child was alive I wept because the LORD might have relented. But now he is dead, and I cannot bring him back."

My breath hitched. Even if I told David about Samuel, he would brush it off. He, who had fathered so many children; what was one insignificant baby?

David tugged my sleeve. "You don't have to attend."

"You should go with her."

He shook his head. "She is but another one of the women. She will stand with her father and grandfather." He coughed. "I can go alone."

I walked to the window. Samuel's burial seemed so long ago, but the pain had not dulled. It stuck like a persistent knife in my ribs right beneath my heart. Again, the sun shone and birds twittered and hopped in the treetops. Again, the world took no note of the passing of a tiny infant.

"You're thinking about Ithream, aren't you?"

David needed me. He didn't have to say it. I would hold his hand. Bathsheba's relatives would hate him. King or no king. All Jerusalem knew David had fathered the baby. Nathan, the prophet, had pronounced the child's death. Another child dead because of his father's sin. Another lamb sacrificed.

"I'll come with you." I took his hand.

He adjusted my veil. Hand in hand we made the long walk down the spiral staircase.

* * *

I opened a scroll and dipped my pen into the inkwell. David barged through the door. "I'm going back to war to claim victory over the Ammonites. Pray for me."

I sheared his hair to a finger's breadth, more silver than copper.

He ran his hands under my gown and roamed the contours of my body. This time he stepped out of the tub and pulled me to the bed. After we finished, I dressed him, strapped on his weapons, and fitted the crown on his head.

We walked to the palace gate, and he bid me farewell. He stood in front of me, not a penitent mourner or a repentant sinner, but once again, a proud monarch—a fierce warrior, favored by God. His crown glinted in the sunlight as he mounted his horse and rode off with his head held high.

I watched him leave, my heart heavy—my David, so troubled, yet so brave. What horrors lurked in that burdened mind?

David returned a few weeks later laden with treasure. The perfect king, he wore a heavy golden crown set with precious stones. He made Bathsheba his queen and called for seven days of celebration. The perfect leader, he sacrificed in front of the Ark. His wives and concubines stood in a train behind him. The perfect ruler, he distributed cakes and goods to all. His kingdom praised him, and their cheers rang to heaven.

I watched from the window, veiled and alone. No one had any idea why he kept me, why he needed me. My heart ached, but I tightened my fists and held onto my resolve. One day, I would be the only one. Ordained by God, created and consecrated for David, one day he'd only want me.

* * *

The nightmares came back with a vengeance. The Ammonite war concluded with great bloodshed. Every man, woman, and child was put under harrows and axes and cremated in the brick-kilns. The smell of blood and burning flesh must have been horrendous. All for a giant crown of gold.

David moaned and clung to me tighter than Eliah, my third son.

"You need to tell me what is wrong." I wiped the sweat from his forehead. "I know what you did to the Ammonites." The words hung in the air. "And before that, the Gittites, the Edomites, the Moabites, shall I continue?"

"They were our enemies. They deserved no mercy."

"So why does it bother you? Why not be glad?"

His squeezed his eyes shut. "Their faces, their cries. The blood." His voice broke, and he clutched me as if his life depended on it. "Do you have any idea what a battle is like?"

I rubbed his neck. "No. I've never seen one."

"You must come with me." He gripped my face with calloused fingers. "I want you to know."

He kissed me, his rough stubble scratching my lips. "You're not afraid of me?"

He pressed me onto the bed, and I tore at him, digging, hurting and bruising. We tangled and sparred, pleasure mixed with pain, extracting the penalty before oblivion crumpled him between my arms and legs.

* * *

Rebellion broke out in Gath. David dressed me in leather armor and a veil, put me on a mule and set out for battle. We camped outside of Gath just past a small hill and next to a winding creek.

He sent messengers to the inhabitants to open the gates and bow to him. I prayed Ittai and my sons would not be in there. Rumor had it they camped in the caves in the wilderness.

David returned to the tent, a marked scowl on his face. "Those infidels. They've killed the messengers and thrown their bodies over the wall."

"So what are we going to do? The walls of Gath are unbreakable. How long will we stay out here?" I had to buy time to find Ittai.

David slapped his thigh. "We're not here to lay a siege, but to teach them a lesson. We start by shooting all the men on the wall. Then we withdraw and let them come out to us."

"What if they won't come out?"

"They will. Or we'll burn their fields. Now wait on this hill behind this rock and watch."

"But... don't you have to prepare first?"

He eyed me. "Why do you want me to delay?"

"I... uh... what if? Oh, David..."

"You can't stand the pressures of war? Pretty little princess, you're falling apart already. Don't worry, we won't offer you in exchange for the king's head." He stomped out of the tent, barking orders to his men.

I huddled in the tent, unable to stomach the assault. Yet, I had to know. An unseen hand drew me out.

I climbed a tree and hid in the canopy to watch. *Oh, God. Don't let Ittai be there.* He would never have rebelled. Perhaps they had been kicked out, or no... No, they had to be away, camped somewhere else. They'd never be trapped inside a fortress like Gath. No, they were outcasts, men without allegiance, outlaws and wanderers.

David positioned the archers. They sallied up to the city wall and shouted, "Ho there, your king is here. Open the gate, or come out and fight."

David divided his men into three groups and rode with the mounted men toward the gate. Another group of men with bows and arrows arrayed themselves in back of the horses near the hill. Finally, the infantry armed with spears and swords flanked the horses near the woods.

The Philistine archers on the wall stretched their arms back. A swarm of arrows soared up like hornets. David's men raised their shields and charged under the first volley. Our archers positioned themselves behind the horses and let loose a barrage of black at closer range. The sound of death pierced the air as men tumbled off the wall.

The trumpet blew, and the gates sprung open. Thundering hooves beat the ground as a mass of chariots and horses charged straight toward us. I clung to the tree, my eyes straining to see, and my heart pounding through my chest.

David and the mounted men surged forward, lances and spears in hand. Our archers launched another volley and pinned the Philistine footmen. The loud clang and screams of the first clash were followed by heavy thuds, cracking sounds, curses and screams. Horses reared, men fell, and chariots turned over. David darted from side to side directing his forces with his sword.

Body after body fell. David's horse squealed, shafted by a spear. My heart jumped to my throat, and I climbed higher. Covered in blood, David hacked his way through a line of Philistines. One man pulled him down. My breath stopped, but Joab cut the man with a swift blade. David whirled and stabbed another man. The Philistines retreated, peppered by the arrows, and chased by the heavy infantry with pikes and clubs.

"Take them all, let none go alive." With a renewed roar, the Israelites pursued them to the gate. The Philistines could not shut the gates fast enough. David's men overwhelmed them and barreled into the city.

Carrion birds flew overhead in large circles and fluttered down onto the dying and the dead. A Philistine covered in blood staggered toward me, his mouth open without sound. His eyes beseeched me, a spear stuck in his back. I pulled the spear out and tore his clothes to staunch the bleeding. He laid his head on my lap and stared, his eyes glazed and hollow. Blood trickled out of his mouth as he gasped and shuddered for breath. I smoothed his hair from his face and sang to him. David's shadow fell on us. He took the man's hand and covered him with prayers. The life drained out, and the eyes went dull.

And so it went, the entire afternoon and into the evening. I searched the dead, dreading lest I find my son or my friend. We separated the living from the dead, the salvageable from the hopeless. David, exhausted and weary, crawled to each man, murmured prayers in his ears, comforted and heard last words. I ministered to the wounded, tied arms and legs, stuffed wool into the wounds, and helped strap men to litters to be borne by their fellow soldiers. Those were the lucky ones; the others lay on my lap and died. Some mistook me for their mother, others cried for their daughters. I kissed them and told them I loved them and laid their heads gently onto the ground to close their eyes.

The stench of blood and death permeated my skin. By the time we had gathered our wounded, David's body was drenched in blood: his armor soaked red, his tunic crimson, turning to rust. Blood flaked off my hands and arms, my face sticky where I received dying kisses, my hair stiffened by bloody hands, and my heart relieved that I had recognized none of them.

After giving orders to his men to march back to Jerusalem, David pulled me on the mule and traveled in the opposite direction. Each in our own thoughts, we didn't talk. We dismounted, and he led me into a rushing river. He grabbed me from behind and dunked me into the water with him.

When I surfaced, he looked like a different man. The shadows of war had been washed away. He smirked with boyish charm. "Now, after all the fighting, comes the fun."

The cold water had lightened my mood also. "Fun? Do you always have fun when you fight?"

"We usually vow not to touch a woman."

I splashed water in his face. "And what am I, a fish?"

"You're a slippery one, now fight me. I won't let you get away."

I pushed and threw my shoulder into his gut, then splashed down the river, stumbling over the rocks. He caught me, tackled me in a pool underneath a spray, and dragged me down. My eyes popping from holding my breath, I clawed at his legs and kicked until he swung me to the surface. I coughed and spat in his face, and he laughed.

"You're my war captive tonight." He swept me in his arms and carried me out of the water, laying me down on a blanket of leaves. He bent over me like a conqueror and opened my legs.

"Why do I have to be the captive? Does this make you feel bigger, like you're always on top?"

"You're talking too much." He bent his head down and kissed the inside of my thighs. "Or would you rather I talk?"

I mumbled something incoherent as he nuzzled me and put his talking muscles to a different task. A warm rumble threatened to overshadow me, and I squirmed and twisted. The leaves tickled my back, and his beard scratched my thighs. His mouth was most sweet and his tongue full of honey. As a spoil of war, I surrendered to his mastery over my body.

CHAPTER 43

Colossians 3:25 But he that doeth wrong shall receive for the wrong which he hath done: and there is no respect of persons.

>>><<<

My sandals slapped on the stones of the women's courtyard. Birds chirped and flitted in the large bay tree. The air smelled sweet and spicy, a mixture of jasmine, myrtle and camphor. With new parchments under my arm, I prepared for a peaceful day of writing. I had my own story to tell in addition to David's turbulent one.

Abital tore around the fountain and clutched my robe. Haggith and Abigail followed close behind.

"My birds are lost," Abital said. "They flew away."

"The curse is upon our heads." Haggith waved her arms, her hair wild and frizzed.

"Haggith, stop fanning fears," Abigail said. Tears streamed down her face, and she wiped it hurriedly with the back of her wrist.

"I don't care what you say. This family is cursed." Two spots of color reddened Haggith's cheeks.

"Wait, wait," I said. "What's happened?"

Abigail drew me aside. "Tamar, Maacah's daughter, was raped by Amnon, Ahinoam's son."

Tamar. David's favorite daughter. Beautiful, meek Tamar. How could this happen? And Amnon, polite and charming. He seemed harmless.

I ran to Ahinoam's door, trailed by Haggith and Abigail.

"She's not talking to anyone." Haggith said.

I pounded on the door. "Ahi, Ahi, open up. It's me, Michal."

"Go away," she cried from inside.

"Please, Ahi, let me talk to you."

"She won't even talk to Abigail. It's no use." Haggith stomped off.

"Ahi," Abigail said in a soft voice, "Haggith is gone now, may we come in?"

352

The door opened, and we entered. Ahinoam's eyes were bright red, her hair unkempt, and her lips cracked.

"It is not your fault." I patted her hand. "What happened?"

"I don't know. I thought Amnon was in love with her. He was always swooning over her, wishing she was not his sister. I told him to look elsewhere. I can hardly believe it. But if it is true, there is no excuse."

"There's never any excuse for rape," Abigail said, her voice choked and harsh.

"But it's not like Ahi did it," I said. "Where's your son now?"

"He's at his house. Do you think David will have him executed?" A fresh set of tears sprinkled from her eyes. "He's my only son."

"Oh, Ahi, I grieve for your heart." Abigail clutched Ahinoam, and they cried together.

I didn't know what to say. Rape was reprehensible, no matter the circumstances. David would have to be the judge. I left them and went to see Maacah, Tamar's mother.

Maacah pulled me through the door. A grim line of hate replaced her usual sultry pout. Her stare pierced through a tangled mat of dusky hair, her face smeared with a mixture of tears and kohl.

I placed a hand on her shoulder. "Tell me what happened."

"Amnon tricked her. He said he was sick, that only Tamar could tend to him to regain his health. He forced her and threw her out like a harlot. Michal, tell David to kill him, to uphold your Hebrew Law."

She clutched the front of my robe and pulled me against her. Her gaze locked on mine, tears swimming in her eyes. "She was only fourteen. Remind David she was a virgin and a child."

Muffled sobs came from Maacah's bed. Tamar hid under the covers with Haggith at her side. I rubbed her back. She trembled and shook, her hands clutching and unclutching the bedcovers, her face hidden.

I lowered my head. "Dear LORD, please look on Your handmaiden, Tamar, a precious lamb. There is no hole too deep Your love cannot fill, no place too far You cannot go. Give her the balm of Your comfort. Hold her close with Your salvation and strengthen her with courage. In Your name we pray, LORD."

* * *

I did not relish breaking the news to David, but they expected it of me. By the covenant, their children were my children and hence my responsibility. I breathed a prayer to the LORD and sent a messenger to David to meet me at our bedchamber.

The door opened with a bang. David rushed in, breathless, his crown hung at an angle.

"What happened? The messenger said you had an urgent message for me."

I threw my arms around him. "David, sit down."

"Tell me, what's happened?"

My chest heaved, and I let it out in one breath. "Tamar's been raped."

David staggered. "No! No! Who?"

"Your son, Amnon." I held him as the blood drained from his face.

"Amnon?" His eyes bulged. He tore out of my grasp and headed for the door.

I ran after him. "David, what will you do?"

He barged into Maacah's house. "Tamar, Tamar, my daughter."

David pulled Tamar into his arms. She kicked and scratched his face and thrashed without regard to her father.

Maacah pulled on David. "Let her go. She's scared. Leave."

Tamar's keening screams pierced the air. David laid her back on the bed and tucked her in. She hid under the blankets. Her mournful shrieks clawed through my heart. David rubbed her shoulders and cradled her head until she calmed.

Her wretched sobs echoed in my ears as I followed David to Ahinoam's house. Before knocking on the door, he asked me, "How is she?"

"Shouldn't you decide what you're going to do about Amnon? Find out the truth?"

"He came to me, asked for permission to have Tamar serve his meals. I never suspected." His voice cracked, and he leaned his forehead on mine. "It's my fault."

"No, you trusted him. It's all Amnon. What are you going to tell Ahinoam? She's distraught. Afraid you'll have Amnon killed."

While we stood there, Absalom, Tamar's brother, met us.

"Execute Amnon." His voice issued like a command. His fist balled at his sides, he glowered at us. "Uphold the Law. Give me permission, and I'll capture and string him up myself."

A vein bulged in David's forehead. "No, Absalom. Leave it to me. Go comfort your mother and sister."

Absalom stood his ground and crossed his arms. "You tell his mother he's as good as dead. Then I'll go to my mother and sister."

David swatted Absalom's head. "No son of mine talks to me like this. Go back to your house. Out of my sight."

Absalom's eyebrows narrowed. He flipped his long, surly locks and strode off, his fists clenched. That boy was too handsome for his own good. No discipline, no respect.

Ahinoam opened her door. "My lord." She bowed her head. "I beg mercy of you."

We stepped in. David put a hand on Ahinoam's back. "Have you seen Tamar? She's been destroyed. What would you do in my place if it were your daughter Sarah?" David referred to the infant girl he had rescued and gifted to Ahinoam.

Ahinoam crumbled to the floor and hugged David's feet. "I will pay. Take me in his stead. Only don't kill my son—my only surviving son."

David crouched and hugged her. "He's my son, too." While he kissed her and wiped her tears, I stepped out.

* * *

David swam in a pool of blood.

The sword hangs over your house, David. You have sinned against God. The sword will pay you back. You despised the LORD and took the wife of Uriah the Hittite. You've slain him with the sword of the Ammonites. Murderer. Adulterer. Rapist.

He cried in the dark. "I'm not a rapist. I treated her kindly. I married her."

The sword knows, David. The sword will pay you back in kind. God is not mocked, whatsoever a man sows, that shall he reap.

"The sword, the sword... no... no... please God, have mercy. I have sinned, oh LORD forgive me."

He moved on top of Michal. "I'm not a rapist."

She opened her arms. "You are not a rapist. Come in unto me, David, and let me love you."

* * *

My head down, I knocked on Bathsheba's door. She opened it and stared at me. She was pregnant again, about halfway along. She cupped her hand over her belly and stepped aside to let me enter.

"You heard what happened?" I asked as she handed me a cup of juice.

"Yes, it's tragic. Why have you come?"

"I need to know," I said, "and I don't know how you'll take it."

"Say on. I've nothing to hide."

"David feels he is being judged by the LORD. Do you agree?"

She shrugged one shoulder and twisted her lip. "I don't think on these things. I have my own problems." She glanced at a round shield and a battle axe mounted on her wall.

"Did you love him? Your husband?"

"Why do you want to know? He's dead now. He was an honorable man—more so than any of us."

"I'm sorry."

"Don't be. I was precious to him, and I would have been happy. His mother died of a broken heart." She popped a grape into her mouth and swallowed stiffly. "So what do you want from me?"

"I want to know about David."

She leaned back, arched an eyebrow and picked at a pomegranate. "You, of all people, know the most about him."

"I want to know if he's a rapist."

Bathsheba dropped the pomegranate. "Heavens, no. Not that I know. Has he raped someone?"

I set the cup down, relieved. "No, he hasn't."

"Oh, I see. You wanted to know if he raped me." She stood and stretched, giving me a full view of her profile. "He's the most loving, gentle and delicious man I know. He looked for you every night, but you took off with your guard, an uncircumcised Philistine. What kind of wife would do that?"

I stood and turned toward the door. "You don't know the circumstances."

"You think maids don't talk? I gave him what he needed, what he craved." She opened the door and cradled her belly. "I'm going to have his son, and he'll be king after his father."

I grabbed her arm. "Then you're coming with me to make sacrifice."

"You dare approach the priests? I thought they'd have your head, daughter of Saul."

I yanked her out. "Do not make a scene. Perhaps the LORD will forgive us and have mercy on David and his house. Do you want your son to pay?"

Surprisingly she did not resist. One side of her face twitched, and she gulped. A guard escorted us to the altar of burnt offering. I bought two ewe lambs and handed one to Bathsheba. She placed her hand over the lamb's head and bowed while the priest slashed its throat.

I hugged my lamb. Her warmth and soft wool filled my heart with guilt. I closed my eyes and placed my hand on her innocent head. She nibbled on the hem of my robe before her blood splattered my feet.

"Oh God, I am so sorry. I regret deeply what I did to David, both in words and in deeds. Pray take my sins away and make me a new creature. I trust only in You, LORD, to deliver me from my sins and to save me from the Hell I so deserve. Have mercy on Your servant, David, and his house. Preserve, O LORD, his seed and forgive his sins. In You, LORD, I rest my soul." I wept with my face in the dust, unaware of Bathsheba's departure.

That evening, I stood at the window of David's tower. Families gathered and young lovers walked in the dark. Bathsheba. Cool, faceless, pregnant. She had a future. And I? Did I even have the past?

Alone, no son, no daughter, only a part of David, the part that comforted him and held him through the night. A pet. His pet, Eglah. Did he truly love me when he had all the others?

David did not return, so I went to bed. A recurring dream nagged me: Ittai hugging my feet and telling me he loved me like no one else.

Ittai, I believe you. Where are you?

* * *

The LORD's judgment sword descended on David's house.

Absalom held a sheep shearing festival. He invited his brothers to join in the celebration. Too busy to attend, David sent them off with his blessings.

A messenger brought the news. "King David, all your sons are dead. Absalom has slaughtered them all."

David staggered against the wall. I led him to the women's quarters, to the gravesites of his young sons and daughters, to Ithream's grave, to the grave of Bathsheba's nameless son.

He threw himself on the earth, flat on his face, and hugged the ground. "Tell the others, Michal."

How could this be? All our sons? Slaughtered like sheep?

Mothers, nurses and maids joined us. A chorus of weeping and screaming resounded on the damp spring earth.

"Mother?" A young male voice spoke.

Haggith cried, "Adonijah? Oh, my son!"

Shephatiah lifted Abital and hugged her. "Mother, it was awful."

David shook Adonijah. "Tell us what happened, what happened?"

Adonijah gaped, wide-eyed and panic stricken.

Chileab threw himself into Abigail's arms. "Absalom killed Amnon. Only Amnon is dead, and Absalom has fled to Geshur."

Ahinoam fainted. Maacah clutched her face and ran back to her apartment. David picked up Ahinoam and carried her back to her house.

* * *

David prayed and wept on the bed. "O LORD, when will you hear me? Remove your lash from my back. My belly is bruised by your blows. Hear my cry, O LORD. Or I am undone."

We stared at each other, face to face, eye to eye, nose to nose, separated by a thin veil of tears.

"Are we being judged?"

He nodded.

"You have sinned, haven't you?"

He nodded again.

"Tell me."

I waited. His chest heaved with his ragged breath. I stroked the cowlicks in his hair, whorled in multiple directions, finding comfort in the repetitive motion.

He stopped my hand. "I took Bathsheba while Uriah was fighting the Ammonites. I lay with her and made her pregnant. And then I had Uriah killed. I told Joab to send him to the wall, where he fell by the hand of the Ammonites."

"Murder?" I sat up.

"I have sinned against the LORD," he cried.

I scuttled away from him. "You killed him. David, why?"

"Don't leave." He touched my arm, and I flinched, my back to the wall.

"I can't. Oh my..." I saw my father's face, the darkened brows, the twisted features, the sweat drops, the red rimmed eyes. "You're mad. Why did you kill him?"

"I don't know." He covered his face and cowered in the corner. "I was afraid."

"Afraid of what? You're the king. You could have asked him to give you his wife. Like you took me from Phalti. What was he going to do?"

"I didn't want her at first. But he wouldn't cooperate. He wouldn't sleep with her and pass the child off as his own."

"But you could have married her to someone else—or sent them both away with gold and silver. Kings and lords do this all the time."

"But I wanted my child." He raised his voice and knocked his head back against the wall.

I paced the room. "I'm afraid. How fearful is the LORD. Well I know. My entire family was destroyed for my father's sins. Have you asked the LORD to forgive you?"

"Yes, he has forgiven me, but I must still pay. The sword shall never depart from my house."

"You mean a curse?" A giant hand squeezed my heart and twisted my stomach. Blood swooshed through my ears, the hammer of judgment pounding my head with sharp pains.

"I'm so sorry. So sorry, Michal." He reached for me. A pitiful look contorted his face.

I clenched my fists. "Was she worth it? Was she?"

"No... I mean..."

"You killed for her. I can't stay in the same room with a murderer." I went to the wardrobe and packed my clothes.

"Where are you going?"

"I'll stay with my maid. Or Abigail. I don't care."

"Michal, don't leave. I can't live without you. Please…"

I opened the door and dared not look at him. How could the man after God's heart be a heinous criminal? Had he killed Ittai also? Used the sword of the Philistines to kill my father and Jonathan? Abner? Ishby? By the sword of Joab and Abishai?

"Don't reject me, my wife. My wife." David took hold of my skirt, and it tore in his hand.

I walked out.

CHAPTER 44

Job 16:15 I have sewed sackcloth upon my skin, and defiled my horn in the dust.

>>><<<

The Ark stood underneath a large blue and purple tent. I lowered my head. David's confession frightened me. The sword of the LORD's retribution had utterly destroyed my father and wrecked our family. Sensing my discomfort, David put his arm around me and held me tighter.

I still lived with Abigail, but agreed to meet David every morning and evening for the sacrifice. It would be our only time together. He wouldn't acknowledge me without being veiled, and I refused to share his bed or comfort him without being acknowledged. The Ark was our common ground.

Songs and chants of praises greeted us from the tabernacle. David had set up musicians to play on harp, psalteries, dulcimers, and pipes. I appreciated that music and singing were a part of worship. I still wasn't sure about exuberant dancing, but surely, the LORD had been pleased with David that day. I hoped the LORD would be merciful today.

"They're gathering the animals," David said. "Seven oxen and ten rams. My sins are many and weigh heavily on my soul."

"Please add a ewe lamb for me."

The animals were brought amidst the music. We bowed low before the Ark, confessed our sins and asked forgiveness and mercy. David placed his hand on each sacrificial animal as the priest slit its throat.

When it was my turn, I closed my eyes and caressed the little ewe lamb. She chewed her cud, and I thought about Ahinoam, wondering if her heart would ever heal. She went among us as a wraith, drained and dispirited, but she would not make sacrifice nor acknowledge the LORD.

* * *

David pulled me to his writing desk. "Michal, I have repented and written a psalm. Do you want to see it?"

Have mercy upon me, O God, according to thy lovingkindness: according unto the multitude of thy tender mercies blot out my transgressions.

Wash me thoroughly from mine iniquity, and cleanse me from my sin.

For I acknowledge my transgressions: and my sin is ever before me.

Against thee, thee only, have I sinned, and done this evil in thy sight: that thou mightest be justified when thou speakest, and be clear when thou judgest.

"It's lovely." I dusted his harp off and handed it to him. "Sing it to me, please."

Create in me a clean heart, O God; and renew a right spirit within me.

Cast me not away from thy presence; and take not thy Holy Spirit from me.

Restore unto me the joy of thy salvation; and uphold me with thy free spirit.

I swooned into his arms and kissed him full on the lips.

O Lord, open thou my lips; and my mouth shall shew forth thy praise.

For thou desirest not sacrifice; else would I give it: thou delightest not in burnt offering.

The sacrifices of God are a broken spirit: a broken and a contrite heart, O God, thou wilt not despise.

* * *

Abigail and I sat at the writing table. She pressed the scrolls while I copied.

"David's new psalm touched my heart deeply," I said, dipping my pen into the ink.

"Yes, I believe he has truly repented. Why won't you forgive him?"

I shrugged. "I'm not the LORD, and there's nothing for me to forgive. I find his behavior reprehensible."

We jumped at the sound of the door opening. David. His face contorted, he came straight toward Abigail.

"It's Chileab… He's been killed," David said between sobs.

Abigail collapsed in his arms with a wail.

"Killed?" A chill drained down my spine. "How?"

"Stabbed in the field. No one saw anything."

I raised my voice and cried with them. Chileab was beloved by all, the sweetest, most adorable young man in the kingdom. He looked almost identical to the young David. And now? Killed in cold blood.

The funeral and burial were a blur. During the months afterward, Abigail lay ill in her bed, nothing more than skin and bones. I sat at her side and nursed her. But her health failed.

One day she coughed blood. I asked a servant to fetch David.

"My sister, rest." I patted her arm. "David is coming."

She made an effort to smile as I wiped her face with a wet cloth. Ahinoam hovered over her, alternately pacing the room and looking out the window.

David opened the door with a rush of wind and knelt at her side. "Dear Abigail, my wife."

Abigail sat up with a fit of coughing. "Don't despair. We'll see Chileab again in the house of the LORD."

I tugged at his sleeve. "Can the doctor do nothing?"

"I've called the best physicians, and you've given her the medicine daily. We must pray."

Ahinoam, David and I bowed our heads at the side of Abigail's bed. We entreated the LORD for her health, to recover her from the sickness, and to comfort her grieving heart. Abigail rested her hand on David's head and seemed to breathe easier.

But when she leaned back, another bout of coughing caught her. In between wheezes, she said, "I must go... Please... do not grieve."

David hugged her. "No, Abi, don't say it. I don't know how I'd live without you. You always see the good in me. You pray for me. You're so wonderful to me."

"You have them. I thank you for taking me in. That day when I met you..." She coughed. "On the road to kill my husband... who beat me and abused me. I so wanted you to kill him."

"No confessions. You were pure and righteous, more righteous than I. You prevented me from a great sin. I only wish you had been with me when I saw Bathsheba on her rooftop. Then none of this would have happened. Tamar, Amnon, Chileab."

"David, don't blame yourself," she said. "I'll always remember the day we met. Remember what I said to you?" She coughed until her face turned red.

David held her in his arms and passed his hand gently over her brow. "Don't talk. You need your strength."

"I need to talk now... because I'm failing. Hear me, David. I told you the LORD... would make... a sure house for you... for you fight the battles of the LORD... and evil has not been found... in you all your days... Do you still believe me?" The wheezing grew into a rasp.

"Oh Abi, I believe you." He wiped the spittle from her lips. "I wish I loved you more."

"You loved me enough. You have dealt bountifully with me." Her body wracked by another violent spell of coughing, she bowed down breathless. I held the bowl while Ahinoam rubbed her back.

"Abi, don't go," David cried. Ahinoam collapsed at her feet and kissed her legs.

Abigail drew a deep breath. "David, The LORD has forgiven you... Else he would have required your life... Why can't you forgive yourself? Are you... greater than the LORD?"

"No, I'm not," David cried. "I'm a worm. I don't deserve you. Oh, dear LORD, don't take Abi from me."

I passed the wet cloth over Abigail's face and held her hand. "Abi, I love you, my friend, don't go." Tears dripped down my face as I kissed her.

Ahinoam held her legs. "My sister, my sister. Abi. My sister, my love. Oh, dear Abi."

Abigail's face shone. She stared a thousand miles away. "Chileab, my boy. Eemah, Abba. I'm coming, dear LORD."

She half-sat on her bed, her eyes wide, mouth open. She didn't seem to see or hear us. Her face glowing with rapture, she breathed one last sigh and fell to the pillow. David closed her eyes.

The three of us fell on her bed and screamed to the heavens. "Abi, can you hear us? Hear us? Hear us?"

The threefold cord forged in the wilderness had been cut. I left David and Ahinoam to work out their grief.

Haggith feared she would pay next. Obsessed with Adonijah's safety, she worried endlessly, went to the tabernacle to offer sacrifices every week and frequented every fortune teller in Jerusalem.

Abital had a sweet, innocent trust in the LORD. She shadowed me, played with her new bird, and asked me to tell her stories. She believed the LORD protected Shephatiah simply because she believed it and asked it of him. Such simple faith. I loved her.

* * *

"I have a surprise for you." David's hands covered my eyes. I startled and swallowed a hopeful flutter. These days we'd settled into a dull routine. Early morning prayer at the tabernacle, walk hand-in-hand in the garden, then sunrise on the wall while breaking our fast.

He maneuvered me behind a set of heavy curtains and removed his hand, but not before kissing the back of my neck. Holy Jerusalem! A gold-plated structure shone in the lamplight. I backed into David's warm chest. His breath sent a flurry of tingles down my spine.

"It's my vision of how the Temple would be built," he said.

I blinked at the intricate detail. Each gold plate was fashioned to cover the entire wall and roof. Narrow windows were cut into the wall, and fluted columns stood outside to support the tiered roof.

David touched the top of one wall and flipped it open. "Here is the inner sanctuary."

The fresh, spicy scent of cedar greeted me. The entire interior was covered with carved, polished wood inlayed with open flowers and decorative almond branches. The carved miniatures of pillars and palm trees held winged cherubim. A curtain of golden chains hid a chamber toward the back.

"I can't show you the Holiest place," David said. "But the Ark of the Covenant will rest there." He picked up a cherub of olivewood with majestic outstretched wings. The boyish exuberance on his face twisted my heart with the old, familiar ache—that of wanting, yet not having.

"It's beautiful." My words stuck to the top of my throat. "Thank you for showing me."

He led me back to his bedchamber and picked up his harp. Heat flashed through my body and flushed my face as he strummed and sang. The intensity of his gaze ignited my heart. He sang of God's glory, His promises, and the Redeemer. And his voice captivated and transported me back in time, to the day I first met him—a time of innocence, of hope, and of blessing. My spirit soared with his song, and I hid my quivering lips behind my fan.

He put his harp down. A wistful smile remained on his face. "I have peace with God. I've cast all my sins under His feet. He is truly merciful and forgiving."

A chord strummed my heart. He had been forgiven. Perhaps he could... I'd make my plea and cast it at his feet.

"David, can you forgive me and restore me to be your wife again?"

He stood behind me and stroked my hair, running his fingers through the waves. "I've already forgiven you of those sins you've confessed to me."

"God has forgiven all of my sins, why can't you?"

He pressed my shoulders. "You have kept something from me."

"You know I'm all yours, don't you?"

"I don't believe so. Am I the only man in your heart?"

I knew who he referred to. I had locked him deep, reduced to a tiny arrowhead, hard and dense, in the core of my soul. I glanced at the silver box and slapped my fan on the table. "He means nothing to me."

"That's what you tell yourself." He traced his finger around my eyes, pressing and smoothing my face. "You decide."

I dug my fingernails into my palms. Why had I been such a fool to want his attention? Wasn't he the murderer of Uriah? And even though he assured me Ittai and my sons were healthy when he last saw them, could I trust him not to lie? The man who plotted his most loyal friend's death? I stood to leave.

"Wait." David caught my arm. His eyes focused on the rolled-up rug. It sat there, a testimony to my misguided attempt at reconciliation, rolled up all these years. We never mentioned it, stepping over it as if it were not there. Bathsheba had complained and urged him to throw it out. But in the end, the rug stayed, a sleeping dragon at the foot of David's bed.

Slowly, he unfurled it. The flaming scarlet shimmered like fire, burning the tree of life in its midst. David held out his hand. "Come, Michal. Lie down with me."

I swayed transfixed as an asp in front of her charmer. His gaze intently on me, he pulled me down on the rug.

He took my shoulders and spread me like an exquisite piece of tapestry. "Keep your eyes open, Michal."

Running his hands over my body, he studied me, arranged my limbs, so that my arms were spread straight out from my sides like branches, and my legs were joined together, straight as the trunk of the tree.

"You were meant to be my tree of life, bear fruit and surround me with children, like arrows in the quiver of a mighty man. You failed me." His words tolled like the final chords of a dirge.

My face simmered. "I gave you two—"

"No!" His hand slapped the rug. "Do you not see the irony? You gave me sons I could not claim. And the ones I could claim could possibly be Amalekites."

"Amalekites?" I lurched to sit, but he pressed me down, his breath hot on my cheek.

"Amnon and Chileab. And now both dead."

"But... Chileab is the image of you... when I first met you..."

David shook his head. "The LORD works in strange ways. If you hadn't been with Phalti, Joshua and Beraiah would be my heirs."

Anger coursed through my veins like a heated plume. "And if you hadn't sent me back to Israel—"

"You would have been raped along with them," he shouted. "Don't you see my sacrifice? Or do you still blame me?"

My lips quivered, my stomach contracted, and I remained still.

His mouth closed into a thin line. "Look at you. Fine lines frame your eyes. Your hair sprinkled with grey. Oh, you're still beautiful, bewitching even. Supple breasts full like the moon, your body toned, oiled, and perfumed."

He inhaled my jasmine scent and pressed his lips to mine, tasted me and drew back. "You have not lived up to your promise. Do you remember what you promised me on our wedding day?"

Tears welled in my eyes despite my vow to keep cool.

"You said you would love only me, Michal. You have not cleansed your heart of him. Do you have anything to say?" His voice sharpened to a tone that clutched and clawed at my heart.

Tears streamed down the corners of my eyes. Pangs of agony shot through my chest and radiated out both arms and down to my toes. When I opened my mouth, my parched throat trapped my words, swallowing them into the depths of my guilt.

He glared at me. "Keep your eyes open. Keep them on mine, and I will divine whether I should forgive you or not."

He peeled open my dress, sat me up and flipped it over my shoulders. Removing my combs, my bracelets, my necklaces, my earrings, and my ornaments, he laid me down naked on the tree. He stripped himself, placed his crown on the floor, and removed his ring, Jonathan's ring. He pried my legs apart with his knee.

He massaged me with his lips and fingers, exploring every sensitive zone on my body. I determined to stay stiff, resist, and give nothing away. But my body trembled, and my throat moaned, and my head flailed from side to side. I closed my eyes as he brought me closer to the warm glow, the heat rising like a kindled fire.

"Open your eyes," he barked. "You left me, Michal. You left your first love. You're thinking about him."

A cold sweat broke over my body, and my excitement retreated. "No, no. I wasn't."

"Keep your eyes open where I can see them." From where his face was, I didn't see how he could tell, but I stretched my eyes wide open and stared at the ceiling.

David resumed his ministrations, but I stopped responding. His accusations hurt me, and images of Ittai came to me, unbidden but delightful. I recalled his cocky grin, his leonine eyebrows, his gleaming white teeth. I felt his hands on me, quivered under his kisses and caresses, and moaned with lust when he rubbed my breasts. He lifted my knees over his elbows, entered me, hard and urgent. I had dreamed of his strong, lean body and imagined what he could do to me. I saw his grin, his black hair as a curtain, his hawkish nose, and I screamed with my eyes wide open.

CHAPTER 45

Jeremiah 3:10 And yet for all this her treacherous sister Judah hath not turned unto me with her whole heart, but feignedly, saith the LORD.

>>><<<

David sat with Michal on top of the palace wall. The sun peeked over the eastern vale, the morning mists rising like steam over a hot bath. Twin hawks glided in intersecting circles, riding in harmony on the currents of the wind.

He never mentioned the rug again and neither did she. Not that he cared. She was his past. He had Absalom, now the eldest—the legitimate heir his kingdom recognized. A hale and handsome man, a leader that men rallied around, he reminded David of his youth.

It was time to bring him back and prepare him to be the next king.

David walked with Michal hand in hand through the garden. The lush, damp scent of the morning earth mingled the flowery overtones of honeysuckle and lilac with spicy punches of bay leaves and myrtle trees. Her presence comforted him despite their distance.

He stretched in the soft rays of the morning sun. "God has forgiven me my sins. He remembers them no more, according to His mercy and goodness. I've slept blissfully ever since."

Michal smiled faintly and tipped her nose up. She picked a sprig of honeysuckle and twirled it around her fingers.

"Today, I will see Absalom," he said. "It's time to forgive him."

"Yes, my lord. If that is what you wish. Absalom was only avenging his sister."

"But I had to put him aside because I'm the king. Everyone is watching me. If I took him back too soon, they would not respect me. They won't follow a weakling."

"No, they won't."

He drew Michal's face to him. "And what about you? Would you follow a weakling?"

The brown flecks in her green eyes flickered as she swept aside her veil. She pursed her lips. "I'm here, aren't I? Veiled, obedient, submissive."

David sighed. "I cannot restore you and appear weak, not in front of my men."

She threw the honeysuckle vine at his face. "I no longer wish to be restored. Not to a weakling. You have your queen. You even killed for her."

She turned on her heels and glided to the steps. David flung the vine her direction and punched the stone wall, bruising his knuckles.

* * *

Four years passed in peace. David withdrew from the audience chamber. He handed his judgments and decisions to Ahithophel, his senior counselor, to train Absalom for the throne. Since Ahithophel was also Bathsheba's grandfather, he allowed Bathsheba to attend all the ceremonies and assemblies in his place.

David retreated to his study to dedicate himself for the building of the LORD's Temple. Even though God had denied him the privilege of building it, he devoted himself to the study of Scripture, writing psalms, and securing the building materials.

He approached Abigail's old house with a servant pulling a wagonload of scrolls.

"Michal," he called. "More songbooks for you to prepare."

She opened the door. Her face radiant in the morning light, she stepped out and poked him in the belly. "My father forgot to tell me being a king's wife was such hard work. I'd say you're using me as slave labor."

David grabbed her wrist and rubbed her fingers. "Such beautiful script should be put to God's use. But how's your book coming along? Will you let me read it yet?"

A side of her lip curved into a smile. "You know it's too personal."

"Even for me?"

"Especially for you, my lord."

Arik and the servant deposited the scrolls and departed after picking up the pile Michal had finished.

David stepped into the room. He sighed every time he spied Abigail's rose-colored robe hanging on the divider. Michal had left Abi's room exactly the same as the day she died.

He unrolled a thick scroll on Michal's desk.

"Stop that." She tugged his arm, her face reddening.

"Why can't I see? Are you writing bad things about me?"

She sniffed. "Arrogant, aren't we? What makes you think you're even mentioned?"

He spun her into his arms. "Well, if I'm not mentioned, I'll have to do something to rectify it." Pulling her face to his, he kissed her.

She tried to turn away.

"You'd deny the king? I could order you back to my bed."

"You could."

He could stare into those eyes forever. "The nightmares are back."

Michal touched his cheek, tracing the scar her father cut. "Is that all I'm good for? Scrolls and nightmares?"

"No, you're much more than that. I wish…"

"You wish you were strong enough to be the actual king."

David stiffened. "Sarcasm does not flatter you."

"Nor does weakness. You don't see what's going on? Absalom, Bathsheba and Ahithophel control your kingdom. You while away your time taking walks with me to the tabernacle and singing praises to the LORD. Consider your nightmares a warning from God."

A red tide boiled in his chest. He clapped a hand over her mouth and pulled her into a chokehold. "You're moving back to the tower. I'll show you how strong I am."

He flung her over his shoulder and stalked out of Abigail's house, deliberately ignoring the stares of his other wives and their children.

Quite out of breath, he stomped up the stairs of his tower and threw her on his bed.

Michal laughed. "You're really getting too old for this, my lord."

"I'm never too old to make you miserable." He flicked his tongue on her long, elegant neck and caressed her full breasts. She responded with a faint indrawn breath.

Since she did not struggle, he found her lips and deepened the tempo of his kiss. A moan escaped her when his fingers probed between her thighs. Her scent, a mixture of jasmine and wild thyme, excited him, and the pulse of his arousal pounded in his heart.

"Michal, I want you. All of you." He tore the front of her dress.

The door pounded with heavy and insistent knocking.

"King David." Arik's voice sounded urgent.

David pulled a blanket over his wife and straightened his clothes. Outside, the sounds of clamoring and outrage filled the courtyard. The door opened to the sight of guards in full body armor.

"Absalom has declared himself king in Hebron and amassed a large force," Arik said. "They are on their way now to take Jerusalem. All of Israel supports him."

David's heart sunk to his knees, and his strength flagged. He ran to the window. Panicked residents of Jerusalem scurried below, packing their belongings. How had this happened? Absalom? His own son?

"We must remove all your wives and children for their safety." Arik marched in and grabbed Michal who still clutched a blanket.

"Wait!" David ordered. "Take my wives. Leave the concubines to keep house."

"My lord," Arik said. "The queen is in Hebron with her grandfather."

"Then rescue her. And hide all my sons, lest Absalom slaughter them." He pried Michal from Arik's hands. "I'll take her. Now go and fetch Bathsheba before it's too late. Take as many men as you need."

* * *

His face lined with weariness and worry, David kissed me half-heartedly and mumbled, "Go help my other wives. I can't be seen with you in public. But remember me."

"Yes, I will behave."

He lingered and gave me one last squeeze. "You know how I feel about you."

I packed a small bag of clothes and went with the guards to the women's quarters.

The guards knocked on all the doors. "Quickly, pack your things and meet us at stables. We must leave Jerusalem."

"What's happened?"

"Where are we going?"

"There is no time," I said. "Absalom has declared himself king and is marching toward Jerusalem with a huge host of warriors. We must escape right now."

We did not have enough animals and provisions to bring our maids. I had set Naomi free long ago, but she stayed because of our friendship. I bade her farewell, pressed some jewels into her hands and wrote a note to Abigail's family to take her in. She would be safer there.

David's younger children were loaded into wagons with their mothers or nurses. The rest of us went on foot: Ahinoam, Maacah, Haggith, and Abital.

We followed David out of the Eastern Gate. He walked unshod, raising his hands to the sky, begging the LORD for mercy. He descended the steep Valley of Kidron, barefoot over the hot jagged rocks. He waded over the Brook Kidron and staggered up the Mount of Olives, winding his way between the old, gnarly trees. He stepped over sharp flint, olive pits, twigs and branches.

I followed his bloody trail. He was not a weak man. I'd follow him anywhere. I should have told him. I should have loved him more, and I should have submitted to him.

David bent as if dragging a heavy load, the wages of sin. Falling down, he crawled on his hands and knees to the top of the broken hill. He collapsed, a man of sorrows, full of grief.

* * *

After David finished praying, he sent the Ark back to Jerusalem. Ziba, an old servant of my father, met us with donkeys and provisions. David ordered the donkeys to be given to his oldest wives.

Once mounted, we took the road to Bahurim, the same road where I gave Anna to Phalti. As everyone shuffled by, I turned and stared at the bend where the stream crossed near the wall. *Phalti's sad eyes bore into my soul. Anna sucked her thumb, dark brown ringlets framed her face. Her bright red lips puckered. She rubbed her eyes and pushed her face into Phalti's neck.*

Abital pushed her donkey close to mine. "Will Buzzi be all right? Miriam said she'd take care of him. Oh, but what if he misses me? I hope she remembers to feed him."

Her attention easily deflected, she observed the trees, the wild birds, the countryside and the terrain, all new sights for her.

Maacah, Absalom's mother, stayed back as far from Ahinoam as she could. Her face tight, she looked like she hadn't slept for days. Ahinoam wore a similarly resigned look. Her long hair covered her face as she rode with a lowered head. Sarah, her adopted daughter, walked at her side.

Haggith pulled up to me. "Bathsheba doesn't want to come along, believe me. She has set herself up no matter which way the wind turns." Haggith sniffed the air. "Where is she anyway?"

"Her grandfather was David's trusted advisor, I'm sure she was only obeying him." I turned away from her and concentrated on the narrow, rocky trail. Flies buzzed and bit us as we plodded toward the Jordan Valley. We were not welcome in any of the towns and villages we passed. The residents threw sticks and stones at us. They cursed David and accused him of usurping the throne from my father. In a perverse way, I was proud they remembered him but sad that David had not captured the people's hearts.

* * *

That evening, we set camp in front of the Jordan River. Sounds of galloping horses thundered toward us. Were Absalom's men closing in?

371

If they came after us right now, we would for sure be slaughtered. We were weak, weary, and dispirited after our hasty flight.

Shouts rang through the camp. "Quickly, saddle up. We must cross the Jordan now. It is too deep and rocky for the wagons, so everyone must ride or wade."

Babies cried, and children clung to their mothers as they tumbled out of the wagons. Bathsheba's nurse-maid struggled with Bathsheba's four sons, an infant and toddler, and two older boys, Solomon and Nathan. Since their birth mother was not present, the nurse turned to me for help. David had required me to hold each infant soon after birth, as if bestowing me a gift with each child he had.

I bestirred my sister wives to help. Haggith turned away, but Abital stepped after me to the wagon, as did Ahinoam and Sarah. The servants handed us mules in exchange for the donkeys that were too short to bear us above the river's rising tide.

The four of us set off, each with a young son of David in our charge. I took Solomon, Ahinoam had Nathan, Sarah grabbed the squirming toddler, and Abital carried the baby. The nurse loaded the children's supplies onto donkeys and followed the other servants to the ford.

Solomon and I kicked off into the river. The swell of the water came up to the chests of our animals, making the crossing slow and not without danger. Several times, when the vanguard came to a rocky place, they would slow down and be bumped by those behind.

Solomon was around ten years old, a small, thin boy. I had taken care of him when Bathsheba was pregnant with Nathan. Later, David oftentimes left Solomon with me to explain the Word of God to him. Even though he was not the heir, having so many brothers older than he, he was dear to my heart. A pensive, serious boy, he paid attention to everything I taught him and read out of the scrolls diligently. I loved the boy. If I couldn't have the love of his father, at least his son would love me. I called him Lemuel. It was our secret, and it rhymed with Samuel.

Our mule kicked another one that scraped too close. When he lunged to nip the other animal, we fell into the water. Cold shock slapped me as I landed on a rock. I grabbed Solomon and hoisted him back on the mule. A swell of water swept me down, and I hit my head. Bubbles blurred my vision. I couldn't tell up from down.

"Auntie, over here," Solomon yelled.

He stopped the mule in the middle of the river. I grabbed a strap and helped myself up, resting my head on the mule while catching my breath.

"Are you okay, Auntie?" he asked.

"Yes. Am I not Saul's daughter? Of course, I'm fine."

Solomon and I were the last to emerge from the Jordan. I pulled him off the mule and gave thanks to the LORD. We huddled together, smelling like wet straw. His teeth chattering, he kissed me and held onto me with bony arms. A flood of love warmed me, and I thanked David for bestowing all his children to my care. Footsteps crackled the leaves behind me.

"Solomon, my son." David picked him up and kissed him. He asked a manservant to find him a change of clothing.

A pang tripped my heart. He acted as if he hadn't seen me. I led the mule to a grassy slope and wrung out my dress. Hot tears dropped on my hands. He could have at least thanked me.

While I shivered, a pair of hands draped a cloak over my wet clothes. "Eg-lah…"

My pulse responded with a quiver, and I bowed to the ground. "My lord, king."

David raised me. "Why so formal?"

"You told me to stay away from you." I trembled from the cold and my proximity to him.

He squeezed my arm. "It'll only be a little while longer. You know it's because of Joab and Abishai. I need their support." He pulled me into his arms. "Maybe after this rebellion is over…" Fingering my wet hair, he kissed me, long and hard.

I clung to him, not wanting to let go, not daring to hope. Would he really consider restoring me after the rebellion? Could I take any more disappointments? I shuddered and clutched tighter.

A manservant cleared his throat. "My lord, the scouts report a troop to the south."

David wrapped his cloak around my shoulders. "Take care of yourself, my love."

I tucked my face into his cloak, still warm with his scent. It was the color of pine leaves, embroidered with vines and green grapes in bright, moss-green thread, a vine of life, full of hope.

* * *

David's spies informed us we were welcome in Mahanaim, the place where my brother Ishbaal ruled and where I lived with Phalti so long ago. Without rest, we rode through the night guided by the moon. At the break of dawn, we rounded the familiar outcropping and stopped at the city gates. It hadn't changed much. The walls were shabbier, and the gates hung at an odd angle. Tall stands of fir trees waved in the breeze, their clean fragrance refreshing and inviting.

Men bowed to David: Machir, Anna's husband, and Barzillai, the grandfather of Merab's sons, Shobi the Ammonite, and Phalti. My heart ached at the sight of him. He was still a large and handsome man, although his hair and beard had greyed. I stood too far away to greet him, and he soon disappeared with David and his advisors behind the palace gate.

The battle plan became clear in the next few days. David gathered the people into the city behind the gates. He did not want to subject the city to a siege, so he sent troops to meet Absalom's forces out in the field. He wanted to lead the charge, but the people begged and pleaded with him to stay. A great outcry of love poured out of our mouths, and David relented.

As the men of war filed out of the city, David ordered them to deal gently with Absalom. Each warrior heard David's order to capture Absalom alive and not hurt a hair of his head.

David stayed by the gate all day. I didn't know what went through his mind as he watched and waited. No matter the outcome, he would be the loser. I longed to go to him, but his counselors surrounded him. As the hated daughter of Saul, I couldn't be seen with him.

The sun traveled to the west. King David stood on the highest part of the gate and maintained a solitary vigil.

* * *

A loud cheer erupted in front of the gate. "Long live the king! His enemies are dead!" I hugged Abital and Ahinoam, and we jumped and cheered with the rest of the people. We milled with the crowd to the gate, but were met with silence.

"Wasn't the news good?" I asked a guard. He pointed to the top of the gate.

David pounded his hands on the wall and wailed, "O my son Absalom, my son, my son Absalom! Would God I had died for you. O Absalom, my son, my son!"

News spread from mouth to mouth. Absalom was dead. We were safe, but David had been stabbed. Three darts into the heart of Absalom drained his life-blood. Three darts into the heart of King David: Amnon, Chileab, Absalom. They killed his spirit. *Oh God, please spare David from more grief. Hadn't he paid enough? LORD, withhold not your tender mercies and loving-kindness from my husband.*

David howled deep into the evening. One by one, he summoned his wives to his side to comfort and grieve with him. Even Haggith, who didn't care about him, was asked to join. I peered after them, but the messenger turned his face as he plucked Abital from my side. David did not want me. Tears rolled down my cheeks. The pain was ever present. David and his wives joined hands in a circle and lowered their heads in prayer.

The soldiers returned covered in blood. Some were injured. Others bore the bodies of their fallen comrades.

"Why is he weeping?" one said.

"Doesn't he care that we bled and died for him?" another said.

"Would he rather we had died and Absalom prevailed?"

"Joab cut Absalom down."

"Good riddance, I say. He was a bad son."

"He cares more about him than us."

The murmuring increased in intensity. Men began to desert.

* * *

Toward nightfall, Joab motioned us to the gate to hear David speak.

"Today God has given us a great victory. I congratulate you and praise you for your bravery and valor. Soon, we return to Jerusalem. Thank you, warriors, for the great victory. This is a night of celebration. We give all praise and thanks to God for His glory."

After David spoke, the camp erupted in festivities. The inhabitants of Mahanaim brought goats and sheep, wine and oil, and lit huge campfires. The men of war changed out of their bloody clothes and joined the women around the campfires. A loud cheer erupted around one fire. Bathsheba wiggled her hips and shook bells in her hands, entertaining a group of raucous soldiers with a harem dance.

Bile rose to my throat, and blood pounded my head. I tore in front of the leering men and yanked her by the wrist. "How dare the Queen of Israel uncover herself in the eyes of the king's servants?"

The crowd jeered and pushed at me to let her go. I dragged her to the edge of the camp. She twisted and turned, but I held her with a strong grip, my middle finger pinched to my thumb. The fumes of hard drink emanated from her mouth, and she shrieked even as tears slid down her face.

"Why aren't you comforting him?" I shook her. "You've disgraced his throne."

"Leave me alone, Michal. You're not my mother. You have no idea what I'm going through."

"I will not have him deprived of a son he loves because of your sins. Do you hear me?"

"What do you care? He hates you. He replaced you. Get away from me." She stomped her foot and pushed me.

I pushed her back. "That crown you wear cost me everything. Do not disgrace it."

"You think I want it? It has cost me. Everyone. I. Love." Her raging breath spit in my face as she detangled the crown from her hair and smashed it into my cheekbone with a bruising clunk. Ahinoam and Haggith broke us apart. Bathsheba sobbed in Ahinoam's arms. I picked up her queen's crown and looped it on my arm.

Haggith sniffed at my side. "She was friends with Absalom. Not surprising, considering she's only a few years older than he."

I walked back to my tent with my head throbbing. The crown. The one I used to wear. If I had been a better wife, none of this would have happened. An enormous wave of grief overcame me, and I sunk into a morass of regret. Hugging the crown, I wept bitterly at the enormity of my mistakes, and I missed David.

CHAPTER 46

Jeremiah 3:20 Surely as a wife treacherously departeth from her husband, so have ye dealt treacherously with me, O house of Israel, saith the LORD.

>>><<<

The next few days were filled with celebrations. The men of Mahanaim and David's supporters organized another feast. The townspeople opened their houses to us for baths, and we were finally able to clean ourselves.

Men told stories and played music. Everyone mingled around giant bonfires. David's younger wives cavorted with the soldiers, and his children made merry with wooden swords and rawhide balls. Even Ahinoam sported a smile as she kept an eye on Sarah who walked with a young officer.

I wandered aimlessly. With no one to celebrate with, I ambled toward the Eastern Palace, retraced the steps to the gate and stopped under an old bay tree surrounded by lilies. Wrapped in David's cloak, I inhaled his woodsy scent. Bathsheba's crown encircled my wrist. Perhaps I could gain an audience to return her crown. Would he see me? Would I be welcome? David had told me to stay away. But his kiss had to have meant something.

A hand covered my eyes. I jumped, taking a breath to scream. Bearded lips covered my mouth, and the scream dissolved into his throat.

"I've captured you, dear Princess." Ittai's voice rumbled deliciously.

My breath hitched. "I thought you were dead, and my boys?"

"We're all fine. Come, I can't talk to you here." He let go and beckoned me around an outcrop of rocks and down a path into the forest. My heart raced after him. My legs matched his strides.

Once we were remote enough, Ittai pulled me into a grove of willow trees. "Michal, I've missed you so much."

My blood pulsed from my heart to my fingertips. "I missed you, too."

I touched his stubble, sprinkled with grey and ran my fingers through his long, smooth hair. His skin was still unlined, and a jagged scar traced his left cheek. His smile twinkled, every bit as rakish as I remembered.

"Didn't you believe I'd show up someday?" he said. "I brought an army. We chased Absalom's men into the forests. Your boys were with me."

My heart rate quickened. "They're here?"

"They were, but they've gone to Jerusalem to look for you, to rescue you, if needed." He tilted my chin. "But look what I found."

"Who told you I was in Jerusalem? Don't you know me better? Even if David had ordered me to stay, I would have come anyway."

"I didn't see you at Phaltiel's house that first night David conferred with us. When I asked about you, no one would give me an answer. But now I have you, and I'm not letting you go."

His strong arms squeezed the breath out of me. He lowered his forehead to mine, and I melted to his chest. Our lips met. My restraint evaporated as the dew on a hot spring morning, unleashing a raging wildfire.

"Ittai," I said breathlessly, "how is it that David has allowed you to return?"

"He needed me." His white teeth gleamed in the dusk. "After he drove me away, I recruited an army and prepared for a time to serve him again. Absalom gave me the perfect opportunity. All Israel had turned against David. All the archers and horsemen went after him. David only had the loyalty of a few aging mighty men, his nephews and the palace guards."

"How did you know all this?"

He wiggled his eyebrows. "I, too, have spies. Your David has been somewhat of a recluse these last few years. Rumor says he keeps his secret queen in his tower. Rumor says he's executed her, and rumor says he talks to her ghost."

I lowered my head. David had been negligent of his kingdom, and he had mooned over me and dreamed of God's Temple.

Ittai touched my cheek. "You look and feel nothing like a ghost. Solid, flesh, hot, breathing, irresistible." He traced my lips with his fingers, and his eyes beckoned my soul. "I've always loved you. From the moment I saw you, when you ran from me and tumbled into the river, I loved you."

He leaned to kiss me, but I held my hand to his jaw. "You? You were the boy?"

His grin tilted one side of his face. "Took you long enough to remember. Do you still have my cloak?"

I shook my head, stunned. "I've often thought about you, whether you made it back home."

He tugged David's cloak and gazed into my eyes. "I was the first to wrap you in my cloak and claim you. You're really mine."

The heat of his chest cradled me, and his lips found mine again. I kissed him furiously, the fire licking the hem of my dress jumped to singe the hairs of my head. Ittai picked me up and took me deeper into the grove, laid me on a pile of leaves and transported me back in time to another tree near Delilah's house in the Valley of Sorek.

He stroked me with his tongue, sending delicious pulses through my body. The stubble of his beard tantalized and evaporated my reason. Crouching on his hands and knees, he worshipped me with his entire body, touching and filling the empty corners of my heart.

"Do you want me? Don't deny me." His love tugged at my heart, fondled it, and snatched it.

A great need overwhelmed me and I pulled him down. His entrance, a rebirth, displaced a lungful of air. His movements danced rhythmically, teased and stroked, intensifying into deep cleansing thrusts, thrusts that claimed and conquered my soul.

A monstrous tidal wave of pressure hammered me with swell after swell of raw delight. My body jerked in spasm with the overspreading of an exhilarating and calming glow. Curled in an envelope of warm bliss, his heartbeat lulling me to sleep, his arms encircling me, love never ending, we lay on the bed of leaves and moss, our bodies entwined in a sheet of sweat and love. Ittai's hair covered my face like a groom's wedding shawl.

* * *

David's eyelids flickered in sleep. He stared at the tip of his sword. It was covered in blood. He turned over the body and pulled the man's hair back. It came off in his hands, seven locks woven in crimson threads.

Absalom. His eyes opened, and a cheeky grin slashed his face. "You killed me. You killed your own son. You should have let me win."

Absalom tossed his bald head back and laughed with blood stained teeth. Laughed and laughed and laughed.

David tossed on the bed. Where was he? And Michal?

She clung to him. She smelled of amber, not jasmine. His head hurt, and he remembered. He should have left her in Jerusalem.

Ittai had shown with six hundred men. Now he had taken Michal.

"David, David?" Maacah's voice called to him, through a dark mist, far away.

He struggled, swinging through the thorns and brambles.

"David, you're hurting me." A stinging slap woke him.

He blinked, once, twice. He waved his hand in her face. It did not change.

"Maacah?"

She lit a lamp. "I should leave now."

"No, don't leave." His gaze darted across the room.

Her eyes watered. "But our son, Absalom. Why? David, kill Joab."

He clutched her hair. "I can't kill Joab. He's saved my life too many times."

"I'm leaving you. Let me go," she screamed.

"Why? You're my wife."

"You had another nightmare. I'll get Michal."

"No, I can't be seen with her," he said. "Not in front of my people, my army."

"Why? All your wives know. You think you hide your insanity so well."

He slapped the edge of the bed. "I am not weak. I am in control of my kingdom."

"You're the king," she said in a sing-song voice. "Everyone should respect you, reverence you, and obey you."

"Like Absalom did?"

Her brows lowered, and the left side of her lip rose in a snarl. "He would have been a better king than you. He cared about the people. You lock yourself in your tower writing songs, wooing your disposed queen, lovesick. You think he didn't know? Or the rest of your kingdom?"

He raised his hand and put it down.

Her eyes narrowed. "Or do you want me to lie to you?"

He lay back. "Yes, Maacah. Tell me sweet lies, Maacah, you're so good at it. Lies like soft pillows, warm sheepskin, lies, Maacah. Tell me."

"Everyone loves you, David. Especially Michal. All your wives reverence you, and the people adore you. You're King David, the mighty, the glorious, the beneficent, all powerful, all good. You're the anointed of the LORD. God shines his favor on you."

* * *

My heart burned with guilt. No question Ittai's six hundred men had saved David's kingdom. But my disloyalty could not be excused. I washed myself in the river, scrubbing my skin raw. *Oh, God, I'm an adulteress. I should be stoned.*

Ittai whistled a tune, intruding into my agony. "Michal, I brought food. I'm betting you're famished." He licked his fingers. "Chicken."

I pulled on my clothes and sat on the rocky bank, hugging my knees, my head bent forward.

"Will you now run away with me?" he asked.

"I've sinned." I hung my head as sobs bubbled from my throat.

He waved a piece of chicken in front of my nose. "Don't think about it."

"How can you sit there and eat as if nothing happened?"

He arched a single eyebrow. "I'm Philistine. Sin is not in my vocabulary."

"I can't face David anymore. I'm ruined. Just kill me."

He smacked his lips on another piece of chicken. "It's not every day a woman wants to die after being with me."

"Is everything a joke to you?"

"No, you're not a joke. Come here." He rolled me into his arms. I cried in his chest until my tears were spent.

"It's getting late," I said. "I should go back to my tent. Abital will worry."

He handed me a bowl and a wineskin. "Eat something first."

The aroma of the spiced chicken watered my mouth. I didn't know when my next meal would be, or what David planned now that Absalom's forces had been scattered. A lingering sob shook my chest. I could never face David again. I sipped the wine while Ittai took his horse to the river.

Crickets chirped in cadence to my pounding heart. The wine warmed my bowels. I breathed the tangy scent of the evening and drank more. Ittai returned and offered me his hand.

I stood too quickly and stumbled. To deflect his concern, I tapped his bicep. "I meant to ask you, my dear Ittai. Have you married yet?"

He snickered. "And I meant to ask you, my dear Michal. Have you been widowed yet?"

"But, my dear Ittai, hasn't it been your doing that I'm not?"

"So, my dear Michal, I have no choice but to resort to kidnapping." He led me to his horse.

"You're not serious, are you?"

He pushed me on his horse. "I don't see you struggling." He jumped on behind me. "Why would you think I'd marry anyone but you?"

"I figured you'd eventually find someone and settle down."

"The only someone I want is you," he said. "Now if you could get over your obsession for the king, I'd have a chance."

"If I could split myself into two women…" I laughed at the thought. "Have you heard the ridiculous nickname David calls me?" My words slurred. "Eg…g-lah."

"Oh, you mean Eglah, the cow? Yes, while you were on your deathbed."

We both laughed as if my deathbed scene came from a Philistine comedy.

"I've an idea," he said. "I'll take Michal, and we'll leave Eglah for him, wouldn't that be funny?"

I giggled while he tickled me to make me laugh more. "But Eglah would be so boring. Do you know she sits in his tower and pen scrolls for him all day long?"

He yawned in an exaggerated manner. "And what does she do at night?"

"She is his blanket, his comforter. She keeps him from having nightmares. She trims his beard, gives him baths, rubs his back. She loves him when he's sick, especially when he's sad."

"She sounds sweet. What does she do for him in bed?"

I elbowed him. "Why? Are you jealous?"

"Of Eglah? Not one bit. What I want to know is how Michal's been doing all these years."

I took a deep breath, and the crushing pit in my stomach returned. "Michal has been hiding. No one cares about Michal. Michal wants to die."

My breath shuddered, and I lowered my head between my hands.

He kissed my neck and the side of my head. "It can't be that bad. It can't be."

"I went back to him because I wanted to help him, but part of him still hates me. He spread me on the rug on top of the tree of life and told me I was a failure, barren—that I didn't keep my vow to love only him."

"What a rotten thing to say. Does he love only you?" Ittai spurred his horse up a cliff-side trail.

"It's not the same. He's a man. He expects his wives to be loyal."

Ittai huffed. "But Eglah, if she exists, loves only David. Isn't that true?"

"Yes, she does. She walks with him every morning to the tabernacle and prays with him. They watch the sunrise together, and he requires her to be veiled. But Michal? Michal is too naughty, and Michal has been unfaithful."

"Unfaithful? Do you mean just now?"

"Yes, Michal should be stoned."

Ittai squeezed my shoulder. "Not where we're going, you won't. So tell me, if Eglah loves David, who does Michal love?"

I sucked on the wineskin before turning it upside down, empty.

Ittai took it from me. "You know that was Phaltiel's best vintage, and you guzzled it like water?"

I hiccupped and leaned against his chest. Did Michal even know who she loved?

We traveled until the night became too dark. Ittai pitched his tent on top of a bed of pine needles near a trickling brook. The crisp, spiny scent soothed my bruised soul. We lay outside the tent and sang the song of Samson and Delilah, lovers separated forever.

He placed his cloak over my head and brought me into his tent. He told me he had a wife. Her name was Michal. He made love to Michal all night, and he filled her with boundless pleasure while raking her back with pine needles of guilt.

* * *

There was no turning back. I would never see David again. I sat in the tent, twirling Bathsheba's crown. With nothing but the clothes on my back, David's cloak, and a few pieces of jewelry, the garnet bracelet, and the emerald diamond necklace sewn into my robe, I faced exile.

We rose mid-morning, packed our camp and resumed westward toward the Jordan River.

"Where are we going?" I asked.

"Gibeah," Ittai said. "I have to check on my daughter, Kyra."

"Daughter? You liar. You did marry. Let me off right now."

"Michal, I can explain."

I wagged my head and said in a sing-song voice, "I can explain. I can explain. Let me off."

He halted the horse and slid me off. "So long, Princess. Let's see if your husband comes after you. I've a daughter to tend to."

He flipped his hair over his shoulder and trotted off.

Teardrops rolled down my cheeks. Ittai had taken my virtue, mesmerized me with his honeyed tongue, and pushed me off the slippery slope of sin. My utter loneliness and destitution was hardly an excuse for unfaithfulness.

I banged my head against a tree trunk, waiting for him to return. Several minutes passed. A biting breeze rattled leaves from the tree. A scurrying noise pattered behind me. The hair on the back of my scalp tingled. The forest crept with silent feet. The absence of bird sounds meant a predator lurked.

The bushes rustled behind me. The fear of wolves crowded my mind. I had to get back on the road. The tree shadows mocked me. A menacing presence stalked me.

"Ittai!" I cried, "Where are you?" Crunching steps came toward me, and I screamed. Something charged, grunting and breathing hard. I stumbled through the bushes and tumbled into a water hole. A loud thwack sounded on my right.

"Got it." Ittai wiped his sword on a tree stump and sheathed it.

"What was it?" I crawled out soaking wet.

"Stay here." He crept over and laughed loudly. "It's a wild boar, Michal. A wild boar charged you. You fell into his drinking hole."

Drenched and humiliated, I crouched on the bank and covered my face. Ittai had lied to me, but at least he saved me from the boar.

Thumping and dragging sounds proceeded from the thicket. Ittai whistled while I wept. He slung the boar over a tree branch, slit its abdomen, and pulled out the sack of entrails.

Then he tied the boar on the back of his horse and washed his hands in the pool. Still sniffling, I put my head between my knees when he stomped his feet at my side.

"Are you going to let me explain?" he said.

"All men lie to me."

"You're not going to listen, are you?"

After a few moments of silence, he squatted at my side and sighed. "The problem with princesses, they're always right."

He tugged my shoulder. "Come on."

Having no better alternative, I followed him mutely and allowed him to place me on the horse with the boar. I held my tongue about the unclean animal in back of me. Ittai walked in front at a brisk pace.

We forded the Jordan at the town of Adam and camped in the hills just west of the river. With winter upon us, temperatures dropped as soon as the sun set.

Ittai chewed on a cinnamon stick. "I was angry with you for assuming the worst of me. But my mother told me never to let the sun go down on my anger. So I've let it go. Let me know when you're ready to talk."

He lit a fire and cut a few strips of meat from the carcass, roasting it. My mouth watered, but the boar was unclean and against the Law. Ittai wiggled a strip under my nose. The smell was delectable but I clamped my jaw and rolled into the tent. My clothes still damp from my fall into the pool, I shivered and thought about David. I had betrayed him and no longer deserved to be called by his name. Ruined and desolate, I sobbed.

Ittai crawled into the tent and stretched. Without asking, he wrapped me in his arms and rubbed my shoulders. "We need to get you warmer clothes. Tomorrow morning we'll be in Gibeah. We would have made it if we had ridden on. But now, we'll have a feast. At least some of us will."

His arms comforted me, and his chest warmed me. I tried to hold onto my anger, but he melted it with kindness by rubbing my cold feet and covering me with his cloak.

"I'm ready," I said.

"You have to stop being so jealous." His coal black eyes stared at me. "I found Kyra abandoned in a cave, but even if I had fathered her, you should understand and accept it."

His words shamed me. I clasped the back of his neck and kissed his cheek. "You're right."

CHAPTER 47

Song of Solomon 2:8 The voice of my beloved! behold, he cometh leaping upon the mountains, skipping upon the hills.

>>><<<

David slammed his fist on the oak table. "Ahithophel is dead, you say? Good. I should never have trusted him with Absalom."

Hushai the Archite, his loyal advisor, passed him a goblet of wine. "I did as you asked. I defeated the counsel of Ahithophel. He advised Absalom to send twelve thousand men to pursue you the first night. It would have been a disaster."

David rubbed his beard. "Yes, we would have been slaughtered."

"Ahithophel also advised Absalom to lie with your concubines. What shall we do with them?"

"Put them in a locked section of the women's courtyard. They shall live as widows."

"Some are quite young. Shall we marry them off?"

"Maybe. Lock them for a month. Those without child can be sold if they wish."

A courier dropped to the ground with a scroll. "King David, Joab sends a message."

Hushai opened the message and read, "Permission sought to pursue Sheba the Benjamite. He has gathered all tribes of Israel except for Judah."

"Granted." David wiped his forehead. A Benjamite, Michal's tribe. And where was she? Ittai had also disappeared. Ittai was a Benjamite from his mother's side. Enemies surrounded him.

"Send a contingent to Gibeah and apprehend Ittai." His spies informed him that Ittai's mother still lived in the house of Ribai, her father. "Bring him back alive, and only him."

He didn't ever wish to see Michal again. How could she abandon him in his grief? She had betrayed him. She could rot and bury herself in

Gibeah. He didn't care. The pain in his chest belied his thoughts, but he couldn't admit how much she had hurt him.

David adjourned court and walked to the women's courtyard. Of his many wives, only Ahinoam and Abital returned. Maacah had gone home to her father, and the rest had run off. Bathsheba stayed back in Mahanaim, too ashamed of her grandfather's role to return to Jerusalem so soon.

He greeted Ahinoam and Abital with long hugs, taking comfort in their loyalty. "Tell me about your journey."

He took Abital in one hand and Ahinoam with the other. The three of them walked out the gate and alongside the palace wall.

* * *

Ittai and I arrived in Gibeah in the early morning. He handed the boar to the camp cook and ran to his grandfather's house. Men greeted him. Four of my sons surrounded me with hugs.

Before I could ask where Joshua was, Joel said, "Kyra's missing."

Ittai slapped the wall. "What do you mean she's missing?"

"We think she left with her friends on an adventure," Gaddiel said.

"Why aren't you looking for her?"

They shuffled and stared at one another. Joel spoke. "We've pledged our allegiance to Sheba. Haven't you heard? He will restore the throne to our tribe. Eleven tribes are united against David."

"You can't do that," I said. "David is God's chosen king."

"No, he's the usurper." Joel glared at me. "We saw what kind of man he was when we fought for him. His own tribe supported Absalom, but he rewarded the men of Judah who returned to him and spurned the rest of the tribes, as if we had no part in the kingdom."

Ittai threw up his hands. "Boys, this is rebellion. Treason. I won't allow you to leave this farm."

"You cannot stop us," Gaddiel said. "Look at the way he treated our mother as a common harlot. He cast her out and kept her on the side."

I slapped him so hard his head jerked. "I didn't bring you up this way. No one is going anywhere."

Eliah hugged me. "Mother, we have to go. We've suffered enough under the king. He raises taxes every year and conscripts forced labor, even among freedmen. You must understand. Israel will be in ruins."

Beraiah stood back, rocking on his heels, looking from brother to brother.

"Where's Joshua?" I asked him.

He shrugged. "He went off with Rachel to look for his son."

"Who's Rachel?" I asked, but nobody took notice.

Joel and Gaddiel slung their satchels and headed for the door. Ittai rushed to block them. Gaddiel knocked him on the head with the hilt of his sword, and Joel tied him up. Eliah tied my hands. "I'm sorry, Mother."

The hoof beats of their horses faded in the distance. I wiggled to Ittai's side and nudged him. He groaned but did not regain consciousness. I could do nothing but wait.

I turned to the LORD. *Please forgive me this sin. Don't hold the sword over my heart continually. I've sinned against you and David. But let me have peace with David. Don't let me be dead to his heart. And protect David's kingdom, for he is your anointed.*

The more I prayed, the more anguished I became. Did I not pray properly? Or had God turned his back on me? *My sin is always before me. I wet my bed with tears. LORD, I'm sorry, forgive me my iniquity, O LORD, and fill me with your mercy.*

A sharp rap on the door interrupted me. "Open up. King's guards."

My heart froze. David had tracked us. They flung the door open and wrestled Ittai to his feet. He swung as if drunk. One man took a pitcher of water and doused him. "How nice of you to be tied up already."

Ittai struggled to speak. "What? Where?"

They dragged him to the door. "King David demands your presence."

"Wait," I called. "What about me?"

Arik stuck his face close to mine. "His orders were to take only Ittai. He specifically said, 'No one else.' And that means he doesn't want you."

"At least cut her bonds," Ittai said.

"That wasn't part of our orders." They sneered and marched off with Ittai.

I lay on my face and wept. *David, you hate me. God, let me die.*

Several hours later, maybe even a day or two, a pair of wrinkled hands put a water skin to my lips and untied my bonds. Tora's scarred lips kissed my cheek. "Michal, I remember you. David's wife."

* * *

David thumped his spear. Arik threw Ittai onto the ground, almost knocking Hushai over.

"Untie him and leave us alone," David said, wrinkling his nose. Ittai smelled sour, like burnt pig. David spat on him.

Hushai stepped back. "Are you sure? He's a warrior and dangerous."

"Are you saying I can't overpower him?"

Arik untied Ittai and shoved him. "You touch a hair of his head, and we'll skin you alive and fry you." To David, he said, "I'll be right outside."

David pulled Ittai to a seat at the table and pushed a platter of food. "Eat."

Ittai shook his head and stared at his feet.

David leaned back and steepled his fingers. "What do you have to say, brother?"

"Kill me, but do not touch Michal."

A gravelly chuckle scratched David's throat. "I have no intention of touching her, I can assure you that. Never mention her name to me again."

"Yes, my king."

"Now, as for you. Did you mean it when you gave me your oath of loyalty?"

Sweat popped over Ittai's forehead. He raked his disheveled hair and scratched his stubbly face. "Yes, I'm still your loyal servant."

"Then why did you aid the rebels? Sheba's men?"

His red eyes blinked. "I did no such thing. Whatever you will have me do, my lord, I shall do it."

David's fingers tapped at a faster rate, his fingernails making a sharp clicking sound. "First, you shall never speak to or see my queen again. If she comes to you, you will walk away. If she calls for you, you are to shut your ears. You are not to write her, take any messages to her, nor receive any sort of communication. She shall be dead to you. Since you cannot communicate with her, either yourself or through third parties, you shall give her no reason for your refusal."

A tear slipped from the corner of Ittai's left eye and traced the scar David gave him. "I'd rather die than see her hurt." His lips trembled. "Please, execute me for treason."

"Making love to the queen is treason. You're right. But I refuse to execute you. It would be too easy for her. She must pay."

David sipped water and cleared his throat. "You will serve me as my armor bearer. Your first task is to defeat the rebels. You will return to Jerusalem until I either release you, or I go to my fathers. Should you step outside of Jerusalem without my permission, I will tie her on the highest tree, alive, and let the birds pick her eyes out."

"You wouldn't. She's your—"

"You control her fate."

Ittai raised his head. "My king, you are too generous. I shall fight for you. Wherever my lord, the king lives, I will live, whether in death or life, I will be your servant."

* * *

David punched his bed, his empty bed. He tore his sheets, his skins, his clothes. Why Michal, why? Did she have no idea how much she hurt him? How much he loved her?

The nightmares had returned. He thought he had peace. But there was no peace.

The sword knows. Spinning, spinning, where it would stop, only God knows.

He opened his window and leaned out.

"David."

He startled.

Abital hurried in, her cheeks two spots of red. "What are you doing?"

He stepped back, dropped his hands, and smiled. "Fresh air."

"Joab has the head of Sheba the Benjamite."

"Wonderful, we celebrate tonight."

Betrayers, Michal, and her sons. Traitors. The seed of Saul, the seed of the serpent.

* * *

I opened the door, and Tora stepped in. Her eyes were red with weeping.

"Do you know what's happened to Ittai?" I asked. "He came by but did not speak to me."

Tora's eyebrows creased. "He's not allowed to speak to you, by order of the king. He's captured Joel, Gaddiel, and Eliah, and brought them back. He had them flogged."

"Flogged!" I shrank in horror. "Where are they?"

"You're not allowed to see them, by order of the king."

I stomped my feet. "Forget the king. They're my sons."

"The king has spies in this village. Do you wish to bring the king's sword on us?"

My throat dried, and I swallowed the rising lump of acid. "You're right."

I paced across the room. My sons, why did they turn against David and incur his wrath? I stopped at the window and bent over the sill. A two story drop would not kill me. I could be maimed and live. *Oh God, save me and help me, for I am undone.*

Tora stroked my hair. "There is a cave where I used to play as a girl. Let's take a hike, just me and you."

"But my sons, are they hurt badly?"

"They'll live. Ittai did the flogging himself. The important thing is that David knows they were punished. You know they should have been hanged, but the king forgave all who rebelled."

A hike would help me. Could David forgive my betrayal? Ittai would obey David. He was the loyal one, and I'd never see him again. I grabbed my cloak, David's cloak, and wrapped it around me as if it were his arms.

Tora packed a bundle of food and slung a blanket over my shoulder. Arm in arm, we walked with our baskets past the gate of Gibeah. The guards took no notice of two women, no longer young, who gathered plants along a path through large outcroppings of boulders and scattered fig trees. Small patches of cucumbers and melons were cultivated on the terraces between the hills. The fresh loamy smell of the tilled earth signaled warmer weather.

We cut through a narrow path between two large table-like boulders and emerged near a feeble spring. A stand of red and black berries provided good pickings. Following the spring, we climbed a boulder and stepped behind a sharp escarpment. A dark crack hidden behind the rock led to a cool cavern.

I froze at the entrance. The odor of a recently quenched campfire warned me to tread carefully. Tora stepped in without hesitation and waved me into the cave. She dropped her basket and took the rolled blanket from my shoulder.

"Someone's been here," I whispered.

"Relax. It's a private place. Not many people know of it. An earthquake shifted those two tables of stone together since I was a girl." She sat on the blanket and leaned against the cool wall. "I wish I had been here when the Philistines came that day."

I squeezed her hand. "I, too, have so many regrets."

"But I've never regretted Ittai," she said.

I closed my eyes and leaned against her. "Me neither."

A footstep thumped. My head jerked and hit a jutting rock. The shadow of a large man obscured the cave entrance. Tora had dozed off. I backed slowly into the darkness, afraid to rouse her and draw attention. My stomach tightened.

The man drew a sword. Measured steps hesitated outside the cave.

Tora snorted in her sleep and woke. "Ittai?"

The man dropped over her. "Mother, did you bring her?"

"Ittai," I cried.

"Michal, mine." His deep voice echoed in the cavern.

CHAPTER 48

2nd Samuel 21:1 Then there was a famine in the days of David three years, year after year; and David enquired of the LORD.

>>><<<

David sorted through Abigail's belongings. These days, he found solace sitting in her room. He picked up a scarf and smiled. Abigail's embroidery was detailed and delicate, each stitch a stroke of a pen, a swish of a brush. She had stitched many of the hangings, table clothes, and altar pieces that would serve at the Temple.

He opened a moss green purse with fall leaves, red, orange, and yellow—fluttering and twirling in a light blue and silver breeze. He drew out a rolled parchment. His heart stuttered. A love note? But from who, her first husband? He was a churl, cruel and hateful. But maybe at the beginning they had loved each other.

He shouldn't read it. Yet, his hands shook as he untied the strings and unfurled the note. Michal's script jumped off the page.

My dearest David, I have borne you two sons. We are living at Adriel's house in Abel-Meholah. Adriel and Merab have passed away. I have adopted their sons. It is dangerous here with many bandits. If you could spare a guard, please send for us. Phalti is with me, but only as a friend. Please consider taking all of us under your protection. Your loving wife, Michal.

Tears seeped into his eyes. Joshua and Beraiah were his sons. Ittai claimed they hadn't joined the rebellion, but their names were listed on Sheba's roster. And Michal. He'd check with his spies and ensure she still lived in Gibeah with Ittai's mother, a strict follower of the Law.

"David?" A pair of female hands rubbed his neck.

Ahinoam bent and kissed him. "I miss her, too."

She picked up the purse and examined the fine stitching.

"She's at a better place now. No tears, no sorrow, no loss." He held Ahinoam's hand and squeezed it. "When will you make a decision to trust in the LORD God?"

Ahinoam lowered her face. "How can I trust him when he's taken all my children? All I have left are those jars."

"He blessed you with Sarah. She's marrying, isn't she?" He hugged her. "You will become a grandmother. I know it. And many little hands will hold yours, little mouths will kiss you, and little feet will follow you."

"Oh, David. You are the best husband any woman could have asked for. You saved me from the Amalekites, and you saved Sarah from the hands of your own men."

"My wife of the wilderness." He kissed her as a squawk deafened his ear.

"Buzzi, you bad bird," Abital's lilting voice called.

Buzzi lighted on David's shoulder and crooned in his ear. "I love you, David."

Both Abital and Ahinoam laughed as David swept the bird away.

* * *

I ran toward Ittai and jumped up and down while hugging him.

His laughter bounced off the walls of the cavern. He stepped back and pulled me to the entrance, into the sunlight. "You didn't think I'd actually obey David to the letter, did you?"

"Tora said the consequences are dire. He'd string you on a tree and have the birds pluck your eyes."

His eyes twinkling, he grinned sidelong. "He only said to ignore his queen, and you, my darling, are no longer the queen. As long as I do as he says, go where he sends me, and serve him faithfully, he will do me no harm."

"Will he try to capture me?"

Ittai shook his head, his eyes moist. "He made an edict. No one in his kingdom is to mention your name. No, I wouldn't worry about him. Would it hurt you to know he no longer cares?"

I gripped his biceps and drew strength and fortitude from him. "It hurts, but in some ways it makes it easier. Easier to love you, Ittai."

"Oh, dear Michal." He moved to kiss me. All the tension of the last few months melted as our lips touched. For once, I could let my guilt fly and love this stalwart man, my closest friend, as he deserved.

A woman's laughter, like tinkling bells, startled me. Ittai wiped his lips and turned to the boulder cleft. A young woman appeared, her hair glinting in the breeze. Her gown, a translucent pearl, was beaded with silver and turquoise tube beads. A cloak of brilliant colors embroidered with Philistine sea shapes angled over her shoulder.

Ittai cleared his throat. "Michal, do you remember Zina?"

She held her hands out, and I grasped them. "Oh, you're all grown. Where's your mother?" *Our mother, Jada.*

"She's waiting for me to give her the signal." Zina smiled. "Ittai didn't tell you, did he?"

Ittai shuffled and drew his hand into his robe as Zina took hold of his arm. Perspiration dampened his forehead, and he coughed. His gaze flitted to the cavern.

"Tell me what?" I didn't like the look Zina gave me, too smug and knowing.

"Mother," he called. "They're here."

Tora walked out, her knees popping. "Oh, I'm stiff."

She prodded me toward the cave. Ittai hurriedly wiped his brow and glanced in the direction of the spring.

Tora patted my hands. "I guess it's time."

"For what?" I said.

"The switch." She grabbed a skin of water. "I'll find Ittai. You two make yourselves comfortable."

Zina stepped into the cave and looked around, as if checking for spiders. "I'm sure we weren't followed, but Ittai seems worried."

"Why?"

"The king has spies. Now, take off your clothes and give them to me. I'll wear your clothes and go back to Gibeah with Tora."

She handed me her cloak, and her gown slipped off. With fumbling hands, I removed my clothing. "This doesn't seem to be a fair trade. My clothes are plain, and yours are exquisite."

"Consider these a gift from Mother. Now, your cloak."

I hesitated. My cloak, David's dark green cloak was the only item I had that linked me to him, not counting the jewelry. Tears stung my eyes as I rubbed my face on it before handing it to her.

Zina flung it over her shoulders and hurried out of the cave. I followed her into the sunlight. The gown flowed like liquid moonlight overlaid with twinkling stars.

Ittai sat on a rock. His eyes widened. He dropped to his knees and grabbed my hands, kissing them.

"Marry me, Michal, daughter of Saul. Join your life to mine."

The earth shook my legs from under me. I gulped and leaned on his shoulders. High above, a lone hawk circled, dipped his wings and caught the updraft. He screeched and a second hawk joined him. The sun glared in my eyes as they disappeared.

Ittai buried his face in my chest. His shoulders tensed.

My heart swelled with affection. I hugged his head and stroked his hair. I wondered at the legality, but pushed it aside as he trembled for an answer. I lifted his face and stared into his deep, lustrous eyes. "Yes, I'll marry you, my love, my Ittai, my prince."

He handed me a necklace, garnet drops on a golden chain. "With my blood, I thee wed."

"Wait, wait!" A melodious voice cascaded over the boulder.

Jada streamed toward me, slightly out of breath. "My daughter."

I fell into her arms. "Mother, oh, I missed you. Why did you leave?"

"Let's not ruin the occasion and speak about it. I'll tell you later." She tapped Ittai's chest. "And you, impudent fellow, have not asked me for her hand."

Ittai coughed and blushed, his bronze skin darkening. "I thought... may I marry your daughter?"

Jada pretended to ignore him. She straightened my gown, picked a twig and a few burrs off the hem and brushed the beads to lie straight. "I wish I had time to do your hair. Ah, I see a few silver strands, not many though. Your father never greyed. Virile fellow."

She fluttered over me while Ittai shifted his weight from one leg to the other.

"Mother, you haven't answered him," I whispered.

Zina giggled, and Tora shuffled with her walking stick. "I'll cane you, boy. What were you going to do? Abscond with your bride before the wedding?"

Ittai rocked on his heels and finally tore off into the bushes. Everyone laughed.

"I guess he did have to go." Tora chuckled. "Now," she said to me, "I'm going to miss you, darling. Take good care of my son."

"I will, dear Tora. He's precious to me." We kissed each other on both cheeks.

Jada clutched my shoulders and stared at me. "Promise me you'll be good to him. He's a good man. Loyal, kind, and generous."

Tears blurred my vision, and I hugged her. "I will cherish him."

Zina returned with Ittai. "Mother, he's back. Can we proceed?"

Ittai knelt at Jada's feet. "Honored Priestess. Bless me, I pray and allow me to take your daughter's hand in marriage."

Jada put her hands inside her sleeves and pulled out two serpents. I gasped and stepped back. Tora clutched my sleeve and shuddered.

Jada waved the serpents' heads in front of Ittai's eyes. Their forked tongues flitted and touched his eyelids. "They have determined you are sincere. You may marry my daughter."

She motioned for me to stand next to Ittai and threw off her full-length cloak to Zina. She wore nothing above her waist but a jeweled scapular laced with snakeskin. The twin snakes curled around her wrists. Below her hennaed breasts, a wide leopard skin belt held up an elaborately embroidered double apron shaped like a double-sided axe, one head in front and the other in back. A colorful, tiered bell-shaped skirt flounced underneath, each layer woven with either a checked pattern, interlocking spirals of stylized flowers or leaves, or intricate mazes. Golden anklets tinkled over her hennaed feet.

Jada snapped her fingers. "Will you two quit staring and join your hands?"

Ittai's throat wobbled, and he took my right hand with his. Jada grasped our joined hands and set the two snakes around our wrists. They wrapped their tails and necks to each other, locking us together. My hand shook at the slithering sensation, but Ittai squeezed and held me firmly, reassuring me with his strength.

As dashingly handsome as the day I met him, his grin still disarmed me. I hadn't noticed the fine lines of amusement radiating from the corners of his eyes. And his hawk-like nose only strengthened his face—a man of distinction and character—a man I had always loved.

Jada intoned, "Oh, great Goddess Asherah, bless Ittai and Michal. They have come to be joined as husband and wife. Bless these hands that hold each other in passion and love. May these hands strengthen one another in sorrow, share with one another in gladness, and be companions to each other in times of silence. Bless Ittai and Michal with both love and happiness in their life together."

The love in Ittai's clean-shaven face shone as he lifted one eyebrow and flashed me a confident grin before joining his lips with mine. Jada removed the snakes, and Ittai whispered, "Just be glad she didn't take out her bronze knife."

I recoiled, and he showed me his wrist. Two thin, pale scars cut across it. Jealousy surged. Ittai backed me into the mouth of the cave. "It's not what you think, my love. I've two brothers bond by an oath of blood, but you're my only wife." Sweeping me into his arms, he carried me through the cave entrance and laid me on a pallet covered with wool.

* * *

Three years had passed since Absalom's rebellion, but the kingdom had no peace. A fierce, unrelenting drought gripped the land, and the people murmured.

David thumped his scepter, silencing the court. "Hushai, bring in the stewards."

Hushai motioned the men forward.

"The storehouses are almost empty. We have not had a decent harvest in three years."

"The entire barley crop is lost. The fields are dry and barren, and there will be no harvest this year."

"The people clamor for grain. Many villages have been abandoned. Dogs terrorize the countryside."

David held his scepter to the priests. "Make inquiry of the LORD for the cause of this famine. Ask him to send me a sign, a raindrop on the tip of my nose. Then shall I know his anger has ceased."

To Hushai, he said, "Cut the rations of my household. We must not eat more than the people on the streets. And bring Ittai to me. I want a complete tour of the Jezreel Valley, the state of each farm, each olive grove, and each vineyard."

He adjourned court and retired to his chamber to pray. He dared not go to the Ark of the LORD, afraid the famine was caused by his sin. *Oh, LORD, I will pay. Whatever you ask of me. Only do not let the people suffer and starve. Show me what I must do.*

David unrolled the rug, the one Michal had given him, and his thoughts returned to her. For three years, she had lived with Tora, alone and without Ittai. They observed the Sabbath and every ordained feast, going often to the high place in Gibeon to pray. David's spies assured him they never saw Ittai go near her. She deserved to suffer the way she made him suffer. Beautiful daughter of Saul. The day he laid eyes on her was the day of his ruin. Yet his heart ached for her. What hold did she have on him? Bewitching daughter of Saul.

A sharp rap on his door brought him to his feet. Nathan, the priest entered, his eyes weary. "I have inquired with the LORD. The famine is for Saul and his bloody house, for he slew the Gibeonites. He broke the vow our fathers made promising the Gibeonites safety within our borders."

Relief swept David's brow. It was not for his sin, nor the sin of his house. But then a chilling knife skidded down his spine. The bloody house of Saul brought this disaster? Would he ever be free of Saul?

He rubbed sweaty palms on his robe. "What is the remedy?"

Nathan raised his hands. "The LORD did not say. Since the Gibeonites are the injured party, they should decide."

David dismissed the priest. He paced his room and rolled up Michal's rug. He'd have to make the inquiry personally, so he'd hear the exact letter of the penalty. He opened his door. "Arik, when Ittai returns, send him to me directly."

David squeezed his eyes and rubbed his face. His shoulders stiffened and his neck ached. 'God is hard on kings.' That's what Michal had said. Being the king destroyed her father. It devastated his sons and daughters. And yet, Saul's sins were forever before them, even affecting his kingdom. What could he give to atone for this sin? Would he part with half his kingdom? Or half of the gold he collected for God's Temple? Could he give them their freedom? A territory to rule? Could he give them his throne? What would they ask for?

* * *

Ittai fell on his face in front of David. "My king, I'm here as you commanded."

"Get up," David said. "We're going to the Gibeonites to inquire of a suitable atonement to put away the famine."

Together they mounted the fastest horses. Ittai carried David's armor and shield. They approached the Gibeonites without a large contingent lest they believed they were under attack.

Heading north, they passed between Gibeah and Nob before swinging west through a series of small villages interlocked within the rocky hills. A conical hill, about five miles northwest of Jerusalem, marked the burial place of the Prophet Samuel. David had gone to the old prophet's funeral in disguise. King Saul's men had posted watch for him, but no one recognized the ragged beggar as the future king.

"My lord, the horses are tiring," Ittai said. "Let me lead them to water."

A village with two large cisterns stood to their right. David dismounted and planted himself under an old oak tree. The sun's rays burnt through the dried branches. A few wrinkled leaves lingered, cracked and grey. Two women gossiped under the tree, and scrawny children, their ribs clearly visible, lolled in the dirt nearby.

Ittai drew back the cover. The cistern was almost dry. He dangled over the side and filled their water-skins with the murky water.

David swallowed grit. The people were suffering. The formerly lush meadows of Gibeah were but stubble, choked in dust. Did Michal have enough to eat? Were her lips cracked? Had her hair fallen out? His heart tugged and he longed to hold her in his arms. He'd stop on the way back and check.

His head aching from the heat, David mounted his horse. They rounded the bend and ascended the smooth hill. Five Gibeonite tribal elders walked down and met them in front of a cracked, parched expanse—it had once been the pool of Gibeon where Joab had fought Abner during the protracted civil war.

Ittai dismounted and bowed. "King David has a request. The LORD has informed him of the cause of the famine. His predecessor, King Saul, had slaughtered your people against the solemn vow our fathers took. Pray tell what my lord, the king, may do to atone for this sin, so the LORD God will once again bless his kingdom."

The eldest Gibeonite, a wizened old man with wisps of white hair over a harsh, weathered face raised his hand to speak. "We Gibeonites desire neither silver nor gold. We do not wish the king to kill any man for us." The old man paused. He stared past Ittai and blinked at David.

David said, "What you shall say, that will I do."

The old man strode in front of David's horse and planted his staff. "Let seven sons of the man who harmed us, seven men of his house, be given to us and we shall hang them up to the LORD in Gibeah in place of Saul, the LORD's chosen one."

Ittai's eyes widened. David pressed his lips and inhaled the arid dust. Seven men of Saul? That would include Michal's sons.

Ittai staggered backward. "Seven? Sons? To die?"

David put his hand over his heart. Michal would never forgive him.

"I will give them over to you." He almost choked on the answer.

God is hard on kings.

CHAPTER 49

Hosea 3:1 Then said the LORD unto me, Go yet, love a woman beloved of her friend, yet an adulteress, according to the love of the LORD toward the children of Israel.

>>><<<

"What do you mean she's ill? Is she hungry?" David tore past Ittai's mother into her modest mud-brick home. "Where is my wife?"

Ittai shifted behind his mother, holding her shoulder and steadying her.

Tora wrung her hands. "My king, pray kill me now. She does not wish to see you."

Red anger burned in his chest, and he stomped past the beaded curtain to the bedchamber. A woman's form lay under a thin sheet. Her dull brown hair flowed over her face. He pulled back the cover and exposed a bony shoulder.

"Eglah." David sat at her bedside. "It's me, your David. Are you sick?"

The woman did not move, although her shoulders tensed.

David gently wiped the hair from her face. The woman's eyes squeezed shut. She looked like Michal, but yet—David fingered the skin around her eyes. Where had the lines gone? His gaze paused at the top of her left eyelid. The scar was missing.

His blood froze, and he yanked the woman out of the bed. "Who are you?"

The woman put her hands over her face and trembled.

David pulled her hands back. "Open your eyes. This is your king's command."

Golden-brown eyes. His indrawn breath sucked the blood out of his heart. He tossed the imposter back on the bed and yelled, "Ittai! My wife. Where's my wife?"

Ittai fell to his knees with Tora joining.

"Get up, you goats, and stop groveling. I want to see my wife. There is a matter that concerns her. You heard the Gibeonites' demand."

Ittai stood first. "My mother had no fault in this matter. Please, my lord, execute me now."

David shoved him against the wall. "I'll deal with you later. What have you done with the woman called Michal? Michal David to be exact. Or if you prefer, Michal, daughter of Saul, wife of King David."

"She's at Jada's house in the Valley of Sorek," he replied. "I will fetch her right away."

"I will go with you." David mounted his horse. "Lead the way, traitor."

David kicked his horse into a gallop. The horses were lathered, but he didn't care. He had to see her, tell her, and if she would allow it, comfort her. Yet she had betrayed him, mocked him, made him a fool.

They doubled back to the village with the two dried cisterns and turned southwest down a curvy, narrow valley. The usual creek beds were dry, but Ittai located a seeping spring of muddy water. After the horses drank, they descended bleak ridges of sandstone and entered the Sorek Valley. What once had been a lush forest had now been reduced to dried shrubs and charred bushes. David's head throbbed, and his vision blurred. After meandering several miles, Ittai pulled in front of a recently repaired house of stone and mud-brick. A broken, charred wall stood beside spindly, bone-dry trees.

Without waiting for introduction, David barged over the threshold and slammed into a vase, toppling it and spilling the precious water onto the stone floor.

Michal and Jada jumped from the grindstone where they had been pounding meal. Dried spices and herbs hung in bundles above the doorway. David's rage dissipated with a single look from Michal's lovely eyes. She was thin, but her face glowed when she saw him.

He pulled her into his arms. "Isha, I pictured you hungry and sick." He kissed her and tasted her invigorating scent, like spices and wild thyme and mint. "I couldn't bear to think of you dying of starvation."

Her gaze faltered, and she lowered her face. A flush rose from her neck to her cheeks. "David, I'm sorry."

He remembered his reason for coming, and his heart scraped the stone floor. Jada and Ittai had stepped out, no doubt to concoct a story he had no luxury to listen to.

He pressed a thumb to Michal's chin. "You're not going to like what I have to say. Do you want me to tell you now, or back at the palace?"

She stared at him. "If it's bad, tell me now."

And so he told her about the cause of the famine, her father's sin, and the penalty the Gibeonites would extract. And she wept in his neck, and he wept and told her he loved her. He picked her up and set her on his horse. And he took her back to his palace and laid her on his bed. Tomorrow, the order would go out to round up the sons of Saul. Tomorrow, he'd deal with Ittai and his treachery. Tonight he'd make love.

* * *

David lined up the nine surviving sons of Saul. Meribbaal, son of Jonathan, son of Saul. Micah, son of Meribbaal. Joel, Gaddiel, Eliah, sons of Adriel, by Merab, daughter of Saul. Joshua and Beraiah, his sons, by Michal, daughter of Saul. Armoni and Mephibosheth, sons of Saul, by Rizpah.

They stood straight and tall, except Meribbaal who tried to sit erect in his wheelchair.

"Let me, my lord, pay the entire penalty." Meribbaal's voice quavered. "I am old and useless, but do not take these lads."

"Did I say you could speak?" David snapped. The five who rebelled were easy choices. "Separate Joel, Gaddiel, Eliah, sons of Merab, and Armoni and Mephibosheth, sons of Rizpah."

The guards grabbed the five men David designated and led them away. David scratched his beard. How could he decide between the sons of Jonathan and his own sons? How could he let any of these men die? But the famine raged and thousands starved. He toughened his face. Saul sinned by breaking the nation's solemn oath, and the LORD demanded that Saul must pay with seven men of his house.

"Meribbaal," David said. "Did not Ziba testify that you and Micah were against me during Absalom's rebellion?"

Meribbaal lowered his face. "Ziba did testify against me, but not against Micah."

"Did you wish to restore the kingdom of your grandfather Saul?"

"I will not say, my lord." His jaw trembled as he gripped the arms of his wheelchair.

David turned to Beraiah. "My son, did you join Sheba's rebellion?"

Beraiah blinked. "I intended to join. Yes, but I did not go."

"What made you change your mind?"

"My brother needed me. But my lord, do not spare my life. Spare my brother Joshua."

David thumped the blunt end of his spear on the ground. "Shut up. I ask the questions. You answer them."

He stood in front of Joshua. "You did not fight for me against Absalom. I heard you made quite a commotion. You stole an Israeli woman and deserted."

"No excuses, my lord." Joshua's hard black eyes stared straight at David, so different from the exuberant boy who used to say, 'More candy, Uncle David, more candy.'

"And you, Micah. Your father had reason to stay in Jerusalem because of his feet. But you played around with Absalom's men. You also enjoyed my concubines. Is that not true?"

Micah shook his sandy hair.

"You dare lie to the king?" David growled.

"Please, my lord," Meribbaal said. "He is but a lad. He was only fifteen at the time."

"Shut up!" David pounded the spear. "Take these men back to the ward. I shall make my decision tonight."

His knees shook, and he sat back on his throne. Hushai leaned forward. "There are two more petitioners."

"Petitioners? I thought today's session was private."

"They are here for this matter," Hushai said.

"Let them step forward."

Hushai clapped his hands, and the petitioners stepped up, dressed in sackcloth and covered in ashes. They prostrated themselves. Phaltiel and Ittai.

David held his scepter. "Each of you may speak once. Phaltiel, you first."

Phaltiel crawled to his knee. "My lord, let me die in place of one of the young men."

"Denied. And you, my armor bearer, what do you want?"

"Michal and I will die for your sons, Joshua and Beraiah."

"Denied. The Gibeonites were specific. Seven men of Saul. Go back to your duty before I arrest you for dereliction. Put your regular clothes on and meet me in my chamber."

Acid crawled in David's stomach. If the LORD would accept it, he would sacrifice himself for these seven men. *Saul, Saul, why do you persecute us? Even in death, your shadow falls on us. Wasn't it hard to kick against the pricks? What man of your house shall I spare?*

* * *

I stood as soon as Ittai's form appeared at the window. "So, who did David choose?"

My heart jittered at an alarming rate. I had bitten my fingernails to the stub, and my hands were rubbed raw from wringing.

"He chose five already," Ittai said. "He is to decide on the remaining two."

"Who?"

"The five are your three eldest and Rizpah's two boys. They had joined Sheba's rebellion, so David set them aside already. He questioned the rest and will determine their fate tonight."

Ittai rattled off David's question and answer session, but my heart had already splattered like an overripe melon. I loved Joel, Gaddiel and Eliah as if they were sons of my body. *Why, why, why? Oh, God. Oh, my sister, I have failed you.*

"Michal, are you listening? He turned down Phalti and my request to die for the boys."

"Let me beg of him. I am the daughter of Saul. I should be worth at least a few of them."

"He's denied it already. I'm to meet him at his chamber. Do you want to come and wait outside?"

My pulse swishing in my ear, I wrapped my hair in a mourning shawl and hurried after Ittai's long strides.

"David made a vow with Jonathan to preserve his seed," I said. "I can't believe he is considering Micah. He was only a lad."

"Meribbaal volunteered. He wants to spare his son. So David may let Micah live. The question is whether he would pick Joshua or Beraiah."

"My guess is Joshua."

"To be spared?" Ittai's eyebrow arched.

"Yes, Joshua did not rebel."

"That's true, and Joshua is his oldest surviving son, older than Adonijah."

I bit my lip. Ittai and David both believed Joshua and Beraiah were mine. My head throbbed with indecision. Should I tell David the truth? But if I did, he'd forsake both of them. And he'd hate me forever for lying to him.

We stopped outside David's door. Arik glared at me. "The king did not ask for this woman."

Ittai stared back. "Respect the king's wife, or I'll break your neck."

Arik announced Ittai and stood in a way where I could not intrude even had I tried. I backed to the outer wall and rested against a window in the stairwell.

My head ached and tears swirled. The sudden events of the past week left me no time to reflect. One minute I was crushing spices and grinding meal with Jada. I was Ittai's wife. I had pledged to love and cherish him. We were happy, very happy. And David toppled everything when he charged in and overturned Jada's vase of divination water.

David's behavior puzzled me. After he brought me back, he planted me in Abigail's house without a guard. While we waited for my sons to be arrested, he asked no questions. He acted as if Ittai were his loyal servant. He even rewarded him in court for finding me. Hushai and all his courtiers had clapped and given Ittai a standing ovation. Only I understood the pain and sadness behind Ittai's downcast eyes as he accepted the reward—the city of Gezer.

What has happened? Oh, why did my father disregard the LORD and the holy oath? And why now? Oh, God, withdraw your curse from our house. Have we not paid enough? I repent of all my evil, dear LORD, only do not harm my boys, my brothers and my nephews.

Ittai stepped out of David's chamber and pulled me aside, away from Arik's glare. We walked halfway down the stairs. "He's going to spare both Joshua and Beraiah because they're his sons."

My intense relief was throttled by increasing dread. "But Jonathan's seed…"

"He questioned me about the twins, whether I saw you suckle them with my own eyes. Phalti swears on the Holy Scripture he's not their father."

I grabbed his wrist. "We must go back and talk to him."

"But, Michal, he spared your sons."

My face chilled as if a biting wind had blasted from the north. I headed up the stairs, pushing Ittai aside. "He made an earnest vow with Jonathan. He'll incur God's wrath. What do you think this entire affair with the Gibeonites is about? Do you not understand how God holds us to a vow? It would be better to not make a vow than to break it."

"Why? Explain."

"Later. Right now, help me get past that guard dog."

True to form, Arik jutted his jaw and blocked my passage.

Ittai placed a hand on my shoulder and addressed Arik, "Tell the king his wife wants a word with him."

Arik entered the king's chamber and shut the door firmly behind him. A minute later he stepped out and waved both of us through.

David looked up from the table. His face ashen, he raked his hair. "Michal, if you're here to propose yourself as a substitute…"

I knelt and hugged his knees. "I'm here as the sister of Jonathan, son of Saul."

He caressed my hair. "Say on."

"My brother loved me and looked after me when I was a young, mischievous girl. He got me into as much trouble as he got me out of. But whatever else he did, my brother was a man who kept his word."

David cleared his throat, but I raised my hand to stop him.

"You and I both know he could have forsaken my father and joined you. Perhaps he would have lived and not died on Mt. Gilboa." Tears formed and dropped onto David's robe.

David sniffed loudly.

"My brother took an oath of loyalty to my father." I continued. "The only time he disobeyed my father was when my father ordered him to kill you."

David shuddered. "My dear, what are you asking?"

I crumpled on his knees, my heart radiating pain through my limbs. I was asking for the death of my sons, Joshua and Beraiah. What kind of mother was I? But the consequences would be dire if God was not appeased. Our sin would multiply and overtake the entire nation.

Ittai interjected. "I also took a vow, a blood oath with Jonathan. I'm here to speak as his brother."

David pushed me from his knees. "What has happened to you two?"

Ittai pounded his own chest. "You took a vow with me, David. If you break the vow with Jonathan, then break ours too. Kill me now, for I deserve to die for what I've done to you."

He drew his dagger and held the hilt to David.

I collapsed onto the floor at the edge of my rolled-up rug, unable to speak coherently.

David paced the room. "Meribbaal has released me from Jonathan's vow."

I grabbed the hem of David's robe. "Take me instead. I'm Saul's daughter. Let me bear the sin for him."

"You can't even bear your own sin, Michal. And you're not a man, you're not a son."

"Oh, David, what choice do you have?" I wet his feet with my tears and brushed my hair over his sandals.

"Are you asking me to kill my own sons? Your sons?" David lifted me from the ground and stared at me, his left eye twitching, a vein bulging from his temple. "Being my sons meant they are not Saul's sons."

Roiling waves of agony clutched my throat. Memories of Joshua and Beraiah at my breasts fought with those of Jonathan reading the Word of God to me. I stumbled to my table and opened the silver box. "Jonathan's blood cries from these arrowheads."

David gasped and closed the lid with a snap. He rubbed his eyes and whispered, "I will split the decision. Meribbaal dies, and you chose, Joshua or Beraiah."

I shook my head, unable to grasp or choose between my precious twins.

"Speak, woman."

"Da...vid." I wailed and clutched his robe. "Don't..."

"You now see how hard it is for me? Do you understand why I cannot sleep? Why I have nightmares? Why I hate myself?" His voice jittered and broke, and he gulped loudly and fell on his couch.

My breath blew so hard my fingers tingled, and I almost passed out. "Do… what's right, David, or the famine will continue and many more will die."

He pulled me onto his lap. "My love, how can I when it hurts so much?" He tilted my mouth and kissed me. "You must help me. I… cannot… bear it… alone."

Ittai backed out of the chamber and shut the door.

Our kisses became bites. He ripped my gown, and I clawed his chest. Pain, the need for it, to feel it deeply, to dissolve the pain in my heart, numbing pain. His intensity burned, as he drove himself deep. My arms tightened over his shoulders, and I dug my nails into his back, spurring him to batter me harder. Pain, pain, pain, pounding pain, as if we could extinguish all the hurt we dealt, the agony of our existence. His ferocious grunts accompanied my wild cries. Screaming, howling, crying, tearing, ripping, the line between pain and pleasure blurred into a maelstrom of anguish and an avalanche of oblivion.

We wept and sorrowed and ran out of tears. We lay across from each other, forehead to forehead, nose to nose, fingertip to fingertip. I smoothed an errant lock of silver hair from his brow. "Remember when Abigail kept you from doing wrong?"

He grimaced. "Yes, how can I forget?"

"She's not here now, so I have to be the voice. When the LORD asked my father to complete the job and slaughter every single Amalekite, my father saved one, a single man."

"The LORD does not compromise," he said.

"No, he doesn't. He ripped the kingdom and all His blessings away from my father and plagued our house with curses."

David gulped. "As long as you won't hate me, or blame me later. Promise me."

My bowels ached, and I shivered with a surge of bile. "I can't promise you. I'm not that noble."

"At least you're not a liar," he said.

I kissed him.

PART IV

CHAPTER 50

Isaiah 54:6 For the LORD hath called thee as a woman forsaken and grieved in spirit, and a wife of youth, when thou wast refused, saith thy God.

>>><<<

The next morning, I rose early and wrapped myself in mourning garments. Ittai accompanied me, Phalti and Rizpah on the four mile trek to Gibeah. David assured me he would arrive before the execution and bless the sons of Saul.

Seven wooden crosses greeted us at the city gate.

"Stop, who goes there?" yelled a Gibeonite guard.

"Where are the prisoners?" Ittai said. "I've brought their mothers."

"No one can see them."

"The king requests you to let their mothers console them." Ittai produced an official looking parchment which neither of the guards could read.

They stepped aside to let me and Rizpah pass, but pushed Ittai and Phalti back.

"Please," I said, "let the fathers give their sons the blessing."

The guards looked at one another and said, "Unhand your weapons and put your hands behind you."

Ittai dropped his sword and his dagger. Phalti removed the knife from his robe. The guards tied their hands and allowed them through.

I stepped into a cell. The acrid smell of fear, sweat, and straw hit me as seven pairs of hollow eyes beseeched. *I must be strong. They must not fear or see me crack. I'm their mother, their aunt, their sister.*

I dropped to Eliah's side. Ittai rushed to Beraiah and Joshua and leaned close to both of them. Phalti crouched near Joel and Gaddiel, while Rizpah kissed Armoni and Mephibosheth. My sons scooted around me.

"Boys," I said, "do you know the LORD? Have you called on His name to deliver you?"

"Yes, Mother, remember, when we were little?" Joel said. "We all believed on the LORD. We called on Him to save us."

"Let me give my blessings. Joel, you first." I cupped his face. *On his thirteenth birthday, Joel recited the Ten Commandments in front of King David and his priests. He stood straight and tall and received a medal. My heart burst with pride, and I wiped a tear for Merab.*

"Joel, I'll never forget when Merab and Adriel brought you to my wedding. You were an active baby, your little legs kicking nonstop. You are the strongest of my sons. You helped me with the little ones. You made me proud of you. O LORD God, please be merciful, let him see Your face and take him to Your everlasting home." I kissed Joel. "I love you, son, remember me when you're in glory."

Gaddiel and I played dueling harps. I led with a lick, and he wove around it. I climbed and pranced up a run of notes, and he leapt off a precipice, tumbling melodic turbulence on the downbeat. I stroked his hair. "My sweet boy, you were always so scared when you were little, but you turned out to be the bravest. You brought such joy to me with your music and your song. O LORD God, take Your son Gaddiel into Your presence and give him a white stone with a new name." I kissed him. "I love you, son. Keep your chin up until we meet again."

I put my arm around Eliah next. *Eliah sat on my lap and spat peas in my face, grinning through his gapped teeth. I blew bubbles on his chubby tummy. He squealed and slobbered me with a wet kiss.* "Let me hold you. You were my most cuddly boy. I used to lie on the bed with you on my belly and we'd nap. You grew into an affectionate and loving man. O LORD God, flood Your loving-kindness on Eliah and hold him in Your lap and comfort him." I kissed Eliah. "I love you, son, don't forget to save a big hug for me when I arrive."

"Joshua." I leaned in hugging him. *Joshua galloped after Ittai, his black hair streaming. Ittai turned and charged and hit him with a blunt spear. Joshua's horse did not slow. He swung to the side of the horse, gripping onto its mane and tripped Ittai's horse.* "My rambunctious boy, full of life, full of mischief. You were always playful, never shy, and whenever there was any trouble, you were sure to find it. O LORD God, grant Joshua the peace that passes all understanding and let him eat of the hidden manna." I kissed Joshua, holding him tightly. "I love you, son. Let me ride with you when I see you again."

I held Beraiah's head to my breast. *I wiped Merab's blood off Beraiah's still face. I breathed into his mouth the breath of life. Beraiah opened his eyes and became my son.* "Beraiah, you were a fighter from your mother's womb. I loved you the moment you were born. You healed my broken heart. Beraiah, out of calamity came blessed joy. And you are a joy, so very sweet." I kissed him. "O LORD God, take special care of Beraiah, give him the morning star to light his way. My son, hold a special room in your mansion for me."

They crowded around me, their bodies pressed against mine, their warmth enveloped me, our tears mingled with the dry dust of the ground. I cried, "Oh, God, let this be my sepulcher. Let me lie here with them. Oh, God, let the daughter of Saul pay. Oh, God, where is Your Redeemer? Where, where, where is Your Redeemer?"

David entered with a loud cry. He went around the room. He talked to them, consoled them and gave his blessing to all seven sons of Saul. But the two he hugged and cried over the longest were Joshua and Beraiah.

* * *

The guards led my sons out to the river to wash their faces. They set food in front of them. A crowd gathered around, some with stricken faces, most in gleeful anticipation. A slight commotion amongst the guards drew my attention. Anna, my daughters-in-law, Phalti and Rizpah's other children, and the wives of Rizpah's sons stepped forward in a group.

David motioned to the guards. "Let the men have some private time with their wives, brothers and sisters."

Joshua kissed his wife, Rachel, and held her swollen belly. Beraiah hugged me and Anna. The sound of sobs and last minute pleas surrounded me with unbearable pain.

"Mother, remember the last New Moon's Feast when we were all together?" Beraiah's thatch of hair, rusted iron-grey, glinted in the morning sun.

I held his head and tickled the patch of freckles over his fine-boned face. "Yes, we were all together then, as now. Oh, God. How can I bear this? I love you so much."

Honey-amber eyes, so much like David's beseeched me. "Don't cry, Mother. Today I'm going to God. It'll be my birthday up there. I'll see Ithream again."

And I held him, remembering the night when he first blinked at me, torn from the bloody womb of my sister. Joshua swung his arm around me, and I hugged them both, my twin boys. What was left of my heart crumbled and dissolved into a brackish, stagnant pool. The guards motioned me back, but I could not loosen my grip. David and Ittai gently pried my arms open, and the guards took my boys to the crosses waiting for them, their faces covered by black hoods.

"You don't have to watch," Ittai whispered as he held me in his arms.

"I have to. My sons, oh, my sons." I could not catch my breath. Next to us, Phaltiel and Rizpah stood together, weeping.

David took me from Ittai's warm chest and gripped my stiff shoulders. I bit the inside of my cheeks and stared at my sons through blurry eyes. One by one, they were lifted to the top of the cross, the rope secured to their necks, and dropped. Each jerk ripped a piece from my heart. Each spasm wrenched my stomach. And as they went limp and their spirits ascended to God, my soul dug deeper to the depths of hell.

David walked to the front of the platform and cleared his throat. "There are times when a few must die for the many."

How could he speak at a time like this? Platitudes, political platitudes.

"There are times when the iniquities of the father are visited onto the children, to the third and fourth generation."

What a miserable excuse, David. What about your iniquities?

"Armoni, Mephibosheth, Joel, Gaddiel, Eliah, Joshua, and Beraiah, your deaths are not in vain."

Hypocrite. They are dead already. They can't hear you.

I yanked my sandal and threw it at David. It hit him on the forehead.

"Liar. They should not have died so needlessly." I rushed the platform and threw my other sandal. David stared at me as it struck his face.

A shout. Somebody grabbed me and pushed, followed by a swish of a sword. I hit my head, and the crowd screamed. A warm wet liquid soaked my chest, and I saw black.

* * *

Rizpah sat with me inside the dank cell. Her eyes were swollen and bloodshot.

I rubbed my aching head. My robe was soaked crimson.

"What happened?" I patted myself to check for wounds.

Rizpah handed me a cup of water. "It's not your blood."

I stared at her, the blood draining my head. "Whose?"

"I'm sorry."

"Ittai?"

She shook her head. "Ittai's mother. She jumped between you and the guards. She's dead."

My shrieks echoed in the small cell. I pounded my head against the wall, scratched myself, and tore my hair. Several hands pushed a vile, bitter liquid into my mouth. I choked and grabbed at them, but they tied my hands.

* * *

Time stood still. I floated into a world so awful, so desolate, that hell itself seemed like paradise. Voices, faces, fire, pain. *Ittai, my love. Don't hate me.* Ittai's scowl grew larger and larger. His eyes darkened and he snarled. 'I hate you, I hate you, I hate you.'

I burned hot and cold, my mouth dry and soggy, my nose swollen and pinched. My head blew bigger than a melon, and my heart crushed flat in a winepress.

My hands were tied, wrapped around with linen cloth. Darkness surrounded me. I lay in a sepulcher. The door opened, and someone lit a lamp. I squinted, unable to focus. My hands were freed. A distorted face hovered over me. *Am I not dead? Why?*

David waved a palm over my face. "Can you hear me?"

I nodded.

He held a wineskin to my lips. "Drink. Go ahead. It's my best wine."

My throat burned when I swallowed. My stomach clenched, and I blew my breath to keep from throwing up. David wiped my forehead with a wet cloth.

"Wh-where am I?"

"You're in my dungeon. Attacking the king calls for death. The people almost strung your daughter up a tree in mistaken identity, but I rescued her."

My heart shuddered. "Where is she?"

"Safe. I've a triple guard at her house. Be glad I pardoned you. You only have to serve a six month sentence for appearance's sake."

"Where's Ittai?"

David patted my shoulder. "He'll never want to see you again. His mother took the sword meant for you." He leaned to embrace me.

I slapped him. "You hateful, smug, prideful, vile rogue. You had my sons killed because you didn't know the Law. Have the rains fallen? Or is the land just as dry and barren as ever."

David winced. "No, the rains have not fallen. Perhaps there is still a member of the house of Saul who has not learned her lesson." He stood to leave. "Is there anything you want from me? Anything I can do for you?"

"No, I hate you with a perfect hatred, and I count you my enemy." A cold frost descended on me, drawing a net from my head to my toe, crystallizing my hair, my face, my skin, freezing me to the core of my soul. "There is nothing you can do for me. Leave me alone."

* * *

My cell had a tiny window too high to reach. No beams with which to fasten a noose. A solitary guard pushed in a platter of food and changed the pot. I banged on the walls. Silence. I screamed and yelled at the guard. I taunted him, called his mother all sorts of names. I even smashed the chamber pot. All he did was open the door, sweep up the shards and replace it with a brass one. He did not hear me clap my hands behind him—a deaf-mute. I retreated into waking dreams.

I'm in a sepulcher. A dark, dank sepulcher. My family surrounds me. See, there's Merab and Mother. Father and Jonathan playing a game of bones. And my babies are alive. Samuel and Ithream. And my boys, all handsome and tall, sit at the table for the New Moon Feast. And Tora is pretty again. The sepulcher is lit with a thousand lamps, and we sing, and we're together, together, together, forever. No David to ruin everything.

The guard splashed water on my face. He'd left a filled tub. It was not deep enough to drown me. My family leaves. I wash and scrub and clean. Oh, who can wash away my sins? Who can take them under His blood? My sins are always before me. They have separated me from my David, my husband, my love. And Ittai, do you hate me? Please don't hate me. I used you, but don't hate me. I recite David's psalms. I recite and recite and recite. But David does not come, neither does Ittai.

And I dream of David, and in my dreams he loves me, and we ride on flying horses and walk on clouds across a golden staircase. We sing like children and splash in pools of silver. He pulls me to the top of a rainbow. And he loves me. I open my eyes.

The cell remained empty.

I broke a bowl and kept a shard in my pocket and slept with it under my pillow. My friend. I named her Tora. And I talked to Tora. I kissed her and told her how sorry I was. And Tora always forgave me. Tora told me to seek David's forgiveness. I had sinned against him. Tora told me her son loved me and would always love me. Tora asked me to tell Ittai about God. I promised Tora I would and asked her to find Ittai and send him to me. Tora said he would come. Tora loved me. Tora understood. I love you, Tora. I kissed the shard and tucked her under my pillow.

* * *

David slipped down the stairs underneath his tower. The Jebusites had kept prisoners below, but he had never used this particular section before. The thought of human beings living beneath his bedchamber disturbed him. He slid silently to the door. She talked to Tora, but her diction had become slurred. She wanted Tora's forgiveness and love. She cried for Ittai, and she never asked for David.

David hated himself for his insane jealousy. He hated that Ittai's mother, a God fearing woman, had to die for Michal's mistakes. When Ittai asked to be set free from his vow, he let him go. Ittai wandered off, a vagabond. No sons, no wife, no mother. David didn't hate Ittai. He rather liked the man. Too bad he loved David's wife.

David held onto his anger as a talisman. Anger covered doubt. Anger drove away niggling thoughts of inadequacy. Anger was his triumph and meant he was right. How dare she love another man? How dare she blame him for hanging his sons? How dare she forget that he, the king, was her rightful husband? Despite proclaiming Ittai a hero for finding his wife, David knew the truth. They had secretly married and mocked him for three years. How they must have laughed at him, scorned him, disdained him.

Every night he lay on the hard, dusty floor, listening, and his heart yearned for her, and he grew concerned for her. Oh, he'd let her out, or he'd go in. He would, if he could. He scraped his fingers over the cold stones. He reached for the door, grasping to be let in, begging to be let in, desperately needing to be let in. But she counted him an enemy.

His hands balled into fists. She would not get the better of him. No, not David, the great king, David, God's anointed, David… the servant boy. David hung his head. Who was he fooling? Underneath his golden crown, beneath his kingly robes… he was just David, the servant… the boy who wanted to do better. But had he done right by her?

A voice—a still, small voice—told him he had been wrong, so utterly wrong. He saw her tender little girl's heart, so freely given to him. She had looked up to him, a man of God, the LORD's anointed. And what had he done? Hurt her, trampled her feelings and forced her to fit a mold, to play a role, fulfill a dream that existed only in his mind. She deserved another chance and a husband who'd love her and cherish her. If only he could have been that man.

A pulsating web of pain expanded and contracted in his heart. He loved her more than he knew what to do. *Michal, let me in. Let me into your heart. Michal, I'll bring you peace. Peace in Israel. Just call on me. Call my name.*

* * *

A masked man followed the prison guard. The guard balanced the food with one hand while he opened door at the base of the tower. The man struck the guard. The bowls broke on the stone floor. He bound the guard and gagged him.

Ittai took an oil lamp and descended the steps noiselessly. A warren of cells opened in front of him. Cobwebs hung amongst the dank stones. Several corridors opened in different directions. Which way? The dust was disturbed on one of the corridors. Ittai followed the trail and came to a closed door. He set the lamp down and tapped at the door.

A woman moaned and sobbed, speaking to another one. He stepped back. Perhaps he had taken a wrong turn. He listened.

"Are you sure he'll come?"

"Yes, Ittai loves you, he'll forgive you."

"Will he? Why hasn't he come yet?"

"Maybe tomorrow. Maybe he'll remember."

"I can't wait any longer. Dear God, let me speak to Ittai before I die."

Ittai pushed the trapdoor open, before noticing the simple bar on the door. He pulled the bar aside and let himself in.

Michal sat on the solitary bed rocking herself with her hands around her knees. Ittai pulled her into his arms. She smelled like dirty laundry and accumulated sweat.

"Michal, mine."

"Tora said you'd come." She picked up a pottery shard and kissed it. "Tora, I love you, Tora."

Ittai hugged her. David had exiled him, so he hid during the day and paid travelers to send the king letters. After months of excavation, he had finally completed the tunnel under the palace wall in the women's compound and into the stone grotto where David's infants used to be interred.

"Michal, I love you." He kissed her.

"I need to tell you about the LORD. Tora said—"

He pressed a finger to her lips. "Later. We have to get out of here."

He yanked her to her feet. She wobbled, barely able to walk. He pulled her over his shoulder, latched the door, and retraced his steps.

The guard was still unconscious, so Ittai untied his hands and feet. He placed the lamp at his side and closed the door behind him. With Michal on his shoulder, he skirted the edges of the palace and trekked to the back of the women's courtyard and through the stone grotto.

"Can you crawl?" He pushed her through the tunnel, and they emerged behind an abandoned cistern. Jackals yipped in the night, and an owl's silent wings floated by. Ittai hoisted Michal onto his horse and walked the horse to the gate. A hefty bribe later, they rode west toward Philistia.

* * *

David opened the dungeon door and stumbled on a body. The man grunted. He kicked the broken bowls. The deaf-mute guard snored and turned on his side.

He ran down the corridor, careful not to spill oil on his feet. The door swung open. Empty. His pulse thundered erratically. He tore out of the dungeon and saddled his horse.

CHAPTER 51

Hosea 2:20 I will even betroth thee unto me in faithfulness: and thou shalt know the LORD.

>><<<

We arrived at Jada's house just after midnight. Water was still precious, but Jada brought a basin and washed me from head to toe. Her loving touch revived me, but she insisted I sleep.

"I've been doing nothing but sleeping in the cell. How long was I there?"

"Five months. Ittai worked on the tunnel for three months. The first two months he mourned, of course. He was devastated, but he doesn't blame you."

"Where is he now?"

She put a finger to her lip. "He's sleeping in the front room."

"Does he think I've gone back to David?"

Jada twisted her lip. "Everyone knows the king gets what he wants. When your father wanted me, he locked your mother in her room. When he wanted me to leave, he threw me out. He took your mother from a man who loved her. Perhaps you were not aware."

I chewed on a crust of bread. "No. I only know my mother was unhappy. She tried to cover it with clothes and jewelry, but nothing makes up for the emptiness."

"No, nothing will." She put oil in my hair. "But Asherah has shined her face on you. You have Ittai."

Warmth stirred in my chest. "Did you know I made a wish with Ittai long ago on the wishing tree?"

Jada chuckled. "Ah, yes, the wishing tree. It's not far from here. I made a wish there when I was a girl."

"What did you wish for?"

"I was not careful," she said. "The tree takes you literally. I asked for a man to love me. I should have prepared a detailed list of conditions—

no kings and no heroes. And I should have said no other wives, women, concubines, boys, men, animals, creatures, gods and goddesses. So beware of that tree. You get a single wish. What did you wish for?"

"It hasn't come true yet. Besides I've lost the leaf."

Jada flicked a loose thread off the new gown she made for me. "Perhaps it has. You just don't know about it." She went to her wardrobe and opened a box. "You left it at my house that day I prepared you for the rug. What did you wish for?"

Ittai stuck his head through the door. "She won't tell."

I flew to his wide grin like a moth to a lamp and kissed him.

He sniffed me exaggeratedly. "You were quite a stinker when I brought you in. Now what did you want to talk to me about?"

Jada stood to leave, but I held onto her fingers. "Stay. I've lost so much time with you two."

She fluffed a pillow and handled me a few grains of parched corn.

Ittai arranged the blankets and pulled me between his legs, hugging me from behind. "If you don't start talking, I'm going to send your mother away and do my kind of talking."

I traced the veins on the back of his hands. "I'm very sorry about Tora." A lump rose in the back of my throat. "I lost control. And she paid with her life."

"I don't blame you. I'm the one at fault. I should have held onto you when David approached the platform to speak. Instead I was angry because he took you from me."

I rubbed his knuckles. "Don't blame yourself."

He kissed the back of my neck. "Then you should also stop blaming yourself."

"While I lay in that cell, my worst thought was being away from you."

"We're together now."

"Yes, but not always. Remember Delilah? And Samson?"

Jada coughed and fanned herself.

I took another sip of wine to wet my throat. "Delilah cries because she is lost in the world below. Samson has gone to God, to paradise, the home for the redeemed. They are apart not just today, but tomorrow and tomorrow, forever and ever."

Ittai traced the tear that slid down my cheek. "Will I see my mother again? What is paradise, this home for the redeemed? She always talked about it."

"Did she tell you how to get there?"

"She said I could not find it myself—that I must trust the God of Israel to take me."

"Have you trusted Him?"

"Have you?"

I kissed his cheek. "I have. I believe He would forgive my sins if I would ask Him to. I believe what He told Moses and the Prophets. And I believe He will send a Redeemer to take our sins away. David told me in his psalms."

"Why would He just forgive us if we ask?"

"He forgives sin because of His great mercy, because He loves us." I jabbed him in the ribs for emphasis.

Ittai rubbed his chin. "Do you have to promise not to ever sin again?"

"You'd be lying if you promised, and lying is also a sin. God does judge sin, so we must take care for our own good to avoid it." I sounded so much like Abigail.

"So how do I ask?"

"Do you believe His promises? Trust in God only, and not in man?"

"You sound like my mother. I wanted to believe, but I wanted you more. I wanted to have you for my wife."

Jada yawned loudly. "All this talk about sin is making me sick. Who can dictate where the heart goes? If you two love each other, there is no sin."

I took a deep breath. "God set up marriage between one man and one woman. He made Adam first, and then Eve to be a helper for Adam. Rules against adultery help to keep the husband to his own wife and the wife to her own husband."

Jada slapped the couch. "David took other wives. What were you going to do?"

"I should have lived as a widow."

"Your God winks at men who take multiple wives, but a woman is stoned for adultery." Jada stood and dusted the breadcrumbs off her gown. "I'm sorry, you two continue with your googly-talk. I'm going out for some fresh air."

As soon as Jada exited, Ittai kissed my neck. "I want you so badly. Think she'll be back anytime soon?"

His hands moved to my breasts, eliciting a bloom of tingles. His heated lips sighed against mine as he lowered me to the lambskin bedding.

"Mmm…" I struggled to retain consciousness. "Let me finish…"

"You can talk after I'm finished with you." He trailed kisses to my breasts.

"Stop. I need to tell you about sin." I squirmed from beneath him. "It's too important. Tora made me promise. Do you want God to save you from your sins?"

"I can't stop sinning. I love you too much." He reached for me.

"I love you, too." I backed away. "No one can stop sinning. Not even David. And he trusts God and believes His Word."

419

Ittai chuckled and slapped his thigh. "Especially David. He is sin in a bucket. Is he a hypocrite?"

"No, he's only a man. Even a man after God's own heart sins. It's our weakness, and God does not wink at it, but He forgives. And He judges you whether you believe Him or not."

"Come here." Ittai pulled me into his lap. "I want God's forgiveness, but I want you too. It is a sin, isn't it, for us to be together?"

I bent my head. "Yes, it is."

Ittai's eternal soul hung at the tip of a sharp two-edged sword. I closed my eyes and prayed silently.

He shifted beneath me and rubbed his calf. I scooted to his side, afraid to prod him, afraid of an interruption, afraid he'd reject my message.

He twirled my hair. "Well, if that rascal David can be forgiven, I suppose I have nothing to lose by asking. I do believe God means well for us, and He makes the rules. I'm just a dirty Philistine. Will He save me also?"

I clasped Ittai's big hands. "Yes. Yes. Believe and ask God to save you. Tell Him you're a sinner, but you're trusting only in Him to save you and forgive your sins. Will you do that now?"

He lowered his head. "I will. Mighty God of Israel, can you look on me, a sinner, and forgive my sins? Please save me and take me as your servant. I forsake all other gods and trust only in You, LORD God of Israel, to be my God forever."

I hugged him. "You did it."

The shadow across his brow cleared, and his entire face brightened. "Thank you, Michal. Thank you for telling me."

"I'm so happy for you." I wiped my eyes with the back of my hand.

Tears dripped down his cheek, and his grin split his face. "Your God is my God."

Humbled and awed, I thanked my God for saving Ittai, my Gittite. "Yes, and we'll be friends forever, even after we die, and you'll see Tora again. Tora will be so glad."

"Yes, but…" He cupped my face. "I sinned tonight by stealing you away from the king."

"He had me in the dungeon. You didn't exactly steal me. You rescued me from that monster."

"But he's your rightful husband. And even if he treats you badly, you said you should live as a widow. Maybe that's why he threw you in the dungeon."

Tears threatened. "That's what Tora said to me while I was in there. She said I had not reverenced him and been the wife he should have had. I broke my promises too. I've betrayed him, and I deserve to die."

"But you said God forgave your sins." His voice was comforting.

"He has, but I must make amends. Everything is my fault. Tora said I should—"

"Stop blaming yourself." He pulled me into his warm chest.

"I agree. It's time to stop the blame." David stepped in, his crown in his hands.

Ittai and I jumped apart. I clutched my robe, my knees weak.

David placed his crown on the table and opened his arms. "Come to me."

He looked grim and tired. I hesitated.

Ittai gave me a gentle push. "Go to him, Michal. Obey your lord."

David stepped forward. He stared into my eyes for a long moment, his gaze solemn and defeated. "I'm going to take you home and treat you well. I promise."

My lips trembled but I took his hand. Ittai stood at the doorway as we walked out of the house. I crushed the terebinth leaf and blew the pieces into the wind.

* * *

David's heart burned. He had heard everything they said about him. But he had also prayed for Ittai's soul. And he rejoiced when Ittai received the LORD God of Israel. But Michal had called him a monster, and that hurt.

He adjusted Michal across his horse. She sat as if he were a stranger. He wanted her to lean her head on his chest, as she did on Ittai's. He wanted that easy familiarity she had with him, how she laughed and her voice inflected and trilled. She had sounded so happy and carefree. And most of all, he wanted to be her friend, the way he had been when they were first married.

He touched her shoulder. "May I call you Eglah?"

"You may call me anything, my lord."

He pulled her back to his chest and hugged her. "Please don't be formal with me."

She bristled and remained stiff. "Your request sounded quite formal."

"I'll call you Michal, if it's what you prefer."

"Call me Eglah," she said, her face pointedly averted from his.

"Sure? I don't want you to dislike it."

"I'm sure." She softened slightly. "You're my husband, and I must obey the LORD in all things."

David's heart ached. During her time in the dungeon, she never once cried for him. He wished she'd obey him because she wanted to, not because she must. He wished she'd encourage him instead of blame him at every turn. But mostly he wished she would trust him and depend on him.

They cut back on the trail toward Jerusalem. The full moon had set, and the faint traces of dawn peeked from the ridge above. Unlike the misty dawns of the past, this one rose bone dry and stark, not a drop of moisture in the air.

"Eglah, are you tired? You've been up all night."

"I've spent more than five months sleeping in your dungeon." She took a deep breath. "The sunrise is so beautiful. I haven't seen the sun or moon for so long. Why did you lock me up?"

"You tried to kill yourself and had to be sedated. I didn't want you to become used to the poppy. So I locked you in a safe room where you couldn't throw yourself out any windows, or stab yourself with a weapon. You spent almost two months immobile. I fed you by hand."

"You cared for me two months? How come I didn't know?"

She had alternated between raving and frozen, had not recognized anyone. And David had neglected his duties, held her in his lap and prayed for her, coaxing every drop of sustenance into her mouth, and kissing every tear from her cheek.

His hands tightened on the reins. "You retreated into a cocoon. And when you woke, you hated me. You... called me... enemy. I got angry and left you alone."

"You were mad at me for months?"

He squeezed her between his forearms. "Yes."

"Didn't you care?"

His heart cringed with a hollow ache. "I did. I came every night and sat outside your door."

"Why didn't you come in?"

"You needed the time, and so did I." God had put them both in the wilderness, the crucible, to try their hearts.

"When were you going to let me out?"

"I was waiting for you to say my name." He sounded pathetically like a small boy. Cords of pain twisted in his heart, and his voice cracked. "I just wanted you to call for me."

For a small moment have I forsaken thee;

David reined the horse up a set of switchbacks, leaving the Valley of Sorek. The soulless sun scorched the barren wasteland they passed. Bleached bones stuck through the sand. Michal shielded her eyes. He stopped the horse and pulled her sideways away from the blood-thickening rays.

She pulled the scarf over her face and rested her head against his chest. David fingered the waves in her hair. If he could only go back in time, back to the beginning, to the day he first met her.

...but with great mercies will I gather thee.

"David?"

His name sounded sweet on her lips. He kissed her cheek.

"All I had to do was say your name?"

"Yes."

She nudged him. "The drought hasn't lifted, has it?" Her voice was soft, without a trace of accusation.

"No. But I didn't know that before we carried out the sentence."

The famine had not abated, and the seven sons hung, with no relief in sight. The burden in his heart grew until he could barely breathe.

Her throat rippled, but she did not speak.

"I wish you wouldn't blame me," David whispered. The familiar weight pressed his shoulders, and he hunched away from the stinging blast of the east wind.

"But you're the man after God's own heart, a hero favored by God."

"I'm nobody's hero." His voice broke. "I can't bring the boys back. The drought continues. And the LORD has not answered me."

In a little wrath I hid my face from thee for a moment...

David's heart drained as dry as the cracked, parched earth they trod on. The dust-laced wind irritated his throat. He slowed his horse, wanting to prolong the contact. He had lost her, the woman God made for him. He had allowed anger and pride to snuff out the love she had for him. He inhaled the fragrance in her hair, jasmine and thyme. The pain in his chest grew and surrounded him in a wasteland of broken dreams.

They arrived at the palace gate and dismounted. Michal pulled her shawl over her face.

He placed her hand on his shoulder. "These shoulders are not strong."

He touched his chest. "And this heart is crushed."

He lowered his head. "And this man needs you."

Her eyes were watery, and she squinted in the sun. "You left your crown."

"I know. I'm not your king. I'm only a man—your man."

She closed her eyes and turned around.

He could not beg. He could only let her go. He carried her to Abigail's house.

...but with everlasting kindness will I have mercy on thee, saith the LORD thy Redeemer.

CHAPTER 52

Proverbs 5:18-19 Let thy fountain be blessed: and rejoice with the wife of thy youth. Let her be as the loving hind and pleasant roe; let her breasts satisfy thee at all times; and be thou ravished always with her love.

>>><<<

David lay face down on the floor. He had been fasting for days.

"O LORD God, restore me my wife Michal. For I have espoused her in my youth. Oh, if I had only the faith of Isaac, I would have prayed for her, and You would have raised a king from her womb. Restore her heart to me. I made a vow with her, to love her and cherish her. Give me another chance. Hear me, O LORD."

I have both heard you and seen your faith. Solomon, your son, shall be your heir, and I will place him upon the throne of the Kingdom of the LORD over Israel. He shall build my house and my court, and I will establish his kingdom forever. As for your wife, Michal, I will bless her and make her a fruitful vine to dwell with you in my house forever.

* * *

I twirled Abigail's spindle repetitively. *Why did God keep me alive when my existence brought a curse to all those around me?* I cried out to the LORD.

"Be still and know that I am God." *I know you are. But was I really made for David or was I mistaken? Why do we hurt each other? And why has all this evil happened to us?*

"I know the thoughts I think toward you, thoughts of peace, and not of evil, to give you an expected end." *LORD, you've stripped me naked, made me destitute, show me, LORD, the expected end.*

"Call on me, pray unto me, search for me with your entire heart, and I will hearken to you and you shall find me."

I shut myself in Abigail's house, asking the servants for water only. I fasted and prayed, beseeching the LORD to take the curse away, to show me David's heart.

After days of hunger, the LORD let me recall the first time I beheld David, a young man. He stripped him bare of all his glories, his kingdom, his power, his might, and his failings. And He showed me a man who loved the LORD God above everything.

David had sacrificed everything to please God. Everything to obey God, to do His will. Everything.

And I had been so wrong about him. Could he ever forgive me? The jealous, spiteful, selfish daughter of Saul. Was his heart big enough, or was it too late?

* * *

David seated his wives in order: Ahinoam on his right, Abital in front of him, and Bathsheba to his left. Sweat prickled his brow, and he bent his head to pray. He had sought the LORD, and the LORD had answered him. Now, he had to obey.

"Women, I have sinned," he said. "God gave Adam a woman, Eve, fashioned out of his rib. One. Single. Rib."

Ahinoam clutched her shawl. Bathsheba blinked and lowered her eyes. Abital nodded, encouraging him.

"I have dealt deceitfully, gone the way of the kings of the world, taken what was not mine. And the LORD has heaped his judgment on me and my house."

He paused. The tension was as palpable as his thickened pulse. "Women, I intend to provide for you, to be your friend, and to love you as a brother. Choose any house, and I will buy it for you. I will serve and support you all the days of my life."

Bathsheba shuddered, and David grasped her hand. Her blue eyes were sodden with tears, and she slumped over the table.

Ahinoam hardly breathed. Her face ashen, she regarded him with a look of reproach. David placed his hand on her shoulder and kissed the side of her face. "Ahinoam, wife of the wilderness, you've suffered more than anyone. My love for you is rooted in the thorns, and thistles, and parched creeks, and dusty cliffs, and the calling of the LORD in the day of my distress."

She sobbed. "My lord. You have been so good to me. More than I deserve. I love you, David, and I thank you." Her lips trembling, she fled with a rustle of skirts.

"Abital, I have loved you with brotherly love. You may think you're weak, but you are strong. You've kept the word of the LORD and have not denied my name. Our son, Shephatiah, will be a mighty warrior and serve the next king with truth and loyalty."

She bowed her head. "Thank you, my lord. I will not cease to pray for you." She kissed him on the beard and patted his shoulder. "I love you, David." Looking back, her sweet apple cheeks dimpled.

Bathsheba raised herself into his arms. "My lord, forgive me for all the trouble I caused."

He held her tightly. "Beautiful Bathsheba, I regret our sin, but I will never regret the love we had. Out of the ashes of wreck and ruin, we've sought redemption and purified our hearts. God has selected our son, Solomon, to be king after me. You shall be his queen and sit at his side. Guide him as you are guided by our merciful LORD."

She lifted her chin. "I will. And I love you, David, always."

He held her a bit longer and kissed the tears off her face. "You shall be the mother of kings, and I shall never forget you."

* * *

David asked a messenger to bring Michal to his bedchamber. He had left her at Abigail's house and had not made an attempt to see her after he brought her back to Jerusalem. He had failed to reach her, and he couldn't force her to come to him. He wanted her to choose him freely, even if it meant letting her go. But first, he needed to set his house in order.

The famine raged and the people reproached him. Unbelievably they murmured that he had caused the famine by harming Saul's house—Saul, the people's choice, exalted by the people, the people's king. Oh, how short were the memories of the people.

The door opened with a knock, and Michal stepped in. The messenger bowed and retreated.

She stared at his feet. Her face had hollowed, and she appeared frail.

He took her hand and kissed it. "I have something to ask you."

She flinched and clutched her throat with her other hand. The centers of her lovely eyes pinched as she took a step back.

He ached to draw her into his arms, to touch her cheek, to kiss her soft lips. "It is nothing to be afraid of. It concerns our sons and their bones."

"Aren't they buried already?"

"Sadly not. The Gibeonites desecrated their bodies by leaving them on the crosses for these last six months."

Michal's eyes widened. She shook her head as a choke tore from her throat. "Why? How can this be?"

426

He drew her into his arms. "Rizpah and her family have been guarding them these six months. It's time to give them a proper burial. I will take Joshua and Beraiah's bones and put them in my sepulcher in Jerusalem. We'll collect the rest of the men's bones, along with the bones of your father and brothers, and inter them in the sepulcher of your grandfather Kish."

Michal pushed back and trembled. David could feel her apprehension and reticence. She covered her face with both hands and wept.

"What's wrong? Do you not like my plan? I'll also set you free. Your six month sentence has been served. You may go and see whoever you wish." She deserved to be happy, even if it was with another man.

She appeared not to have heard him. Her shoulders shook, and she pounded the wall with her fists.

David held her from behind. "Did you hear me? You're free. You can leave after the burial if you wish."

His fingers ached where he touched her, and his chest warmed where he held her. "I should like it if you'd stay, but I won't force you."

"Oh, David. Don't hate me."

He turned her around. "Why would I hate you? I forgive you for everything."

She wiped her eyes furiously. "You're going to hate me when I tell you."

"Tell me what?"

"You can't put Joshua and Beraiah in your sepulcher."

A spear lanced David's heart. He staggered back as if the earth heaved and bucked. "What do you mean?"

"I lied to you." Her voice lowered to a whisper. "They're Adriel's sons. Merab and Adriel's."

A cold, heavy fist punched the wind out of him. Michal had lied? She might have been stubborn and willful, sarcastic and bitter. But always honest.

His voice broke. "Go away. Just go away."

* * *

Covered in a heavy veil, I rode on a mule behind David. He led the solemn procession from Jerusalem to Gibeah. He had not spoken to me since the day he told me to depart from him. But his messenger urged me to attend the burial. It would not do for the daughter of Saul to miss this event. My father and brothers' bones rode in an ox-cart. Crowds thronged the streets. The entire tribe of Benjamin and many onlookers came to honor my father and his house.

David's men entreated with Rizpah to leave her post as they took down the bleached bones of our sons. The men placed all the bones on the ox-cart, and we rode to Zelah where the sepulcher lay.

It took the procession some time to gather around the entrance to the cave. Dry, chalky dust clogged my nose, and I craned my neck to see the large stone as it was rolled from the entrance of the tomb. The bundles of bones were lifted one by one and carried into the cave. My eyes blurred in memory.

"Walk for Eemah." I held my hands just out of reach. "Joshua, come to me. Beraiah."

They stood and stumbled a few steps, then fell in a pile of squealing, laughing arms, tummies, and legs.

"Try again. Come to Eemah." They climbed over me, grabbed my hair for leverage, and tumbled into my lap. Two sets of eyes, two gapped-tooth smiles, two blessings from God.

I swept a hand behind my veil to wipe my eyes. The stone had been rolled back in place, and the people played music. David handed the parchment bearing my father's genealogy to Meribbaal, Jonathan's son.

He stood on a platform and spoke, "Saul and Jonathan were mighty men. The beauty of Israel is slain upon thy high places: how are the mighty fallen! Saul and Jonathan were lovely and pleasant in their lives, and in their death, they were not divided: they were swifter than eagles and stronger than lions. I am distressed for you, my brother Jonathan, very pleasant have you been to me, your love to me was wonderful, passing the love of women. How are the mighty fallen, and the weapons of war perished! Saul and Jonathan, may my house and your house be joined together in peace as brethren."

"To brethren! To brethren!" cheered the people. "Long live King David. Long live the king!"

As the mourners departed, I dismounted and fell to the parched ground to say my own prayers. When I rose, Ittai passed under a nearby tree with his daughter Kyra and her Egyptian maid.

I stepped toward him, and the women walked away.

"Michal." Ittai's eyes held tears. My veil still in place, I embraced him. His throat bobbled. "Are you free now?"

"David has let me go. I'm free."

He lifted the side of my veil. "What will you do now?"

I gazed into his loving eyes and traced the scar on his left cheek. His arms had supported me, and his chest had warmed me. I hugged him tighter. "I'll go back to Jerusalem and live as a daughter of the Law should."

"I'm proud of you," he said. "I'll never forget you. Michal, mine."

His declaration brought a lump to my throat. "I can still remember the time I saw you in that clearing."

He grinned sideways. "You were watching?"

"Jada told me to hide."

"Tell me what you were thinking."

I must have blushed because a smirk split his face, and he wiggled his eyebrows. "You wondered what it'd be like to run your hands over my body and reach under my leather kilt."

"Ittai! You're incorrigible."

"Did you like what you found?"

The lump swelled to fill my throat. I placed my face on his chest. "I found a loyal friend, a comforter, and more, much more."

He stroked my hair. "And I love everything about you—even dragging your stinkiness out of jail." He kissed the top of my head. "You taught me how to love. The day I married you, I believed we would never part. I believed you would be mine forever."

"Are you disappointed now?" The lump rose in my throat.

"No, never. It's why God chooses not to tell us the future. He gifts us only with the present, so we can love to the fullest, without fear or reservation. I love you, Michal, mine."

"I love you, too, Ittai, my Gittite." A tear rolled down my cheek. "I have to go."

He pulled my veil aside. "Let me look at you. If I could have been David, I would never have let you shed a single tear." His lips pressed together, he forced a smile. "No more tears. I don't want to carry your weeping face in my mind for eternity."

He poked my belly and wiggled his fingers under my smaller ribs where I was most ticklish.

I laughed and slapped his hand. "Stop it."

"I'm not going to stop until you tell me what you wished for."

"You never give up, do you?"

"No, and I'll haunt you."

"Is that a promise?" I chuckled, and he kept tickling me.

"You know you can't stop thinking about me." He circled his tongue around his lips and smacked them.

"My wish won't come true because I crushed the leaf and blew it into the wind."

He wagged a long finger at me. "The tree keeps her promise, whether you threw the leaf away or not. My leaf crumbled long ago."

I pulled a long face. "Oh my, so it looks like neither of us will get our wish. You can tell me now. What did you wish for?"

He snickered and pointed to the tree. "I'll tell you if we climb that tree."

"You can't be serious."

His face cracked into a wolfish grin. "Have you ever known me to be serious?"

He hoisted me onto the low branch of the nearby oak and climbed beside me. "Do you want to go higher?"

I poked his ribs. "No more delaying."

He put an arm around me. "Well, it might feel better if we share a kiss, I mean, of course, a brotherly-sisterly kiss."

I pouted and turned my chin away. "Is this your new rendition of the chaste and pious kiss?"

He pulled my veil up. "How did you guess?"

Licking his upper lip in a highly ornamented fashion, he tongued my mouth lightly.

"Eww… that's a puppy dog kiss."

"Fine, here's a kitty cat kiss." He purred and brushed his mustache across my lips.

"Your delaying tactics are too obvious, Prince Ittai."

He caressed my face. "You're smiling, Princess Michal, and your tongue is still sharp and yummy."

Our lips tangled, and I kissed him, roping, and tugging, wrestling with my fate, and screaming inside, knowing it would be the last time.

"You're making it harder." My voice balled in my throat.

"I never said I was an easy man. Okay, I'll tell you now. My wish for you is a husband who loves and cherishes you, and only you."

I rubbed his shadowy beard. "I had that for a while. With you and with Phalti."

"Yes, like I said, the tree had loopholes. I forgot to specify the time. I should have said one man for your entire lifetime." He kissed my lips. "Your turn."

"I wished the same for you."

"No!" He pushed me. "A husband for me? Are you crazy?"

"I meant a woman, a wife."

"The wording is important. Your exact words, please."

I flicked my veil shut. "Oh, I can't remember. It was a long time ago."

"Stop teasing. You promised to tell me." He squeezed me until I could hardly breathe.

I patted him to loosen his hold, caught my breath, and stared into his soulful eyes. "I wished for you to have your very own woman—who never loved anyone before, whose heart is solely and purely yours." I lowered my face. "It meant I could never be that woman."

Ittai tilted my chin. "Why did you wish that for me? I'm an old man now. Where am I going to find a woman who has never loved before? Whose heart had never known the seed of love?"

I jumped off the branch, sending jolts of pain through my feet. "It means you better start looking and not waste any more time."

"I happen to prefer more mature women. You've set me an impossible task." He swung his legs to tap me with his sandals.

I exhaled slowly. "So long, Prince Ittai."

He did not reply. His pensive eyes stared at me, unblinking. I left him on the branch, swinging his legs. I adjusted my veil and turned toward my mule.

"Hey, Princess, you're going the wrong way. I hear the beaches of Gaza are nice this time of year."

A dart pierced my heart, and I ran. The ache expanded with each step I took. I passed Phalti, Rizpah and Anna in a blur. I would see them later for the New Moon Feast.

I stumbled over the rocks near the burial cave and skinned my palms and knees. *Oh, God, it's so hard to do right. Examine my heart and cleanse it. And let my wish for Ittai be fulfilled.*

David pulled me from the gravel. He tucked my face in his neck and hugged me. "Where do you want to go?"

"Home. I want to go home." I sobbed without control. David held me with no trace of anger, just tenderness and caring.

"Where?"

"Jerusalem. Abigail's house." *With you, my lord.*

CHAPTER 53

Luke 7:47 Wherefore I say unto thee, Her sins, which are many, are forgiven; for she loved much: but to whom little is forgiven, the same loveth little.

>>><<<

We dismounted. David dismissed his contingent and handed the mules to a servant. He touched my elbow and placed his fringed shawl over my head. All around us, the rain sprinkled the thirsty ground with the fresh scent of hope.

One more lie stood between us.

I followed him to his tower. He asked for refreshments and bid me to sit across from him. He gave thanks for the food and looked at me. The once confident face of youth was lined with years of worry and exhaustion. But the boyish tilt was still there in his jaw, and the spark in his eyes had not died.

He broke bread and handed me a piece, slipping a crust in his mouth, chewing deliberately. He looked at the wedge in my hand. I rolled it between my fingers. Even simple things, such as eating, felt strange. I swallowed and peeked at him. He tilted his chin and ate another piece. Slowly I brought the crust to my lips and took a small bite. His eyes clutched my heart with their intensity, but he did not smile.

He poured wine into two golden goblets and pushed one to me, brushing my hand with his fingertips. He swirled his goblet and brought it to his lips. Peering over the rim, he waited for me. He dropped his eyelids briefly before holding my gaze again. Taking a deep breath, I touched the goblet to my lips. He sipped and nodded. My hands shook, and I tilted the goblet too fast. Wine spilled down my chin.

A lopsided grin crept on his face. He held a grape and touched it to my mouth. I took it from his hand, and he caressed my face as I chewed and swallowed it. I plucked a grape and touched his lips. He made a kissing motion and sucked it from my hand.

I stared, entranced, into his luminous eyes. The old sensation quickened deep inside of me, taking my breath hostage. He dipped his fingers into the honey-pot, his eyes glittering with mischief, and tickled my tongue. Licking, tasting, imbibing, I recalled the first time I laid eyes on him. I interlaced his fingers with mine and held his gaze.

Like desert wildflowers after the rain, my heart bloomed. The familiar ache rolled back the heavy, sealed stone. The young red-headed harpist sat in front of me. He spread my fingers like harp strings and stroked them one by one.

"Why did you lie to me?" His tone was gentle, without bitterness.

Words and emotions jangled in my heart, jostling for the truth. I wanted to spare him the pain of knowing. Yet I had replaced it with a more horrendous burden. I studied his strong fingers, the square palm, his sturdy wrist. Why had I lied? Could he forgive me? His liquid amber eyes beckoned for an answer.

"Samuel died."

David's face crinkled, puzzled. "And?"

His fingers tightened around mine, waiting.

"Not the prophet, but our... real... son, Samuel."

His sharp gasp was followed by a heartrending groan. "How?"

"He... never opened his eyes... He died as he was born. I never heard him cry."

David came around the table and knelt by my side, holding my waist, his head resting on my chest.

"And when I pulled Beraiah out of my sister's dying womb, I wished so much... I wanted it to be true."

"You don't have to explain. I forgive you." He crushed my breasts with his face and shuddered. "My son, Samuel. I would have loved you so."

The splatter of rain mirrored the tears from our faces. I drank in the cool, damp air and the sizzling freshness of lightning. Thunder rumbled as sheets of blessed water washed the dust from our window. David stood behind me, his arms wrapped around my waist. Life giving water, showers of blessings, joy, and peace.

A bolt of lightning crackled in multiple directions, followed by a majestic shake of thunder. David pulled me from the window, took a step forward and back. He moved in a circle holding me. I followed. Another step and he turned and twirled me completely around, wrapping my arms with his around my waist. I leaned against his hard body, still muscular after all these years. He caught my sigh and swayed me, his hot breath in my ear, his beard nuzzling the back of my neck.

Without warning, he turned and lifted me off my feet and lunged. I lost my breath and balance as he bent me backward until my hair touched the ground, his strong arms wrapped securely around the small of my back. Blood rushed to my head, and the room spun with dazzling stars.

He pulled me up as ripples of laughter trickled from my lips. He spun me until I didn't know up from down. His deep, rumbling laughter in my ear lightened my heart, leaving me breathless, heady with the excitement of a young girl.

"You're dancing, Eglah. Do you still think me a base and vain fellow?"

I tangled my fingers in his hair. "Of the basest sort, and you can be as vile to me as you please, and I shall honor you."

He unrolled our rug and laid me on top of the tree of life. "Eglah, you are my tree of life. Without you, life would not be worth living." He spread my arms out to the sides and ran his hands over my body, down my legs, straight as the trunk. "You have borne the fruit of love, peace, and faith. You have captured my heart."

His gaze roved over my body. "You are beautiful, a woman who fears the LORD, a woman who comforts my bones, and a woman who sings to my soul."

I parted my lips and received his kiss, tasting and inhaling all of him, my husband, my David.

He caressed the dress off me, removed my combs, earrings and ornaments, stripping everything from my body except for my garnet necklace and matching bracelet. Red drops of blood embraced in gold. He took off his crown, his rings and his clothing.

He lay over me, bare skin on bare skin. His hands formed and fashioned my desires and stroked my innermost passions. Like the fullness of pregnant rain clouds, a torrent of wanting flooded me head to toe. David responded and filled my emptiness. The pent up emotions heightened the pressure channeling deep inside of me. A swell of sweet pleasure inundated my body, drenching me with complete surrender to my rightful husband, my lord, my life.

Wrapped around each other, our damp bodies cleaved to the rug, embraced by the crisp scent of lightning and the balmy, moist air of renewal. The LORD had brought me back to him, the man of my heart, my David.

* * *

The haunting fragrance of jasmine and sandalwood drifted among the willow trees. David held Michal's hand as the keepers rolled back the stone. They had traveled the two-day journey to Abel-Meholah to retrieve Samuel's bones. Phaltiel and Rizpah stepped in behind them, followed by Machir and Anna. The dank, slimy air and the tang of cold stone, dust and old bones trickled a chill down David's spine.

Phaltiel pointed to a tiny skeleton wrapped in strips. A woven fringe of red and gold, dancing lions for the tribe of Judah, encircled the collar and shoulder bones. All was silent except for the muffled sniffling of the women and the croak of a persistent toad.

David clutched Michal's shoulders and stared at the remains of his son, his firstborn son. His heart tightened as he handed her a linen sack.

Michal reached, but faltered. With a choked sound, she gave the bag to Phaltiel. Instead of picking up the bones, he lifted the tiny slab on which the baby lay. Reverently he took it out of the cave and placed it in the covered cart.

David hugged Michal tightly. She leaned on him for several long moments. He couldn't find words for the sorrow they shared, so he closed his eyes and inhaled her breath and allowed the steady beat of his heart to comfort her.

No one made a sound. Michal led him among the markers until she found her sister. She stared for a long time. She stroked a gauzy piece of cloth over the ribcage.

"Are you ready to go?" David asked softly.

"Not yet, my lord. I wish to pay respect to my mother."

Phaltiel guided her toward the back of the cavern. Michal knelt and knocked her head on the ground. "Mother, I understand now. You used to tell me about Barzillai. How huge his farm was: the well-watered land, the meadows full of sheep, vineyards that rolled for miles and miles, olive trees and fruit trees. You told me how you used to play together as children and how Barzillai's parents liked you best. You never told me he loved you. Mother, I forgive you, and I love you."

David caught his breath. Barzillai, his loyal friend, had died shortly after his three grandsons were hung. No, five grandsons. Had he known about Joshua and Beraiah?

Michal moved to the freshly wrapped body next to her mother's. David's heart smote him. *Oh, my friend Barzillai. Forgive me for taking your grandsons. You have sacrificed much for my kingdom's sake. May God richly reward you and bless your descendants.*

David took Michal's hand and led her out of the burial cave. The sorrowful drizzle misted over the tears on his beard, and the chill seeped deep into his bones. He wrapped Michal in his cloak and lifted her into the cart with Samuel's remains.

* * *

The wind whipped through my hair and tickled my face. I leaned back in David's arms as we rode to Gibeah. We bypassed the killing field and headed to the market square. The heavy winter rains had revived the meadows. Trees budded and the scent of spring and fresh earth and the sweet fragrance of grape blossoms filled the air with promises of God's bountiful blessing.

David pointed to a part of a broken wall jutting between the stalls of two vendors. "Can you picture the old guard shack?"

We dismounted and walked around the pottery, fruit and vegetables. David placed his hand on mine, and we touched the rough stones, tracing the mortar, looking up to our special place.

I leaned against his broad chest. "Yes. I can hear you coming up the steps. Feel you behind me."

He held me closer, oblivious to the sounds of the marketplace. "I fell in love with you up there."

Winding our way between the hawking merchants, we came to the wizened olive tree, its fragrance still pungent and peppery. It stood in the center of a square where the villagers gathered. Children darted around, and little boys climbed its gnarly branches, its silvery green leaves dancing in the breeze.

We stepped into the canopy. David held my hands and drew me close to him. "Will you marry me, Princess?"

We kissed, deep and lingering. The air hushed, even the birds stopped chirping, replaced by the strains of many harps, a train of heavenly chords.

* * *

I sat with David in the garden, holding his hand, my head on his shoulders. A couple of years had passed since the famine, and the warm summer air lulled me. Israel was finally at peace, the wars had ended— David's dream fulfilled, my bride price paid.

"Eglah, are you happy now?" he whispered.

"Yes, I'm happy, very happy."

"Is there anything you regret? Anything I can make up to you?"

"No, nothing. You've given me everything I desire. I just wanted you to love me. Nothing more."

"Are you sure?"

My heart squeezed around a small pit of pain. "We don't have a surviving child."

I stared at the pool; the sun reflected golden waves, beckoning.

He traced a finger in the water, breaking our reflections. "You have something better than a physical heir."

"How is that?" I turned to look in his liquid eyes.

"You were meant to have my love for always, not only in this world but the next. Our souls knit together forever, is that not better than our bloodlines?" He spoke the truth, although I still would have wanted both.

"I love you," he said. "I've loved you since the moment I saw you. And I never want it to end."

A flame of joy anointed my chest and I sang:

Our love tried by fire, and purged of the dross,
Melted together as pure as fine gold.
God tried our hearts, and revealed His plan.
In darkness of spirit, He comforts us still.
And we shall rejoice in the LORD and sing Him a song.
And follow His Word, in His steps we will trust.
When it is time, to lay down to rest, we will appear as Him.

David smiled broadly. "That was beautiful. Seems I'm not the only psalmist in Israel."

We walked to the scroll room. David pointed to a tiny scroll on the top shelf. He brought it down and blew off the dust. "My wife, you shall dwell with me in the House of our LORD forever."

Our marriage covenant. He unrolled it and smoothed it on the table. We read the words together. "David, son of Jesse of Bethlehem is hereby joined in marriage to Michal, daughter of Saul of Gibeah, in front of the LORD God. Presided over by Elihu, the Priest of the LORD. Witnessed by Saul, son of Kish and Jonathan, son of Saul."

He pointed to the tear mark and kissed it. Holding my hand, he led me to our bedchamber where we dwelt the rest of the day as lovers, a man and a woman.

* * *

The pestilence raged three days. David held her, praying, begging, entreating the LORD for mercy.

"David, my love, meet me at the window," she whispered as her spirit departed.

The sword fell and pierced straight through David's heart. His sin. He had numbered the people against God's will. Always his sin. Seventy thousand people died. Not a family in Israel escaped grief.

Peace I leave with you.

Her maid handed him three boxes, sandalwood, silver and jade, and three items, a cloak, a thick scroll, and a shepherd's harp. He opened the jade box. A single moss green river stone lay inside. He kissed the stone and placed it in her hand.

They put her in his sepulcher, next to the place where he would lie. He placed the cloak over her heart and the harp at her side. He kept the scroll. The boxes he would send to her daughter.

My peace I give unto you.

He prepared his son for the throne. He freed his concubines.

He lay down with her scroll.

He read every word.

Not as the world giveth, give I unto you.

He looked over his list of mighty men and penned, 'Ittai the son of Ribai out of Gibeah of the children of Benjamin,' and lastly 'Uriah the Hittite, thirty-seven in all.'

He turned to his genealogy.

And unto David were sons born in Hebron: and his firstborn was Amnon, of Ahinoam the Jezreelitess;

And his second, Chileab, of Abigail the wife of Nabal the Carmelite; and the third, Absalom the son of Maacah the daughter of Talmai king of Geshur;

And the fourth, Adonijah the son of Haggith; and the fifth, Shephatiah the son of Abital;

And the sixth, Ithream, of Michal, daughter of Saul king of Israel. These were born to David in Hebron.

He dipped a reed in the inkwell and struck out the words, 'Michal, daughter of Saul king of Israel'. In big bold letters he wrote:

EGLAH DAVID'S WIFE.

Let not your heart be troubled, neither let it be afraid.

He was tired. It was time. David lay on his bed with his wife's words on his chest. He closed his eyes.

His breath departed.

EPILOGUE

I stand at the window of my mansion, peering out at the golden lane. The evening sky glows crimson, purple, brilliant. I pull aside the silken curtains and lower the scarlet cord. I linger, taking in the indescribable glory and beauty in front of me. Fruit trees dot the landscape, set along a sparkling brook of diamonds.

Jewel colored birds sing overhead. Flowers and herbs grow on the walls of my mansion, setting root between gemstones, bright and dazzling. Rivulets of water trickle over the stones, glistening in the setting sun. The sweet scent of jasmine and sandalwood heighten my bliss. I check the cord again. Maybe tonight will be the night of his coming.

I lie in my bed of pearl and wait. Angelic choruses stir in my dreams. Tonight, a rat-tat-tat of drums accompanies the sweet tunes with the sound of marching men. A presence arouses me, and I glance toward my window. The cord tightens.

I rush to the window, the swelling strums of the harps intensifying. David! Young, handsome, and smiling. His eyes sparkle with love and devotion.

"Isha, my love. I've come as I promised." He leaps into the room and cups my face with both hands, and I behold his face as if it were an angel of God.

Psalm 17:15 As for me, I will behold thy face in righteousness: I shall be satisfied, when I awake, with thy likeness.

THE END

CAST OF CHARACTERS

Bold - Name Mentioned in the Bible

Bold Italic – Fictional Character, or name not mentioned in the Bible

Abiathar. Son of the priest of Nob, Ahimelech, who escapes to David in the wilderness after King Saul ordered the slaughter of the priests of Nob. Served David.

Abigail. Wife of Nabal, the Carmelite, who disobeys her husband and gives food to David and his men while on the run from Saul. After Nabal's death, David takes her as his third wife. Mother of Chileab, David's second son.

Abishai. Nephew of David, a son of David's sister, Zeruiah. He is one of David's notable warrior and a mighty man. He accompanies David in the cave when they discover Saul.

Abital. David's sixth wife, and mother of Shephatiah, David's fifth son.

Abner. Son of Saul's uncle Ner. Serves as Saul's commander in chief. He also serves and betrays Saul's son, Ishbaal (Ishbosheth) in the civil war after Saul's death.

Absalom. Third son of David by the princess Maacah of Geshur and brother to Tamar. He plots to overthrow his father and took the throne temporarily.

Achish. King of Gath, who provides sanctuary for David while he flees Saul. He cedes the town of Ziklag to David as a reward for raiding his supposed enemies.

Adriel, the Meholathite. Husband of Merab, Michal's sister, hence brother-in-law to David. He is the son of Barzillai, David's friend.

Adonijah. Fourth son of David by Haggith. He attempts a coup in David's old age to prevent Solomon from taking the throne.

Ahinoam, daughter of Ahimaaz. Saul's wife, and mother to most of Saul's children, including Jonathan.

Ahinoam, of Jezreel. David's second wife who followed him faithfully through the wilderness during his days of exile. Mother of Amnon, David's firstborn son.

Ahithophel. David's counselor, Bathsheba's grandfather, and chief conspirator with Absalom during his rebellion.

Amnon. Firstborn son of David by Ahinoam of Jezreel. He rapes his half-sister Tamar and is killed by Absalom.

Anna. Daughter of Michal and Phalti, born during the civil war between David and Ishbaal (Ishbosheth).

Arik. David's chief guard.

Barzillai. The Gileadite of Abel-Meholah. He is the father of Adriel, who is the husband of Merab, daughter of Saul, and sister of Michal. He is the grandfather of the five sons of Merab whom Michal adopts. Loyal to David during his escape from Absalom.

Bathsheba. Daughter of Eliam, wife of Uriah the Hittite, one of David's mighty men. She commits adultery with David and becomes his wife and mother to Solomon, David's heir to the throne.

Beraiah. Fifth son of Adriel and Merab, whom Michal adopts.

Beulah. Abital's cockatoo.

Buzzi. Abital's parrot.

Chileab. David's second son, by Abigail.

David. Son of Jesse, a Bethlehemite. He is anointed by Samuel, the Prophet, to replace King Saul on the throne of Israel. Marries King Saul's youngest daughter, Michal. He eventually attains the throne after King Saul and his sons die.

Doeg. The Edomite. Saul's chief henchman who observes David being succored by the priests of Nob. He carries out the execution and elimination of all the priests along with their wives and children.

Eglah. Pet name for Michal, David's first wife. She is the mother of Ithream, David's sixth son.

Eliah. Third son of Adriel and Merab, whom Michal adopts.

Elihu. Priest who serves King Saul. Tutors Michal and her siblings.

Gaddiel. Second son of Adriel and Merab, whom Michal adopts.

Goliath of Gath. Champion of the Philistines who challenges King Saul to find a man to fight him. David defeats him with a stone from a slingshot.

Haggith. David's fifth wife and mother to Adonijah, David's fourth son.

Hushai the Archite. David's chief advisor, who pretended to join Absalom's rebellion, so he could undermine Absalom from the inside and thwart Ahithophel's clever counsel.

Ishbaal, **Eshbaal (or Ishbosheth).** Son of Saul who survived the war with the Philistines. He is installed by Abner on the throne after Saul dies. He ruled from Mahanaim during the civil war against David.

Ithream. David's sixth son, by Eglah, his wife.

Ittai, the Gittite. Loyal friend of David. He commands an army of six hundred men to save David's kingdom when Absalom rebels. (also Ittai, son of Ribai, of Gibeah, a Benjamite, one of David's mighty men).

Jada. Priestess of Asherah who befriends Michal when she is estranged from David.

Jehiel. Tutor to David's sons.

Jesse. An Ephrathite of Bethlehem in Judah. Father of eight sons, the youngest of whom is David. Grandson of Boaz and Ruth.

Joab. David's nephew and chief commander.

Joel. Firstborn son of Adriel and Merab, whom Michal adopts.

Jonathan. Son of Saul, brother-in-law to David. He dies with his father and brothers at the battle of Mount Gilboa.

Joshua. Fourth son of Adriel and Merab, whom Michal adopts.

Maacah. David's fourth wife, daughter of Talmai, king of Geshur. She is the mother of Absalom and Tamar.

Merab. Older daughter of Saul. First offered to David, but marries Adriel.

Meribbaal (or Mephibosheth). Crippled son of Jonathan, father to Micah.

Micah. Grandson of Jonathan, son of Meribbaal.

Michal. David's covenant wife. Younger daughter of Saul, given to David for a bride price of one hundred Philistine foreskins, also known by the pet name of Eglah.

Nathan. David's court prophet who pronounced God's sword over David's house over David's sin with Bathsheba and murder of Uriah.

Naomi. Michal's maid.

Phalti, Phaltiel, son of Laish. *A scribe* from Gallim who takes Michal for wife, after David flees into the wilderness. *Father of Anna.*

Rizpah. Saul's youngest concubine. She bears him two sons, Armoni and Mephibosheth.

Samuel the Prophet. A priest of the LORD, who anoints both Saul and David to be king of Israel.

Sarah. Adopted daughter of Ahinoam, David's second wife. David saves her as an infant when her mother was slaughtered by David's men.

Saul. Son of Kish. A handsome Benjamite who stands a head taller than everyone else. He is anointed as king of Israel by Samuel. He rules from Gibeah.

Sheba, son of Bichri. A Benjamite and leader of the Israelite rebellion against David after the defeat of Absalom.

Solomon. David's son born by Bathsheba. He is the eventual heir to David's throne and rules from Jerusalem after his father's death.

Tamar. Daughter of David by his fourth wife Maacah and a sister to Absalom. She is raped by Amnon, her half-brother, precipitating a cycle of violence and revenge in David's family in fulfillment of the judgment sword hanging over David's house.

Tora. Daughter of Ribai of Gibeah. Friend of Michal and Ittai's mother.

Uriah the Hittite. One of David's mighty men and husband of Bathsheba. David murders him to obtain Bathsheba as wife.

Uzzah. Young man on the cart escorting the Ark of the Covenant to Jerusalem who touches the Ark and is stricken dead.

Zina. Jada's daughter.

AUTHOR'S NOTE

This work is fiction based on historical characters. For the true story, please read the books of 1st and 2nd Samuel and the many Psalms attributed to King David in the Holy Bible. There is no evidence whatsoever that any of King David's wives were disloyal. Their use in this story is to illustrate God's love for Israel and the Gentiles. Characterizations of King David's wives were taken from Revelations Chapters 2 and 3. Michal is a type of Israel and her story illustrates God's covenant with the nation of Israel.

Rabbinical literature suggests Michal and Eglah are identical, and indeed no other woman is named in the Bible with the title "David's wife" other than Michal and Eglah. Inspiration for this story comes from 2nd Samuel 3:5.

ABOUT THE AUTHOR

Rachelle Ayala was a software engineer until she discovered storytelling works better in fiction than real code. She has always lived in a multi-cultural environment, and the tapestry in her books reflect that diversity.

Rachelle lives in California with her husband. She has three children and has taught violin and made mountain dulcimers.

You can contact her on Facebook:
http://www.facebook.com/RachelleAyalaWriter

Twitter: http://www.twitter.com/AyalaRachelle

Blog: http://www.rachelleayala.com

GoodReads: http://www.goodreads.com/rachelleayala

DISCUSSION QUESTIONS

1. Women's roles in Biblical times were circumscribed by their relationship to their father or husband. How well did you think Michal asserted herself with her family? With David, and later on, in the harem?

2. Physical cruelty was practiced routinely in ancient times. To what extent did that exonerate David in his treatment of non-Israelite people groups?

3. Who was your favorite character? Was it Michal or David? If not, why?

4. David made many mistakes, but he is most famous for his repentance and love for God. To what extent did his love for God cause him to overlook his family and his responsibilities as king?

5. Which man did you like for Michal? If it is not David, how do you think he would have reacted given the king's role and responsibilities?

6. Would you have been capable of loving David as deeply as Michal did? How did her love change as she matured?

7. Polygamy was accepted and even expected of a king. Do you think David cared for his other wives? Was he wrong to take them?

8. Do you agree that a vow, once made, must be kept at all costs? Have you read the story of Jephthah and his daughter? Joshua and the Gibeonites? How does this principle apply to marriage vows? To the vow David made to Jonathan?

9. What event do you think marked the main turning point for Michal, where she would no longer accept whatever David dished out?

10. Do you think Michal succeeded in getting David to love her on her own terms? What would you sacrifice for love? Did you like the ending?

COMING November 2012!

Broken Build (Romantic Suspense)

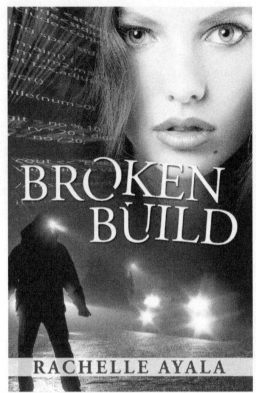

Twenty-five-year-old Jennifer Cruz Jones is a software build engineer with a new job, a new car, and a new apartment. Athletic and trim, she worked her way through college and 24 Hour Fitness. But she cannot hide from her past when the brother of her ex-fiancé is killed in a hit-and-run.

Startup founder Dave Jewell thought he needed one more cash infusion to launch his social shopping network. But when Jennifer finds blood on the frontend of his car, he is forced to protect her from a gang of ruthless thugs intent on blackmailing her for the software that drives his company's success.

Jennifer falls in love with Dave while fearing he'd recognize her from the past. Her vulnerability triggers Dave's protective instincts, and he believes she can heal the hole in his heart.

Together Jennifer and Dave must thwart a killer and avoid the police who suspect both of them, while keeping his startup from folding. A hostage is taken. Dave discovers damaging information about Jennifer and must race against time to deliver the ransom while Jennifer avoids becoming the next piece of roadkill.

Made in the USA
Las Vegas, NV
14 August 2021